DRAGON'S TIME

Also by Todd McCaffrey

Dragonholder
Dragonsblood 22
Dragonheart
Dragongirl

By Anne McCaffrey and Todd McCaffrey

Dragon's Kin
Dragon's Fire
Dragon Harper 20

DRAGON'S TIME

ANNE McCAFFREY

and

TODD McCAFFREY

BANTAM PRESS

LONDON • TORONTO • SYDNEY • AUCKLAND • JOHANNESBURG

TRANSWORLD PUBLISHERS
61–63 Uxbridge Road, London W5 5SA
A Random House Group Company
www.rbooks.co.uk

First published in the United States
in 2011 by Ballantine Books
an imprint of The Random House Publishing Group
a division of Random House, Inc., New York

First published in Great Britain
in 2011 by Bantam Press
an imprint of Transworld Publishers

A CIP catalogue record for this book
is available from the British Library.

ISBN 9780593066201

Addresses for Random House Group Ltd companies outside the UK
can be found at: www.randomhouse.co.uk
The Random House Group Ltd Reg. No. 954009

The Random House Group Limited supports the Forest Stewardship
Council® (FSC®), the leading international forest-certification organization. All our
titles that are printed on Greenpeace-approved FSC®-certified paper carry the FSC® logo.
Our paper procurement policy can be found at
www.rbooks.co.uk/environment

Printed and bound in Great Britain by
CPI Mackays, Chatham, ME5 8TD

2 4 6 8 10 9 7 5 3 1

For
Eliza Oriana Johnson
first granddaughter, first niece:
gentle, loving, brave heart

LETTER TO READERS

Dear Readers,

When Todd and I were casting about for ideas for our next collaboration, we tossed around working on my novel, *After the Fall Is Over,* together, but contractual obligations took that out of the running—and, I must confess, I still am a bit possessive when it comes to the futures of F'lar and Lessa. Still, I did talk over some of my ideas with Todd, and he sent me a long list of questions in response that proved thought-provoking, inspiring, and challenging.

I had read and enjoyed his *Dragonheart* and *Dragongirl,* and the truth is, the excitement was catching. And so I said: "You know, Todd, how hard it is for me to share. . . . Maybe you could show me how?"

Todd got the message and quickly agreed. And it's been a lot of fun. Not only have I enjoyed helping Todd wrap up this very dramatic part of Pernese history, but my own creative juices have been flowing thick and furious: I've been writing up a storm on my own, too. I think that *Dragon's Time* is one of our best, and we're both eager to get started on the next one, *Dragonrider.* Already we know that *Dragonrider* will break new ground and old tradition; still, Todd'll do most of the writing and I'll do the tweaking and critiquing, just as before.

And after that, who knows? He's been so good about allowing me to take part in moving *his* characters around the playing board . . . maybe I'll finally let him play with *my* characters!

Ciao,

Annie

FOR READERS NEW TO PERN

Thousands of years after man first developed interstellar travel, colonists from Earth, Tau Ceti III, and many other origins settled upon Pern, the third planet of the star Rukbat in the Sagittarius sector.

They found Pern idyllic for their purposes: a pastoral world far off the standard trade routes and perfect for those recovering from the horrors of the Nathi Wars.

Led by war hero Admiral Paul Benden, and Governor Emily Boll of war-torn Tau Ceti, the colonists quickly abandoned their star-traveling technology in favor of a simpler life. For eight years—"Turns" as they called them on Pern—the settlers spread and multiplied on Pern's lush Southern Continent, unaware that a menace was fast approaching through space.

The Red Star, as the colonists came to call it, was actually a wandering planetoid that had been captured by Rukbat millennia before. It had a highly elliptical, cometary orbit, passing through the fringes of the system's Oort Cloud before hurtling back inward toward the warmth of the sun, a cycle that took two hundred and fifty Turns.

For fifty of those Turns, the Red Star was visible in the night sky of Pern. Visible and deadly, for when the Red Star was close enough, as it was for those fifty long Turns, its indigenous lifeform could cross the void to Pern. Once these alien spores entered the tenuous upper atmosphere, they would thin out into long, narrow, streamer shapes and float down to the ground below, as seemingly harmless "Threads."

However, Thread was anything but harmless. Like all living things, Thread needed sustenance, and it ate voraciously of anything organic: wood or flesh, it was all the same to Thread.

The first deadly Fall of Thread caught the colonists completely unawares. And, having abandoned their high-tech weaponry and tools as part of their idealistic move to Pern, they barely survived. In the aftermath, they came up with a desperate plan to design a shield against the recurrent threat: they used their knowledge of genetic engineering to modify fire-lizards—six-limbed, winged Pernese life-forms that had natural resources against Thread—into huge, intelligent, telepathic dragons. Able to instantaneously travel from one place to another—by going *between*—and to "breathe fire," the dragons could intercept Thread and burn it out of existence before it could reach the ground. Telepathically linked to their riders from the moment of Hatching and thus able to work as fighting units in perfect tandem, these dragons formed the mainstay of the protection of Pern.

The approach of the Red Star not only brought the mindless Thread but also caused the tectonically active Southern Continent to heave with volcanoes and earthquakes, causing the colonists to seek refuge on the smaller, stabler, though less temperate Northern Continent. In their haste to flee, they lost many important resources and, over time, much knowledge was forgotten.

Huddled in one settlement, which they called Fort Hold, the colonists soon discovered themselves overcrowded, particularly with the growing dragon population. So the dragons moved into their own high mountain space, Fort Weyr. As time progressed and the population spread across Pern, more Holds were formed and more Weyrs were created by the dragonriders.

The combined needs of the holders and the dragonriders resulted in a complex societal structure. Settlements called holds fell under the authoritarian jurisdiction of major Holds, each run by a Lord Holder, who could maintain control over terrified people and limited resources during the years of Threadfall. The Weyrs, under the leadership of a Weyrwoman—rider of the senior queen dragon—and a Weyrleader—rider of whichever male dragon flew the senior queen in a mating flight—were unable to both provide for themselves and protect the planet. They were forced to rely on tithes from the Holds to keep them provided with food and supplies.

And so the two populations grew separate, distant, and sometimes intolerant of each other.

The Red Star grew fainter, Thread stopped falling. Then, after a two-hundred-Turn "Interval," it returned again to rain death and destruction from the skies for another fifty-Turn "Pass." Again, Pern relied on fragile dragon wings and their staunch riders to keep it free of Thread. And, again, the Pass ended, and a second Interval began.

At the beginning of the Third Pass, a new disaster struck—dragons started dying of an unknown disease. These deaths, added to the losses from fighting Thread, decimated the Weyrs. K'lior, Weyrleader of Fort Weyr, decided upon a desperate course of action and sent his injured dragons and riders ten Turns back in time to abandoned Igen Weyr where they might heal and return in time to fight the next Threadfall. Their desperate jump *between* time—led by young Fiona, rider of gold queen Talenth—proved fabulously successful. After spending three Turns living and growing in the past, they returned to Fort Weyr, recovered and trained to fight, a mere three days after they'd left.

Upon her return, Fiona discovered that while not much had changed at Fort Weyr or Pern in the present time, she had changed greatly. She was three Turns older—and wiser. When the dragonriders of Telgar Weyr were all tragically lost *between*, Fiona volunteered to go to Telgar Weyr to revive its Thread-fighting forces. She was accompanied by bronze rider T'mar and many other dragons and their riders who, during their sojourn in the past, had grown to know her, love her, and respect her.

But at Telgar, tragedy struck again: More dragons, including Fiona's beloved Talenth, were stricken with the same illness that had already killed so many of the dragons of Pern. It looked as if Fiona would surely lose her dragon . . . until ex-dragonrider Lorana and Harper Kindan arrived from Benden with a cure—a cure won at the cost of Lorana's own queen dragon.

An extraordinary and unusual relationship arose among Fiona,

Lorana, and Kindan, in which Fiona bonded with both of them—and discovered a strange telepathic connection with Lorana. This three-way bond, as well as her special relationship with bronze rider T'mar, bolstered Fiona as the Weyrs struggled with the knowledge that even though the deadly dragon illness was no more, the surviving numbers were not nearly enough to protect the planet from Thread.

Losses continued to mount. Lorana, who had the rare ability to bespeak *all* dragons, felt every death, and despite the wonder of her newfound pregnancy, and everything Fiona and Kindan tried to do to protect her, she grew increasingly desperate . . . until that desperation forced to her to attempt a bold plan. . . .

CHRONOLOGY OF THE
SECOND INTERVAL/THIRD PASS

DATE (AL)	EVENT	BOOK
492.4	Marriage: Terregar and Silstra	*Dragon's Kin*
493.10	Kisk Hatches	*Dragon's Kin*
494.1	Kindan to Harper Hall	*Dragon's Kin*
495.8	C'tov Impresses Sereth	*Dragon's Fire*
496.8	Plague Starts	*Dragon Harper*
497.5	Plague Ends	*Dragon Harper*
498.7.2	Fort Weyr riders arrive back in time at Igen Weyr	*Dragonsblood, Dragonheart*
501.3.18	Fort Weyr riders return from Igen Weyr	*Dragonheart*
507.11.17	Fiona Impresses Talenth	*Dragonheart*
507.12.20	Lorana Impresses Arith	*Dragonsblood*
508.1.7	Start of Third Pass	*Dragonsblood, Dragonheart*
508.1.19	Arith goes *between*	*Dragonsblood, Dragonheart*
508.1.27	Fort Weyr riders time it back ten Turns to Igen Weyr	*Dragonsblood, Dragonheart*
508.2.2	Fort Weyr riders return from Igen Weyr	*Dragonsblood, Dragonheart*
508.2.8	Telgar Weyr jumps *between* to nowhere Fiona, T'mar, H'nez to Telgar Weyr Kinden, Fiona to Telgar Weyr	*Dragongirl*

On Pernese time:

The Pernese date their time from their arrival on Pern, referring to each Turn as "After Landing" (AL).

The Pernese calendar is composed of thirteen months, each of twenty-eight days (four weeks, or sevendays) with a special "Turnover" day at the end of each Turn for a total of 365 days.

CONTENTS

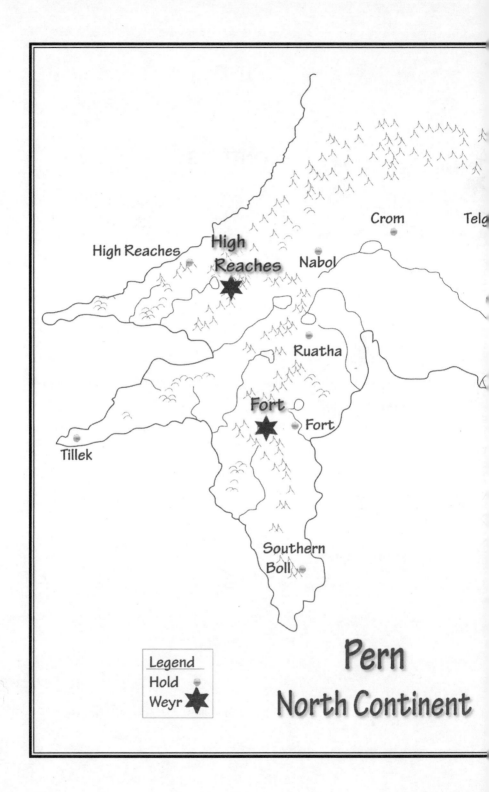

High Reaches

High
Reaches

Crom

Telg

Nabol

Ruatha

Tillek

Fort

Fort

Southern
Boll

Legend
Hold
Weyr

Pern
North Continent

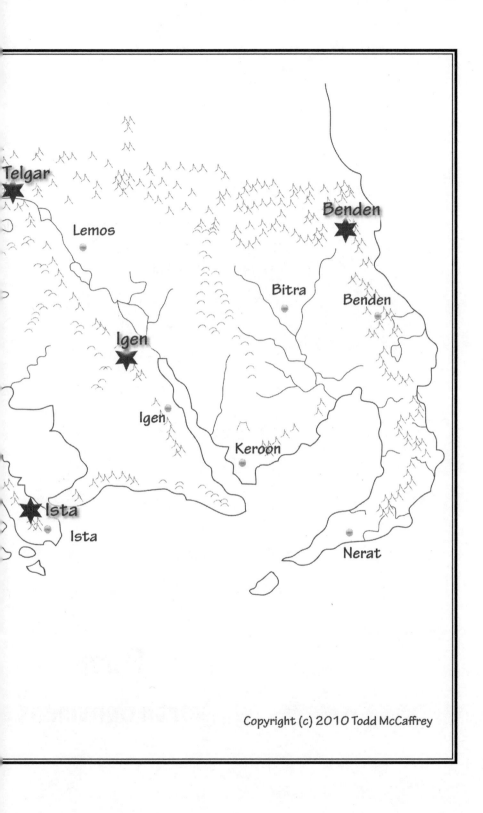

Telgar

Lemos

Benden

Bitra

Benden

Igen

Igen

Keroon

Ista

Ista

Nerat

Copyright (c) 2010 Todd McCaffrey

DRAGON'S TIME

ONE

The way forward is dark and long.
A dragon gold is only the first price you'll pay for Pern.

Cold. Black. Silent.

Deadly.

Between. That strange nothingness where dragons can go that can only be described as *"between* one place and another."

"Between only lasts as long as it takes to cough three times." For a short journey, yes. For a journey from one place to another, anywhere on Pern—yes, three coughs is enough. But when traveling *between* one time and another—it takes longer. A cold, silent, freezing longer that saps life.

Lorana felt nothing, not the warmth of the queen dragon beneath her, not even the tiny, tender presence that warmed her womb.

I'm sorry! Lorana cried, her hand going to her belly. *There was no other way!*

No response.

Pern was dying, there were too few dragons and riders to protect it from Thread. Slowly, steadily, inexorably, the protection of Pern was being eroded, was dying out. The dragonriders, including Weyrleader T'mar, Weyrwoman Fiona, and all the Weyrleaders of the four other Weyrs, had tried their best, had developed new tactics, had kept adapting, kept striving, kept searching for some way out of their trap. But the problem was that there were too few dragons, less than a third the number required, and more were being lost each Fall.

The dragons' numbers were so few because of the strange sickness that had come upon them just before the start of this new Pass of the Red Star. Lorana, with Kindan's stout aid, had succeeded in finding help from the distant past and that help had led them to a cure for the sickness. In the meantime, however, too many dragons had succumbed to the sickness—and more to Thread—leaving too few dragons to protect the planet. In desperation, because no one could conceive of getting further help from the past, Lorana had decided to jump forward in time, to jump ahead to a time after the Third Pass and beg for aid from the future.

She was the only one with a sure sense of time and place—a gift, she thought, from her special link with all the dragons of Pern—and only she could make the journey forward to such an unknown, unseen time. She used the Red Star to guide her, picturing it and the stars in their stations where they would be fifty Turns from her present.

Using her gift came at a price, however. A jump of this length would be a terrible strain on her and gold Minith. But it would be fatal to the life stirring inside her.

Lorana wailed silently. Go back! she urged herself. Go back before it's too late.

I can't, she decided a moment later. It's too late. I'm all alone.

I'm here! Minith called to her feebly, her touch full of support. *You are not alone.*

Lorana made no reply. She knew she couldn't explain herself to the gold dragon, to a queen who laid eggs.

Everything I've loved, I've lost, Lorana thought to herself, letting her hand slip, unfelt, unfeeling, from her belly.

I've lost my own queen, my beloved fire-lizards, and now . . . She couldn't finish the thought.

Tears froze on her cheeks, her heart beat at a slow, glacial pace, as the cold of *between* sapped her strength, her life.

And stilled the life of the other inside her.

A dragon gold is only the first price . . .

The cold *between* gripped her and she knew no more.

Lorana closed her eyes in a spasm of pain. She was in a bed, in a nightgown. Fearful, her hands went to her belly—it was flat, lifeless.

"You lost the baby," a voice said. It was old, hoarse with age, but somehow familiar. "But you knew that. You planned on it."

Tullea. Benden's Weyrwoman, Minith's rightful rider.

Minith? Lorana called.

I am here, the queen responded quickly. There was no echo to her voice: no sign that an older Minith—a Minith of this future time— had heard her call.

"Don't," Tullea warned harshly. "You are still too weak. I wasn't sure that you wanted to live yourself." She paused for a moment, then added, "Perhaps you didn't, really."

"Where am I? Is the Pass over?" Lorana asked, her eyes still closed. Her mouth was dry; her voice was slurred and felt awkward.

"The Pass is over," Tullea affirmed. "That much I'll tell you and no more."

"Help?" Lorana said. She realized that word wasn't enough and, after another breath, asked, "Will you send help?"

"Dragons from the future?" Tullea said. "Simple, quick, efficient! Oh, yes, no worries for those left behind." She snorted and added viciously, "Oh, no! No, dragon-stealer, you won't find any dragons in the future."

"None?" Lorana opened her eyes only to find the room completely dark.

"None for you," Tullea snapped back. "You were always meddling when you should have left things alone."

"Where's B'nik?" Lorana asked.

"Where's his jacket?" Tullea retorted. She barked a bitter laugh. "*Between,* that's where! Where you left it!"

Lorana wondered for a moment if the old queen rider had gone insane.

"Where you must go, now!" Tullea went on, and Lorana gasped as, abruptly, the blankets were pulled off her. "Get up, your things are over there!"

"But—I want to talk—"

"You've talked enough!" Tullea snapped, grabbing Lorana's hand and feebly pulling on it. "You're well enough to travel; it's time— long time—you were gone." Tullea seemed to think her last comment funny and let out another bitter laugh.

The faintest of glows, smaller than any Lorana had ever seen, was turned. It provided only a dim light, which revealed bare stone walls, the rude blanket thrown over her, and the rough, reed bed beneath her. And Tullea—old, bent, white-haired, almost unrecognizable.

"Take my dragon with you, dragon-stealer!" Tullea said, throwing clothes toward her.

"Can't I talk to anyone?"

"What makes you think there's anyone to talk to?" Tullea asked sharply.

Lorana started to answer, then stretched her senses, searching for someone, for a dragon or even a watch-wher, but—

Slap! Her cheek was suddenly aflame with stinging pain.

"Don't do that!" Tullea barked. "Don't make me remember!" She shoved Lorana. "Get dressed, get going! Now!"

Shocked and depressed, Lorana wordlessly slipped back into her riding clothes. Her undergarments were unwashed; they smelled of sweat and the fear she'd felt when she'd made this journey to the future.

So far. She'd come so far. She'd given so much.

"Get moving!" Tullea hustled her along. "Time enough to think later."

"Please, we need help," Lorana said even as Tullea nudged her. They walked down a slope on a cloudy, starless night. She heard more then saw Minith in the distance.

"You'll have to fly high and south to get above the clouds and see the Red Star," Tullea told her as she tried to push Lorana up onto the gold dragon. "Be quick about it! I want to have as much time with *my* dragon as I can!"

Lorana found herself perched on Minith, wondering if the poor gold queen had been wearing the riding harness the whole time Lorana had been a babbling wreck in bed. Had she even been fed?

"Of course she was fed!" Tullea declared irritably. "Now, go! Go back where you belong!" She barked another dry laugh. "The Red Star will guide you, just as it did when you came here!"

Without another word, Tullea turned away, heading back up toward the cave from which they'd emerged. Lorana watched her in the dim light, frowning. Wasn't there anything she could do?

"Go!" Tullea wailed.

Come on, Minith, let's go, Lorana said sadly to the queen. In a moment they were airborne, climbing toward the clouds. As they rose higher, the clouds thinned and she could see the Red Star faintly through the breaks.

She brought the image of Red Butte into her mind with stars, moons, and the Red Star to mark the time, thankful for the very small favor of Tullea's, and gave Minith the coordinates.

All this way, she thought to herself as they entered the cold of *between.* Involuntarily her hands went to her belly. Her cold, flat, lifeless belly. All for nothing!

Tullea turned back when she heard the sound of Minith going *between.* Her shoulders slumped and she let out a deep, regretful sigh.

Minith, tell her it's done, Tullea thought, stretching her mind into *between* in the special way she'd been taught.

A moment later the air was full of the sound of dragon wings. A pale yellow specter, a ghost of the young fertile queen who'd been here just moments before, landed daintily in front of her with the grace of long years.

Beside her, another queen landed. And another.

"Stay there!" Tullea called up to the two queen riders. "I want to get back to the Weyr and feel some warmth in my bones."

"How did she take it?" the older of the two riders asked, her face bleak with sorrow.

"Just like you said she would," Tullea snapped waspishly. For a moment her habitual mask slipped and she asked, "Why couldn't I have told her? Why did I have to be a monster to her?"

"Because that's what she said," the woman replied. Her hair was mostly white with only a few streaks of blond left in it, but her eyes were still the sea green blue they'd always been. "She said that you were horrible to her, gave her not one moment's kindness." She paused and added, "Nor one clue."

"So she'll never know," Tullea mused to herself. "She never found out."

"No," Fiona replied sadly. "She never had a chance to learn how you'd changed." She smiled at the older woman. "But I did."

Tullea snorted in disbelief.

"Why do you think I insisted on that glow?" Fiona asked.

"Because Lorana said that's what there was," Tullea said.

"Because if there'd been more light, she would have seen your face clearly," Fiona told her.

"So?" Tullea barked. "It's old, it's creased." Her tone changed as the feeble spark of anger in her dimmed. "I've lived a long life; I'm ready for my rest. We go back to the Weyr, I say my farewells, and you keep your part of the bargain."

"Of course," Fiona agreed.

Tullea mounted, moving slowly with care for her old bones even as she cursed her age. It was time, she thought to herself. She'd seen enough, lived enough. It was time.

Before she urged Minith back to the Weyr, she turned to Fiona. "What about the light?"

"The lines in your face," Fiona said by way of explanation. "They're not lines of sorrow. If she'd seen them, she'd have known."

"Oh," Tullea replied. Her face grew brighter and she shot the younger woman a smile as she added more emphatically, "Oh!"

It was only when they were back in the Weyr, when Fiona was helping Tullea down off the aged Minith, that the older Weyrwoman had time again to think of what she'd done.

"Will you ever tell her?" she asked without hope.

"About you?" Fiona asked sadly. At the old woman's nod, she shook her head. "No, I never knew. Never knew until it was too late."

"Pity," Tullea said. She glanced toward the clouds and the night sky, which threatened rain later. "I would have liked for her to know." She snorted. "It's the least I could do, for all that she's done."

Above them, the sky was torn open as wing after wing of dragons appeared overhead and spiraled down gracefully into the Weyr below.

"Don't tell him at least," Tullea pleaded as she glanced upward at the returning dragons, with Benden's Weyrleader in the vanguard.

"That his mother was here tonight?" Fiona asked, looking over toward the Benden Weyrleader. "Or how surprised she'd be to know that he's partnered with your daughter?"

A streak of light burst from the Dining Cavern and a young form raced into sight, stopping with sudden concern for Tullea's old bones.

The dark-haired little boy looked up at Tullea and she knelt down.

"I'm too old to pick you up, you know," she said as she drew him into a great hug. "I think I'll miss you most of all."

The boy looked at her in confusion, his dark brown eyes were deep and thoughtful, slanted just slightly and shrouded by the thick dark hair that made him the near-twin of his great-grandmother.

"He'd be proud, you know," Fiona spoke up quietly from Tullea's side, with a brief tilt of her head toward Benden's Weyrleader.

"I'll have to be proud enough for all of them," Tullea replied, her eyes spangled with tears.

Again Lorana was numb, voiceless, shocked by the length of the cold *between*. She had followed Tullea's image blindly, and so it came as a shock to realize that she and Minith seemed to be *between* for even longer than on their jump forward. Where was Tullea sending her?

Suddenly, as if in a clear instant, Lorana froze, thinking that she heard voices. She strained her senses, reached out, and caught— panic, fear, despair!

A man's voice cried out. And a woman's, too. Fiona?

Lorana started to worry that she had jumped blindly *between* forever, like D'gan and the Telgar riders, and that perhaps she was hearing Fiona's voice calling for her. She tried to reach out, to touch Fiona, to find her and then—

She burst forth into a cold night sky. It felt as cold as *between*, and as dark—except she could see a spattering of stars in the sky and a small light below.

She realized suddenly where she was—she had drawn a picture of it once long ago—Red Butte, the massive uprising of rock in the center of the Keroon Plains. Minith, without urging, began a slow, steady spiral down toward the light.

It was a campfire, warm and inviting. Lorana saw one figure rise from beside it before exhaustion overtook her once more and even that small light went dark.

"The soup is warm, you should sip it slowly," a young man's voice said. A hand covered her eyes briefly as he added quickly, "Don't open your eyes until you've sat up, or you'll stare straight into the sun!"

Lorana was lying on the ground, its rock-hardness eased by a layer of soft cushions, perhaps a pile of reeds. She sat up slowly and opened her eyes.

An earnest young man smiled at her, proffering a steaming bowl of soup.

Thirsty, cold, and fatigued, Lorana took the bowl and drank a quick, small sip.

"It's good!" she said, taking a longer drink.

"Finish it, I'll get more," the young man offered, pointing at a large cauldron resting on the side of a neat ring of rocks.

Lorana gladly complied. At the man's gesture, she handed him the bowl and he scooted over to the cauldron to dip out another serving. He coughed once and shook his head with a frown.

As he handed the bowl back to her, Lorana looked at him closely. Had she come back to the time of the Plague?

"It's not the Plague," he said, as if guessing her thoughts. "This is my own doom." Another cough rattled through him and it was a long moment before he could take another breath. Once his breathing eased, he told her conversationally, "I won't have it much longer. I'm going to die tomorrow."

Startled, Lorana made to rise, saying, "We can get help! Minith will take us—"

"That won't be necessary," he told her, shaking his head. "There is nothing that can be done."

"But you're so young!"

"I've had my Turns, now it's my time," he said. He held a hand out to her. "Until now, you've never met me, but I've already seen *you* several times."

"Seen me?" Lorana asked, bewildered. "At a Gather?"

"No," he said, smiling sadly and raising a hand to his head. "In here. And in the flesh." Another cough wracked his body. "My name is Tenniz; I think you've heard of me."

"Tenniz?" Lorana repeated. "The trader?" Her hand went to her chest, where she wore the unusual brooch that had been left for her at Telgar Weyr—a strange gift with an even stranger message. "You sent me this."

"I did," the young man said with a grimace. "I wish it were not so." He cocked an eye at her. "You've returned from the future?"

"You knew?" Lorana said, surprised. *"The way forward is dark and long. A dragon gold is only the first price you'll pay for Pern,"* she went on, quoting the note that had accompanied the brooch.

Tenniz shook his head. "I only knew a little," he told her, tapping his head. "I see the future only in glimpses."

"Please," Lorana said, "what did you see?"

"I saw a long, cold darkness," Tenniz said. "I saw a face you knew, but older. I felt a loss, a numbness, a warmth gone cold." He looked up at her, his eyes troubled. "What was it?"

"My baby," Lorana replied softly.

"Oh!" Tenniz cried, "I didn't know! I'm sorry!"

His expression so unnerved her that Lorana found herself sobbing as she saw the sympathy in the eyes of the young man who would die the next day.

It was a long time before she could draw a shuddering breath and ease the pain in her heart. "Have I paid enough?"

Tenniz shook his head. "I don't know."

Lorana looked at him, examining his face carefully for the first time. The face was not that old, certainly younger than her, but older than Fiona. The thought of the irrepressible younger woman brought a slight smile to her lips and instinctively she reached out—

"I can feel her!" Lorana said in surprise. "Twice!" She explained, "I can feel her baby self at Fort Hold and her older teen self, here now in Igen Weyr." Her smile slipped as she added, "Baby Fiona is so *cute*!"

She felt the slim child's mind start to turn questioningly toward her, heard Talenth at Igen Weyr respond to her dreamily, and felt, behind the dragon's query, a more tenuous strand of thought from the teen Fiona and abruptly pulled herself away from them. Neither baby nor teen had yet met Lorana and she didn't want to frighten them.

"You brought her back to Igen," Tenniz guessed.

Lorana shook her head. "I haven't."

"Yet."

Lorana considered that for a moment, then nodded. "I suppose at some point, I could do it."

"Either you or someone else from her future must do it," Tenniz said.

"Must?"

"It is said that there is no way to break time."

"There are ways to cheat it," Lorana said.

"Cheat it?"

She gave him a sad nod. "Yes," she said. She told him about Ketan—the ex-dragonrider who had lost his brown to the sickness—and how, at Tullea's urging, Lorana had taken Minith back in time with the older Ketan to give the dragonrider one last chance to ride his beautiful brown dragon and, at the same time, save Weyrleader B'nik from death by taking his place.

"That's amazing," Tenniz said. "But, of course, it had always been that way, hadn't it?"

"I suppose you could look at it that way," Lorana replied.

"I see it differently."

"Things that happen differently?" she asked.

"No," he said. "What I see happens. It's just that it may not happen the way I see."

Lorana was growing more confused.

"For example, I saw that you would suffer another loss, but I did not see *what* it was."

"You said you see glimpses."

"Yes," Tenniz agreed.

"Did you see me coming here?"

"It was one of the first things I ever saw," he replied. "Among those born with this gift, it is common that the first thing they see is their own death."

"Your death?" Lorana asked, wide-eyed. "Here? With me?"

Tenniz nodded twice.

"That must be horrible!"

"Not really," Tenniz said. "I first started *seeing* around my eleventh Turn, and so seeing myself all 'grown up'—as I thought then—seeing myself talk to someone whom I was really pleased to meet, was quite an enjoyable image." He shook his head and smiled fondly at the memory of his younger self. After a moment he added, "It's almost easier to *see* things about myself than others."

"What about Pern?"

"I see glimpses of the future, people in them," Tenniz said. "It's like dreaming but different; there's a sense of *purpose* to these dreams, like they're important."

"So you don't know what will happen?"

Tenniz sat silently for a moment before answering, "Even before I met Fiona, I knew the dangers of talking too much about the future."

"What does it matter?" Lorana asked. "You say the future can't be changed."

"And you say that it can be cheated," Tenniz replied. "Just like Fiona, I learned that telling too much can be harmful."

"How?"

"By making it harder to cheat," he said.

"Pardon?"

"If you think you know how things will go, then why would you try anything different?" he replied. "Consider your friend Ketan."

"Well, what I know right now is that no one survives," Lorana said bitterly.

"How do you know that?"

"I told you, I met Tullea, I couldn't hear any dragons—"

"I thought you said that she slapped you," Tenniz interjected.

"She did," Lorana said dismissively.

"Just when you were reaching out, right?"

"Yes," Lorana replied, wondering suddenly how Tullea would have known that she was reaching out. How could she know that unless . . . Her eyes widened. "And she sent me here, to you." She looked at him quizzically. "Why?"

"Why indeed?" Tenniz said. "I didn't tell her that I was coming here."

"But now I would know, I could tell her in the future," she said.

Tenniz frowned while he considered her notion. "But why send you back here, then?"

"So you think she had something in mind?" Lorana asked. "And she slapped me so that I wouldn't reach out to find dragons?"

"I don't know," he said. "She could have slapped you just because she was mad."

"She *was* very angry," Lorana agreed.

"She might also have been mad, too," Tenniz added with a bleak expression.

"Mad enough to send me back here?" she wondered.

"You have another thought?"

"Perhaps she *wanted* me to find you," she said. "In which case . . ."

"Nothing," Tenniz said, shaking his head gently. "It would seem that Benden's Weyrwoman, in her old age, has grown more cunning than I would have expected."

"Or someone else suggested it to her," Lorana said. The image of a smiling blond-haired, green-eyed young woman came readily to mind. "They could all have hidden *between*," she added. "I wouldn't have been able to find them, then."

"How would they know when to come back?"

"There are several ways," Lorana said after a moment. "Because this happened to me already, anyone I tell would know what happened and could tell Tullea in the future."

"Or you could be grasping at straws," Tenniz said.

"I could," Lorana agreed, "but that's better than what I thought before."

"So you get my point," Tenniz said with a grin. "It's important not to give away too much so that we can cheat time."

"It still doesn't solve our problem now," she said with a grim look.

"You mean *then*," Tenniz corrected. Lorana made to answer but he held up a hand, adding, "Your 'then' is ten Turns in our future, when the dragons have stopped dying of this sickness, but are too few to protect Pern."

"Yes, that *then*," Lorana agreed.

"Time-travel must be very confusing," Tenniz said.

"It is," she agreed. "And tiring."

"And dangerous," he said, blowing out a sigh that turned into another hacking cough. He held up a restraining hand as Lorana moved to his aid, and in a few moments the cough subsided. When he recovered, he gestured for her to get up. "I must show you some things while I still can."

Bemused, Lorana rose, only to reach out to the thin man for support. Tenniz gave her an apologetic look and a firm grab, helping her to steady herself on her wobbly legs.

"Not far," he said. "I hope you'll have your energy back soon."

"You didn't see that?"

"What I saw was that you came from a dark, cold place, through a darker, colder place, suffering a great loss, feeling a great sadness and despair," he told her. He smiled for a moment. "I saw us laughing together and looking up at the stars—" He glanced up at the daylight surrounding them. "I expect that will happen later." He paused as he steered her toward his destination. It was a pile of rocks. "And, I'm sorry to say, I saw you crying as you piled the rocks."

"Piled the rocks?" Lorana repeated, looking at the neat pile. And then, beyond it, she saw the small depression carved out of the unrelenting stone of the Red Butte.

"Well, it took me a while, but I figured it out, I think," Tenniz said pursing his lips in a quick grimace before adding, "I always liked being out among the stars." He paused, took a quick step in front of her, and, still holding her hand, knelt, looking up beseechingly. "Would you bury me when the time comes?"

TWO

Rise up,
Fly high,
Flame thread,
Touch sky.

Telgar Weyr, evening, AL 508.7.21

"It will turn out all right," Fiona said as Kindan tucked her into bed. She was exhausted. The day had been a horrible drain on her: first with Tullea's unexpected arrivals and accusations, then with the realization that she couldn't *hear* Lorana anywhere, and finally with the growing belief that Lorana had taken Tullea's queen Minith forward in time—at the cost of her own pregnancy. Tenniz's prophecy had come true for Lorana in a horrible way: *A dragon gold is only the first price you'll pay for Pern.* If that prophecy were true, then so must be the prophecy that Tenniz had given Fiona: *It will turn out all right.*

"If you say so," Kindan murmured. T'mar had, with a firm nod, sent him off to guide Fiona to bed while the bronze rider had remained with Tullea, B'nik, and the others.

"*I* don't say, *Tenniz* said so," Fiona replied sleepily. She suspected Kindan or Bekka had dosed her drink with *fellis* juice and she made a note to herself to speak with the younger woman about that—wasn't *fellis* supposed to be bad for a baby?

▼ ▼ ▼

"The fact remains, T'mar, that we've less than a full Weyr's strength still able to fight all the Thread on Pern," B'nik said as he slumped wearily in his chair. He and Tullea, at T'mar's suggestion, had gone into the Kitchen Cavern for wine and a talk.

"If Fiona's right, Lorana has gone ahead—"

"Why?"

T'mar shrugged. "To get help, I'd imagine."

"Help from the future?" B'nik repeated, his eyes narrowing. "Is that possible?"

"I suppose, if we can go into the past to recover, we can just as easily go to the future," T'mar said.

"Why don't we send our injured and our weyrlings back in time?" Tullea asked. The others looked at her. "We've got almost more of them than we have fighting dragons."

"Where would we send them?" B'nik asked. "Igen's been used back in the past, unless we want to go back to the time of the Plague."

"I wouldn't recommend that," Kindan's voice carried to them as he strode up to the table. T'mar gestured him toward a seat, asking, "Fiona?"

"Sleeping," Kindan replied. A small smile tugged at his lips as he added, "I convinced her that Bekka had dosed her mulled wine with *fellis*."

"What good did that do?" Tullea asked.

Kindan shook his head, his smile widening. "Weyrwoman, for many, it's not so much the deed as the belief that makes things happen."

"Well, she would certainly qualify!" Tullea replied with a derisive snort. "She's willing to believe anything."

"I don't think so, Weyrwoman," Kindan replied.

"You're no judge; you're besotted with her," Tullea snapped.

"She's got a good heart, Weyrwoman," H'nez spoke up in Fiona's defense. "And she's done a great deal of good for this Weyr."

Tullea frowned. "I suppose you're right." After a moment's

thoughtful silence, she shook her head again. "It's not a question of heart, it's a question of numbers, and we don't have enough."

"So, if Fiona is right, Lorana has gone to the future to ask for dragonriders to help us," C'tov said, looking to T'mar and Kindan for confirmation.

"Yes," Tullea agreed, glancing toward the door. "So where are they?"

"I imagine it would take time to convince them," H'nez said.

"Time *then*, not now," Tullea said, shaking her head. "If Fiona was right, then Lorana would already be back and our Weyrs would be full."

She glanced from B'nik to T'mar for confirmation.

"Perhaps—" C'tov began.

"I think we've been through enough for an evening," B'nik said, rising and yawning widely. With a wry grin, he gave T'mar and the Telgar riders an apologetic look.

"It's later at Benden than here," T'mar said, rising as well. He nodded to Tullea. "I'm sorry we kept you so long."

Tullea waved the apology aside. "It wasn't you, it was Lorana."

"All the same," B'nik said as they walked out into the darkened Weyr Bowl, "she did save my life."

"And for *that*," Tullea said with a heavy emphasis on the last word, "I am grateful."

"Kurinth's hungry," Terin said the next morning as she heard F'jian mumble behind her in the bed. It had been a strange night for the both of them, with Terin railing at F'jian about his drinking and the bronze rider trying to avoid the issue, but, in the end, with the air cleared, Terin found herself snuggling up close to the taller bronze rider and drifting off to a sleep more peaceful than she'd ever had before.

"I'll come with you," F'jian offered, stirring beside her.

"No, you're going to drill today and you need all the rest you can get," the young queen rider assured him. She turned around long enough to catch his eyes as she added, "With all this timing, you'll need to be at your best."

"Tomorrow's never certain," F'jian said, sitting up and looking around blearily for his tunic. "I treasure every moment with you."

Terin smiled at him, quickly pulled herself together, and raced out of his weyr down to Kurinth. She was surprised to see Fiona waiting for her, a bucket of scraps in her hand.

"I was just about to feed her."

"Thanks!" Terin said, taking the bucket and going into Kurinth's weyr, calling out happily to her beautiful baby queen dragon.

"Good morning, F'jian," Fiona called as the bronze rider rushed up the queen's ledge into Kurinth's weyr.

"Good morning, Weyrwoman," F'jian returned jauntily as he raced past.

"Well, I'll leave you to it," Fiona said, with a smile and a wave as she turned back to her own weyr.

A commotion from the weyrling barracks distracted her and she turned to see all the newly Impressed dragonriders race off for buckets of food. She wondered how quickly they'd settle down into a regular routine and wondered if they, too, would suffer from the strange fatigue that bothered her, T'mar, and the weyrlings who had accompanied them back in time to Igen Weyr.

A growl from her stomach forced Fiona to realize that the dragonets were not the only ones needing food. With a mental caress for Talenth, she started down the ledge across the Bowl to the Kitchen Cavern, following the marvelous smells of breakfast and freshly baked rolls.

She was not surprised to find T'mar, H'nez, and C'tov already seated, looking as though they'd finished a hasty breakfast. T'mar nodded politely to her, rose quickly, and pulled back a chair in which to seat her.

"Thank you!"

"How are you feeling?" T'mar asked conversationally.

"I'm feeling hungry," Fiona said, smiling up as a sound from behind alerted her to Shaneese's approach with a basket of fresh rolls and a pitcher of juice. "Oh, thanks. I'm not sure I could stomach *klah* this morning."

"You wouldn't get it anyway," Shaneese told her. "Bekka's orders."

"That young girl takes on entirely too much—"

T'mar snorted and Fiona glared at him. "I recall saying exactly the same thing about *you*!"

"I can't imagine where she'd learn it," Shaneese said in agreement.

"Her mother, probably," Fiona said, trying to hide her chagrin. Fiona glanced around the Cavern before asking, "Where is she, anyway?"

"Doing her rounds," T'mar said. "She was up early with one of the injured dragons—"

"Dragons!" Fiona exclaimed. "Where is Birentir?"

"Leading the way," H'nez said.

Fiona pushed a roll into her mouth and started chewing urgently even as she rose from the table.

"Where are you going?" T'mar asked, brows furrowed.

"After them," Fiona said. "It's my duty as Weyrwoman."

"Sit," T'mar said, jabbing a finger toward the chair. Fiona shook her head and then turned in surprise as she felt Shaneese's arms going to her shoulders, pushing her back down.

"T'mar's right, you need to eat," Shaneese said.

"But—"

"Weyrwoman, please listen to them," H'nez said, his dark eyes grave.

"But—"

"Fiona, you've got to take care of yourself if you're to be of any use to the rest of us," T'mar said. "And you've got more responsibilities to consider now."

"Especially with Lorana gone," C'tov added quietly.

Fiona allowed Shaneese to guide her back into her chair and carefully chewed her roll. They meant well and she knew what they meant—she not only had a responsibility to the Weyr but also to the stirrings in her belly.

"Lorana's coming back," Fiona said after she swallowed. The

others looked away, unwilling to comment. Fiona's lips tightened as she realized that even if she came back, Lorana would have gone too far forward *between* for her pregnancy to survive. Fiona's eyes misted as she recalled the tiny kick she had felt from Lorana's belly. Sometimes, Fiona thought sadly, there are no good choices.

"Our next Fall will be over lower Crom in five days' time," T'mar said to the wingleaders with a side glance toward Fiona.

"We have seventy-four fighting dragons," H'nez pointed out.

T'mar nodded. "B'nik's offered us a wing from Benden."

"That'll help," C'tov said.

F'jian raced in, rushing through the Kitchen Cavern entrance and nearly bouncing off some of the weyrfolk as he ran over to join the discussion.

"Sorry I'm late."

"I meant to say that F'jian was helping Terin feed her dragon," Fiona said hastily in the cold silence that fell.

T'mar smiled and shook his head. "I've just started," he said. "If I'd felt your presence was critical, I would have had Zirenth bespeak Ladirth."

H'nez gave the younger bronze rider a dry look while C'tov merely pulled back the seat beside him invitingly.

"As I said," T'mar continued while F'jian poured himself some *klah*, "our next Threadfall is in five days' time and we're getting a wing from Benden to help."

"That's good," F'jian agreed.

"If we need to," T'mar continued, "we'll time it. If we do that, as I've told B'nik, we'll do it without the Benden riders."

"Well, let's hope we get all the Thread the first time, then," F'jian said. He opened his mouth for a smile and was startled when it expanded into a huge yawn.

"Somebody had a good night," C'tov muttered to H'nez.

"F'jian, you'll take the light wing," T'mar declared, glancing over to catch his reaction. "You'll be responsible for firestone and our reserve."

F'jian nodded glumly; he'd expected no less for being late.

"You'll have some company," T'mar declared, "as I'm going to fly solo to coordinate with the three wings." He nodded to H'nez and C'tov. "That will leave you two your wings intact."

"Half of my people are injured," H'nez said.

T'mar nodded. "Which is why it's vital that we spend the next several days training with our new organization."

"How do you want to do that?" C'tov asked.

"I think first we'll set up the new wings and then give you the day to train them separately," T'mar said.

"Just a day?" H'nez asked.

"Let's see how we do," T'mar said, shrugging. "I expect that coordination will shake out pretty quickly." He gave them all a wry grin. "After all, we *have* done this before!"

"And after that?" C'tov asked.

"We'll train for a day or two as a Weyr. B'nik's offered us a day of training with the Benden wing after that," T'mar said. "The day before the Fall, we'll rest." He glanced at F'jian as he added, "Some of us may need it more than others."

The younger bronze rider raised his hands in surrender. "All for the best of reasons, Weyrleader."

That evening, F'jian invited Terin to dine in his quarters. The drill throughout the day had been hard and they had not had a moment alone together since the morning, so Terin agreed.

She was disturbed by F'jian's silence as they climbed the stairs to his rooms.

"Tired?"

"Thinking," F'jian told her with an apologetic look.

F'jian had arranged to have their meal sent up before they'd started their climb and it was waiting for them when they entered his quarters.

"Ladirth, how are you?" Terin called politely as they crossed to the small circular table where they took their meal. She frowned when the dragon made no response.

"Sleepy," F'jian told her with a wave of his hand. He gestured to one of the chairs. "Sit! I'll get the food."

Terin was delighted at his graciousness, but sat dutifully. F'jian paused on the way back with their dinner tray, looking at her intently.

"What?" Terin asked, wiping her face in search of any stray hairs or dirt.

"You're so beautiful," F'jian said, placing the tray between them and carefully setting the dishes in front of her. Terin was amazed; F'jian often just wanted to eat straight off the tray.

"What's wrong?" Terin asked, suddenly uneasy with his behavior.

F'jian shook his head. "Nothing," he said softly, "nothing at all."

Terin woke suddenly in the night, cold. F'jian was out of bed. He'd insisted, strangely, on having her sleep further in on the bed—closer to the wall—which was not their normal routine. Terin had relented grudgingly, but soon fell asleep in his rangy, strong, comforting arms.

Now those arms weren't around her. She started to call out but stopped as she heard voices from the direction of Ladirth's weyr. One of the voice's was a woman's, speaking quick and low. She heard F'jian answer and then the flutter of wings as Ladirth flew off.

Concerned, she sent a tendril of thought toward her Kurinth—the young queen was sound asleep. Terin stretched her senses, listening in the dark of the night, but heard nothing untoward. After a while she drifted back to sleep once more, determined to talk to F'jian when he returned.

She woke to the feeling of hot tears on her cheek. She turned over to see F'jian leaning over her, his eyes full of tears.

"What?" she cried. "F'jian, what is it?"

"Nothing," the dragonrider told her huskily. "It's just that you're so beautiful." He paused and leaned down to kiss her cheek. "I love you so much. Don't ever forget that."

Tenderly, Terin turned to kiss him properly but, to her surprise, he turned from her, kissing her on the cheek firmly.

"Sleep," he said, allowing himself a huge yawn. "Sleep, I'm sorry I disturbed you."

Terin murmured a response and lay her head back down on her pillow. She opened her eyes again as F'jian's fingers brushed her cheek and he leaned closer, wrapping his warm, strong arms around her once more. Terin sighed happily and drifted back into a deep sleep.

Terin found herself glancing at F'jian nervously throughout the next day, trying to figure out what had happened. He seemed both more at ease and sadder at the same time. He would always smile when his eyes found hers, but he'd never allow her to catch his expression unguarded for long.

If F'jian's behavior was odd, Fiona's announcement that morning was completely disturbing.

"She's all right!" Fiona shouted as she bounced into the Kitchen Cavern that morning.

Kindan, who was at the weyrlings' table, glanced up.

"Lorana!" Fiona said, rushing over to him and grabbing his hands. "I saw her, she's fine!"

"Where is she?" Kindan asked even as T'mar and the other bronze riders rushed over, glancing around in a vain attempt to spot the ex-queen rider.

"She left," Fiona said airily. "She said she'd be back, though."

Kindan's expression grew troubled and he glanced imploringly over at Birentir and Bekka, who responded by joining them.

"You saw her?" Bekka asked. "How was she?"

"She drew a picture for me," Fiona said. She glanced at Kindan. "I didn't know you'd given her your colored pencils."

Kindan shot her a troubled look.

"Fiona, why don't you sit down and tell us while you're eating," Birentir suggested, gesturing for one of the weyrlings to yield his seat to the Weyrwoman.

"All right," Fiona said, with a touch of annoyance entering her voice. She sat, pulled over a roll, and buttered it. Chewing quickly, she swallowed and looked up to Kindan. "As I said, I saw Lorana this morning."

"And she drew you?"

"Yes," Fiona said. "I sat on my bed while she drew."

"Can I see the picture?" Kindan asked.

"She took it with her," Fiona said. She frowned. "She seemed sad, now that I think about it."

"How did she look?"

"I didn't see her too much, she was in shadow," Fiona said. "She wanted the light on me, so it was coming over her back."

"Did she say where she had been?" T'mar asked.

"Did she say when she'd be back?" Kindan added.

Fiona frowned and shook her head. "She just woke me, said she had to draw me, made her drawing, and left."

Kindan exchanged glances with T'mar, then Birentir. The older healer sighed.

Bekka spoke up, her tone gentle. "Sometimes when people are pregnant they have strange dreams," she suggested.

"It wasn't a dream!" Fiona declared. "I was awake!"

"You said that Lorana woke you," Bekka said. "I've heard of people who think they're awake and having conversations and they're only dreaming."

"It was real!" Fiona cried, her voice rising as she glanced around at the disbelieving faces gathered around her.

"I dream of my daughter sometimes," Birentir said to her gently. "I dream of her being almost as old as you are now, Weyrwoman."

"It wasn't a dream!"

"Could it have been?" Kindan asked her gently. "Could it not just have been a pleasant dream?" He paused, glancing into her eyes as he added in a wistful tone, "Sometimes I dream of your sister and she's smiling at me."

"It wasn't a dream!" Fiona roared, flying to her feet and glaring angrily at everyone. "I know when I'm dreaming. It was real!"

She glanced around, saw no acceptance in the eyes of the others, and, with a sob, raced out of the Cavern.

"Could it have been real?" T'mar asked Kindan as the others recovered from her abrupt departure.

"If so, then why didn't she stay?" Kindan asked. "Where is she now? Can Zirenth hear her?"

T'mar relayed the question to his bronze dragon, received his reply, and shook his head. "No."

"She's been under a lot of stress," Birentir said into the silence that followed.

The others nodded, but Kindan caught T'mar's eyes and they exchanged a worried look.

"I'll have Shaneese bring her breakfast," Bekka suggested. "She'll feel better with something in her stomach." She paused thoughtfully before glancing up at Birentir. "I think this backs my guess."

"Twins?"

Bekka nodded. Kindan and T'mar glanced at her with wide eyes, so she added, "It's too early to be certain. Shards, it's even too early to be sure of the pregnancy, but the way she's been eating and . . . well, the way she's been eating makes me think she's eating for three."

Fiona found herself in the Records Room, searching through Records. She'd show them!

Where to begin? The Records at Telgar weren't the dry, warm parchment of Igen, some of them were the thin, fragile slivers of hardstone with the words deeply chiseled into them.

The mustiness of the Records and the room made her stomach roil and turn. Fiona toyed with the idea of leaving for better air, but decided stubbornly to continue with her work.

She moved the Records more slowly, took smaller stacks, and read them more carefully than usual.

How it happened, she could never recall, but Fiona woke up hours later with the imprint firmly in her cheek of the Record she'd laid her head on while she'd nodded off. With a quiet snarl of anger, she pushed herself up, left the Records where they were, walked back to her quarters proper, and took a long, soothing bath, hoping that the water would ease the imprint out before anyone noticed.

Footsteps coming toward the entrance alerted her and she called out, "Don't come in!"

"Fiona?" T'mar's voice echoed into the room. "Are you all right?"

"Of course," Fiona said quickly. "I just felt like a bath."

T'mar made a noncommittal noise. Fiona glowered unseen in response.

"Bekka and Birentir wanted me to tell you that they'll manage just fine on their rounds," T'mar said.

Fiona murmured in reply. "That's good, because I think I'll look in the Records."

"The Records?" T'mar repeated. "I went there first, did you know that someone had left piles on the table?"

"Mmm," Fiona returned noncommittally.

"And one of them was wet," T'mar added, his tone full of humor. "It seemed like someone had fallen asleep on it and drooled."

"Drooled," Fiona muttered to herself, chagrined.

"Pardon," T'mar called, "I didn't catch that."

"That's interesting," Fiona called back loudly. "I suppose I'll have to clean that up." Fiona's brows creased as a thought came to her. "Aren't you supposed to be training?"

"We're just back for lunch," T'mar replied easily, in a teasing tone. His tone changed as he added, "Has Terin spoken to you about F'jian?"

"Why?"

"Because it was everything he could do to stay on his dragon at drill," T'mar said. He added in a thoughtful tone, "I know that all of us are still muzzy-headed, but he seemed worse than most."

"Kindan thinks we're timing it," Fiona reminded him. "Maybe F'jian feels it worse just now."

"Or maybe he's timing it more," T'mar murmured thoughtfully. "We know that the effects of going *between* times are cumulative—if he were timing it more than once a day, then he'd feel it worse than others."

"There could be another perfectly reasonable answer," Fiona answered after a moment. She flushed as she explained, "I mean there are other ways to get tired than simply going *between* times."

"One for which congratulations would be in order?" T'mar asked with a grin.

"I suppose that depends upon who you're asking and how they feel about it," Fiona said.

She could almost *feel* T'mar thinking furiously as he stood outside her bath, deciding upon a course of action.

"Would you like me to talk with Terin?" Fiona offered.

"When you're done with the Records," T'mar replied with a renewed spark of humor in his tone. Fiona growled at him and the Weyrleader laughed easily in reply. "I'd best get back to lunch, we'll be practicing this afternoon, too."

"Keep an eye on F'jian!" Fiona called to the sound of his departing steps.

"Indeed," T'mar's distance-muffled voice replied. A moment later his steps faded from her hearing. Fiona lay back in her bath, thinking.

The next Fall was over lower Crom in four days' time. It was an evening Fall, starting just about the seventh hour after noon. She frowned, realizing that, stretching for six hours, the Fall would go into the early hours of the next morning.

Talenth, Fiona reached out to her queen who responded drowsily, *has T'mar asked Nuella about training with the watch-whers?*

In another two days, Talenth replied after a short pause to relay the question to her mate, Zirenth, and receive his rider's response.

Having the watch-whers flying with them would certainly help and a night Fall had less live Thread than a daytime Fall. Idly, Fiona wondered how the watch-whers were faring and whether their numbers were as precipitously low as the dragons'.

Kindan had told her that what had killed Lorana's queen Arith had been the contents of the fourth vial found in the Ancient Rooms at

Benden—the one meant to change a watch-wher into a dragon. In her ignorance, Lorana had mixed all four vials together in her desperate attempt to save her queen's life. It had been Arith's death—and Lorana's frantic grab for her across nearly five hundred Turns of time—that had warned the Ancient Timers of the peril of the sickness in the present time. Lorana had only used a little of each vial, thankfully, so there was enough left to save the dragons of Pern—and provide, in that fourth vial, a chance to turn watch-whers into dragons. Did Lorana tell Nuella *when* to use that scary vial that would make watch-whers into dragons? Had she somehow *known* that it would be needed?

Fiona let out a sad sigh as she asked herself honestly, Could Lorana have gone *between* forever? Fiona shook her head, reminding herself: I saw her, she came here, drew a picture of me.

Lorana could have come back from the past, she thought in response. In irritation with her own thoughts, Fiona stirred and pulled herself from the bath into the cold air of her bathroom. She stood there for a moment, her face set in a frown, her skin freezing, as if in punishment, before reaching determinedly for a towel. I saw her!

THREE

In darkest night I find you,
The sisters of tomorrow:
Heralding the dawn.

"There's no chance you could be wrong?" Lorana asked the young man hopefully.

"There's every chance I could be wrong," Tenniz agreed. "And imagine how embarrassed I'd be to find myself not dead."

"Have you ever been wrong before?"

Tenniz shook his head slowly. "No." He added, "I've wished it several times but—no, I've never been wrong."

"But you said that you see only glimpses," Lorana reminded him.

"Some glimpses are more definite than others," Tenniz said. "As I said, I saw you crying and piling rocks on the cairn." He turned back toward their camp and gestured graciously for her to accompany him.

"But you could die another day," Lorana protested as they walked back slowly. "It doesn't have to be today."

"Tomorrow, in the morning, I'll be dead," Tenniz assured her. A cough wracked him and he gestured at himself with a hand as if in proof. "All that really matters is now and what we'll do with our time together." He smiled at her. "I, for one, am hoping to spend it in pleasant conversation."

"I'm not prepared to die."

"Pardon?"

"I'm not prepared to die," Lorana repeated. "I'd much rather talk about how to save Pern."

Tenniz nodded in understanding. "I would like to know that my son and daughter will grow up in a world free of Thread."

"You've a son and a daughter?"

"I've nearly twenty Turns," Tenniz said.

"But you knew you were going to die," Lorana said.

"I did and I do," he said. He gave her a wry look. "As are we all in our own time."

Lorana accepted that with a nod. "It must be hard on you," she said.

"No harder than it was for you," the young man replied. Lorana's eyes misted as she caught his meaning. "We faced hard choices."

"Where are they now?"

"Safe, with their mother," Tenniz replied, a wistful look livening his face. "My son's the elder, my daughter's not yet born."

"How old is he?"

"Jeriz's just turned a very difficult two," Tenniz said with a rueful look. "I'm sorry to be leaving him for Javissa to deal with, but"—he dipped his head—"we traders look after our families and no one was ignorant of my fate."

"They're trying to keep this Sight of yours alive, aren't they?"

"Among the traders it has saved countless lives," Tenniz told her. "Even for myself, I would say it was more blessing than curse."

Lorana cast a quick sad glance at her flat belly and gave Tenniz a fierce look as she asked, "And your daughter, how do you know she'll be born?"

Tenniz gave her a sympathetic look before telling her, "I've seen it."

"And what else, to save the traders, have you seen of the future?"

"All that I could say to you, I have," Tenniz told her in a pained voice. "You know that we can't break time."

"J'trel tried," Lorana said, more to herself than the trader. With a sad smile, she recalled the old blue rider who had brought her out of her misery, succored her after the death of her father, and set her on the path that led to Benden Weyr and her beautiful gold Arith. She recalled him telling her how he'd tried to go back in time to show his dragon to his mother and how he'd found that he couldn't.

"Many more will try," Tenniz said, "none will succeed."

Lorana gave him a sharp look. "You say that for me, particularly."

Tenniz regarded her silently. Finally, he said, "I think you must have some trader blood, some of the Sight."

Lorana shook her head in irritation.

"Who else hears the dragons the way you do?" Tenniz prodded gently. "I think that you are a distant relative."

"My father was a beastman near Benden."

"A traveling man," Tenniz said. "Your family moved a lot, with the herds, as he bred for the best."

Lorana was surprised.

"You've been seen by others," Tenniz said.

"Your father?" Lorana guessed.

Tenniz shook his head. "My mother," he told her. "The Sight can go to either man or woman."

"But only one," Lorana guessed. "The Sight only comes to one in each generation."

Tenniz gave her a wry look. "See? You prove my point," he told her triumphantly.

"It was a guess," Lorana said acerbically. The wind, which had been light and steady, gusted suddenly, catching Lorana off guard.

Tenniz nodded toward the bedrolls. "It can get very cold up here," he said. "You might want to wrap in a blanket." He moved over to the fire, stirred the embers with a nearby stick and threw some more light kindling on to keep it going. "If you're hungry, we can heat up lunch."

"How did you get all your supplies up here?" Lorana wondered, glancing around at the gear of the camp and appraising the effort it must have taken to transport to the top of the Butte.

"I have my ways," Tenniz told her drolly, reaching back for his pack and quickly pulling some strips of dried meat from a bag. "We've water enough, if we can wait, that this will cook into a nice stew with a good broth." A cough distracted him and he frowned in mild annoyance until it passed. He rummaged in the pack some more and, with an amused glance at Lorana, pulled forth a bottle. "And some wine for later, if we feel like it."

"You plan on drinking at your own wake?"

Tenniz shrugged. "I merely hope to spend time with a friend."

The wind died down and Lorana shrugged out of the blanket, rose quickly, and came over to Tenniz, reaching for the pack. "Let's see what you have in here," she said.

There were several large flasks of water laid near the pack and Lorana once again felt surprise at the provisioning of this temporary camp.

"Put some more wood on the fire," Lorana told him. "We're going to need a lot of heat to stew that dried beef." She took the pack from his hands as he rose to comply and peered into it. While Tenniz built up the fire, Lorana rummaged in the pack and found several savory dried herbs. Her eyebrows lifted in wonder; someone had good taste. Perhaps Nuella had packed for him? Someone had to have brought him up here and with Nuella nearby and the relations the traders had established with the wherhold, she was the likely choice.

The gold watch-wher was large enough to have managed carrying the two of them and the supplies, but probably not all in one trip. Back in this time she had yet to meet the Wherwoman, but she could easily imagine the delight Nuella would have had in arranging the journey and completing the trip, probably all in alarming darkness. If that was what happened, Lorana was amazed that Tenniz wasn't still in shock.

"There's another pot in that large bag," Tenniz said as he caught Lorana eyeing their breakfast pot warily. He added, in an oddly amused tone, "We don't have enough water to wash them out, afterward."

"Hmm," Lorana agreed, not entirely surprised. "I suppose if we left them up here long enough, the grit in the wind would be enough to clean them."

"We traders have done that in the desert sometimes," Tenniz agreed.

Lorana fetched a flask of water, unstoppered it, and poured a generous amount into the new pot, throwing in the herbs she'd gathered in her other hand before setting it atop the stones centered in the fire.

"There's another lid over there," Tenniz said, pointing with the stick he'd used to prod the fire to greater life. As Lorana turned to spy yet another sack, Tenniz added from behind her, "Three of them, in fact."

"So we're set for three meals?"

"We prepared for four," Tenniz said. "Breakfast, lunch, dinner, and"—his eyes cut away from hers—"well, food for the morning."

The sun rose, reached its noon height, and presently began to sink again. She and Tenniz had fallen into a companionable, thoughtful silence as they'd watched the dim flickers of flame in the bright sun, had felt the winds gentle with the nooning, had watched Minith dozing comfortably.

Presently Tenniz rose and busied himself with some long poles. Lorana watched him curiously for a moment, then rose and helped him assemble a crude awning.

"Too long in the sun up here and we'd both be burnt crisp," Tenniz explained as he finished tying the last of the stay ropes to a large rock. He gestured for Lorana to join him and together they put themselves in the shade, out of the worst of the sun's rays, pulling in the bedrolls and spreading them out to ease the bite of the hard ground beneath.

"So, what is your daughter going to be named, or do you know?" Lorana asked conversationally.

Tenniz shot her a startled look. "We agreed—" he stopped and took a quick breath, looking away from her as if to re-collect his control. "That is, we were hoping, with your blessing, to call her Jirana," Tenniz said after a moment, speaking as though choosing his words carefully.

"My permission?"

Tenniz's eyes darted away from hers with the same look Lorana had come to associate with Fiona when she was caught scheming. "I told Javissa what I saw of you," Tenniz responded shortly, "and we agreed that if you wouldn't mind, we would include part of your name in our daughter's."

"I'd be honored," Lorana told him. She cocked her head at him, giving him a thoughtful look. He raised an eyebrow questioningly. "I was trying to imagine your features on a girl."

Tenniz chuckled. "I'm not certain that's wise, my lady," he said. Lorana started to protest, but he raised a hand, gently forestalling her. "Fortunately, Javissa is much prettier and I hope our Jirana will take after her."

"She must be quite a person, your wife," Lorana said.

"Kind and wise beyond her years," Tenniz agreed, his expression dreamy. "And patient, very patient. She'll need it with my son."

"So, your son will get the Sight?" Lorana asked.

"No," Tenniz said with a sigh, shaking his head. "I'm afraid that will go to Jirana."

"Are you afraid it will be a burden for her?"

Tenniz gave her a small smile, shaking his head. "I am sure that she'll thrive."

"Does it hurt a lot," Lorana asked, "knowing that you'll never hold her in your arms?"

Tenniz shot her a startled look and took a deep steady breath as he shook his head once more and said, eyes downcast, "No, no, I've seen enough to be content."

Lorana nodded, rising from her cross-legged squat to move out from the awning toward the fire. With a stick, she lifted the lid and looked inside. She sniffed the fragrant steam wafting up and turned back to Tenniz. "If you're ready to eat, it's done."

At Tenniz's urging, she left the stew to cool while they opened the wine that the trader had wisely placed in the shade along with them.

"Benden white!" Lorana exclaimed as he displayed the bottle to her. "Your friends know how to treat you."

"I am blessed in my friends," Tenniz agreed, nodding to include her among them.

Two small but clean stone goblets had been packed for the wine and Lorana was surprised to realize how relaxed she felt as she savored the taste of the liquid in her mouth before swallowing. After she swallowed, she lifted her goblet higher and gestured to Tenniz, "To Pern!"

"To Pern!" The trader raised his goblet and inclined his head as he repeated the toast. Sipping his drink, Tenniz raised it once more and added, "And to the women who guard it!"

Lorana raised her goblet once more, but before she could drink, Tenniz's words startled her, "Don't drink, I was toasting you."

"And who else?" Lorana asked as she recovered from her confusion.

"Those who guard Pern," Tenniz returned cryptically, seeming annoyed with himself. Lorana glanced at him shrewdly for a moment, thinking how thin the man was and how strong wine could inspire loose lips.

"To Fiona, then!" Lorana said, raising her goblet and deliberately taking a small sip, while tipping her drink far back. Tenniz followed her toast and Lorana reached forward for the wine.

"I need more," she said, pretending to top off her goblet and pouring a generous amount into Tenniz's. She raised her goblet again, saying, "To J'trel!"

Tenniz did not follow her, saying instead, "I never met him."

"He was a good man," Lorana said, masking her annoyance at his reluctance to follow her toast. "If it weren't for him, we wouldn't be here now." She raised her goblet once more, repeating, "To J'trel!"

Reluctantly, Tenniz followed with his drink.

"You have mentioned your wife," Lorana said, trying a different tack, "tell me about her."

Tenniz thought for a moment before answering. "She has the prettiest green eyes," he said. "I fell in love with her the moment I saw them." He glanced at her wryly. "Green is such a dangerous color here on Pern, I suppose it seems strange of me to admire it so."

"We need green to grow," Lorana said with a flick of her fingers. "Just as Thread needs it to survive."

"And sucks the land dry," Tenniz said, his voice suddenly cold and hollow. Lorana met his eyes, but the trader lowered them.

"To the dragonriders of Pern!" Lorana said, raising her goblet once more and taking a deep drink.

Tenniz followed her action wordlessly. After a moment, he searched for a flat place and carefully placed his goblet on it, rising and heading toward the stew.

"If we keep drinking, we'll get light-headed," Tenniz said, as he reached for one of the bowls and the stirring ladle. He turned back to Lorana. "Are you hungry?"

"Starving," Lorana admitted. Tenniz smiled at her and passed her the first bowl. "Whoever picked your herbs knew my tastes perfectly."

"These herbs are common in the desert," Tenniz said, his back to her as he filled his bowl. He put the ladle back in the pot, spun on his heel, and quickly sat once more under the awning, a small pinch of herbs in his free hand, which he crumbled into his stew as he added, "Although I prefer it a bit spicier."

"If that's spark pepper, you like it a *lot* hotter," Lorana replied, her eyes wide as she took in the sprinkling of bright red-orange spice flakes on top of Tenniz's serving. "You'd best top your glass."

Tenniz shook his head. "Water first, then wine, with this mix." He jabbed his spoon into his bowl, took a large portion and wrapped his mouth around it, his eyes closing blissfully.

Lorana took a bite of her stew, and quickly sought out her wine goblet to cut down the spicy heat that assailed her. The stew itself was nearly cool, but the spices caused her to break into a sweat. "This wasn't hot enough for you?"

"Heat helps in hot climes," Tenniz said in the singsong tones of someone repeating a proverb. He helped himself to another large spoonful of the stew before adding, "They do say it's an acquired taste, though."

"I can see that," Lorana agreed firmly. Actually, now that her mouth was used to the spicy heat, she found the stew only pleasantly hot and the overall taste full of complex flavors. She closed her eyes for a moment, savoring the stew as she chewed. She opened them again when Tenniz chuckled at her. "See, a few days in the desert and you'd be ready for robes!"

"Ready for robes?" Lorana repeated in confusion.

"People who aren't used to the desert spend a lot of time wearing clothes suited to cooler climes," he told her. "We say someone is ready for robes when they've learned to respect the desert and seek ways to keep cool."

"Fiona and Shaneese mentioned—"

"Shaneese? You met Shaneese?"

"Of course."

"Did she spit in your stew, too?" Tenniz asked with a grin. Lorana shook her head and the trader laughed. The laugh lurched into a long hacking cough and Tenniz turned an alarming shade of puce before he managed to find another breath. "Another good thing about spices," he said weakly when he could speak again, "they keep the lungs clear."

"Have you seen a healer?" Lorana asked.

"Several," Tenniz agreed. "Some think it's left over from the Plague, but others say it is something I was born with." He waved the issue aside. "It is not important now."

"I can't imagine Shaneese spitting in anyone's soup," Lorana said.

"Ah, but she was much younger—she *is* much younger now," he said. "You met her when she was a grown woman, correct?"

Lorana nodded.

"At this moment she is even younger than I," Tenniz told her. "And she didn't like what I had to say."

"And what did you say to her that made her spit in your soup?"

"I told her that she would gladly share her man," Tenniz said. He shook his head at the memory. "I should not have spoken, but I was in the grips of a seeing and it was a good thing." He cocked his head at her questioningly. "Do you know of it?"

"You've met Fiona?"

"Fiona!" Tenniz said, his eyes suddenly going wide. "But—" he cut himself off, shaking his head fiercely as if to drive the words out of his head. "So I was right to think she was lucky."

"Perhaps," Lorana agreed. "The relationship is still new, still—"

"It has something to do with you, too," Tenniz said, with more than just a guess. He smiled fondly as he added, "She is a special person, and special to you, isn't our Fiona?"

"She is," Lorana agreed. A moment later, she added in a different tone, "Although I don't think she can ever forgive me—"

"For the baby?" Tenniz guessed.

Shakily, Lorana nodded. She piled her spoon high with spicy stew and shoved it into her mouth, allowing the heat to distract her and provide her with a moment's silence. When she spoke again it was in a small, troubled voice. "Was it worth it?"

"Your price?" Tenniz asked.

Eyes bright with tears, Lorana nodded. Again, she said, "Because I don't think Fiona would forgive me—"

"No," Tenniz cut her off. She glanced at him in shock. In a hard voice, he continued: "You know better. She's no stranger to hard choices. Tell the truth."

Lorana let out a small sob and lowered her eyes. "I don't know if *I* can forgive myself."

"Yes," Tenniz agreed. "That's the truth."

"And?" Lorana prompted, her tone pleading.

"And that's the question only you can answer," he said, pursing his lips in a grimace. "Always, in the end, only we can answer our own questions."

"Have you answered all your questions, then?"

"No," Tenniz admitted. He raised his eyes to meet hers, his lips curving upward. "I have many questions I think I'll never get answered."

"But you've got more answered than most," Lorana said with a touch of anger in her voice. Tenniz raised his brows questioningly. "You know that the dragons survived the sickness, for example. So you know that your daughter will have her eighth Turn."

"No," Tenniz said with a quick shake of his head, "that is not given to me."

A breath of cold air whipped over her and Lorana jerked upright. The sun was setting, the evening winds had picked up. Lorana's surprise faded as she remembered lying down, her lunch warm in her stomach, the last sip of wine, Tenniz's companionable silence. It had been all too easy for her to just close her eyes and drift without effort into a heat-induced sleep.

"Tenniz, I'm sorry!" Lorana said, turning toward the now-shadowed spot where'd she last seen the trader.

"Sorry for what?" Tenniz asked, accompanied by sounds of stretching.

"For falling asleep," Lorana said. "If this really is your last day . . ."

"Traders nap in the heat of the sun," Tenniz said, dismissing her concern gently. "Anyway, I think I was asleep before you." Another cough shook him and it was a long while before he recovered. So long, in fact, that Lorana went over to him only to see the darker shadow of his hand waving her away.

She turned to the outdoors and went to the fire, carefully finding more kindling and building the last of the embers back into flickering flames, all the while keeping her hearing stretched painfully to the sounds of the young man behind her. She turned when his coughs ceased, worried that she had heard his last breath. The sound of rustling blankets and of Tenniz rising came to her ears before her eyes could make out his movements in the shadows. She let out a quick sigh of relief, unaware that she'd been holding her own breath in sympathy.

"The stars will be out," Tenniz said, glancing up at the darkening horizon as he approached her. He dropped his gaze toward her, adding with a smile, "They'll be beautiful."

"When I was with J'trel," Lorana said, "we had time to look at the stars." She shook her head. "I don't think I've done it since."

"Well, then, it's certainly past time that you did again!" Tenniz glanced around, wandering over to the supplies and rustling among them. "Tonight," he said, as he saw Lorana eyeing him, "I cook for you." He raised a hand as she started to protest. "It is a special meal and it would honor me if you would take of it."

"Gladly," Lorana said, moving toward him. "How can I help?"

"Clear the old pots, see to the fire, get it hot again," he said. "We won't be eating until we see the right stars, so you won't want to freeze."

"And what about you, won't you want to stay warm?" Lorana asked. Tenniz opened his mouth, closed it again and shook his head. "Is it possible that you see too much of tomorrow? That seeing what you see causes you to give in? That you might die because you catch your death of cold tonight?"

Tenniz was silent for a long moment. "That is the greatest danger of knowing too much of the future."

Lorana absorbed his words thoughtfully, lowering her eyes. For a long moment her mind churned on his meaning, on all that it meant and then—"You tricked me!" she shouted with a laugh. "You just wanted to teach me the lesson *you've* already learned Turns before!"

"Yes, my lady," Tenniz agreed with a light chuckle, "I did."

"How can you be so happy at a time like this?" Lorana asked him, suddenly serious and angry, really angry in a way that embarrassed her, made her feel small and vindictive.

"If I thought being somber and serious would give me another day with my wife, I wouldn't be here," Tenniz replied. He stood up with his supplies and moved toward the fire. "But I've known for Turns that this day would come, I've had Turns to adjust to the notion that I would die before my daughter was born, would never live to see my son a man." He turned back to her. "I cannot see how being angry or solemn would make it any easier for me."

He gestured around the plateau and beyond to the beauty that was unfolding in the setting sun; the promise of a brilliant night of stars. "I choose not to wrap myself up in grief over things I cannot change, cannot control, and, instead, take joy in all the gifts I've been presented. Rather than rail against the moments I cannot have, I will cherish those I do—instead of squandering them in useless rage."

There was a long silence.

"It is strange," Tenniz began again, in a softer, less emotional tone, "how those who expect to see tomorrow have so little appreciation for it."

"I was talking to myself, wasn't I?" Lorana said after a moment.

"'All the words we say aloud are heard by at least one pair of ears,'" Tenniz agreed with the tone that made it clear he was reciting another trader proverb. He took the largest flask of water, unstoppered it, and drank deeply.

"Ah!" he said with pleasure. He twisted his body to offer it up to Lorana. "Tell me what you think."

Gratefully, Lorana accepted the flask and, sensing ritual, took a long drink herself. The water was perfect, not too cold, not too warm, full of the sort of satisfying flavor that only water can have when found at the end of a hot day or when thirsty from wine.

"Perfect," Lorana said, passing the flask back to him.

"Only a parched man really knows water," Tenniz said, again in the tone of a trader saying. He poured a generous amount into the pot, stoppered the flask and slid its strap over his shoulder so that it hung down at his side.

"Only a dying man really knows life," Lorana said, glancing at Tenniz.

"So it is said," Tenniz agreed quietly. "But just as it is the path of wisdom in the desert to bear water, so it is the path of wisdom to learn life."

"And cherish it," Lorana said, her eyes suddenly wet with tears, her hands unconsciously moving toward her flat belly.

"My wife was right," Tenniz said huskily. Lorana glanced down at him and saw him looking up at her. "You are the right one for my last night."

"You could have spent it with her," Lorana guessed.

"One of the gifts of the Sighted is to know our last night," Tenniz said. He gave her a crooked smile. "It's more of a blessing to know of a certainty that this night, and no other, will be my last."

"I could see how, knowing that, you could have a very special night, one for the memory of all times with your wife," Lorana agreed. She frowned as she added, "It would have been a great gift to her, to your son as well."

"And now you come to wonder why I spend it with you," Tenniz said, nodding. He reached into the pack and brought out some carrots, somewhat wilted from the earlier heat of the day but smelling ripe, fresh, and savory. A knife and a cutting board came out of the pack. He deftly chopped the carrots and put them in the pot, along with some fully ripe tubers, quickly chopped; fresh onions; crisp celery. He looked amused as he pulled out a small packet of herbs, sniffed appreciatively at the gorgeous scent wafting up, giving Lorana a strangely thankful look as he carefully chopped them finely and poured them in.

"You are giving me a great gift," Lorana said in awe.

Tenniz gave a quick chuckle, rooting once more in the pack and drawing a bunch of fresh herbs. "As are you, me!"

Lorana moved toward the fire, throwing on more kindling and working in silence to build it up to a proper size and heat.

"Is there a shroud?" Lorana asked, looking across the now bright fire toward Tenniz, who was only visible as a shadow, with firelight gleaming in his eyes.

"Pardon?"

"Is there a shroud I should put you in," Lorana said, taking a deep breath to finish, "for tomorrow?"

"That would be awkward," Tenniz said. "I've some robes I'll put on tonight, before dinner; they'll be fine."

"And we'll drink more wine," Lorana guessed.

"Oh, no," Tenniz corrected, "water only."

"For those crossing the desert," Lorana guessed.

"'Parched, you shall drink,'" Tenniz quoted.

"'Hungry, you shall eat,'" Lorana said, hearing the catch in Tenniz's voice confirm that she strangely knew the right words.

"'And—'"

Lorana joined in with him—"'the stars shall guide you to your sleep.'"

"There's another," Lorana said, craning her neck up into the slowly darkening sky above her.

"Three," Tenniz agreed, the sound of his voice changing as he lowered his head. "It's time."

The trader had long since changed into his robes. Lorana was not surprised at the fine fabric nor at the simplicity of the design; she could see the loving care that had gone into its making, the delicate darker embroidery along the cuffs, the care that had gone into the stitches. She guessed that more than one hand had prepared the outfit, that perhaps Tenniz's mother or even Fiona's friend, Mother Karina, had sewn parts of it, making the whole a covering of love.

"You have to see the back," Tenniz said proudly as Lorana had admired it. With a smile, he twirled so that the firelight picked up the brilliantly colored embroidery.

"A dragon?" Lorana exclaimed. "A queen? Over water?"

Tenniz spun back again quickly, his smile slightly strained as he told her diffidently, "It's a pretty image, don't you think?"

"Certainly," Lorana agreed, feeling once again that the younger man was desperate to divert her. Lorana raised a hand with one finger stretched out and twirled it, gesturing for him to turn around again. "I'd like to see more of it."

"There's another," Tenniz said, pointing up the sky. "There's the fourth star." He glanced back to her as he added, "They made a cloak, too, which I can wear if it gets chilly."

"Is it as pretty?"

Tenniz shrugged. "More plain but still white. I think the fabric is the same." He gave her a shy look. "I don't think I'll need it, I'd be happier if you took it with you."

"But then your beautiful emblem would get all dirty," Lorana complained. She cut herself off abruptly, realizing that she was talking about the time after his death.

"I think we can spare a blanket instead," Tenniz said, gliding over her chagrin. "As you say, it *is* nice fabric."

"But won't it seem . . . wrong if I were seen with it?"

"Those who see you will know it was my gift to you," Tenniz told her. "'The dead have no belongings.'"

"But it's not right to take what they were left with," Lorana protested.

"True," Tenniz agreed, taking a deep breath and breaking out into yet another long, wracking cough before adding ruefully, "but as I am *still* drawing breath, I can freely give it you, and you can freely accept with no guilt."

Lorana sensed that the robe seemed important to him, that there was more than mere kindness in the offer, but that he could not tell her more.

"Another prophecy?"

Tenniz gasped, sounding surprised, but he covered it quickly, saying, "Hardly."

"Very well, I accept and with thanks," Lorana said, deciding that it would only be cruel and heartless to press the younger man.

"We should eat, so that we have time to enjoy the full dark of the night," Tenniz said, rustling about for another set of bowls and spoons.

Together they pulled the stew off the fire. Tenniz ladled the hot, pungent mix out of the pot and presented Lorana with the first bowl. Sensing tradition, Lorana took it with a grateful nod, then passed it back to him. Tenniz's eyes lit as he took it and nodded in thanks.

Lorana took her bowl and spoon and stood, gesturing for Tenniz to follow her. The trader rose, his brows furrowed questioningly.

"Minith," Lorana called, "how are you doing?"

I'm fine, the queen responded.

"Would you like some company?" Lorana asked. To Tenniz, she said, "Have you ever warmed yourself against a dragon's belly?"

The trader's eyes widened in wonder and he shook his head, his mouth open in awe. "No, my lady, never."

Invitingly, Minith rolled on her side and moved her forearms out, creating a large sheltered spot.

Lorana carefully chose her position, turned, and deftly squatted with legs crossed and her back against the warmth of the huge golden hide. She glanced up to Tenniz, a hint of challenge in her expression. Still awed, Tenniz followed her example and sat next to her.

"She won't mind, will she?" he asked, craning his head over his shoulder and peering up and up at the mound of her stomach.

Not at all, Minith responded. Lorana heard Tenniz's gasp of surprise at the draconic surprise.

"I guess you didn't see *that*," she teased him gently. To ease the sting, she directed her next question to Minith, "Aren't the stars lovely tonight?"

They are, the queen agreed, raising her neck to crane her head up into the sky. *The trader is right, we do not look at them enough.*

Lorana took a taste of the stew and found herself gasping, fanning her mouth for the fire that burned inside. Wordlessly, but with palpable mirth, Tenniz passed her the water flask even as he, with his other hand, raised a full spoonful to his lips.

"It is better to take fully of life," he told her as he chewed and swallowed with a sigh of contentment. "Savor it, feel the spice, acknowledge the heat and the tears."

Lorana did as he said. After the first few spicy-hot mouthfuls, her tongue and throat grew more accustomed to the heat and she began to experience the flavor.

"Babies cry and howl because they do not understand what they are sensing," Tenniz said, taking another mouthful. "Later, they grow accustomed to harsh things."

Dutifully, Lorana took another mouthful, chewed slowly, and swallowed. Life: hot, spicy, painful, unpredictable, tasty, chewy, beautiful, searing. Life.

Lorana took another bite, a bigger mouthful, forcing her protesting tongue and throat to accept it.

Life. She'd had a life growing inside her. She remembered the cold, the numb of *between*. The sense of loss.

The heat of the spicy food roiled her stomach. She couldn't argue now that she wasn't alive. Tears streaked down her face and she realized that only some were the tears of hot food.

"It's dark," Tenniz said, rising a hand toward the sky.

Dark. Lorana looked up, into the deep black of the night sky. The stars above filled the sky with pricks of glittering light. A soft breeze blew, bringing a waft of cold air over her and she drew it into her lungs.

So many things I would have given you, Lorana thought to the emptiness of her womb. Before the lump in her throat could grow unbearable, Lorana spoke up, and grasping for anything to say, she said to the trader, "The stars are beautiful tonight. I haven't truly looked at them in such a long time."

She felt ritual engulf her once more. "Even in the dark, there is still light."

"'We are stars in the darkness,'" Tenniz replied with agreeing ritual.

"We burn bright, beacons for others," Lorana said.

"'We cannot see our own light, only those of others,'" Tenniz continued.

"Our light lights others," Lorana said, suddenly chilled with the power of the words, the sense of meaning that grabbed her, held her.

"'As their light lights us,'" Tenniz agreed, translating her words into the trader sayings of old. He glanced over to her and told her quietly, "You do not know our words exactly, but you have a trader's ear for truth."

"And so while there are stars, there can never be darkness," Lorana said.

"'And in the darkness, there is always light,'" Tenniz finished.

Silently, Lorana passed him the flask. Tenniz took it, drank deeply and passed it back to her. Lorana nodded in thanks and drank deeply, her tears drying on her cheeks, her throat no longer raw and protesting.

Life.

Lorana woke. She craned her head around quickly but she knew what she would see even as she turned. It was too quiet. There was a stillness, a respectful silence as though all Pern itself were paying homage.

She was glad to see that she had held his hand in hers, even as her eyes started to stream with tears.

Something slipped off her shoulder and it took Lorana a moment to realize that it was the white robe Tenniz had promised her. He was sitting on the old blanket and had it wrapped around his shoulders. His eyes were closed and his mouth was set in an expression of peace and joy.

He looked—and Lorana could not contain a sob—as though he'd spent the night with a friend.

Above her, Minith crooned anxiously.

"I know what to do," Lorana said to the queen, rising and wrapping the white robe around her shoulders. Gently she let go of his cold hand, caressed his face for the first time, but more in promise, as if she could embody the gentle touch of the woman she knew he'd loved. Gently she laid him out fully on the blanket, grabbed it firmly with two hands by his head and slowly trudged toward the dug-out ground and the pile of stones laid beside it.

Occasionally, she glanced over her shoulder to verify her course as she walked backward. Often she found herself glancing down at his face and wondering what sort of child he'd been, what memories he had had that he could never share again.

She pulled him and the blanket into the hollow. She hesitated for a moment near his head, then caressed it one more time and finished wrapping his body.

It was still dark out. The stars were fading. The sun was only a threat on the horizon.

Lorana had no trouble finding the stones, bright white even in the deep dusk. Her fingers grew cold, stone after stone, but she did not falter, never slackened, moved at the same pace.

Rock after rock, stone after stone, she built Tenniz's cairn.

Finally, she stood, wordless, staring down at her finished work. All the stones had gone to cover him. Two hundred and fifty-seven; she'd counted them absently.

"It's still dark, Tenniz," Lorana said, surprised at her own voice and the renewed tears in her eyes. "And it's darker now, for there's one less light in the sky."

She glanced upward, toward the fading stars.

. . . in the darkness, there is always light. His words echoed back to her.

Again, an echo: *. . . All the words . . . are heard by at least one pair of ears.*

"This was for me, too, wasn't it?" Lorana said to the cold, white rocks before her. "This wasn't just for you, or even just about you."

And the realization dawned on Lorana: This wasn't just to bury one person.

It was to bury two.

Her fingers stroked the fabric of the white robe idly as she realized that just as she had lost a child, a child of Tenniz's had lost a parent.

"I still don't know what to do," Lorana said miserably, shaking her head at the dead, silent rocks. She glanced up to the sky once more. "The stars are going out, Tenniz, there's only me and—"

She stopped abruptly, her eyes going wide.

One last star burned bright, flaring with the rays of the morning sun. One star that was no star at all.

"I know what to do, Tenniz!" Lorana cried, tears streaming down her face.

"And you knew!" She almost laughed at the trader's trick and she quoted him once more: "In the darkness, there is always light!"

"I *know* what to do!" Lorana cried loudly, startling Minith. She raced toward the queen, shouting, "Come on, Minith!"

She pointed a finger skyward, straight at the brilliant light in the sky. Dragon and rider rose into the cold morning air, circled once, and then winked out, *between.*

FOUR

Dragons and riders rise
To the sky
Look above you, scan wise
Time to fly
Time to flame
Thread from sky.

Telgar Weyr, AL 508.7.23, later that evening

"Have some more *klah*, F'jian," C'tov said, pushing the pitcher toward the younger bronze rider. "You practically fell off your dragon tonight."

"I'm all right," F'jian said, only to be overtaken by another yawn. "It was a long day."

"Probably a longer night before that," J'gerd added with a knowing grin from farther down the table. F'jian ignored him, pouring himself some more *klah*.

"J'gerd, you should drink less of that wine," H'nez said, "unless you *like* flying sweep."

The brown rider gave the wiry bronze rider a startled look and shook his head swiftly. He apologized to F'jian, "Sorry, I meant no disrespect to your lady."

"You're a good lad, J'gerd," C'tov said, coming over behind the brown rider and resting his hands on the other's shoulders. "Not too bright, but good."

The others roared with laughter at C'tov's ribbing and J'gerd turned red, shaking his head in chagrin.

"Don't listen to him, anyway, F'jian," another rider called. "You know he's just jealous."

"All of you should get sleep while you can," T'mar called as he strode over from the high table to the gathered riders. "We've plenty of work to do in the morning."

C'tov and H'nez rose immediately, as did F'jian a scarce moment later, and the remaining brown, blue, green, and bronze riders all followed suit, filing out of the Kitchen Cavern and into the darkened Weyr Bowl to seek their quarters.

At a nod from Kindan, the weyrlings rose from their table and commenced to clear the dishes from all the dragonriders' tables.

"I presume you're going up," Fiona said to Terin as they sat at the Weyrleader's table, playing idly with the last of their desserts.

"You don't mind, do you?"

"No, I think I'll see Kindan after he gets the weyrlings settled," Fiona said. She glanced at Shaneese; the headwoman dipped her head in acknowledgment. "Shaneese will probably manage to get T'mar into a bath long enough to work the worst kinks out of him and he'll be asleep as soon as his head hits the pillow."

Terin rose from her seat and stretched, the stretch abruptly transitioning into a long yawn.

"How are *you* feeling?" Fiona asked, her brows narrowed with worry.

"Tired," Terin confessed.

"You've looked it, too," Fiona remarked thoughtfully. "Ever since you Impressed."

"I thought all new riders were tired."

"Of course," Fiona said with a wave of her hand. She did not fool Terin.

"What is it?" the young redhead demanded, glaring down at the still-seated Weyrwoman.

Fiona rose and shrugged, stretching and yawning in turn. She pursed her lips as she toyed with an answer, then said, "Are you feeling more muzzy-headed than usual?"

"Yes," Terin said, eyes going wide in surprise.

"Ever since you Impressed, right?"

"Probably," Terin agreed. "I was so happy at the time, that I didn't notice."

"So *you're* not the reason F'jian is so tired," Fiona guessed.

"Fiona!" Terin said with a bite in her voice. Heads swiveled in their direction and Terin's face blushed to match her hair. More quietly she added, "I told you, I'm not ready."

Fiona cocked her head inquiringly.

"Closer to when Kurinth rises, that's when," Terin said. "There's no point in rushing things."

"And F'jian has no problem with this?"

"No," Terin said quickly. The Weyrwoman's eyebrows rose. Just as well as Terin knew Fiona's mind, Fiona knew Terin's. "Well, maybe."

"What?" Fiona prompted, gesturing for Terin to sit back down and seating herself, leaning forward so that they could talk in low, quiet voices.

With a feeling of relief, Terin lowered herself back into her chair and leaned forward, confiding all the events of the night before to Fiona.

"And you're sure it was a woman's voice?" Fiona asked when Terin had finished.

"I'm not *sure* of anything," Terin replied. "It could all have been a bad dream."

"It could be," Fiona agreed halfheartedly. She saw Terin's hurt look and added quickly, "One thing I'm certain of, F'jian wouldn't do anything like that without telling you."

"Maybe he's too worried."

"Why don't you go up and see?" Fiona suggested. "He's probably dead to the world, as exhausted as he was." She saw the troubled look in Terin's eyes and rose once again from her chair, reaching out a hand to the younger woman. "I can come with you, if you'd like."

Eagerly, Terin rose and grabbed Fiona's hand.

Shaneese saw them heading off and stopped them long enough to thrust a glowbasket at Fiona.

"You need to remember that you aren't a watch-wher," Shaneese told her.

"Watch-wher?" Terin asked as she and Fiona continued into the darkened bowl.

"They can see at night," Fiona explained, her tone dancing with humor at Terin's muzziness.

"Why aren't you still as muzzy?" Terin asked when she realized that Fiona was making merry at her expense.

"Shaneese says that it might be the baby," Fiona said. "Or it might be that I've gotten used to it." Just then, Fiona stumbled over a small pebble. She laughed. "Or it might be that I'm still as fuzz-brained as before."

As they started up the stairs to F'jian's weyr, they stopped talking and walked quietly, as if better to hear. Only the noises of the Weyr at night greeted their ears, comforting but subtly different from the warm, dry night sounds of their old Igen Weyr.

As they got nearer, Fiona turned the glow partly so that it shed only the barest light. "No sense in waking him."

Fiona, sensing Terin's nerves, went first through the thick curtain that separated F'jian's quarters from the corridor, raising them for Terin to follow. As they crossed inside, Fiona was pleased to see the bedsheets wrapped around the large form of the bronze rider.

Tenderly Terin leaned over and stroked F'jian's cheek only to jerk back with a startled gasp.

"Fiona! He's cold!"

Fiona glanced sharply down at the bronze rider. Perhaps *that* explained his exhaustion.

Talenth, she called.

Yy-YE-eE-Ss-S, came the pounding, blaring, dizzying response. Talenth was twice as loud as usual, her touch warbling, spinning, flickering, slurred.

Dimly Fiona heard Terin shouting, "Fiona! Fiona, what is it?" as the world spun around her and she fell, the glow spilling out of its basket and spinning wildly on the floor, casting a whirling set of shadows that seemed all too bright to Fiona's dazed mind.

"She's all right," someone said as Fiona felt her breath slowing down, her pulse returning to normal, the cold sweat on her forehead warming.

"Terin?" Fiona asked.

"No, silly, you," the voice said. Bekka; Fiona recognized Bekka's voice.

"What happened?"

"We were hoping you could tell us," Birentir's deep voice replied.

"Should I open my eyes?"

"Go ahead," Bekka said. "You didn't catch anyone this time."

Slowly Fiona opened her eyes, recalling her concussion Turns before at Fort Weyr.

The room was normal. She was in her bed, Kindan was standing nearby, as were T'mar and Shaneese. Fiona spared a quick smile for the headwoman, recognizing the way the other woman was exercising tight control on her own emotions. Shaneese returned the look with a relieved nod and grabbed T'mar's hand, gently pulling him away, back to his own weyr.

"Where's Terin?"

"With F'jian," Bekka said.

"They're probably both asleep by now," Kindan added. He nodded toward Birentir. "They had wine dosed with *fellis*."

"So what happened?" Fiona asked. "Terin said something about F'jian being cold and I reached for Talenth—" she stopped and reached, tentatively, for her queen. Instantly she felt the warmth and love of the great dragon, followed a moment later by a soft fluffing rumble from the weyr beyond.

You worried me, Talenth said. *I called Bekka.*

Bekka, eh? Fiona thought to herself. She knew from all her reading and time in the Weyrs that a dragon referring to a person by name was rare. What she also knew, and had decided to keep to herself, was that many of those so dragon-friended themselves later Impressed.

"I felt confused and the room spun," Fiona finished, hastily editing her story. Until she could get to the Records again and read some more, she decided to keep her odd reaction to Talenth's voice a secret. "How is F'jian?"

"There was no sign of a chill," Birentir told her.

"You need to rest," Bekka added firmly. She cast the older healer a meaningful look.

"We'll check on you in the morning," Birentir said, taking his lead from the young girl at his side and stepping toward the queen's lair and the ledge beyond.

"I'll stay with her," Kindan said, giving Fiona a look that tried to hide his worry.

"It's either you or Xhinna and Taria," Fiona told him tartly. "And I'm certain they'd prefer their own quarters."

"Perhaps not," Kindan said even as Bekka and Birentir departed. He waved after them.

"Bekka's worried about something and won't say it in front of me," Fiona said, smiling fondly at the memory of the forceful youngster.

"We're all worried," Kindan said, even as he changed into his night clothes. "We've got a lot to worry about. Worrying about you relieves us of other worries."

Fiona sighed at his words, too tired to argue, too sleepy to care.

Kindan must have understood, for he climbed quickly beside her, wrapped her gingerly in his arms, and leaned over to kiss her cheek lightly.

"It will be all right," Fiona assured him dreamily, eyes closed even as she relaxed against the warmth of his chest.

"Every day with you is a treasure," Kindan told her feelingly.

Fiona found herself idly amazed at his words; they were the nicest thing she'd ever heard him say.

Sleep came and Fiona fell into it with the certainty of someone held in strong arms, loved and cherished.

"**Y**ou're certain you're all right?" Terin asked for the third time when she found Fiona in the Kitchen Cavern the next morning.

"Absolutely," Fiona assured her. "Bekka and Birentir have pronounced me fit."

"Though not fit enough that they have you on rounds," Terin noted.

"Fit enough to do the rounds without me," Fiona replied. She was tired of the topic and switched it. "What about F'jian?"

"What about him?" Terin asked. "He slept all night, the same as me—they gave us fellis juice."

"You said he was cold," Fiona reminded her.

"It was probably just a chill, a breeze from Ladirth's quarters," Terin said, waving a hand airily.

Fiona frowned thoughtfully before saying, "Keep an eye on him."

Terin's eyes narrowed. "Why?"

"Just keep an eye on him," Fiona said, rising from the table and turning toward the Weyr Bowl.

"Where are you going?" Terin asked. "Aren't you supposed to be resting?"

"No one said so," Fiona called back over her shoulder. "But they wouldn't complain if they had: I'm going to look at the Records."

"Hoping to find other dizzy Weyrwomen?" Terin called back and then blushed as she saw all the weyrfolk in the Cavern turn at her in surprise.

Fiona kept moving, shaking with laughter and raising a hand in farewell as she turned to the queens' quarters.

Terin followed after her a moment later, nodding in thanks to the young weyrboy who handed her a bucket of tidbits for her young queen.

I ignore you shamefully! Terin called contritely to Kurinth as she picked up her pace and raced over to the queen's weyr.

I itch, Kurinth said with factual directness.

I'll get you oiled immediately! Terin promised. She paused in her stride as she heard the rustling of wings behind her and turned to see a wing of dragons lifting into the air. Behind, still on the ground, were F'jian and the reserve wing. She spotted him and was thrilled when he waved in her direction. Still concerned about Kurinth, Terin could only spare him a quick, jaunty wave in response before she bounded up the ledge and into her queen's weyr.

Soon she was too engrossed in oiling and feeding the most marvelous, the most brilliant, the most lovely queen dragon ever to grace all Pern to notice anything else at all.

Fiona, true to her word, made her way through her quarters and into the Records Room. Warily, she eyed the stacks she'd left on the table the day before, before letting out a deep sigh, picking them up, and carefully putting them back in their proper places.

They wouldn't have the sort of information she was looking for. She turned her head to a different section, with a sense of foreboding. The Weyrwoman Records were broken into several sections through hundreds of Turns of practice. Some sections were devoted to the tallying of goods received, some to the parceling of those goods throughout the Weyr, others again to injuries and losses. And then, dusty and disregarded, was a special section set aside for the musings of the Weyrwomen themselves.

At Igen Weyr, Fiona had quickly grown bored with the sort of gossip she'd read in the old Weyrwoman Records. At the time, her interest in babies lasted long enough to coo over them and hand them back to their rightful owners.

Now, as she glanced ruefully down at her belly, she accepted that she needed a slightly more enlightened outlook.

She was always going to have children, there was never any question in her mind. And she was going to have girls and she was going to have boys and she was going to love them all. She knew that a large part of that was her reaction to being an only child after the devastating Plague that had killed so many throughout Pern—including

all her brothers and sisters. But she was also honest enough with herself to accept that she liked the idea of babies, that she liked the idea
of toddlers. She knew enough, from her Turns in Fort Hold, about the
problems each presented, but she had grown up in a world where
each new child, each squall, each smelly diaper was something quietly treasured. There was always a small pang of sorrow in the coos
and aahs of the older folk around Fiona as they eyed new babies. She
could see the babies that they'd known before the Plague echoed in
their sad eyes.

And Fiona also recognized that part of her wanted babies to make
up for those that her older sister, Koriana, could never have.

And now, apparently, she needed to know a lot more about the
whole situation, particularly those babies with dragonrider parents.
She knew Bekka too well now, and the look she'd given Birentir had
been a special look, the look Bekka gave when she was afraid and
didn't want to scare anyone else.

Unfortunately for Bekka, Fiona had seen and recognized that look.
And, fortunately for Fiona, the Weyrwoman knew just what to do
about *that*—even if it meant pouring through stacks and stacks of
musty, old, boring Records.

Xhinna and Taria rousted her out for lunch. The blue rider took one
look at the stacks before Fiona and snorted knowingly. "You'll be fine,
Fiona," Xhinna assured her.

"You heard?"

"Everyone heard," Taria said. Xhinna nodded.

"The weyrlings hear everything, of course," Xhinna added.

Fiona cocked her head thoughtfully. "Have they heard anything
about F'jian?"

The room grew suddenly tense and Fiona felt Taria try to shrink
into herself. Fiona gave Xhinna a challenging look.

"Only talk," the blue rider said. "We're all too tired to do more than
drill, feed the beasties, and sleep."

Taria nodded fiercely in agreement.

"Come on, Fiona, we'll be late," Xhinna said, gesturing for the Weyrwoman to procede them.

Fiona grabbed Xhinna's arm as she went by and held it as they negotiated their way through her quarters, past a sleeping Talenth, and out into the brilliant warmth of the noon day.

"What sort of talk?" Fiona asked as they started down the queens' ledge.

"He's worried, Weyrwoman," Taria spoke up, much to Fiona's surprise. She'd always seemed the more diffident of the two, silent and willing to let Xhinna take the lead, but it was clear that Taria had her own mind. That much had been clear for a long time, really, just as it was clear that Taria had spent much of her time since meeting Xhinna exalting in her presence. "He's worried that he won't survive, that he'll leave Terin before . . ."

"Before his time," Xhinna finished diplomatically.

"I see," Fiona said. They walked halfway across the Bowl in an uneasy silence before Fiona added, "And do you hear anything about him trying to do something about that? With someone other than Terin?"

"No," Xhinna said, shaking her head firmly. "Nothing like that at all."

"You'd tell me, if you heard?" Fiona asked.

"You're the Weyrwoman," Taria said, as if that was answer in itself.

Fiona glanced challengingly at Xhinna, who looked uncomfortable.

"You're the Weyrwoman," Xhinna said finally. "You've the right to know."

"Even if it hurts me?"

"I haven't said anything about Lorana," Xhinna responded tightly, indicating that there were some things she would not bring up with her Weyrwoman and friend for fear of causing her pain.

"Why don't you two eat with me, alone, when we get to the Cavern?" The question had all the weight of a Weyrwoman's orders behind it.

Fiona sensed T'mar's surprise and saw Kindan's strained look when she led the two young dragonriders to a separate table.

"All I can say is: About time," Shaneese said as she set out the servings in front of them. "And I'll be back with more, never you fear," she added with a special look for Xhinna.

"Hungry?" Fiona asked.

"And tired," Xhinna replied.

"Too tired," Taria added.

"How many others are tired?" Fiona asked, glancing over her shoulder to the werylings' table. And why hadn't Kindan commented on it to her?

Fiona noticed that the answer was longer in coming than it should have been. Gently, she said, "Xhinna?"

It was Taria who answered. "There's nothing wrong, is there?" She flicked a troubled glance toward the Weyrwoman.

"Wrong, how?"

"Wrong with us," Xhinna said, her voice edged with anger. Under that anger, Fiona felt raw, deep, desperate fear.

"Tell me," Fiona ordered, emphasizing the command with a raised, clenched fist.

"It's not the others," Xhinna said. "Kindan wouldn't let them and—"

"They're a good lot, all round," Taria said. "I've known most of them all my life and they've never said a mean word—except when we were all little and silly."

"But the dragons—" Xhinna started.

"I can't help if I don't know," Fiona told her friend in a calm voice.

"Fiona, is it possible that it's wrong for the dragons to Impress women?" Xhinna blurted.

"No," Fiona said instantly. "Not at all."

"Golds, sure," Xhinna agreed in a contentious tone.

"No, your Tazith chose *you*, Xhinna," Fiona said. She glanced toward Taria. "Just as Coranth chose you."

"But we're *so* tired," Taria protested. "All the time."

"And you feel like you're walking through thick mud," Fiona said. The other looked at her in surprise even as Fiona continued, "And you're slow, you can't do sums, you'd do anything for a nap, and when you wake, you still feel tired."

"Yes," Xhinna agreed. "That's the muzzy-head?"

"Yes."

"You don't seem muzzy-headed," Taria spoke up and then blushed, abashed at gainsaying the Weyrwoman.

Fiona laughed. She surprised herself with it, it was so natural and yet so perfectly just the thing the other two needed to hear. "Didn't you hear about me last night?" she asked as she recovered.

Xhinna's lips twitched, then pulled back in a full grin even as Taria shot her partner a nervous look.

"In this Weyr, Taria, it's okay to laugh with the Weyrwoman," Fiona assured her. Taria's lips twitched, but no more; she was still uneasy.

"So, why are we muzzy-headed?" Xhinna asked. "And couldn't that be a sign that—"

"That we're not going to make it," Taria finished solemnly. She looked at Fiona expectantly, but not nervously. Fiona could tell that the green rider had heard about Lorana's loss, had heard Tullea's rage—who couldn't?—and had drawn her own conclusions.

"Perhaps," Fiona said quietly. "But I grew up around Kindan; I absorbed his determined outlook while still a child." She glanced back at the harper, who was gazing intently in their direction. "'Step by step, moment by moment, we live through another day,'" she quoted. "And we will." She glanced down at her belly. "Lorana paid a terrible price. I intend to be here when she returns, to show her the value of that price."

Xhinna nodded in agreement. Taria looked away uneasily.

"For now," Fiona said in a quiet voice, "drink plenty of *klah* and make sure all of you do."

"I don't like *klah*," Taria confessed.

"It keeps you from muzziness," Fiona told her. She smiled sympathetically at the girl. "M'tal thought that there was a reason, that perhaps we were too much in the same time—"

Fiona broke off, her eyes suddenly wide as inspiration struck.

"Weyrwoman?" Taria ventured.

"Fiona, what is it?" Xhinna asked urgently.

"'In the same time,'" Fiona repeated to herself. She glanced toward Xhinna and Taria. "What would it be like, do you think, if your dragon spoke to you twice in the same time?"

"You were very silent at dinner," Terin said that evening as she and F'jian prepared for bed. She'd suggested that they sleep in her quarters and he'd accepted with alacrity. Thinking on it, she found the walk to her weyr had been much more pleasant and much shorter than the walk up to his weyr.

"I was tired," F'jian replied, punctuating his remark with a long yawn. Terin struggled and failed to avoid a yawn of her own and glared at him in mock anger. "And we'll be up early."

"The Fall's at night," Terin protested.

"The drills will be in the dark of the night, then some rest, then another drill near lunch, then another rest, then a night drill," F'jian told her. "We're drilling with the riders from Benden and both T'mar and B'nik are determined to keep the casualties low."

"But doesn't that mean you won't have anything to do?" Terin asked as she crawled into bed. "You're leading the reserve wing."

"And carrying firestone," F'jian reminded her as he got in beside her. "I thought T'mar was punishing me by not letting me fly the Fall, now I know that he was giving me the harder duty. Not only will my wing have to provide the firestone, but we'll also be the reserve."

"I could talk to Fiona," Terin suggested.

"And have me leading a fighting wing?"

"Well, perhaps that's not a good idea."

"Shh, it will be all right, love," F'jian said, leaning close to her and stroking her soft hair tenderly. "Sometimes it might not seem like it, but it will be all right."

"You sound like Fiona," Terin murmured with a touch of annoyance.

"Fiona is a smart person," F'jian said. "You know that."

"Mmm," Terin murmured in agreement. Presently she drifted off to a warm, comfortable sleep.

▼ ▼ ▼

Terin woke. A gust of cold air disturbed her. She flailed in her sleep and felt F'jian grab her hands.

"Shh, it's all right, there's nothing to worry about," F'jian whispered quietly. "Hush, now! Hush, love, get some rest."

"F'jian," Terin asked a moment later, "why are you crying?"

"I'm sorry," the bronze rider said, his voice harsh in his own ears. "It's just that—you're so lovely, you're so beautiful. I love you so much."

Terin turned toward him, reaching up to kiss him, but F'jian ducked aside, grabbing her chin with his fingers and caressing it, stroking her lips with his index finger.

"Sleep," he told her. "Go back to sleep."

She did as she was told, only a little annoyed with him. Just as she slid into a deeper slumber she thought she heard the rustling of wings, the sound of a dragon going airborne. She started to move, to come awake, but F'jian moved against her, stroked her hair, and whispered soothing sounds. Terin cuddled in close against his warmth and drifted back to sleep.

"Fiona?" Terin's voice roused the Weyrwoman from her stupor, perched over another set of Records. She heard Terin enter the Records Room, stop, and scan the mess in surprise. "Xhinna said you'd be here."

"It's a Weyrwoman's job," Fiona said. She turned to give Terin a sour smile as she added, "You should try it, you might be Weyrwoman yourself one day."

"Weyrwoman!" Terin said, startled. "I've enough to do just keeping Kurinth fed." And keeping an eye on you, Fiona heard the unspoken words.

"You can't fool me, Terin," Fiona said, rising and stretching before pointing to the stacks in front of her. "There are *numbers* there and we know how you are about them."

"What are you looking for, anyway?" Terin asked, eyeing the stacks with more interest.

"Oh, lots of things," Fiona returned airily, realizing that she wasn't sure she wanted to discuss her explorations with others, even Terin.

"Like how to fight Thread when each Weyr has less than a full Flight?"

"That, too," Fiona agreed. Her stomach rumbled. "I'm hungry," Fiona said in surprise, glancing over to Terin. "Were you sent to remind me to eat?"

"Shaneese suggested you might be here," Terin said, her eyes dancing in amusement as she made her indirect agreement.

"Well, then, let's get out of this dusty place and into the sunlight," Fiona said, turning toward the exit and frowning at the darkness of the hallway.

"Hmm," Terin said, "Shaneese should have sent me sooner."

"It's not lunchtime?"

"Dinner," Terin said.

Fiona groaned.

"I'm going to speak to Shaneese," Terin said firmly. "Someone's got to watch over you and *force* you to eat."

"I guess so," Fiona agreed in a troubled voice. "I hadn't realized how much time had passed."

"You're worried," Terin guessed as they crossed from Fiona's quarters into Talenth's weyr.

"You're not hungry, are you, Talenth?" Fiona called to her queen, rushing to her and showering her with affection that ended with a good solid scratching of both of Talenth's eye ridges.

Not hungry, only sleepy, Talenth replied, not at all disturbed by the attention of her rider.

"Get some sleep, then, love," Fiona said, failing to stifle a sympathetic yawn that was immediately picked up and repeated by Terin, who grinned at her with a cross look.

"Are you muzzy-headed, too?" Fiona asked, eyeing the younger rider carefully. "You *are*, aren't you?"

Terin finished her yawn and shook her head. "I don't know what you mean, Weyrwoman."

"How much *klah* did you have today?"

"One pitcher?" Terin thought out loud. "Two?"

"Is that what's affecting F'jian, then?"

"He's worse," Terin said, her lips turning down in a frown. Her eyes grew wary as she debated revealing her worries to Fiona.

Fiona knew Terin too well and gave her an inviting gesture, saying, "Share the burden."

Terin's frown deepened and she hesitated, but Fiona's expression made it clear that, now that the Weyrwoman had tumbled to Terin's mood, it would only be a matter of time before Fiona wormed it out of her.

So, Terin told her about the night before.

"He's not seeing anyone else," Fiona said firmly. "I would have heard if he was."

"Then what is he doing?"

"I hate to say it, but could you be dreaming?"

"Like you about Lorana?"

"Perhaps," Fiona said, waving a hand to ease the tension. "And for the same reasons, it would make sense for both to be dreams." Terin's eyebrows went up. "Me, for dreaming what I'd like, you for dreaming what you fear."

She gestured for Terin to precede her down the queens' ledge and they walked in silence until they reached the Weyr Bowl.

"It could be that he's training, in secret," Fiona suggested.

"He's so tired now that I don't see how it could help," Terin said, frowning once more. They spied a group of weyrlings drilling and another group cleaning outside the barracks. "How many of them are muzzy-headed?"

"All of them," Fiona said, her voice full of concern.

"Well, they can't go back to Igen," Terin said.

"I'd thought the same thing."

"Somewhere else?"

"Where?" Fiona asked. "And when?"

Terin shrugged. A moment later she said, in a quiet voice, "You'd take me, wouldn't you?"

Fiona glanced at her, her brows raised.

"If you found a way, you'd let me and Kurinth come, wouldn't you?" Terin said. A half-smile crossed her looks. "If we went, then I'd be old enough . . ."

"If it comes to that, I couldn't imagine leaving you behind," Fiona agreed. She shrugged. "But I have no idea where we could go."

"Southern?"

Fiona shook her head. "Too dangerous. We might get infected with the dragon sickness or worse."

Terin grimaced at the thought.

They continued in silence into the Kitchen Cavern and made their way to the Weyrleader's table. T'mar and the other wingleaders were already there, as well as a grizzled old rider wearing the shoulder knots of a Benden wingleader. Kindan was talking animatedly with the Benden rider.

When they approached, Kindan paused and gestured to the other rider, who spotted Fiona and Terin and rose, giving them a gracious half-bow.

"L'tor, Nimith's rider, Weyrwoman," he said to Fiona, with another bow to Terin, "Weyrwoman."

"I'm pleased to meet you," Fiona said, extending her hand into the grasp of the older man's rough, dry one. Terin followed her and they took chairs near T'mar and the others.

"I've sent F'jian to bed," T'mar murmured to Fiona, clearly expecting her to relay the news to Terin. He grinned, looking behind the Weyrwoman to the redhead as he added in a quieter voice, "I don't know what they're doing, but she should stop before he fades *between*."

"They're not doing anything," Fiona replied, her eyes worried. "Terin says that they just sleep, but she's been afraid that he gets up in the middle of the night."

"Another woman?"

"Not that we know."

T'mar frowned.

"Terin thinks perhaps he was practicing."

T'mar shook his head. "If so, it's on his own. Not even the reserve riders know of it."

Fiona raised a hand to forestall him while she turned to Terin to explain F'jian's absence.

Shaneese approached with fresh settings and a look that made it clear to Fiona that her absence at lunch had been noted.

"I think we need to assign me a guard," Fiona confessed.

"Well, it can't be me. I'm keeping an eye on *him,* which is taking all *my* time," Shaneese said, pointing a finger at T'mar. The two women exchanged conspiratorial grins.

"And Bekka and Birentir are too busy with the wounded," Fiona declared.

Shaneese accepted that with a nod and then her look transformed into a grin as her eyes took in Terin. But it was still to Fiona that she said, "I've heard that you've a knack for taking 'difficult' characters and managing them. If you're up to handling another, I think I've got just the person for you."

"Hey, I wasn't difficult!" Terin said.

"No, silly, she means you were the source of her information," Fiona said consolingly, thinking back to a particular time when some of the young riders had fought at Igen Weyr.

"Remember, please, that I'm pregnant," Fiona pleaded. She doubted that anyone this headwoman classified as "difficult" would be an easy acquaintance.

"Well, then you'll deserve each other," Shaneese said. She saw Fiona's alarmed look and waved a hand. "Oh, nothing too drastic, well within your talents, I'm thinking."

Fiona gave her an encouraging gesture.

"And you might like him, he being a reminder as it were of your time in the past," Shaneese allowed. "It might be fitting; after all, he was sent here by Mother Karina."

"He?" Fiona said.

"A trader's son, someone you might recall," Shaneese said, her eyes clouded.

Fiona cocked her head challengingly.

"The lad's name is Jeriz," Shaneese said finally. "He's been here less than a Turn." She bent down to Fiona's ear as she added, "I kept him away from the old riders; D'gan would have sent him packing."

"Where are his parents?"

"His mother's got her hands full with the daughter," Shaneese said. "The boy's got a strangeness to him, but not the Sight."

"He's Tenniz's son?" Fiona guessed, eyes going wide. "Why didn't you introduce him to me sooner?"

"I wasn't sure . . ." Shaneese's voice faded out and she shook her head. "I'm still not sure," she corrected herself. She met Fiona's eyes firmly. "I'll need your word."

"My word?"

"If he turns out to be too much, you'll tell me," Shaneese declared firmly. "You've enough on your plate."

"But you want to send him to me anyway?"

Shaneese snorted. "Let's just say that you might be what he needs."

"My word," Fiona affirmed.

"Good," Shaneese said with a nod. "I'll have a cot put in your quarters."

"A cot?"

"Unless you want him sharing with Kindan," Shaneese said blandly. Fiona gave her such a look that Shaneese grinned. "I thought not."

"But he won't be freezing if it gets too cold, either," Fiona warned, wagging a finger at the headwoman.

"That's one of the reasons I thought of you," Shaneese said. Fiona raised an eyebrow questioningly. "Traders have the same sensibilities with cold."

"He must be freezing," Fiona said.

"He hasn't said so."

"Stubborn," Fiona guessed.

Shaneese, diplomatically, said nothing. After the headwoman left, Terin said to her, "Are you sure this is wise?"

"Well, it's certain that you can't be looking after me all the time," Fiona assured her.

"But from what Shaneese said, I'm not sure who will be looking after whom."

"Everything all right?" T'mar asked as he saw the two break their head-to-head conversation.

"Just making some arrangements," Fiona assured him. She nodded toward L'tor. "And you?"

"We'll be drilling tomorrow," L'tor said, cutting across T'mar's answer. "I think it's wise, as we've not flown together before."

"Eat, Fiona!" Terin spoke harshly before Fiona could respond. To L'tor she said, "She's pregnant and forgets."

"I quite understand," the bronze rider replied. "I sometimes forget myself with hardly half as decent a reason."

Dutifully, Fiona ate.

After dinner, Shaneese brought over a young lad, who looked to have no more than seven Turns. His expression was grim, just less than a glower, and he kept his eyes downcast.

"Weyrwoman, this is Jeriz," Shaneese said, with one hand firmly on the lad's shoulder.

"Jeriz," Fiona said, holding out a hand, "I'm pleased to meet you."

The boy continued to glower at the floor. Shaneese shook him. "Answer the Weyrwoman."

The boy looked up and Fiona was pierced by his brilliant green eyes, eyes that were set in a swarthy trader face and looked out from under unruly, long black hair. Fiona was shocked at the beauty of the boy just as she caught his hidden fury, anger, rage, and—beneath all them—his great fear and loneliness.

Fiona rose out of her chair and moved it aside, squatting down to meet the boy's eyes. He flicked them up to her, surprised. She held out her hand again. After a moment he lowered his eyes again, letting them settle on her hand before glancing once more to the floor.

"The Weyrwoman hasn't got time for this, boy," Shaneese hissed angrily.

"Your father was a friend of mine," Fiona said. The boy's eyes jerked up slightly, then fell. Fiona glanced up to Shaneese, deciding on a different tack. "I'm going to need some oil, Talenth has another spot of patchy skin."

"Of course, Weyrwoman."

Jeriz's eyes flickered and lowered again.

"Have you ever seen a dragon, Jeriz?" Fiona asked the boy.

His shoulders twitched.

"Have you ever seen a queen?"

He nodded.

"Up close?"

Jeriz shook his head, but his eyes darted upward once more, his expression changed for just an instant before he schooled it once more into solemn blankness.

"Have you ever wanted to Impress?"

"I'm a trader," Jeriz said proudly.

"And traders are never Searched?"

"Sure, loads of them," Jeriz said, his pride pricked. "Some have Impressed bronzes."

"Would you like to Impress a dragon?"

"I'm too young," Jeriz said.

"You'll get older," Fiona said. "And, if you know more about dragons, you're more likely to Impress."

That information was news to Jeriz.

"I'm too small," Jeriz said. "They said I'd get crushed."

"Have you seen Jeila?"

"She's trader-bred," Jeriz said again, his voice full of pride.

"And not all that big," Fiona agreed. "And yet her queen is the biggest queen on Pern."

"She's trader-bred," Jeriz said again, as if that explained everything.

"I need someone trader-bred to help me," Fiona told him. He glanced up at her, his eyes widening just slightly. She held out her hand again. "Are you willing to make a trade?"

"What for? I've got nothing."

Ah! Fiona thought to herself. Another who cannot see their own worth.

"I could trade you nothing for nothing, but it seems a poor choice," Fiona said. She frowned for a moment. "How about this: I help you and you help me."

"You're a Weyrwoman, you don't need my help."

"Then you'll come out best in the bargain, won't you?"

Jeriz's eyes widened, once again surprised.

"In fact, however, I do need help," Fiona told him. He gave her a dubious look. "I'm pregnant and I've gotten forgetful. I don't want anything to happen to our baby and I need reminding."

"Of what?"

"I need reminding of the time," Fiona told him. "Of when to eat."

Jeriz twitched a foot and rubbed it on the ground, clearly impatient to be away.

"Anyone can do that," Jeriz decided. A moment later, he added boldly, "And if I do that, what will you do for me?"

"What's the most important thing for a trader?"

"Trade," Jeriz said simply.

"Knowledge," Fiona corrected him. He gave her a thoughtful look. "Trade is easy, knowing *when* to trade and *what* to trade, that's hard."

"She's right," Shaneese put in, giving Fiona a surprised look.

"What I offer you is knowledge, Jeriz," Fiona said. "I'm going to be spending a lot of time with the Records."

"The Records?" Jeriz asked with more interest than he'd ever shown before.

"I'll let you read what you want and keep that knowledge for yourself," Fiona said. "You can learn all about the Weyrs, the dragons, and our trade."

Jeriz's breath caught and then he exhaled, his shoulders slumping, his eyes going back to the ground. He seemed to completely fold in on himself even as he shook his head once, silently.

Suddenly, Fiona had a thought. "I can teach you to read, too."

Jeriz's eyes suddenly locked on hers and he took a step forward so that he could whisper into her ear, "And you won't tell anyone?"

"No one," Fiona swore solemnly, hiding her exaltation at having guessed correctly. She lowered her voice so that only he could hear her, "Not even Shaneese."

Jeriz stuck his hand into hers and shook it firmly. "Deal."

"It'd help if I could tell Kindan," Fiona said later, as she walked up the queens' ledge with the boy by her side.

"I told him I could read," Jeriz said doubtfully.

"It means a lot to you, doesn't it?"

"A trader who can't read is worthless," Jeriz told her, frowning.

"Then I think you'd want to do everything to fix that," Fiona said.

Jeriz fidgeted but said nothing.

"Are you afraid to tell Kindan that you lied?" Fiona asked.

"My honor."

"A stain on your honor, is it?"

Jeriz nodded.

"Which stains more, the lie or not being able to read?"

"Reading," Jeriz said as if it were obvious.

"Not everyone on Pern reads, you know," Fiona said as they reached Talenth's weyr.

"Traders do!" Jeriz stopped, looking at the huge queen who lay in front of him, her head raised, staring at him intently.

"Here, you're weyrfolk," Fiona told him.

"They said you knew how to trade," Jeriz said, unable to tear his eyes from Talenth.

"I'm flattered," Fiona said. "But I'm a Lord Holder's daughter, I was taught since I was very young." She paused. "And I read a lot."

Jeriz tore his eyes from Talenth just long enough to give her a questioning look.

"As I said, reading helps," Fiona told him. She gestured for him to cross to her quarters.

Jeriz hesitated. "Shouldn't I say something to her?"

"What would you say?"

"I don't know," Jeriz confessed, looking to her for suggestions.

"She's as smart as most, so why don't you just say hello?"

"Hello?" Jeriz's brows narrowed. "That doesn't seem respectful."

"What would you say, then?"

"Talenth, senior queen of Telgar Weyr, I, Jeriz of the traders, give you greetings on bended knee," Jeriz said, sinking to one knee and bowing his head as he said the words. "I greet you and honor you for all that you and yours do for Pern."

"Well said!" Kindan's voice called out from behind him, causing Jeriz to startle and nearly tumble. "I doubt I've heard half as courteous from Lord Holders."

Fiona raised Jeriz back to his feet and turned him to face Kindan. The harper was dust-covered from his day drilling the weyrlings and Fiona could see the exhaustion in his eyes even as he shot her a questioning look.

Jeriz shot Fiona another imploring look and it took all of her father's training in manners to keep her from laughing at the boy's discomfort.

"*I* call him Kindan and friend," Fiona said. "What would you say to him?"

"He's a weyrlingmaster and a harper," Jeriz said, clearly torn as to which honor ranked higher. Decisively he squared his shoulders and looked up at Kindan. "Harper and Weyrlingmaster, I hope I cause no offense."

"None at all, provided you are willing to call me Kindan in private," the harper returned easily, striding forward with a steady gait and extending his hand. "And how shall I call you?"

"My name is Jeriz," the boy said. "I'm the Weyrwoman's drudge."

The swat to the back of his head was neither hard nor expected.

"No drudge," Fiona snapped. "You're here to help as weyrfolk or trader, whichever you wish."

Jeriz raised his hand to his head, but said nothing.

"You remind me of someone," Kindan said, looking at the youngster critically.

"From what you told me, he shares many traits," Fiona said, giving Kindan a meaningful look. She grabbed Jeriz's hand and tugged him gently toward their quarters. Over her shoulder, she called to Kindan, "I'm giving this one a bath. Would you send for some late snacks?"

Kindan followed, brows raised as he took in her comment and then noticed the cot placed on the far side of their room. In the days since Lorana had disappeared, he spent more time here with Fiona than he did with the weyrlings. When asked, he'd said that it was to comfort Fiona. Xhinna and Taria between them did a good job of covering for him and he made sure that he was up early in the morning and stayed with the weyrlings until late at night.

In the bathroom, Jeriz eyed the large warm water pool warily.

"How many Turns have you?" Fiona asked, wondering at his behavior.

"I've nearly ten," Jeriz said.

"Small for your age: I would have guessed you no more than seven," Fiona said, her lips pursed thoughtfully. She saw the flame flare up in his eyes and nodded to herself. "You've had your share of fights over it, haven't you?"

Jeriz nodded.

"And didn't win many of them, going against those so much bigger than you," Fiona guessed. Jeriz said nothing.

"Are you bruised?"

Jeriz's eyes melted and, reluctantly, he nodded.

"I've patched and healed far worse, I can assure you," Fiona told him. "When I was your age, I was always getting scraped up going after tunnel snakes."

"I've never seen one."

"I hope you don't," Fiona told him. "Nasty things, sharp teeth. And fast." She gave him a thoughtful look. "They'd probably send you after them, too, if you were in Fort Hold, 'cause you're small for your age." She pointed at the pool. "You get in there, have a good soak, dry off with those towels over there, and come wake me when you're done."

Jeriz made to protest, but Fiona shook her head. "The water's warm, it'll be good for bruises."

With that, Fiona turned and left quickly, lying on her bed and listening for the sounds of the boy getting into the pool.

"Don't forget to use the soapsand!"

She heard the boy groan in response and smiled to herself.

A while later, a splash alerted her that Jeriz had gotten out. She rose as she heard him grab a towel and dry himself quickly. "Are you decent?" she called. "I'm coming in." The boy let out a garbled noise that cut off abruptly as Fiona entered and gestured toward a stool.

"Do you want help drying your hair?" she asked. "Sit there and I'll do it."

"I thought I was supposed to help you," Jeriz complained.

"You are," Fiona said. "Sometime not too long from now, I'm going to be doing this with my own child." She wiped the comb dry and ran it through the boy's fine black hair. "I'm going to need the practice."

"Ow!" Jeriz complained.

"See?" Fiona said, easing off on her pressure. "That's exactly what I mean."

She must have gotten it right, for presently the boy was silent and a short while later, let out a sigh of contentment that he tried desperately to hide and which Fiona pretended not to notice.

The next morning Fiona was awoken by the sound of someone clearing her throat. Terin. Fiona turned toward the noise, only to discover herself wedged with a small body on one side and Kindan's larger body on the other. She was quite warm and toasty, Fiona noticed with a self-satisfied expression. She remembered coaxing Jeriz in with her when it became apparent that he was shivering and bravely trying not to show it. She wondered how many cold, shivering, sleepless nights he'd spent since coming to Telgar. He was so small he was barely noticeable, once she insisted forcefully that he get in on the far side of her, nearest the wall.

She could sense his unease and waited until his breathing eased into sleep before finding a more comfortable position herself.

She had just drifted off to sleep when she heard Kindan's trudging footsteps approach, his slow, trudging step seeming all full of contrition. She heard his sharp breath when he noted that Jeriz was with her and his sigh as he decided that it didn't matter and he slid, quietly, gently in with her.

"I love you," she whispered softly as he lay his head on the pillow. His arms tightened around her in response and they drifted quickly to sleep.

"Have you got room for another?" Terin asked, her voice sounding teary.

"It'll be tight, but I think we can manage," Kindan said, gallantly rising and offering her a space next to Fiona. Terin smiled thanks at him and crawled in, patting the space at the edge of the bed invitingly. With a grin, Kindan eased back into the small remaining portion of the bed.

"Hang on," Fiona said, gently moving the boy who'd sprawled in his sleep further into the bed. "That's better," she said as she scooted over more. She pulled Terin closer to her, close enough that she could whisper to her, "Rest first, talk later."

The redhead nodded and closed her eyes.

Much later, Fiona sent "the men," as she carefully referred to them, into the bathroom first to get dressed and changed while she lay with Terin.

"What is it?"

"He was gone again last night," Terin said. "I woke when he came back and I challenged him." She sniffed. "He told me that he couldn't say where he'd been, that he'd given his word."

"And?"

"I told him that I loved him," Terin replied. "He said that he would always love me."

"And?" Fiona asked again, knowing there was more.

"I asked him again and he said that he couldn't tell me," Terin said, sounding miserable. "He said that I'd understand." She sniffed angrily. "How can I understand if he won't *tell* me?"

"Terin," Fiona began slowly, feeling out her words. "Do you love him?"

"I don't know," Terin said quickly. Then she shook her head. "No, that's not true. I love him, I just don't know if I can trust him."

"I understand," Fiona said. Terin wasn't a jealous soul, Fiona knew, but she wanted certainty in her life. Fiona was sure that if F'jian had another love and was honest with Terin about it, she'd eventually come to accept it. She merely wanted a solid relationship, with the rules known.

Even though, with nearly fourteen Turns, Terin was as old as some who were already settled, she was still young enough to be unsure of herself, to want to take things slowly. Perhaps more slowly than F'jian, but that was her right and her decision. Fiona couldn't fault her; she'd waited for her own time.

"The question is, can you live without him?" Fiona asked and just as instantly regretted her words. No one could say how long any dragonrider would survive in these perilous times.

"I don't know," Terin sobbed. "I don't think I could ever let anyone fly Kurinth but Ladirth."

"Shh," Fiona said, running her hand through the younger woman's hair. "Shh, it'll be all right."

"That's what *he* says," Terin complained. She flipped her head from under Fiona's hand and looked her in the eyes, "What if it isn't?"

"Terin, you know better: 'Ifs and ands are no work for hands.'"

"That old saying!" Terin snorted. "And what's it mean, anyway?"

"It means that if you spend all your time worrying about the future, you'll never enjoy today," Kindan's voice spoke up. Neither Fiona nor Terin had noticed his return to the room. He nodded to Terin. "It means that you've got to hold on to what you can hold, and not what you can't."

His eyes flicked toward Fiona as he found other meaning in his own words. He smiled at the redhead, adding, "I don't know what you were talking about, weyrwoman."

Terin sighed. "That's fine, you've answered my question anyway."

"Why don't you two go off to breakfast, we'll be along," Fiona said to Kindan and Jeriz. Kindan nodded and beckoned to the youngster, who followed with a backward glance at the Weyrwoman. She waved him on, smiling.

"So that's Tenniz's son," Terin said as she watched the small boy follow Kindan out. She waited until they were out of earshot before adding, "He's cute!"

"It's the eyes," Fiona agreed. "He has the most beautiful eyes."

"He is going to have a full Flight of admirers when he gets older," Terin predicted.

"Two, if he's not picky," Fiona agreed. "That is, if he decides to stay with the Weyr."

"How is it that you collect so many people, Fiona?" Terin asked.

"I lose some of them, too," Fiona added sadly, thinking first of Lorana and then of F'dan. The blue rider had been a marvelous person, a great help to her back in Igen Weyr—as surrogate parent, part-time conscience, and good friend. She'd been devastated when he'd been lost to Thread. She realized that he came to her mind because of the luxurious combing Jeriz had given her the night before, insisting on repaying her after she'd combed out his hair.

"We've all lost them," Terin agreed sadly.

"Come on, let's get up," Fiona said, shoving Terin toward the edge.

They found T'mar, F'jian, C'tov, H'nez, and L'tor just finishing their breakfast at the high table when they arrived in the Kitchen Cavern minutes later.

"How is it working with your new helper?" T'mar asked when he got a chance to talk with Fiona alone.

"He's settling in," Fiona said, glancing at T'mar's long hair. "Have you ever thought of braiding your hair, T'mar?"

"Pardon?" T'mar asked, moving away from Fiona's greedy fingers.

"Later, perhaps," Fiona said regretfully as he rose. Shaneese came directing two others burdened with food trays and settled it in front of Terin and Fiona.

"You can't expect us to eat all that!" Fiona declared, eyes wide in horror.

"Kindan, Jeriz, Xhinna, and Taria are joining us," Shaneese said as she sat down with them.

"You haven't eaten yet?" Fiona asked in surprise. "You must have been up for hours already."

Shaneese shrugged her comment off even as she gestured for Kindan and the others to join them.

"I've heard some disturbing rumors," Shaneese said as the others were seated.

"What about?"

"I've heard that the weyrlings are worried that they're going to die," Shaneese said, glancing to Xhinna and Taria for confirmation.

"Yes," Kindan said, glancing toward Fiona. "I've heard it, too." He gave a wry smile. "They don't come out and say it, though, they mostly talk around it. And—" He nodded toward Fiona. "—they confessed to feeling muzzy-headed, all of them."

"But you've got a plan to deal with it, haven't you?" Fiona asked.

"How many of the others are still feeling muzzy-headed?" Terin said, glancing at Fiona.

"I can't say about me for certain," Fiona said. "I've got a baby to muddle things up as well."

"T'mar for certain," Shaneese said, giving Fiona a worried look.

"F'jian," Terin added. She yawned and, red-faced, admitted, "Me, ever since I Impressed."

Fiona waited until the yawns that Terin's action had initiated had passed through the group before asking, "How bad is it?"

"I wouldn't know compared to Igen," Terin said. "It didn't affect me."

"Well then, none of the weyrlings would be able to gauge," Fiona said with a frown. She thought for a moment, then said to Kindan, "How about we do some tests?"

"Tests?" the harper asked so blandly that Fiona guessed that she'd stumbled upon his plan. "What sort, Weyrwoman?"

"Two of them, actually," Fiona said. "Well, maybe three, come to think of it."

Kindan gave her an inviting look. She thought of kicking him under the table, but decided it was beneath her dignity as a Weyrwoman.

"First, we have Talenth and myself drill with the weyrlings," Fiona said. She grinned at the reaction of the others. "That'll give us a chance to see how they compare to me." She cocked a head at Terin. "You can join, too, it'll do you good."

Terin turned a girlish groan into a womanly "ah-hmm" of agreement.

"Let's ask Jeila as well, as she and Tolarth seem immune," Fiona said. And that, come to think of it was an odd thing, given that Jeila and Tolarth had been back in time three Turns. None of the dragons Minith hatched at High Reaches Weyr had displayed the muzzyheadedness, as far as Fiona knew. Why was that, she wondered. Was it something that affected only those from Fort?

"You said three things," Kindan reminded her politely.

"Well, we should compare the weyrlings to someone who hasn't Impressed." She turned her eyes to Jeriz who struggled to master his alarm. "I think Jeriz should join us and we'll see if he's as tired afterward as they are."

"And the third?"

"If he's not too tired," Fiona said, smiling at the small green-eyed boy, "I'm thinking that we might arrange for Jeriz to spend a night or two in the weyrling barracks." She smiled at Kindan. "He could use your bed."

"And why do that?"

"Because Jeriz might hear something or get a feel for what's happening that we"—she gestured to herself, Kindan, and the rest— "might not hear said in our presence."

"Because he's so young or because he's so cute?" Xhinna asked.

"Both, I think," Fiona said, ignoring the flush that came to Jeriz's cheeks. She pushed the basket of rolls toward him; he took one and wolfed it down.

"That sounds like a good plan," Kindan agreed. Shaneese snorted and Terin's eyes danced with suppressed humor. Xhinna noticed and her eyes widened as she tumbled to the joke.

"Should we mention this to T'mar?" Terin wondered, frowning.

"Yes," Fiona said. She made a quick tour of the cavern with her eyes and realized that it was empty of dragonriders. "When they return from drill."

"Well, then, we should probably get started," Kindan said, rising.

"Now?" Fiona protested. "We haven't eaten!" She pointed at her plate. "Take Jeriz, if he's eaten already; Terin and I will join you shortly."

"It'll give you time to explain to the others," Xhinna added diplomatically.

Kindan gave Fiona a measuring look, decided against teasing her further with a shake of his head, and gestured for the others to follow.

"We've got to check on the quarters, anyway," Kindan allowed as they moved off. He cocked an eye toward Jeriz. "How are you at judging what's clean?"

"Not very good," Jeriz admitted with a frown.

"Well, then it's time you learned!" Xhinna told him with a smile. She glanced up at the harper. "You know, Weyrlingmaster, this may work out better than you imagine."

Fiona didn't hear the answer as the group trailed out of earshot and into the Weyr Bowl.

"Eat!" Terin told her, pushing a bowl in her direction.

Shaneese toyed with a roll and answered the occasional question from one of the polite weyrfolk who wandered her way, but Fiona felt that the headwoman was holding back something that troubled her.

"Terin's worried about F'jian," Fiona began, deciding to provide Shaneese with an opening.

Shaneese's face clouded even as Terin gave Fiona a hurt look.

"We're all afraid," Shaneese said after a moment, giving a comforting look to Terin. Then she turned to Fiona with a thoughtful frown.

"And," Fiona said, reaching a hand to grab Shaneese's, "some of us worry needlessly." She met the woman's eyes as she said, "You have something you want to tell me?"

Shaneese pulled her hand out of Fiona's and shook her head wordlessly. "It's too early."

"'It's never too early for good news,'" Fiona reminded her.

"'Don't count your dragons until they've hatched,'" Shaneese returned with flashing eyes.

"But you're worried," Fiona said.

"Would you two *please* stop talking in sayings and make sense?" Terin broke in.

"Shaneese is pregnant," Fiona said, with a nod toward the headwoman.

"It's too early to be certain," Shaneese cautioned.

"You know," Fiona said with no doubt in her voice.

"I . . . think," Shaneese said, choosing her words carefully.

"And you haven't told T'mar?"

Shaneese let out a deep breath and nodded.

"Well, I, for one, was hoping this would happen," Fiona said, reaching for Shaneese's hand again and clasping it firmly, rocking it to emphasize her point.

"You were," Terin said. "Why?"

"We can swap duties on smelly babies," Fiona said casually. She waved her free hand airily. "Besides, it will give me company."

"You've got Jeila!" Shaneese reminded her.

"And—" Terin cut herself off abruptly. She'd been about to say "Lorana" and they all knew it. The redhead went bright red and lowered her eyes, toying with her breakfast.

"She'll be back," Fiona said firmly.

There was silence with Terin eating slowly to avoid speech and Shaneese eyeing her worriedly, groping for words.

"Well, I've said my news," Shaneese said, pulling her hand out from Fiona's again. "You need to eat, Weyrwoman."

"So do you!" Fiona reminded her, pointing to the food in front of them. "Oh, this will work out perfectly! With you to keep me eating and Jeriz—"

"And how is he working out?"

"Better, with a good night's sleep," Fiona said. "Did you know, he'd been too proud to admit he was freezing sleeping by himself?"

"Traders trade on their pride," Shaneese said.

"And what is the profit on freezing to death?" Fiona asked, brows raised archly. "Anyway, as soon as I realized where the chattering was coming from, I insisted he get in with me—"

"Kindan didn't object?" Shaneese asked.

"Kindan wasn't there," Fiona said, moving on quickly. "Anyway, as soon as I got him in with me he was out like a new-hatched dragon with a full stomach." Terin giggled at the image. Fiona's eyes narrowed as she observed Shaneese's body language.

"What is there between you and this child?" Fiona asked her, her tone serious and authoritative.

"I've nothing against the lad," Shaneese protested quickly.

"I never asked you, how was it you came to be here, a trader in the Weyr?" Fiona pressed.

"L'rat found me," Shaneese said. "I wanted to go. I was young."

"Do you miss him much?" Terin asked softly.

Shaneese frowned before responding, "He was a good man."

"But—"

"I don't think I ever really knew him," Shaneese said honestly.

"Not the way you know T'mar," Fiona guessed.

"You have the advantage of me," Shaneese said, her eyes dim, reserved. "You are younger, prettier—"

"Oh, please!" Fiona broke in. "This is not a competition, Shaneese. I told you that before."

Shaneese nodded, her eyes wet with unshed tears, and she bowed her head.

"I left because I was shamed," Shaneese said. "Tenniz shamed me."

"How?" Fiona asked, eyes wide with surprise, prepared to hear the worst.

"No," Shaneese said quickly, "he did nothing like that." She sighed. "In fact, I think he told the truth. And, perhaps if I'd been older, I would have understood the gift he gave me." She snorted at a memory and looked up to meet Fiona's eyes. "Instead, I spit in his soup."

"Shaneese!" Terin exclaimed.

"I had sixteen Turns at the time," Shaneese said. "I had a lot of pride, too." She added, frankly, "I was beautiful in my youth."

"Still are!" Fiona said, just a moment before Terin joined in agreement.

Shaneese waved their compliments aside. "Traders value the profit and the trade."

"We know," Terin said, with all the feeling of old Igen Weyr's principal negotiator.

"For a woman, a man must be worthy," Shaneese continued. "And so, when Tenniz said what he said . . ."

"What horrible thing did he say?" Fiona asked.

"That you were ugly?"

"He said that I would be second wife and enjoy it," Shaneese said, looking directly at Fiona. "That I would gain great honor and much happiness after a time of sorrow."

"Yeah, he always seemed to speak in riddles," Terin agreed.

"Among the traders, being second wife is considered a great shame," Shaneese said with a sigh. "Rarely do we even consider such things and almost always in times of great hardship." She sighed again. "And then, the first wife is always the one considered the better, the superior."

She shook her head. "I could not believe that he had seen the future and he would not take back his words." Her lips turned down in a frown as she added, "I think he was truly hurt that I didn't find joy in his seeing."

"So you spat in his soup?" Fiona asked.

Shaneese nodded, her dark skin brightening with an underlying blush.

"I suppose that beats tunnel snakes in the bed," Terin said, glancing meaningfully at Fiona.

"It was only one!" Fiona protested. "And you said you wouldn't tell anyone!"

"Seems to me," Terin replied, taking another roll and buttering it, "that if you two are wives to the same man, you ought to share such exploits."

Fiona thought on that and nodded, telling Shaneese, "It was Kindan, Turns back when I was a child and he'd been ignoring me."

"A tunnel snake?" Shaneese repeated.

"It was only little," Fiona said in her own defense. "And I screamed a warning before he got in the bed, so he wasn't bitten."

"Tunnel snakes are rare in the desert," Shaneese said. "But they are very deadly. You're lucky you weren't caught."

"Oh, believe me," Fiona said, rising from her chair and rubbing her behind in painful memory, "I *was* caught!"

Shaneese and Terin shared a laugh at her expense. Fiona joined them, then said to Terin, "We should get going if we don't want Kindan to send the weyrlings after us." She turned and hugged Shaneese. "I can't say what the future will hold," she told the older woman. "But I would like to see it with you—and our children."

"I cannot say that it will always be easy, Weyrwoman," Shaneese told her somberly. "I am not the easiest of persons and I may find it difficult to share."

"I know what you mean!" Terin agreed feelingly.

"This close, this near to the same man, things may not always be easy," Fiona agreed, hugging her again. "We can only do our best."

Shaneese nodded solemnly. "And we'll do our best for our children."

"Always! That's what weyrfolk do!"

Fiona and Terin found the weyrlings and Kindan already arrayed outside the weyrling barracks. Kindan noted their approach and worked them carefully into his speech.

"And here are the Weyrwoman and weyrwoman Terin to show us how it's done," Kindan said, his eyes darting with laughter as he saw how he'd caught Fiona unprepared and how quickly she'd recovered from the sudden introduction.

Fiona eyed the cluster of weyrlings. Forty-two. If only they were old enough and mature enough to fight Thread. Telgar would have a full Flight with reserves and . . . they just might make it. She forced the thought away, concentrating on maintaining a cheerful appearance. "The Weyrwoman is the heart of the Weyr."

"Weyrlingmaster, what is it you want us to do?"

"I was thinking, to warm up, some dismounted drill," Kindan said.

Fiona smiled and nodded, moving closer to Kindan to speak to his ears alone, "May I make a suggestion?"

"Of course," Kindan said out of the corner of his mouth, even as he waved for the weyrlings to spread out. "You know I'm just winging this."

Terin giggled at the choice of words.

"After they've stretched, have them bring out their weyrlings to watch the drill," Fiona said. "And before that, it might make sense if Talenth and I make a demonstration flight."

"It'll be Turns before they can fly," Kindan reminded her.

"True, but we found at Igen that drilling and practicing made their muscles stronger when they could fly."

Kindan nodded at the sense in that. Fiona recalled that not too long ago—just after the weyrlings had Impressed—she had made a note to spend more time with them. It seemed such a long time ago, but it was only a month; the events of Lorana's disappearance and the ever-present dread hanging over the Weyr seemed to make events distant, memories fading.

"And when they got older, they were allowed to practice gliding off the queens' ledge," Terin put in hopefully.

"Well, if Jeila won't mind, I've no objection," Fiona said, grinning. "After all, I could hardly imagine Talenth objecting. Turnabout is fair play."

"You'll say that if you find a tunnel snake in your bed, won't you?" Kindan teased.

"No, I won't," Fiona told him firmly, her hand moving down to her belly. "I have no need of a sudden fright."

Kindan acknowledged her point with a nod, but Fiona suspected that sometime in the future, after the birth, she might find herself the recipient of a tunnel snake shock.

Kindan split the weyrlings into three teams, with X'lerin leading one, W'vin leading another, and Taria in charge of the third. The green rider gave him a startled look when her name was called, but Kindan explained that every weyrling should expect to lead the drill.

"Jeriz here is going with W'vin's group," Kindan said, nodding to the youngster. Some of the weyrlings exchanged surprised looks, but Kindan continued, "For this exercise, he'll be a rider from another Weyr."

Kindan started the weyrlings on simple stretching exercises, going from group to group to provide corrections and examples. Fiona decided to follow along.

"Don't stretch too much," Kindan warned her.

"Bekka would have told me if I couldn't."

"I don't recall you asking her," Terin remarked.

Fiona gave her a mulish look, then thought better of it. *Talenth, could you ask Bekka if I can exercise with the weyrlings?*

A moment later, a thin voice bellowed from a weyr several levels up, "Of course! Just take it slow!"

Fiona smiled and waved up at the small blob of blond hair and the larger form of Birentir behind her. Bekka waved idly back and returned to her rounds. Fiona noticed the shadow of a third person behind them.

"Where's Jeila?" Fiona asked.

"With Bekka," Terin told her, sounding surprised. "Didn't you know? She's been doing it for nearly a sevenday, Shaneese asked her."

"Makes sense," Fiona said. "I imagine Bekka's keeping an eye on her."

"I'm sure."

"You go with Xhinna and I'll go with X'lerin," Fiona said. "We can be extra riders, too." With a wave she headed off, leaving Terin to tromp over to her assigned group, feeling a bit awkward.

Fortunately, Xhinna and Taria greeted her cheerfully and Xhinna worked her into their stretch exercises quickly.

After stretches, Kindan had them run. Fiona joined in, but ran slower than the others. She hated running and Kindan knew it; she planned to plead her pregnancy if he gave her any trouble.

"Come on, Fiona, you can do better!" Kindan called to her as he urged the others on. "You don't want to show the weyrlings that they're faster than you."

Well, naturally, all the weyrlings immediately set about to prove that they were faster than their Weyrwoman. Fiona kept up gamely, glowering at Kindan while arranging to be slow enough that even the slowest of the weyrlings beat her.

"They'll be talking about that for *days*," Kindan murmured to her as she made it past the final mark.

Fiona smiled at him. Kindan gave her a wary look: he'd seen that look on her shortly before he'd found that tunnel snake.

"You know," Fiona said, "we should have them run to the queens' ledge and back."

Kindan cocked his head at her questioningly.

"After a while, tell them that the first one back will be the first to have their dragon glide from the ledge."

Kindan's brows rose approvingly. "A very good idea."

"And I'll be able to run to the queens' ledge and sit out the run back," Fiona added.

Kindan laughed. "Another good idea."

He turned his attention back to the weyrlings as Fiona rejoined X'lerin's group and received their good-natured and high-spirited commiserations with aplomb. He had them space out and started them on calisthenics. It was not long at all before all of them were sweating, hot, and tired, Fiona and Terin among them.

Kindan had them cool down with some simple formation drills: having them form wings and wheel left, right, and form to line ahead. He had them practice "flying" between each other, taking care to avoid touching their outstretched fingers—"wings"—while making the maneuvers progressively more complicated.

The drill lasted less than an hour before Kindan set them loose to look after their hatchlings.

Kurinth came scuttling out of her weyr then, looking for Terin, who raced off to feed her. Fiona and Jeriz, however, joined the hatchlings as they went into their quarters.

"Feed them, then check their skin," Kindan ordered as he looked around for the runner assigned to coordinate getting the raw meat sent over from the Kitchen. He frowned, and nodded toward Jeriz. "Do you think you could run over and tell Shaneese that the hatchlings need their meal?"

Jeriz gave him a slightly troubled look, but nodded anyway, taking off across the Weyr Bowl with his arms slightly outstretched, trying to disguise his self-conscious imitation of their earlier drill.

Fiona followed X'lerin and the werylings she'd drilled with to their dragonets, praising each one and giving advice on feeding when the buckets of scraps arrived.

"You're doing great with the oiling," Fiona told X'lerin as she examined Kivith's skin and stroked the small bronze's eye ridges.

"Thank you, Weyrwoman."

"Could you look at my dragon, please?" a worried weyrling asked and Fiona shortly found herself going from weyrling to weyrling offering advice or encouragement as needed. She was not surprised that Xhinna's Tazith and Taria's Coranth were perfectly groomed: the older girl had spent enough time helping Fiona oil young Talenth when they were together back in Fort Weyr.

"It'll seem like all you do is feed, oil, and—occasionally—sleep," Fiona assured the weyrlings with a grin. "But, ask any dragonrider and they'll tell you that it gets better over time."

"How long?" W'vin asked.

"It depends on the dragonet," Fiona said. "Some start sleeping longer in their third or fourth month, others sooner, others later." She smiled at the chorus of half-smothered groans rising around her. "You get used to it so quickly that when they start sleeping longer or needing less oiling, you'll wonder where you found all the extra time."

That thought cheered them up. She caught several stifling yawns and saw at least one that had to be caught by the others when he stumbled, sleep-weary.

As soon as she could, Fiona caught up with Jeriz and suggested that they tend to Talenth.

"Are we going to have to oil her?" Jeriz asked, his eyes wide in fear of the monumental task.

"Of course!" Fiona agreed impishly, starting her way briskly across the Bowl and smiling at the pounding of the boy's feet behind her as he strove to catch up.

"She's bigger, but not so patchy," an oily Jeriz declared with relief an hour later when they'd finished going over every bit of Talenth's gold hide. He wiped his oily fingers on the rag and, with a disappointed frown when he realized that he hadn't made them any drier, wiped them surreptitiously on the back of his trousers.

Talenth rustled her wings and carefully folded herself into a comfortable ball, placed her head under her wing, ready for a nap.

The air smelled of hot rock, cool oil, and the very special, pungent smell of dragon.

"Be glad she's not Tolarth," Fiona said, patting her queen affectionately. "We'd still be here."

"Tolarth is Jeila's queen," Jeriz said sounding both questioning and proud at the same time.

"She's the biggest queen on Pern, for the moment," Fiona said. "She's the first queen born with the cure for the sickness."

"And that makes her bigger?"

"We'll see," Fiona said. "If the other queens—like Terin's Kurinth—get as big, then probably. If not, well, Minith is maybe better at producing big dragons."

They will all get bigger, Talenth assured her.

I'm sure yours will, love, Fiona thought back affectionately.

"We should clean up and then get lunch," Fiona said to Jeriz.

"And after that?"

"Reading Records," Fiona pronounced. Jeriz couldn't stifle groaning his opinion of that.

▼ ▼ ▼

The afternoon was, as Fiona had said, spent reading Records. But some of it was spent with the boy perched in her lap as she traced out the letters and read to him. He was small enough that his weight didn't crush her and cute enough that cuddling him was a joy; Fiona hoped that her sons would be as cuddly at his age. Jeriz at first resisted the treatment, but relented when it became clear that it was the easiest way to work on reading.

After an hour of working on letters, Fiona switched to reading Records. Not long after she started, she felt the boy's body relax into slumber. She smiled fondly as she heard the slow, steady sound of his breathing and, greatly daring, kissed the top of his head, finding the jet black hair as soft as she'd imagined. How could anyone not love this child, Fiona thought to herself. She bent to kiss his hair once more, but her movement must have startled him, for Jeriz woke and struggled in her lap.

"Get off!" he said, erupting from the chair. He turned back and glared at her. "I'm not your son."

"No," Fiona agreed. "You fell asleep."

"I was tired," Jeriz said, lowering his eyes from hers. "And you were droning on."

Fiona got the impression that Jeriz felt his pride had been assaulted.

"Sorry," she said, nodding toward the nearby chair. "You can sit there, if you'd prefer."

Jeriz idled toward the chair but seemed reluctant to take it. He sat in it for a moment, then got it. "It's hard and cold."

Fiona hid a smile. "I'm sorry," she told him. "You can have your choice of chairs, but they're all pretty much hard and cold."

Jeriz thought that over. "I suppose I could sit with you."

"Certainly," Fiona said. The boy moved back over to her, trying to find the most manly way of sitting back in her lap. "One condition, however," Fiona told him. Jeriz looked up.

"I need to understand how to raise boys, I'll have some of my own, soon enough," Fiona said. "Little girls like sitting on laps and being tickled and falling asleep and being cuddled."

"They're girls," Jeriz said with all the contempt of a boy barely ten.

"Well, I'm used to them," Fiona said. "So, you'll either learn to accept that or you'll have to work out with me the proper way to treat boys."

Jeriz frowned.

"Do boys like being tickled?" Fiona asked.

"Sometimes," Jeriz said doubtfully.

"They don't like sitting on laps, though, do they?"

"Well, sometimes."

"And being cuddled, how about that?"

"Not like girls."

"I see," Fiona said, patting her lap suggestively. "Well, let's try this out, then."

"You won't tickle me?" Jeriz asked.

"Not unless you ask," Fiona said.

"Tickling's supposed to be a surprise," Jeriz snorted.

"So I'm to surprise you?"

"But not often," Jeriz said. "And you're to stop when I tell you."

"And if I don't?"

"I'll get mad."

"I see," Fiona said. She frowned. "That seems rather one-sided. Perhaps you should sit on the other chair."

"No!" Jeriz said. "I mean, I suppose it would be all right once in a while."

"Once in a while is all I imagined," Fiona told him.

"And only in private."

"Naturally," Fiona agreed. "So, should we try again?"

Jeriz nodded and sat back onto her lap. Fiona kept her arms to her side, her back straight. Shortly, Jeriz started fidgeting. "What is it?"

"You're not comfortable," Jeriz said. "You need to sit back and let me lean against you."

"That would be cuddling," Fiona warned him.

"And if you keep your arms like that I might fall off, if I fall asleep," Jeriz added.

"So you don't mind if I put an arm around you?"

"Not too tight," Jeriz allowed, leaning back against her.

"You know," Fiona began conversationally as she wrapped an arm lightly around his midriff, "there's a thing girls do."

"Hmm?"

"Well, mothers, more than girls," Fiona said.

"What's that?"

"Well, when they love someone who's littler, they find it almost impossible," and Fiona wrapped both arms tightly around the suddenly squirming lad, bending over and kissing him lightly on the crown of his head, "not to cuddle and kiss them!"

Jeriz grunted in annoyance and squirmed once more, for show's sake, before quieting and snarling, "That's what my mother said."

"Mothers do that," Fiona told him.

"You're not my mother."

"But I'm going to be a mother and I need all the practice I can get," Fiona said.

"Well . . ." Jeriz stopped struggling. "I suppose if no one else knows."

Fiona smiled, loosened her grip on the boy, raised her head, and went back to reading her Records. A while later, Jeriz turned, resting his head on her chest, his legs over her side, his breath slowing back into slumber. He was still not quite asleep when Fiona leaned over quickly and kissed his head once more, but this time, he only sighed in contentment.

Fiona could feel the boy's trust in her growing, could feel the pain and fear inside him easing.

Somehow, she thought to herself, we must prove worthy of that trust.

She thought of the child growing inside her and added, we must give you both a Pern that lives.

FIVE

Rider to your mate be true
Follow heart in deed and do
All the best your strength can find
So you will rest in heart and mind.

Telgar Weyr, AL 508.7.27

Terin and F'jian had both gone to sleep early that night. Fiona had sent her away early to spend time with the bronze rider, just as T'mar had released all the dragonriders for a day's rest prior to the Threadfall.

Terin was sore from the exercises she'd had with the weyrlings and probably even more sore because she'd been too shy to join Fiona and Jeriz in an after-drill bath. Jeriz might seem small and young to Fiona, but to Terin he was little more than three Turns her junior and she was still young enough to be body-conscious.

Fiona had let her go good-naturedly, even though Terin was sure that she would have preferred her company and, truth be told, Terin somewhat regretted her impulsive rejection of the offer. Maybe it was time to get over such things. Maybe F'jian would be just the teensiest bit jealous when he heard.

So she replayed the conversation with the Weyrwoman and the green-eyed boy over and over as she tried to settle her mind for sleep. A part of her knew that she was avoiding sleep just as she was avoiding the thoughts that would scare her—Threadfall over Crom.

Tomorrow's Fall would be short, only a third of the total six-hour Pass would be over Crom territory; the rest would be flown by High Reaches as the Threadfall passed into Nabol and Tillek, but Terin couldn't control her fears.

She pretended, though, to be sleeping, keeping her breath purposely slow, listening for each new breath from F'jian, trying to burn her brain with the memories lest they be the last.

Stop it, she told herself. He'll be fine. A moment later, she added chidingly, and you're not helping with your worries.

She wondered how Fiona was sleeping. Perhaps she was awake, worried. Perhaps Terin should speak to Kurinth and ask her to talk to Talenth, to see if Fiona was—no, Terin thought as she reached out and found her queen fast asleep.

Tomorrow Kurinth would be itching and creeling with hunger. Terin hid a smile at the thought. It was hard not to be forgiving of her beautiful queen and, after all, it was only normal—and good—that she was hungry and growing new skin daily. New skin needed oiling, and there was always new skin.

At least I've ready hands to help with the oiling, she thought. The little boys were always eager to please, as were the young girls. Released from their chores to help the weyrwoman, they ran screaming across the Bowl only to walk, silently and cautiously, up the queens' ledge, fearful of being rude, hopeful of getting a chance to help. Terin was glad to let them—not only for the ease it gave her but also because she genuinely liked the small ones and loved their wide-eyed prattling.

She decided that, perhaps, she was being just a bit silly not to bathe with Fiona just because Jeriz was about.

A noise startled her. Footsteps. Fiona?

No, not Fiona, Terin decided. All the same, she felt that she knew that walk and that it was a woman's.

F'jian must have been listening, too, for all that he seemed asleep because he slipped the sheets off him and slid quietly out of the bed, grabbing gear and shoes as he went.

"Where are you going?" Terin asked, turning on her side, propping her head with an arm. "And when were you going to tell me?"

"I won't be gone long," F'jian said with a voice torn with sorrow. "I'll be back before first light, I'm certain."

"Who are you going with?"

"I can't tell you," F'jian said.

Terin started toward the edge of the bed. "I'll come with you."

"No!" F'jian said desperately. "You can't come, Terin. Trust me."

"Why can't I come?" Terin asked. "How can I trust you?" Her voice turned bitter. "You're going with some other woman." Tears sprang from her eyes unwanted. "If you didn't want me, you had only to say so."

"No," F'jian said, glancing to the weyr and back to Terin. "No, you don't understand."

"What's to understand?" Terin asked. "You couldn't wait, so you found someone else."

"No," F'jian raced back to her, reaching for her cheek, but she flinched away. "No, never anyone but you, Terin, never!"

"Until now!"

"No, never!" F'jian said, his voice raw with pain. "Never, by the Egg of Faranth. I promise you, Terin, only you! For all my days, only you."

Terin said nothing. She couldn't believe him. In the distance she heard movement. F'jian hesitated, then turned toward his weyr, calling back to her, "I'll be back."

Terin shook her head, too angry, too hurt, too wretched to say anything. She heard his footsteps fading, heard Ladirth move out of his weyr, heard the sounds of wings fluttering into the sky, then nothing.

Fiona woke the instant she heard the steps and elbowed Kindan gently. The harper snorted once, glanced her way, then heard the steps and got quickly out of bed. She heard him murmur something, heard Terin's voice whimper in response and then Terin was in bed beside her, her head buried tight against Fiona's chest, her tears burning hot through her nightdress. Quietly, Kindan sidled into the overcrowded bed.

"Shh, shh," Fiona said soothingly to Terin, cuddling her up tight against her, stroking her hair and sending soothing thoughts toward the distraught young weyrwoman.

Slowly, Terin's sobs ebbed, her tears stopped, and slowly her breathing eased into the depths of sleep.

Fiona felt Jeriz's gaze bore into her back, but the boy said nothing. A moment later, Jeriz said apologetically, "I've got to get out."

Kindan must have heard, for, with a sigh, the harper reached over Fiona and bodily pulled the boy over her and Terin both, setting him on the ground with a whispered, "Go! Hurry back!"

Fiona could hear the amusement in Kindan's voice and reached beyond Terin to stroke his arm in thanks. Kindan grasped her hand with his for a moment and released it, settling back into a waiting doze until Jeriz returned and Kindan, much to the boy's surprise, chagrin, and delight, repeated the maneuver.

"Fiona," Jeriz whispered into her ear a moment later, "there was someone out there."

Fiona nodded absently, reached behind herself to rub his arm comfortingly and slipped back to sleep.

But not for long. It seemed only an instant before she heard voices again. Kindan and another male and then the piping voice of Jeriz, who had somehow crawled over her and Terin without waking them.

"Go to bed, you can talk to her in the morning," Kindan said.

Fiona opened her eyes. It was F'jian.

"I just need to tell her—"

"It can wait for the morning, trust me, bronze rider," Kindan said.

F'jian gave him a final imploring look and, weary and defeated, turned away. A moment later, a rustling sound was followed by the shadowy outline of a dim glow, and Jeriz called quietly, "I'll light your way."

"Thank you," F'jian said, still sounding miserable.

Fiona waited until Jeriz returned much later, hid the glow, and crawled back into bed, this time too tired to do more than snuggle against Kindan who held him close and whispered, "You did well."

Fiona heard the boy's pleased sigh at the words even as he drifted off to sleep.

F'jian was back at first light, bearing a tray with a pitcher of warm *klah* and a basket of fresh rolls.

"Make him go away," Terin said miserably as soon as she heard his voice.

Fiona rose and pulled on her robe even as Kindan greeted the bronze rider with marked reserve.

"You need to go, F'jian," Fiona said before he could say anything.

"Please," he begged, "can I talk to you, Weyrwoman?"

"Come with me, then," Fiona told him sharply, nodding toward Talenth's weyr.

In the morning light reflecting into Talenth's weyr, Fiona could see the misery in F'jian's face. His eyes were red-rimmed, his hair unkempt, and he looked absolutely exhausted.

"She has to know I love her," F'jian began without preamble, his hands raised by his side, clenched for emphasis.

"Actions will tell her that," Fiona said. She sent a thought to Talenth, who passed the message on to Zirenth. "What happened last night?"

"I cannot say," F'jian said, sounding forlorn.

"I can't help you much if I don't know what's happening," Fiona told him reasonably, all the while thinking of the warm *klah,* her still warmer bed, and how little she liked standing in a nightdress with only her nightrobe for warmth. "Who was the woman, F'jian?"

"I can't say," he repeated miserably. He looked into her eyes adding softly, "You cannot break time."

"Break time?" Fiona repeated, her eyes narrowing. "You've been timing it?"

"I cannot say more," F'jian told her. "I wish I could, believe me, but I cannot."

"You've been timing it?" T'mar appeared behind F'jian in response to Fiona's summons. "This near a Fall?"

"I—I had to, Weyrleader," F'jian said, turning to include T'mar in his view.

"You've been dead on your feet for the past sevenday, man, and now you tell me you've been *timing it*!" T'mar shook his head savagely. "You don't fly tonight. You may kill yourself, but I can't risk you killing others."

"I think you should return to your quarters, F'jian," Fiona told him sternly.

"But—" F'jian looked from Weyrleader to Weyrwoman and back. Finally, he dropped his head and slumped away.

"Has anyone else been timing it?" Fiona asked as she watched him make his way across the Weyr Bowl. She caught T'mar's expression and gave him an apologetic look. "I should have kept a better eye on them."

"Affairs of the heart aren't usually conducted in broad daylight, Weyrwoman," T'mar told her gently. "As far as I know, only you operate that way."

"So I should have known better," Fiona repeated.

"Yes," T'mar agreed. "Beyond saving Pern, beyond looking out for strays, beyond your queen and your Weyr, beyond all that you do, you should have known better."

"But she's my friend!" Fiona protested. With a wan look at F'jian's retreating form, she added, "And I thought I knew him."

"You probably did," T'mar said.

"Come in, there's warm *klah*," Fiona said, nodding toward her quarters invitingly. T'mar frowned in thought for a moment, and gestured for her to precede him.

"This is not the best start to a day," Kindan said as he marshaled Terin and Jeriz around the table. There weren't enough chairs with T'mar present, so the boy insisted on standing and serving the others. He conducted his self-appointed duties with skill and aplomb, receiving praise from the four older folk and beaming in response.

"And now we're a dragon short," Fiona added with a grimace.

T'mar nodded, then looked over at Kindan. "I don't suppose you'd—"

"No!" Fiona cut him off harshly. The Weyrleader looked at her expectantly. "If F'jian's been timing it this much, Ladirth is no better than he. They're both too tired."

T'mar reflected on this for a moment and nodded. Sighing, he said, "Well, then we're another dragon short this Fall." His eyes turned to Terin and he gave her a troubled smile. "I'm sorry, weyrwoman, that you've been through so much."

"I trusted him," Terin said with a half-sob. She struggled to get herself under control. "All this time . . ."

Fiona groped for something to say, but could only shake her head wordlessly, sending a beseeching look to Kindan.

"Sometimes," the harper said slowly, "when we're very afraid of losing that which we desire most, we make terrible mistakes."

Terin eyed him bleakly, her tear-stained cheeks and red-rimmed eyes mute testimony to the pain she'd experienced.

Fiona regarded the exchange thoughtfully. She reached over to her friend and grabbed her shoulder comfortingly. Terin covered Fiona's hand with her own and lay her head on the pair. Fiona made a noise and stood up, circling around behind the redhead and resting both hands on her shoulders, moving them in to massage Terin's tense neck. After a moment, Terin sighed and closed her eyes gratefully.

"Terin, love," Fiona told her softly as she sensed the youngster relax, "you're going to have to forgive him."

Terin tensed under her hands and leaned forward out of her grasp. She turned her torso so that she could stare at Fiona. "Forgive him!"

"Yes," Fiona said, nodding grimly. "Forgive him." Terin snorted her opinion of that. "If you don't forgive him, you'll never move on from this—and you'll never forgive yourself."

"She's right," Kindan said, glancing at T'mar for agreement, but the Weyrleader was watching Fiona in amazement. Kindan smiled to himself, realizing that some of his lessons had rubbed off on the impish Weyrwoman. Sensing T'mar's rapid thoughts, Kindan continued, catching Terin's eyes with his own as he said, "It took me a long while to recover from Koriana's loss." Fiona gasped at the mention of her sister. Kindan nodded to her. "I blamed myself for not being quicker, I blamed Lord Bemin for—for anything I could think of." His eyes fell to Fiona. "I blamed you for living and trying so hard to take her place."

"I could never take her place!" Fiona declared. "She was my sister, Kindan."

"You never knew her," the harper told her quietly. His lips twitched upward for a moment as he added, "But she would have been *so* proud of you!"

Tears started in Fiona's eyes.

"And rightly so," Kindan said, lowering his eyes to Terin once more. "You've made great friends and you keep loyal to them." Terin absorbed his words and leaned back once more in her chair in silent apology to Fiona, who held her shoulders once more and grasped them gently in acceptance. "And you're not afraid to tell the truth as you see it, no matter how hard it is on you."

"They say I'm stubborn," Fiona agreed. Kindan smiled at her, joined a moment later by T'mar and Terin. She leaned over Terin to speak in her ear once more. "Which is why I'm telling you: You have to forgive him." She paused to let her words sink in. "You rise above the pain when you do, trust me."

"Who did you forgive, Fiona?" Kindan asked her softly.

"You," she told him, raising her eyes to meet his unflinchingly. "When I saw you with Lorana and, even before, when I'd heard you were with her." She smiled sadly and turned her head down toward Terin. "And it was then, when I could forgive myself for loving him, forgive myself for being jealous of Lorana, that I discovered that I could love them both."

"So if I forgive him, then I can love him?" Terin asked, arching her head back to catch Fiona's eyes. "I don't want to, Fiona. There's too much pain."

"Pain's part of love, sweetie," Fiona said, leaning down and kissing Terin affectionately on the nose. "You know that."

"Pain's part of living," Jeriz piped up. All the others turned to him in surprise. "'Love is extra, pain's a given.'" He flushed as they stared at him. "That's a saying we traders have."

"Well, that's a saying we weyrfolk will keep," Fiona said, including him with a wave of her hand. She looked back down to Terin. "Love is extra, pain's a given."

Terin's lips puffed out in a pout and she lowered her head, shaking it slightly. "So I have to forgive him?"

"Forgive him," Kindan said. "It's not for him, your forgiveness, it's for yourself."

"Because until you do, you lock yourself up in your anger, you can't move on," T'mar agreed.

"All I want to do is crawl back into bed," Terin said miserably.

"Then do so," Fiona told her. "We'll take our breakfast in the Cavern."

The matter was easier said than done, but Fiona, T'mar, and Kindan were soon ready to leave.

"If you would, weyrwoman," Jeriz said solemnly to Terin, "I'll stay here in case you need anything." He gestured nervously to the unused cot in the distance. "I can rest over there, I won't disturb you."

Terin smiled and nodded in acceptance of the offer. "But if I get cold, you've got to snuggle with me."

Jeriz's eyes went wide, but he nodded solemnly. Fiona gave him an encouraging smile before she left, and his eyes lit with pleasure, rising to a blaze with Kindan's curt nod and T'mar's respectful half-salute before they departed.

"How many others are like F'jian—disconsolate?" Fiona asked as she, Kindan, and T'mar trouped across the Weyr Bowl to the Kitchen Cavern.

"Pretty much all of them," Kindan guessed. T'mar nodded mutely.

"You, too?" Fiona said, turning to the bronze rider.

"I want to hope," T'mar said. "But the numbers are bad."

"High Reaches has only seven more dragonpairs than us, Fort only ten," Kindan said. "The best is Benden, with slightly more than a full Flight."

"And likely less after the Fall tonight," T'mar added grimly.

"Likely," Kindan agreed.

"We've pulled through before, we'll do it again," Fiona said.

"Kindan and Lorana found the cure," T'mar said, leaving unspoken the thought that it was too little, too late.

"Worry about today, T'mar," Fiona said, skipping ahead to catch his hand in hers. "You let me worry about tomorrow."

T'mar smiled at her suggestion. "If you don't mind, I'd prefer it if you could worry a little faster."

"Or better," Kindan agreed.

"Of course," Fiona said, keeping her tone light even as her heart skipped in dread. If Kindan and T'mar were this gloomy, how could she hope for better from the riders?

After breakfast, T'mar sought out J'gerd, who'd been assigned as F'jian's second. "You're to lead the wing," he told him. "F'jian's not well enough."

"Weyrleader?" J'gerd said, surprised and off guard. He saw the implacable look in T'mar's eyes and stiffened. "Certainly."

The weyrlings were released from drill to help prepare the firestone for the evening. Fiona noticed the nervous glances of the weyrfolk, hastily averted when she looked, but they could not hide their worry and concern.

They had all seen the older Telgar riders vanish in a single Fall. Now they wondered if they'd see any of the current riders return. And there'd been too many lost, lost timing it, lost fighting Thread.

News of F'jian's relief and the reasons for it spread throughout the Weyr, even though Fiona was certain that no one who was present had spoken about it. Probably, she thought from her experience at Fort Hold, the weyrfolk had noted who was present, who was absent, and had drawn their own—correct—conclusions.

Lorana had been gone for six days and already the morale of the Weyr had plummeted. Fiona felt fears creeping in, humor unraveling, tensions mounting, and she was powerless to do anything about it.

She remained at the high table as T'mar and the others went out to the Weyr Bowl to plan and check their gear.

A man cleared his throat softly from behind her. "I haven't seen it this bad before."

It was Mekiar.

"It was bad back at Fort Weyr when we'd banished the fire-lizards and the dragons were still getting sick," Fiona replied, her voice low. "It was this bad when we came here and Talenth caught the sickness."

"I suppose it was," Mekiar allowed. Fiona raised a hand, inviting him to sit with her. The old ex-dragonrider moved deliberately and sat with a sigh and a nod of gratitude.

"Old bones are hard to move," Mekiar said.

"Hah!" Fiona snorted. "Try pregnant bodies!"

"If you're moaning now when you scarcely show . . ." Mekiar said, shaking his head. Then he stopped and eyed her intently.

"What?" Fiona demanded, wondering if she had to defend her honor.

"I was just thinking," Mekiar said. "I don't recall you to be the sort to complain."

"I don't see how it can help, most times," Fiona admitted.

"So, if you're not complaining over much, you have to wonder why is it you're feeling so poorly this early?"

"It's my first time," Fiona said. "I've never done this before. I thought that was reason enough."

"Perhaps," Mekiar agreed blandly.

"Or?" Fiona prompted.

"Multiple pregancies are noticeable earlier than single pregnancies."

"Multiple?" Fiona repeated, eyes going wide. "Twins?"

"Triplets are very rare," Mekiar agreed, his eyes sparkling. "Although I recall a holder who had four at once."

"Four?" Fiona repeated, aghast. She looked down at her stomach. "Two will be enough, if it comes to that."

Talenth, ask Bekka to meet me in the Kitchen Cavern.

She asks if it can wait, Talenth responded a moment later.

Say to her: twins, Fiona replied.

She's coming, Talenth said a moment later. *What are twins?*

It's when a person has two babies at once, Fiona informed her.

Babies aren't like eggs, Talenth said, sounding slightly confused.

No, eggs are clutched, then hatch, Fiona told her. *Babies clutch and hatch at the once.*

Awkward, Talenth declared.

Fiona snorted at her queen's observation, then replied, *But it keeps the wait shorter.*

Talenth made no reply, but Fiona got the distinct feeling that the queen preferred *her* way. Fiona wondered if she might agree with her before too long.

"We're still not sure!" Bekka called from the entrance of the Kitchen Cavern, bustling toward Fiona with Birentir trundling behind her.

"And you were going to tell *me* when?"

"I thought we had," Bekka said. "I mean, I recall telling you to eat more . . ."

"You said the same to Jeila."

"She's too thin, hardly putting on any weight," Bekka replied immediately. She eyed Fiona. "You won't have that problem."

"Why didn't you tell me?" Fiona demanded.

"It's really too early," Bekka said. "You know that things can go wrong in the first twelve weeks—" Fiona nodded irritably. Bekka frowned. "Well, they can go worse with two."

"They can?" Fiona felt her throat go dry with fear.

"It's possible to lose one and not the other," Bekka said, suddenly solemn and not at all happy with her news. "I didn't want to say anything, in case."

"I see," Fiona said, forcing herself to breathe slowly. "How would I know, if I lost one?"

"We won't really know if you've got two until they're old enough that we can hear their heartbeats," Bekka temporized. "And even then it's often hard to be sure."

"So what makes you think I've got twins?"

"The way you've been complaining," Bekka said. Fiona didn't need to turn to feel Mekiar beside her, nodding. "You're more sore than you should be at this time. And—" Bekka had the grace to flush "—you've been peeing more than usual."

"It could be a bladder infection," Birentir reminded the youngster.

"That's why we've had her drink more fruit juice, just to be sure," Bekka replied waving a hand dismissingly. "I'd say, judging by her behavior, that's not it." She eyed Fiona judiciously and nodded. "No, I'm pretty sure it's twins."

"And I could lose one?"

"You could lose both," Bekka said. "Carrying a child is never certain." She frowned when she saw Fiona's distraught look. "I don't think you will or I'd have the Masterhealer here this instant."

"Or his wife," Birentir suggested, "she's better with pregnancies."

"I'd have *both* of them and you know it," Bekka said. She gave Fiona a frank look and leaned closer. "I'm more worried about Jeila, to be honest."

"Jeila?"

Bekka nodded. "She's thin and small-boned. Even if everything goes well, it may be difficult for her." She puckered her lips. "She's built small like me and my mother, who lost two before she carried one to term." She nodded to Fiona. "I spoke with Kindan, your mother had four children, all full-term and healthy." She smiled at her friend. "There's no reason to think you'll be any different."

"Four," Fiona said quietly, thinking of the four special mounds in Fort Hold's garden, one for each of her brothers, one for her sister, and one for her mother. She glanced up at Bekka. "How would I know?"

"Know what?"

"If I lost one," Fiona said.

"You might feel cramps," Bekka said. "And you might have bleeding more than usual."

"Bleeding?"

"More than usual," Bekka assured her. "You'll tell me or Talenth will tell me if there's anything to worry about."

"Talenth?"

"We talk," Bekka said with a shrug. "Ever since you said we could."

"She's keeping an eye on you," Fiona admitted.

"And you, too, Weyrwoman," Birentir added humorously. "Apparently your queen is a bit of a tattle."

"She just likes people," Fiona said. She cocked an eye at Bekka. "Anything special I should do?"

"Yes," Bekka told her emphatically. Fiona raised an eyebrow demandingly. "Don't worry."

"Worry?"

"Worry," Bekka repeated. "Worrying can cause distress and that can affect the pregnancy."

"It's rather hard to avoid worrying these days," Mekiar observed.

"Don't worry about the babies, Fiona," Bekka said. She pointed a finger at herself, adding, "That's *my* job."

"And mine?"

"Everything else," Bekka told her. "You grow the babies, feed them, keep Pern from doing whatever it would do without you, and I'll see to it that you have two healthy babies when the time comes." She paused, then frowned. "If I can."

"If it's any help, my lady," Birentir put in diffidently, "she's quite good at her job."

"For a girl?" Fiona asked him tauntingly.

"For anyone," Birentir replied staunchly, his hand going to Bekka's shoulder and resting there. "Her father has every right to be proud."

"Where is he?" Fiona asked, suddenly realizing that Seban was nowhere to be seen.

"With Jeila, finishing our rounds," Bekka said in a slightly testy tone.

"He's keeping an eye on her?"

"Two," Birentir said with a wink.

"And don't you tell her, Fiona," Bekka said, shaking a finger at her Weyrwoman. "She's the sort to fret, and fretting would be certain to cause her to lose the pregnancy."

"I'll worry for her then," Fiona decided.

"No you won't!" Bekka told her firmly. "If you do, that's just the same as worrying about your own—only with even less control and you'd be certain to lose them, and then *she'd* probably lose hers in sympathy." Bekka spluttered. "Fiona, you've got to know what you can and cannot do."

"And I can't worry about my babies or Jeila's babies," Fiona said questioningly.

"Not with everything else you worry about," Birentir said, his hand shaking Bekka's shoulder affectionately. "She's right, Weyrwoman. In this, you have to put your trust in us."

Fiona looked at the healer, surprised in the change in him since he'd first arrived full of arrogance and self-importance. More than anything, she realized, it was Bekka's unassuming performance of her duties that had changed him.

"Is she learning enough here?" Fiona asked him. "Or should we send her to the Healer Hall?"

Birentir snorted. "My lady, you should know better! You have a way of attracting strong wills in small packages." He grinned down at Bekka, whose eyes flared in mock anger. "And this is one of the smallest." With a sigh, he continued, "Still, I'm not a Master and she needs one before she can walk the tables."

"Then have Master Betrony come and certify her," Fiona said.

"I don't know if—"

"With two weyrwomen pregnant, I suspect he'll be willing to make a visit," Fiona said.

"And there are some patients here he'd probably like to see," Birentir ruminated, raising a finger to his lips in thought.

"You, Seban, Bekka, and the others have come up with some novel treatments that should be recorded back at the Healer Hall," Birentir said after a moment. "And, I think, the Masterhealer should take more of an interest in the healing of dragons, as well."

"Dragons?" Fiona repeated, surprised. "I would have thought he'd leave that to the Masterherder."

"Who, as we both know, has no interest whatsoever in dragons," Birentir said, shaking his head sadly. "No, I think that those healers who can expect to be assigned to the Weyrs should have an opportunity to learn at least part of that craft in their own Hall."

"That would probably be better than learning it the hard way," Fiona agreed, her lips twitching at the various memories of ichor-soaked nights spent desperately trying to sew Thread-torn wings.

"Precisely my thinking," Birentir agreed.

Fiona sighed. "Well, it will have to wait until after this Fall, as we've no one spare to send."

"What about F'jian?" Bekka asked.

"He's too tired," Fiona said, surprised at her suggestion.

"We could take Talenth," Bekka said, eyes suddenly aglow. "We've done it before."

"I haven't been out of the Weyr for a while," Fiona said, musingly.

"No, you should stay here," Bekka said. "You're needed. Father could come with us."

"There's no certainty that the Masterhealer will be available," Birentir reminded Bekka.

"But you've just got to see me with Talenth!" Bekka said, suddenly excited.

Fiona started to shake her head and squash the notion, but she felt a foot rub against hers and looked up to see Mekiar eye her intently. She caught his look and turned to face Bekka squarely, seeing the joy in the youngster's face overshadowing the fear, sorrow, and pain.

"Let me see if she's up for it," Fiona said. *Talenth, would you take Bekka and some others to the Healer Hall? She needs some cheering up.*

What about you?

If you'll be okay, I'll stay here. Fiona replied, half-hoping that Talenth would object, but honest enough to let her feelings and concern for Bekka slip through to her queen.

She would be happier riding me without you? Talenth thought about that. *We've never tried this before, it could be fun.*

Yes, it could. Fiona agreed. *Would you like to try?*

Yes. Talenth's response made it clear that she'd be just as happy to have her rider along, but also that the novelty intrigued her.

"She said yes," Fiona spoke out loud, and was rewarded with Bekka's whoop of delight. The small youngster sped away, only to return and grab Birentir's hand, forcibly dragging him out of the Cavern in much the same manner as she'd once dragged Talenth off to eat.

"A strong will in a small package, indeed!" Mekiar chortled as they watched them leave. In an approving tone, he added, "You did well, Weyrwoman."

"Well, at least there are two who are not despondent," Fiona agreed.

"Three," Mekiar said, pointing to himself. "I put my faith in my Weyrwoman as she is wise enough to put her trust in others. Even her dragon."

"Well, she is a very *wise* dragon."

K indan gave Fiona an approving look when he heard of her decision. T'mar nodded in agreement.

"The more we show we're not jealous," T'mar said, "the easier it'll be when the need comes."

"The need for what?" Fiona demanded. She narrowed her eyes at him. "You're not thinking of mounting fit riders on other dragons again, are you?"

"If it comes to that," T'mar said. He pursed his lips in a sour look. "As it is now, we've more dragons injured than riders."

"Dragons are bigger, they're more likely to get scored," Kindan said.

"It's surprising, really, that any riders get scored," Fiona added in agreement. "As it is, the amount is nearly one rider for every ten dragons."

"Why is that surprising?" T'mar demanded.

"Well, think about it," Kindan said with a shrug. "A dragon's about—what?—forty or fifty times the size of a rider."

"More for bronzes," Fiona said. T'mar shrugged, still not certain of their point.

"Well, all things being equal, the dragon's a much bigger target than a rider, so there should be more scored dragons to match the proportions," Kindan said.

"I think the riders are more worried about protecting their dragons," T'mar said. "And so we worry more about them than us."

"Which is why there aren't forty or more scored dragons for every rider," Fiona agreed. "Though, honestly, I'd rather there were none."

"Someday there will be," T'mar said. Fiona gave him a questioning look. "When this Pass is over."

"By the First Egg, let it be so!"

Talenth burst out of the skies over Fort Hold and the Harper Hall with a triumphant bugle, announcing to all that a queen had arrived.

Accompanied by Bekka's cries of joy, the queen banked sharply, dipping on her wingtip, and spiraled down to the ground, landing softly.

"Well done, Talenth!" Bekka called, slapping Talenth affectionately on the neck.

Thank you, Talenth said. *I did land well, didn't I?*

"You did indeed," Bekka said, even as Seban started unbuckling the three of them from the riding straps.

The air was warm with summer heat, full of the smells of fields full of crops, though none too near any of the settlements.

"Fiona!" a man's voice called from the direction of Fort Hold. "What are you—" the voice cut off as the man got close enough to distinguish the shapes. "Well, healer Bekka, this is a surprise!"

"My lord," Bekka said, bowing to Fort's Lord Holder—Fiona's father.

"She's not ill, is she?" Bemin asked suddenly, moving close enough to peer into Bekka's eyes while at the same time dismissing her acknowledgment with a wave. He saw Birentir and Seban and his eyes widened.

"She's well, my lord," Bekka said hastily. "Pregnant, worried as we all are, but well."

"Pregnant?" Bemin's eyes rose to his brows even as his shoulders slumped in surprise.

"With twins," Bekka added. "We've come to consult with the Masterhealer."

Behind her, Seban and Birentir nodded in confirmation.

"Twins?" Bemin repeated incredulously. He snorted a laugh and added, "She was never one to do things by halves!"

"Indeed, my lord," Birentir agreed. "We were just on our way to report to the Master, if you'd care to join us?"

"Certainly," Bemin said, joining them. He glanced up at Talenth and then back to Bekka. "She let you ride her?"

"Yes, my lord," Bekka said, just barely containing her excitement. "Talenth says I was very good, too."

Bemin accepted that with a nod and glanced over the small girl's head to the accompanying men, who both added looks in agreement.

Silently the four made their way under the arches of the Harper Hall where they were met by the growing sounds of harpers in various states of motion: some rushing to classes, others playing games, still others playing instruments in groups.

"Perhaps we should have gone around," Birentir said as they made their way through the throng, leaving behind knots of curious harpers whispering amongst themselves about their arrival.

"Nonsense," Bemin said, "Master Zist would have descended upon you—"

"He would have shouted," Bekka agreed in an uncharacteristically demure voice.

"Who would have shouted?" a voice roared from a window above, filling the courtyard and creating an instant silence.

"You would, Master," Bekka said, breaking into a huge smile.

"So Fiona has unleashed you back on us again, has she?" Zist bellowed in a bass voice. "And sent her father to make amends, no doubt."

"No doubt," Bemin said with a chuckle, waving up to the Master-harper. "Should we join you?" With a wry look, he added, "We'd hate to interrupt any important undertaking."

Zist snorted at the jibe. "Most would call it a nap, Lord Bemin," Zist replied. "And it was hard enough"—and here his voice hardened—"to get rest with all the racket in the courtyard." The hush deepened, but Birentir noticed grins on most faces; clearly this discourse from the Masterharper was not uncommon. "Particularly those who in-sisted upon singing out of tune."

"No one was out of tune," Kelsa called out from the archway lead-ing down to the dining hall. "Or I would have heard."

"Nonsense," Zist roared back loudly. "New mothers are always tone deaf."

Kelsa snorted at that and raced up the steps, bearing a tray in one hand and a small sleepy baby in the other.

"Kemin!" Bekka shouted, racing off after her. "Oh, please, let me hold him!"

"I thought she didn't like babies," Birentir murmured to no one in particular.

"Not this one," Bemin said with pride. Kemin was his son.

"Is he over the colic, then?" Seban asked.

"No, more's the pity, but he will be soon enough," Bemin said, shaking his head. "In fact, I was on my way down here for night duty when I spotted Talenth."

"We'd better catch up or she'll hand him off to us the moment he gets stinky," Seban said, stretching his legs for a longer stride.

He was not wrong and not at all surprised when Bekka pushed baby Kemin into his arms. "Father, would you please?" she begged with her best wide-eyed innocence. "I need to talk with the Master-harper."

"The Masterharper can wait, young lady, the child cannot," Zist in-toned.

Bekka sighed heavily at the injustice of it all, but took Kemin back and made her way out of the Masterharper's quarters, muttering to herself.

"How is she doing, then?" Zist asked, the moment he was certain she was out of earshot.

"She should walk the tables," Birentir said firmly. "She knows more than most journeymen." He pointed a finger toward Seban, adding, "So should he." He gave the ex-dragonrider a respectful nod, adding, "With more training, you could be a Master."

"I think I'd like that," Seban said.

"If Betrony could rate you Master, Bekka could be your journeyman," Zist mused.

"I don't think that would be a good idea," Bemin spoke up. Zist glanced at him. "She's a good child, but before long she'll be hitting her more rebellious phase and having her father as her Master will help neither."

"Yes, I see," Zist said. He glanced at Birentir. "And you? Would you be her Master?"

"I haven't learned enough, as I'm sure Master Betrony will agree," Birentir said.

Slow footsteps climbing the stairs announced the Masterhealer's arrival. Zist nodded for Birentir to get the door and the healer opened it before the Masterhealer had started to knock, bowing respectfully.

"Birentir, how are you?" Betrony asked cheerfully. He saw Seban beyond him and his smile widened. "And you, too!" He glanced around the room, eyes twinkling. "Have my spies deceived me? I'd heard that my favorite student was here as well."

"Your spies are accurate as always," Zist said. "Just as they've probably made you aware that we've sent the young one away with the baby."

"A babe in babe's arms," Betrony said, delighting in the irony.

"They tell me that Fiona is pregnant," Bemin added.

"Pregnant?" Zist asked alertly. "Kindan or T'mar?"

Bemin added a questioning look of his own to the two healers from Telgar.

"She hasn't said," Seban replied coolly. Zist gestured for him to go on and the ex-dragonrider added, "Honestly, I can't say. It could be either."

"Or both," Bekka added as she pushed open the door with one arm, dangling a burbling Kemin under the other. She passed the baby back to Kelsa. "There, all clean!"

Kelsa took the baby back with a grateful smile and tucked him easily against her side. Bemin reached to grab the boy from her, but the Songmaster shook her head with an easy smile, content for now to have the baby with her.

"I suppose, with that child anything is possible," Lord Bemin, her father, admitted with a sigh.

"We really shouldn't have told you, my lord," Bekka said, suddenly serious. Bemin's eyebrows went up. "It's early and you know . . ."

"I see." Bemin nodded somberly. "So you were hoping to learn some family history from me and consult with the Masterhealer."

"And there were some techniques that we thought you might want to see, Masterhealer," Birentir added respectfully.

"I suppose that the best place to see them would be at Telgar Weyr, would it?" Betrony asked, his eyes darting toward the old Master-harper.

Seban glanced between the two of them and then to Kelsa, who shook her head warningly.

"I suppose if I want to see anything of my journeyman, I should come as well," Zist said with a sigh.

"They're fighting Thread tonight," Seban warned.

"Which makes it a good time, then," Betrony said. He glanced at his three healers, as he added, "It would give me a chance to see how you are under pressure."

Bekka's eyes danced at the notion. "Of course, Master."

"I'm not sure that Talenth is able to carry five," Seban said.

"How about four?" Betrony asked.

"She'd have no problem with four," Bekka swore. She was about to say more, but the Masterhealer laid a hand on her shoulder and clenched it warningly.

"Then I suppose Birentir can remain here while we venture forth,"

Zist said, passing some unspoken agreement to Betrony with his eyes.

"We'd be delighted to have Birentir stay with us," Kelsa spoke up as if on cue.

"And if it would help you, Master Zist," Bemin put in smoothly, "I'm sure I could arrange for him to stay here."

"I promise I won't let him sing," Kelsa said, reaching over to grab the graying Lord Holder's arm.

"Journeyman Birentir?" Betrony asked, inclining his head toward the other man. "Do you feel up to a night manning the Healer Hall?"

Bekka gave him a firm go-ahead gesture.

The older healer snorted and said, "I think, Master, I could use the rest."

Betrony mouthed the word "rest" to himself and then his eyes settled on Bekka and he nodded in understanding.

"Well then, give me a few minutes to brief Birentir on the state of things in my Hall, and I'll be ready to see the marvels of Telgar," Betrony pronounced.

Half an hour later they were airborne, with Birentir, Bemin, Kelsa, and a gaggle of excited harpers and healers waving as Talenth swept upward with her great wings. In an instant, they were *between* and three short coughs later, they emerged into the midday light of Telgar, Talenth warbling happily and telling Fiona excitedly, *We're back, we're back! And we brought Masters!*

"Talenth says that she's brought Masters," Fiona called as she rushed into the Kitchen Cavern and frantically sought out Shaneese.

"I'll get the wine," Mekiar said, rising from his pottery wheel and racing back toward the cold caverns.

"We've something on, as always," Shaneese said, gesturing urgently to a group of cooks. "I'll get the table set."

"I'm not sure they'll be hungry," Fiona called over her shoulder, already rushing out to find T'mar and greet the guests.

Talenth timed her approach more slowly, having divined Fiona's mood, and did not touch the ground until Fiona, T'mar, L'tor, and the rest of the wingleaders were assembled behind her, as were Kindan and the weyrlings.

"Masterharper Zist," Fiona said as the elderly harper was helped down by Kindan, Seban, and several riders. She tried to keep any nervousness out of her voice, but she'd had Turns enough in the old Harper's bad books to harbor some residual misgivings, partly from several still-undiscovered episodes in her childhood.

"Catching tunnel snakes, my lady?" Zist asked, moving forward jauntily and catching her outstretched hand in his. His eyes turned back to Kindan as he continued, "Or merely discombobulating more of my harpers?"

"And Weyrleaders," T'mar put in smoothly, his eyes dancing as he caught Fiona's distraught look. "Don't forget that, Master."

"That's old news," Zist said with a wave of his hand. "As are the rather ribald Records that—"

"Oh, no!" Fiona cried, pulling from Zist's grip and burying her head in her hands.

"—Verilan assures me were not actually written by the Lady Holders to whom they were ascribed," Zist finished, his voice rumbling with humor.

"They were being mean to me!" Fiona said in her defense.

"They most certainly must have been, for you to have created such—interesting—depositions," Zist agreed drolly. He glanced at Kindan. "You really must read them sometime, they are works of art."

"Honing another talent, Fiona?" T'mar teased shamelessly.

Fiona lifted her head and fumed quietly. "It was Turns ago."

"Not all that many," Zist corrected.

"Turns for *me*," Fiona declared. "You may recall that we spent three Turns back in Igen."

"And her behavior was much corrected," T'mar agreed, the twinkle of his eyes belying his words.

"Oh!" Fiona said, stamping her foot in frustration. With a deep sigh, she turned once more to the Masterharper. "We've some wine and food, if you'd desire, Master."

"I would," Zist allowed, gesturing toward Betrony.

"Weyrwoman," Betrony said, with a polite bow. "I hear you've been graced with good news."

"Does all Pern know about this?" Fiona cried in exasperation.

"Not yet," Kindan said, "but if Master Zist tarries the night, I'll be sure to send him back to the Hall with a decent song."

"That is enough to tempt me," Zist said. "Although I understand you'll have Threadfall soon."

"Kindan, as weyrlingmaster, has duties to attend to," Fiona said. She raised a hand and waved toward Xhinna. "I think we can find a deputy for the moment."

Xhinna came forward with an easy air that fooled Fiona not one bit.

"Masterharper, Masterhealer, this is my friend, Xhinna, rider of blue Tazith," Fiona said, gesturing to the younger woman with all due formality.

"Dragonrider," Zist said, extending his hand and nodding courteously.

Xhinna paused just an instant before extending her hand in response.

"Did I hear the Weyrwoman aright," Betrony asked as he extended his hand in turn, "you ride a blue?"

"Five women Impressed in the last two Hatchings," Fiona said. "Only Xhinna Impressed a blue."

"Could you imagine the look on old D'gan's face if he'd seen that?" Betrony chortled in surprise, shaking his head.

Zist nodded in fierce agreement. "I could imagine him bellowing about Tradition until he was blue in the face."

"We've done what we could without him," T'mar said dryly.

"Although now, we'd sorely love all those dragons," Xhinna said. "He had over three hundred with him."

"Even if it meant his displeasure on seeing you?" Zist asked.

"Master," Fiona spoke up, her eyes gleaming, "I don't think D'gan would stand a chance in either a battle of wills or wits with our blue rider here." She caught Xhinna's surprised look, felt the girl's warm appreciation at her words. "Xhinna, the Masterharper wants to let Kindan bend his ear for a while, I was wondering if you could take over for him with the weyrlings."

"It might be better to let X'lerin or W'vin have the duty, my lady," Xhinna said demurely.

"True, but I didn't ask them," Fiona said. "Next time."

Xhinna nodded unhappily and departed.

"You aren't making her position any easier," Kindan murmured in Fiona's ear while they walked toward the Kitchen Cavern.

"She'll never be happy following," Fiona said. "Blue or no, she wants to lead."

"She could lead a wing," T'mar agreed, "if she could get them to follow her."

"Blues don't lead wings," H'nez said, glancing apologetically toward Fiona. "They haven't the endurance."

"Pardon, wingleader, but I have to question that," Seban spoke up diffidently. "My Serth had no problem keeping up with your wing."

H'nez frowned thoughtfully, then nodded. He glanced toward Fiona. "There is a danger of pushing too hard, too fast."

"Yes," Fiona agreed, eyeing the wiry wingleader with respect. She said to T'mar, "H'nez has a point. We need to be wary of trampling on Tradition just for the joy of it."

"*I* don't trample on Tradition," T'mar said.

Fiona grinned and walked silently on.

Shaneese and the weyrfolk greeted the two Masters with a mixture of pride and awe. It was unheard of, T'mar realized, for two craft Masters to appear at the same Weyr on the same day. They would frequent the Holder Conclaves, but never a single Weyr, not in his memory.

Zist and Betrony were excellent guests, insisting upon meeting all the people in the hall, shaking their hands and exchanging quick words. Betrony spent several minutes in quiet conversation with Mekiar and the ex-dragonrider looked very pleased with himself at the end of it.

Shaneese was set at ease by Zist's compliments on the wine and Betrony's compliments on the food. T'mar could see how worried she was that everything be right not just for the honor of the Weyr but also from her desire not to let him—or Fiona—down.

Kindan sent for instruments and Taria arrived, to T'mar's surprise, with a group of the better young vocalists. In short order Kindan and the weyr children were providing light, lyrical, soft music to accompany the meal.

"Bekka tells me it's twins," Betrony said to T'mar conversationally.

"So I've heard," T'mar agreed easily. "If all goes well, it will be good for the Weyr."

"Indeed," Betrony agreed.

"If you're done, Master," Bekka piped up, "we'd like to take you on a tour of the injured."

"Dragons and riders?" Betrony asked.

"Dragons and riders," Bekka agreed. She glanced at Fiona, adding, "Usually the Weyrwoman accompanies us, but she has other duties."

"Be sure, though, that you let Jeila know," Fiona said. H'nez glanced at her and looked distant for a moment and then said, "She's on the fourth level, she'll meet them there."

Fiona smiled at the lanky rider. H'nez surprised her with a nod in acknowledgment.

"See if you can get her to consent to an examination, while you're at it," Fiona said, looking at Bekka and noticing the relieved look on the youngster's face.

"Is there a problem?" H'nez asked, his expression guarded and tense.

Fiona shook her head. "She's smaller than I am and we want to be careful, that's all."

"Perhaps I should come along," H'nez said, rising from his chair.

Fiona grabbed his arm and pulled him back. "Bekka's lectured me already, H'nez," she told him. "She told me that she's in charge of worrying about my twins and Jeila's pregnancy."

H'nez's eyes trailed after the departing healers and settled with a frown on the slight blond in the lead.

"Masterhealer Betrony is here at her request to advise her," Fiona said. "She's not taking any risks with Jeila." She paused and held his eyes. "And if I felt for a moment that she was, I'd have someone else here before you could cough *between*."

"She'll need me," H'nez said imploringly, worried about the petite weyrwoman.

"She needs *us*," Fiona said with emphasis, "not to show worry about her pregnancy."

"Then there's reason for worry?"

"With every small person, there's reason," Fiona said. "More so with a first pregnancy than with later ones, I'm told."

"She could lose the child?"

"If you worry about it and she picks up on it, she'll start to worry and that will *certainly* cause problems," Fiona told him.

"It's just like with your dragon, H'nez," T'mar said. The bronze rider gave the Weyrleader a startled look, surprised that he'd been listening in and confused by the example. "If you worry that Ginirth might get Thread-scored, don't you increase the risk?"

"Yes," H'nez admitted sullenly. "I see your point, Weyrleader, Weyrwoman." He focused on Fiona. "But what if something *does* happen?"

"Then we'll be there for her, with our love and comfort just as we'd be there for Ginirth if he were injured."

"Sometimes it's all we can do," T'mar said, his eyes darting toward Fiona, "to hope that those we love survive."

"Bekka knows what to do, H'nez," Fiona assured him soothingly. "She's shown that by bringing the Masterhealer here."

H'nez nodded.

"And I trust that her sense is right about this, too: that we can't worry overmuch, we need to leave that with her."

"Is that not a rather large load for such a small person?" H'nez asked.

"Wouldn't you say that just as easily of Jeila?" Fiona countered.

"I do," H'nez replied, "often." His lips twitched upward as he added, "I've heard it said that you surround yourself with powerful people."

"The small ones are the most impressive," Fiona agreed. She stroked H'nez's arm. "Don't fear, bronze rider, we'll keep an eye on her."

"And while you're doing that," Shaneese chimed in, "*we'll* keep an eye on you!"

With the two Masters in Bekka's good hands, Fiona made her way to her weyr to check on Talenth. She wasn't surprised to note that her bed was empty. Kurinth was young and for all her unhappiness, Terin couldn't ignore the pleadings of a hungry dragonet.

I'm hungry, Talenth said as if prompted by Fiona's thoughts.

And no wonder with all that you've been doing, Fiona agreed. It had been nearly a week since the queen had last eaten, so it was about time. She escorted her queen to the beast pens and watched, calling out encouragement as Talenth took down a fair-sized meal and ravenously tore it apart. Fiona felt her blood grow hot with the passion of the gold over her meal. She wondered idly if T'mar were free or Kindan, then shook her head, dispelling the notion firmly. Dragon passions were strong, but she would not let them be her master.

Even as she thought that, her stomach rumbled, not pleased with the smells her nose was reporting, and Fiona moved upwind of her queen's feasting.

Once Talenth was sated, Fiona walked her back to their weyr and saw her settled, finding one patch of dry skin and carefully oiling it even as Talenth's inner lids started to close for a well-earned nap.

Fiona scratched the gold's great eye ridges with one hand until she saw that Talenth was fully asleep and, with one final caress, left her.

She did not go far, ducking into Kurinth's lair after a few quick steps.

The little dragonet seemed tiny in comparison with Talenth, but nearly full-scale when compared with Jeriz standing beside her, watching anxiously as he encouraged Terin in her feeding.

"Terin," Fiona said softly as she approached her friend. Terin said nothing, fishing out another morsel and handing it to Kurinth, who took it delicately, her eyes whirling in a hungry red.

"Do you need help oiling her?" Fiona offered.

Terin shook her head, but Jeriz caught her eyes and nodded imperceptibly.

"She's getting bigger," Fiona said, eyeing the gold critically.

"Every day," Terin agreed softly, reaching for another morsel from the bucket. Finally, the queen was sated and Terin pushed the bucket away. She reached for the oil pail only to have Jeriz bring it to her and offer her a rag. She smiled in thanks and proceeded to gently stretch Kurinth's wings, oiling lightly. Fiona, crooning soft encouragements, took another oil rag and started on Kurinth's other wing.

"You're the most beautiful baby dragon on all Pern," Fiona said in a baby voice to the dragonet. "Yes, you are."

Kurinth creeled happily in response.

After watching the others for a moment, Jeriz found another rag and began oiling Kurinth's belly, careful not to get in Terin's way.

"There's something very satisfying about a well-oiled dragon," Fiona said as she soaked her rag in the oil and returned to work diligently on her wing.

"That's not what you used to say," Terin quipped with a ghost of her former humor. Jeriz gave her an inquiring look and Terin told him, "She used to moan every day."

"I was tired," Fiona said in her defense.

"And now that you're pregnant, shouldn't you be even more tired?"

"I suppose I should," Fiona admitted, surprised. "But I'm not so much, it's as if the pregnancy is giving me more energy." This statement was punctuated with a long yawn that caused Fiona to frown and Terin and Jeriz to follow suit, as yawns always do. She glanced at Terin. "Did you know I am having twins?"

Terin frowned then nodded. "Not so much 'know' as guessed," Terin said. Fiona arched an eyebrow demandingly. "Well, I asked Bekka and she told me."

Sheepishly, she added, "Bekka said she'd keep an eye on you."

"And you didn't tell me?" Fiona asked, still feeling a little out of sorts over the whole affair.

"I was . . . distracted," Terin said with a shrug. "I suppose I can do better now."

"You can't hold a grudge forever, Terin," Fiona said, shaking her head. "It's not in your nature."

"Well, I can certainly hold a grudge for now," Terin told her firmly, ducking down to work on Kurinth's hind leg.

"Certainly," Fiona agreed, finishing her wing and ducking down to start on the other hind leg. "I think you could easily go a whole Turn, if you tried."

"No," Terin said, shaking her head. "At this rate, we'll all be dead before Turn's end."

Fiona heard Jeriz gasp but she merely shook her head. "I hope you're wrong."

"Fiona, why would he lie to me?" Terin asked, looking across under Kurinth's belly to meet with the Weyrwoman's eyes in misery.

"I don't know," Fiona told her softly. Her voice strengthened as she continued, "And because I don't know, I have to wonder if he *did* lie."

"But I heard her!"

"You heard someone, true," Fiona said. "He's been timing it, he said that much." She shook her head. "That's all we know."

"Could it have been you?" Jeriz piped up, surprising them. "Could he have been timing it to you?"

"What, going back in time to Igen?" Terin asked, shaking her head. "Or when I was a child at Fort?"

"'Talking angry is better than angry silence,'" Jeriz quoted another trader saying.

"Maybe you should talk to him," Fiona added in agreement.

Terin snorted. "He can wait, he's not going anywhere."

"*I* hope he's sleeping," Fiona said. "He looked nearly Threaded with exhaustion."

"I want you two to come back with us tonight," Betrony said after they'd finished the rounds and returned to the Kitchen Cavern. "Bekka, would you be willing to give a lecture?"

"Tonight?" Bekka said. "There's Threadfall, we'll be needed."

"Birentir can hold your place," Betrony said, adding with a stern look, "unless you don't think he's ready."

"We'd only be a dragon's flight away," Seban reminded her. "Three coughs, no more."

"The Weyrwoman—"

"The Weyrwoman has no objection," Fiona cut across Bekka's objection smoothly as she, Kindan, T'mar, and Master Zist finished their private conversation. "Unless, of course, you don't want another chance to ride Talenth?"

Bekka's eyes went wide with excitement and then grew thoughtful. She gestured for Fiona to come closer and whispered accusingly, "What are you planning?"

"You'll find out," Fiona said, grinning. "I think you'll like it."

"So, it's settled then," Zist said. "Kindan, Bekka, and Seban will return with us."

"Kindan?" Fiona asked, turning to the Masterharper in surprise.

"I didn't forget that song he promised," Zist said, wagging a finger at her.

Fiona slumped, saying dejectedly, "*I* did." She glanced at Kindan. "The weyrlings will be able to manage without you?"

"X'lerin will be in charge," Kinda assured her, adding, "Although, I'd appreciate it if you could keep an eye on them."

"I could put Terin in charge," Fiona said musingly. She nodded firmly. "Give her something to do."

"Then you've no objection?" T'mar asked. Fiona shook her head, "No, I suppose not."

She gave Bekka a huge grin, which alarmed the younger woman greatly. "Sometimes, it's hard to recall that you've over thirteen Turns."

"I'm small for my age," Bekka agreed, glancing toward her father. "I get that from Mother."

Seban smiled and nodded. "We should arrange to visit her soon."

Bekka nodded firmly, eyes shining in agreement.

"Maybe I'll take you," Fiona said. "After all, if you ride Talenth anymore by yourself she might forget who Impressed her."

"Never!" Bekka said. "I won't let her."

"Besides, you'll have your own queen soon enough," Fiona predicted.

"I've got enough work to—"

"I think I've heard enough of that excuse," Fiona interjected. "If I can do it, you can."

Bekka, wisely, said nothing.

"Well, if all's settled," Zist said, glancing toward T'mar and Fiona, "and you'll excuse us, Weyrleader, Weyrwoman, we'll take our leave. The sooner we get them to the Halls, the sooner we can return them to you."

Talenth circled once above the Star Stones and winked out, *between* to Fort Hold.

T'mar glanced over to Fiona admiringly. "I don't know how you can do that so easily."

"Twins," Fiona said, lowering a hand toward her belly. "That, and I know what Zist has got in store for them."

"Well, yes," T'mar agreed, his eyes lighting. "It will make this evening's work more enjoyable."

"It certainly will," Fiona agreed. "And we'll have a Master to tell the tale."

"You *do* realize what Master Zist is hoping, don't you?" T'mar asked, his eyes taking on a worried look.

"To promote Kindan to Master, and maybe groom him as his

replacement." She shook her head, adding, "I think he might find himself surprised. Although, even if he isn't, Fort is only a *between* away."

T'mar snorted humorously at her words.

"Well," Fiona said with a dismissive shake of her head, "we've lots to do and I'd best be started." She roused herself. "I've been practically indolent this past sevenday."

"Indeed," T'mar agreed in facetious deadpan.

Fiona ignored him, setting her course for Terin's weyr. She heard Talenth cheerfully announce their arrival and wished her queen good choice in ledges, picturing one in particular just above Fort Hold itself where Talenth could keep watch on her father. The queen agreed, glad to oblige her rider, and quickly settled herself in the suggested spot even though some of the Fort guards seemed unduly concerned by the prospect of a gold dragon perched above them.

"Terin!" Fiona called as she entered Kurinth's weyr. "Enough sulking, we've got work to do!"

Terin, after an initial burst of anger, had settled down quickly to join Fiona and Jeila in organizing the Weyr for the evening's Fall. She and Fiona, after one quick consulting glance, had ensured that Jeila's assignment required the least exertion or moving about. That left Jeila with a lighter load, but not so much that she was not being asked to do her share.

Terin and Fiona exchanged looks when H'nez happened by and the two lovers exchanged heartfelt caresses punctuated by a long, steamy kiss. For all H'nez's stuffiness and bristly exterior, it was clear to the both of them that his love for the diminutive weyrwoman was strong.

Finally, all was ready. Fiona forced a cheerful look on her face even as she compared the scant Flight of dragons to the full one hundred and eighty-five fighting dragons that had arrayed before her not more than half a Turn before. Even as her heart shrank in fear, she schooled her expression and forced herself to project confidence and ease for the dragonriders about to start their Fall in the growing gloom of the evening.

T'mar came to her and she hugged him fiercely. "Come back to us," she said, letting him go and pulling Shaneese over to take her place.

She sought out and hugged C'tov and H'nez in turn, then surprised gruff L'tor by hugging him as well. "Fly safe."

"Always, Weyrwoman," L'tor assured her with a tone that fooled her not one bit. She eyed him and leaned up to whisper in his ear, "Don't try to fool me, just come back safe or Weyrwoman Tullea will have my ears for losing another of her dragons."

That brought a sharp chuckle from the old rider, who added drolly, "Under those circumstances, I am doubly inspired."

At last the wings rose into the air, circled the Star Stones, and winked out, *between*.

Fiona gathered the weyrfolk assigned to the aid stations and broke them into groups, sent a third to rest, another third to eat, and remained on watch with the final third.

J'gerd and the reserve wing arrayed themselves near the weyrlings, who eyed the older riders with awe, instantly ready to meet their every wish.

Of F'jian, Fiona noted with narrowed eyes, there was no sign. She thought that odd, even given his shame, for he was usually well-liked and his absence would be noted. She didn't say anything to Terin, but Jeila caught her look and nodded understandingly.

"Terin," Fiona said suddenly, "can you keep an eye on things here? Jeila and I will have a little sit-down." Terin nodded blankly and Fiona gestured Jeila toward a pair of chairs set far enough from Terin that the younger weyrwoman wouldn't be able to hear them as Fiona quickly brought Jeila current on the events regarding F'jian and Terin.

"I don't think he was lying," Jeila said thoughtfully when Fiona had finished. "He's always seemed truthful and devoted to Terin."

"That's what I thought," Fiona said. "But why did he time it? He had to know that it was exhausting him, that T'mar couldn't allow it."

"From what you say, he did his best to hide it," Jeila pointed out. "But I don't think you're wrong, T'mar would have noticed. Or H'nez."

"Or C'tov," Fiona agreed. "In fact, T'mar did notice it. He remarked on it to me, even."

"And now we fly a dragon light," Jeila said with anger in her voice. "What could have been so important?"

"All he said was that he could not tell me, he'd promised."

"Which again leads me to believe that he was honest with Terin," Jeila replied.

"Either that or he's become a gibbering coward," Fiona said.

"That's not without possibility," Jeila agreed. She glancd at Terin, who was engrossed in a conversation with one of the weyrfolk. "But what about her?"

"I've got Jeriz watching her," Fiona said. She explained about her need for a minder and how Shaneese had supplied her with Jeriz.

"He's Tenniz's son?" Jeila asked, eyes wide. "Does he have the Sight?"

"He says no, that it will go to his sister," Fiona said, shaking her head.

"That must be hard on him," Jeila said. "Losing his father and growing up in the shadow of his sister."

"Well, we'll have to see to it that his life has a different course," Fiona said.

"You can't simply expect to supply everyone with dragons, Weyr-woman," Jeila upbraided her in a tolerant voice. "As I recall, the dragons *do* have a choice."

"True," Fiona agreed. "But they seem to find trader stock most appealing."

"That's because they have excellent taste," Jeila agreed with a laugh. "And I suppose, being Tenniz's son, he might be particularly acceptable."

"That was my thinking," Fiona agreed. Jeila eyed her thoughtfully. "Didn't Azeez say you must have had trader stock yourself?"

"I haven't heard of many blond traders," Fiona replied.

"There have been some, particularly in far Keroon," Jeila said. "We're not all dark-haired and dark-eyed."

"And incredibly gorgeous," Fiona agreed. "Although Jeriz—"

"Weyrwoman?" Jeriz called out upon hearing his name. Fiona recovered quickly, gesturing for him to join them.

"Have you met weyrwoman Jeila?" Fiona asked. Jeriz shook his head and extended his hand, bowing courteously. "Weyrwoman, my pleasure."

"You're from the desert?"

"You're from the north?" Jeriz asked, taking in her features and that special look that seemed to mark most traders.

"I am," Jeila said smiling. "I was Searched three Turns back, but before that I was daughter to those hauling goods to the Fire Hold."

"Herdbeast or ship?" Jeriz asked, sinking into trade talk.

"Both, actually," Jeila said. Her eyes lit with memory. "There were summers we spent with cargo from Tillek to Southern Boll."

"Fish down, spices up?"

"Indeed," Jeila said. "I see you were well trained."

"Many came to see my father," Jeriz said, his tone going flat. "After, not so many to see my mother."

"I see," Jeila said. "And how came you to be here?"

"My mother sent me to the one who spit in Father's soup," Jeriz said. "She said that she might teach me manners."

"She still has some way to go, I see," Jeila replied, her tone going colder.

"Jeriz, keep an eye on Terin, please," Fiona said. Jeriz nodded in response, dipped his eyes to Jeila, and sped off.

"So who spat in his soup?" Jeila asked quietly as she watched the small figure dart toward the cluster around Terin. "And doesn't he have the most amazing green eyes?"

"Shaneese spat in his soup," Fiona said, delighting in Jeila's surprised look. "And, yes, he has the most amazing green eyes."

"Shaneese?" Jeila repeated in surprise. "Why?"

"Because Tenniz predicted that she'd be second wife and like it," Fiona told her, eyes dancing.

"Oh!" Jeila said understandingly. "She must have been very young."

"And very angry," Fiona agreed. "Although perhaps not so young; she had sixteen Turns at the time."

"For a trader woman, what he said was a deep insult."

"And, as it is, the complete truth."

"Around you, Weyrwoman, the truth takes the strangest directions."

Fiona laughed.

It was not the best time to fly Thread, T'mar mused as the wings formed up in front of him, two Telgar and one Benden. The sun had not yet set, edging toward the horizon with its last rays blinding the riders. While the Thread that fell between the sun and the dragonriders would be highlighted, Thread that fell from the east could easily be lost in the shadows behind the riders.

T'mar's plan was to avert that problem, with himself set well behind the fighting wings. J'gerd and the reserve force were there to provide additional eyes. T'mar swore bitterly at F'jian for his foolishness; not only was the wing deprived of his leadership when it was most needed, but his fatigue had made him slow and thoughtless in their drill so that the reserve wing was only half as effective as it should have been. T'mar cursed himself for not taking action sooner. Beneath him, Zirenth rumbled reprovingly.

You thought you were doing best, the bronze told him with uncharacteristic forcefulness.

I should have known, T'mar said.

Like Fiona?

T'mar's lips edged upward at the comment and he slapped the bronze's neck affectionately in acknowldgment of the jibe.

What's done is done, T'mar agreed. *Now it's up to us to deal with here and now.*

Zirenth agreed firmly, swiveling his head from one side to the other while T'mar turned around to peer behind them. He had half of the reserve wing doing the same, the other half scanning the backs of the leading dragons.

It was not yet dark enough for the watch-whers, nor cold enough for Thread to freeze.

Not the best time. T'mar had placed H'nez in the center, C'tov on the right, and L'tor on the left. All three wings had drilled in all three different positions: left, right, center. T'mar had made the assignment based on H'nez's pride and skill and C'tov's marked proficiency flying on the right.

The winds were light, but apt to whip up as the sun continued to set; a dangerous combination.

T'mar spotted an ominous streak of white in the sky to the right and behind him. Zirenth quickly turned and beat his way upward to let them get a better look before T'mar realized he was seeing only the wisps of the high cirrus clouds, lit by the sun's last rays.

He had just returned to the flight level when a dragon bellowed behind him and, in an instant, a third of the reserve wing went *between*, dodging Thread.

Thread behind! T'mar warned, even as he and Zirenth wheeled, flaming, toward the danger.

Fiona winced as Talenth relayed the first clash of the fighting dragons to her. Three at once! Fortunately, they were all back immediately, their injuries light. But she could imagine the disarray of the fighting wings, learning that the Thread was behind them.

Jeila had the same information from Talorth and the two weyrwomen exchanged nervous glances over the head of Terin.

"What?" the youngest weyrwoman demanded, looking from one to the other.

"Thread from behind," Fiona said. "Fortunately, they ducked *between* and are safe."

"Oh," Terin said glumly. She seemed to shrink in on herself, scanning the horizon near the Star Stones as if hoping to see the battle.

We may need you, Fiona told her dragon.

I have told Bekka, Talenth replied. *She says she's ready if needed.*

▼ ▼ ▼

In fact, Talenth's warning was all the excuse Bekka needed to de-mand that she be allowed to fly back to Telgar *now*, even though Birentir had already returned on a Fort Weyr dragon.

"You've just finished your talk," Betrony told her soothingly, "take a meal with us first."

"You are behind time," Zist agreed, "you won't get a decent meal when you get back and you might need your energy."

He glanced at Kindan who shook his head at the Masterharper, a wry look on his face. Zist winked at him and touched a finger to his nose, daring the younger man to keep the secret.

Bekka started another objection, but Zist caught her hand in one of his. "Humor an old man," Zist implored. "We've missed your com-pany."

"The apprentices would like to have you seated with them again," Betrony added, glancing at Seban, "both of you."

Seban's eyes widened just for an instant before he turned to his daughter. "We should sit with them; who knows when next we'll get the chance."

"Lindorm and Cerra are here, too," Betrony added. "They made journeyman."

"Good for them!" Bekka said. "I'd like to congratulate them."

"Then, it's settled," Zist said. "We'll have a proper feast in your honor and get you back before you're needed in Telgar."

"Let me check with Fiona," Bekka said solicitously. A moment later she had her answer. "The Weyrwoman says that Birentir is doing fine and Talenth won't be needed for a while."

"Excellent!" Zist agreed. He nodded to Betrony, eyeing Bekka's garb. "You know, though, if she's going to eat with the apprentices, she should have proper attire." Zist cocked an eye at Seban. "And you, too."

"I think we can find something suitable," Betrony said, gesturing for the two healers to follow him.

"Dinner will be ready shortly, don't be late," Zist called as they left his quarters. After the door closed, Kindan turned to the old Master, a smile on his lips. "Is it too much to suppose, perhaps, that there is spare journeyman garb for me?"

"I recall Nonala remarking on that a while back," Zist said with feigned indifference. "I think she and Kelsa arranged to get some of your older garments cleaned."

"So I should find Kelsa?"

"No, probably Nonala or Verilan," Zist said.

"Then I'll take my leave," Kindan said with a polite nod to the old Masterharper. Zist nodded, seating himself at his table, pretending to write in his sandtable. At the door, Kindan turned back and poked his head inside. "Don't think I'm fooled, Master."

"Fooled by what?" Zist asked, looking up and managing an irritated look.

"Fooled by you," Kindan said, his eyes crinkling in delight. "It's a good plan, but it won't work, I'm bound to Telgar."

"A wise harper has more than one set of strings," Zist intoned grandly.

"Hmph!"

"Get going, you'll be late," Zist said, making a shooing motion toward the journeyman harper.

"It is an honor that you would think so of me," Kindan said as he closed the door.

"Who said I was thinking about you?" Zist said, raising his voice enough to carry through the thick door to Kindan's ears as he made the way down toward Verilan's quarters.

"Well, it's about time," Verilan said as he and Nonala helped garb Kindan in a very neat, extremely new harper's outfit. It was certainly one that Kindan had never seen before, even if perhaps its measurements were taken from one of his cast-offs. "Now he won't carp on at me all the time."

"Or me," Nonala added.

"Or Kelsa; think what *that* would do to the Lord Holder Conclave,"

Verilan added, bringing a clenched fist to his chest while miming florid anger.

"We'd lose half from apoplexy," Kindan agreed. "Although with Nerra firm at Crom, and the strength of the traders—"

"Not to mention Pellar and Halla in Fire Hold," Verilan added.

"Indeed not," Kindan agreed, continuing, "with all those, perhaps the Holders might be willing to see a woman as Masterharper."

"Gadran would sooner die," Verilan said with a snort, referring to Bitra's irritable Lord Holder while gesturing for Kindan to bend down when the Master Archivist fixed his collar. A moment later he motioned for Kindan to stand once more and cocked an eye toward his mate. "Suitable?"

"Fit for the tables," Nonala agreed from behind. She grabbed Kindan's shoulders and spun him around, hugging him tightly. "This should have happened Turns back."

Kindan wisely said nothing, choosing to smile at the warm loyalty of his friends.

"Come on, Journeyman, walk with us to dinner," Verilan said, managing to sound fierce and formal.

"You've had a lot of practice with that, haven't you?"

"Mostly with the children," Nonala said with a chuckle.

"He's good with them?" Kindan asked, arching a brow.

"If they don't behave, I make them write out lines in fair neat hand," Verilan said in a menacing voice.

"The eldest has—what?—three Turns now?"

"And writes most beautifully," Nonala said with a laugh. She poked Kindan in the back. "Now hush up and move on, or Zist will bark at you."

Kindan, far too used to the Masterharper's barks, still could not stop himself from lengthening his stride.

Bekka was just as glad to get dressed in the fine blue garb with the healer's mark as she was to acknowledge the compliments she received from journeymen and masters on her talk that evening. Seban beamed at her and nodded at others, but kept silent, preferring to let Bekka do the talking.

"This looks like a special meal," Bekka said as she sat down next to the oldest apprentice. Over her head, Seban shook his head warningly at the apprentice whose eyes lit with delight as he played along, saying, "Oh, it's nothing special. Just the cook's way of giving thanks for your talk."

"It's not often healers talk about birthing," a younger apprentice agreed, even as she helped herself to a savory platter of roast meat.

"It certainly shows that we should be talking to midwives about first aid as well," another chimed in.

"They know more than just first aid," Bekka began, diving into the conversation eagerly.

She didn't notice when Kindan entered and was seated at the journeymen's table, but Seban saw him and nodded once, gravely. Kindan shot him a quick smile and then turned his attention to the journeymen, most many Turns his junior, and joined easily in their conversation.

Fiona was torn between her interest in the festivities at the Harper Hall and the battle raging in the skies above Crom. Talenth's vantage atop Fort Hold was no good for information; she had to rely on the scraps that the queen passed on from Bekka, which were tantalizing at best. Her lips quirked upward, though, when Talenth relayed Bekka's request to stay for dinner, and some of Bekka's surprise at the clothes offered her were reflected by the queen. Wait until dessert, Fiona thought with a grin.

Her information on the Threadfall was no better; Jeila relayed what her Tolarth told her. The news wasn't good.

The dragonriders had recovered from their initial shock, but she could feel their worry and the disarray of their wings only grew.

Dark had slipped over the Weyr and the weyrfolk at the aid stations had turned the glows up for light, with large patches of shadow spread between.

In this gloom Fiona suddenly noticed a pair of bright eyes peering down from above: a dragon's whirling multifaceted eyes reflecting the light of the glows.

"Terin," F'jian's voice called from beside the dragon.

"F'jian, what are you doing here?" Fiona called, instantly on her feet, alert—and afraid.

"I need to speak with Terin," F'jian said, moving past the Weyrwoman as if she didn't exist.

"Stay there, I can hear you," Terin spoke up coldly from where she sat.

F'jian sought her out in the dark, guessed her position, and threw himself to his knees in front of her.

"I have to go now," he said, his voice sounding heavy, full of dread.

"Go?"

"They need me," F'jian said. "It's my time."

"Your time?" Terin said, standing up and reaching out for him where he knelt, partly silhouetted by Ladirth's eyes. "No," Terin said, firmly, her hand reaching his shoulder. "No, you need to be with me."

"I will," F'jian told her. "I've got to go." He stood up, cupping her hand to his chest.

"No, you need to stay with me," Terin said again, moving forward and wrapping her other arm around his waist even as Fiona and Jeila found their way to her side. "Stay here, now."

"I can't," F'jian said, shaking his head. "I wish I could, but I can't."

"Promise me that you'll be with me always," Terin said, her voice harsh with emotion.

"I promise you that when you need me, I'll be there," F'jian said, pulling away from her. "By the shell of Ladirth, I so swear."

Behind him, Ladirth bellowed in agreement.

"I must go now."

"Bronze rider," Fiona spoke, commandingly, sternly. "Stand down, return to your weyr."

"Weyrwoman, I cannot," F'jian said with a sob.

Fiona moved to him, close, and spoke for his ears alone, "Why?"

"I cannot break time."

"Will you break your vow?"

"No," F'jian said. "I have not." And with that he pulled away from them all, vaulted to Ladirth's back and the bronze leaped into the night air. A wave of cold air filled the Bowl as dragon and rider slipped into the cold *between*.

The meal was every bit as good as, but different from, the best of meals prepared at Telgar Weyr, and Bekka found herself enjoying the company. She avoided the wine proffered her way, delighting in saying that she was flying Fiona's queen and seeing the astonished looks of the younger apprentices who had never heard of such a thing.

Dessert was served, everyone was relaxing, and Bekka was thinking, with mixed emotions, of her return to Telgar; how she'd love to fly Talenth *between* once more, how she'd regret leaving this good company behind.

Silence descended around her before she noticed and she looked up guiltily to see Masterharper Zist and Masterhealer Betrony standing at the Masters' table for silence. As the last word died, the other Masters rose.

"It is our custom," Betrony said into the silence, "to take apprentices for many Turns, ensuring that their knowledge is up to the heavy burden of a healer."

"And Turns after, those that prove themselves return to the Healer Hall to take their ranks as journeymen," Zist added.

"That custom ends tonight," Betrony said. The room was stunned.

"The Plague wrought many changes," Zist said. "And tonight is yet another of them."

"We cannot always choose where our best learning will take place," Betrony said in agreement. "Nor," and his eyes fell on Bekka, "can we choose by age or gender."

"Bekka of Telgar," Zist called forth in a voice that resonated in every corner of the room, "rise!"

Bekka could not move. She was both alarmed at her frozen limbs and forever grateful to those beside her, positioned on purpose she later realized, who helped her up.

All the journeymen, healer and harper, trouped over to stand behind her. She was glad to realize that Kindan was on her right.

"It's time to walk, Bekka," Kindan told her kindly, resting his hand on her upper arm and guiding her away from the table.

"Daddy?" Bekka asked, looking down at her father's beaming expression.

"Walk," Seban said with a firm nod.

"Head high, Telgar," Kindan told her encouragingly.

Head held high, eyes gleaming with tears, Bekka of Telgar walked the tables to join the journeymen healers of Pern.

"I think we need the set," Zist said as the applause died down and the other journeymen had all clapped Bekka on the back in warm congratulations.

"I agree," Betrony said. "Seban."

The journeymen were quicker to get to the ex-dragonrider, who rose with aplomb and a grateful nod. To Seban's surprise, they took him on a longer walk, insisting upon circling the Masters' table before bringing him to sit with them, opposite his daughter.

"This is the first time in our history that a father and daughter have walked the tables on the same night," Verilan declared in a carrying voice. He raised his glass high.

"I give you Journeyman Bekka, Journeyman Seban!"

"Bekka, Seban!" the room roared back, feet stamping on the hard floor as all rose in toast.

T'mar never knew what hit him until it was over. One instant he was watching over his shoulder to clear the threat of further Thread behind, the next instant he and Zirenth were reeling in the sky, thrown down by the blast of a dragon and rider coming from *between* just above them.

As T'mar craned his neck up to swear at the brazen rider, he saw the scintillating flashes of light as Thread landed, gorged, and grew on the form above him. Before he could even cry in alarm, rider and dragon, seared beyond hope, were gone.

They saved my life, T'mar thought.

Ladirth is no more, Zirenth told him.

T'mar had no chance to recover before the air in front of him erupted with dragons. Above them he caught sight of smaller beasts: watch-whers. It was dark enough for them to fly. High Reaches had taken over the Fall.

D'vin's compliments and they have the Fall, Zirenth told him.

My compliments to High Reaches and good flying, T'mar said, completing the handoff. Wearily, he turned to scan for the remaining Telgar and Benden dragons. *Zirenth, tell them to go back to the Weyr. Have H'nez lead.*

Zirenth relayed the order and H'nez's acceptance.

Let's go, T'mar said wearily, giving his bronze the image and willing him *between.*

Bekka was just overcoming her shock when the room went silent once more. She glanced at the Masters' table and saw that Zist had risen, alone.

"What is it?" Bekka whispered to Kindan.

"Wait," the harper replied.

"**F**'jian?" Terin cried as a dragon streaked in from the night and landed near the aid station. "Is that you?"

Fiona felt the tension ratchet higher; she moved closer to Terin and felt Jeila do the same.

The figure of a rider emerged from the darkness.

"T'mar!" Fiona exclaimed, giving him a welcoming grin.

T'mar ignored her, moving toward Terin. In an eerie reenactment, he went to one knee before Terin.

"Terin," he began softly, his voice full of sorrow.

"No!" Terin said, shaking her head. "No! He promised! He swore! No, it can't be so!"

Fiona raced to her side and embraced her. The younger woman collapsed into her arms, sobbing. Fiona pulled her head tight against her, stroking it with her hand while Terin bawled into her chest. She looked over Terin's head to T'mar.

"There was a clump," T'mar said. "He came out right into it, he pushed me aside." He drew in a long, shaky breath. "He saved my life."

Terin turned in Fiona's arms to face T'mar. "But he promised me! He swore on Ladirth that he would be here when I need him."

She looked widely around and called desolately into the night air: "I need you now! F'jian, I need you now!"

She turned once more in Fiona's arms. "He broke his vow, he's not here. He'll never be here."

"Shh, shh," Fiona said soothingly. Her eyes sought out Jeila's and the older weyrwoman joined her.

"Let me take her," Jeila said to Fiona, leading Terin into her arms.

"I'll help," Jeriz's voice called from the night.

"Go with them," Fiona agreed, waving in thanks to Jeila. "I can handle things here."

"We lost two," T'mar said when they were out of earshot.

"Who?" Fiona asked, bracing herself.

"Z'mos, one of C'tov's," T'mar said. "His Linuth was engulfed at the same time as F'jian, probably by the same freak fall."

"Winds are tricky at that time of night," Fiona said, trying to ease his pain. T'mar nodded. "And the injured?"

"Three badly, two less so," T'mar said. He glanced across the Bowl toward the queen's ledge. "H'nez was one."

A bugle from above announced the return of the rest of the Telgar riders.

"Three mauled, two wounded," Fiona called to Birentir and the weyrfolk as the dragons started to land. "Birentir, you take one of the mauled dragons, I'll take the other."

As Fiona raced toward the dragon landing shakily near her, she heard Birentir say jokingly, "Bet it's nicer at the Hall!"

"I wouldn't be so sure!" Fiona said and then was lost to all banter as she took in, by glow-light, the damage to Winurth's left wing.

"Get him some fellis and get me some numbweed," Fiona called out heedless of who obeyed her orders, only intent on the injuries and the need to calm J'gerd, who looked ready to collapse at the loss of his friend and the pain to his dragon. "I'll need a number three kit over here!"

"On the way, Weyrwoman!" a voice called back in acknowledgment. The first-aid kit was thrust into her hands, needle end first, suture set trailing over her shoulder just as she and Bekka had instructed. She held up her other hand and had a small pin thrust in it with which she quickly pinned the tatters of Winurth's wing, reaching back for another and another until the damage was pinned up and she could sew stitches into the damaged membrane.

"Another kit!" Fiona called as she reached the end of the first string, wiped an ichor-soaked hand on her trousers and moved toward the near section of the long tear. It would be many months before Winurth healed.

Sixty-seven. As of this moment, all Telgar Weyr had was scant more than two wings of fighting dragons. Another four would return to the fight in two days' time.

Fiona thrust the thought brutally from her mind and forced herself to focus on the injury even as she tuned out J'gerd's worried imprecations.

Finally, she was done. She stood up, stretched her aching back, cracked her aching knuckles, and moved over to J'gerd.

"He'll recover," Fiona told the brown rider calmly, reaching out to touch him gently on the shoulder. "The damage is heavy, but he'll fly again."

J'gerd looked at her, his head shaking slowly, his eyes distant. He said nothing.

Fiona was still groping for some way to bring the man out of his pain and worry when she heard a shout from the queen's ledge. She turned even as she saw a small form pitch forward, arms windmilling for balance and failing, falling forward off the ledge and onto the ground below.

"H'nez!" Jeila cried as she fell.

Fiona raced across the open ground even as she screamed in her mind, *Talenth, we need Bekka* now!

"As is fitting with our new custom," Zist intoned slowly, "we must apply it not just to healers but to harpers as well—"

"No!" Bekka's shout cut across everything as she bolted to her feet. "Jeila!"

Kindan and Seban were on her heels and the three were out of the dining hall and in the Harper Hall's courtyard before anyone could react.

Zist managed to make his way through the throng and far enough into the courtyard to yell, "What is it?"

"Jeila's fallen!" Kindan yelled back. "The baby!"

Even before Fiona reached the fallen form of her friend, she heard Talenth's bellow as the queen appeared just above the ground and skidded to a halt just in front of the queens' ledge.

Bekka and Kindan tumbled off just as Fiona stopped in front of Jeila's umoving form. From above, Jeriz called out, "She just ran off!"

"Don't move her!" Bekka shouted as she rushed up beside Fiona. "Father, get a stretcher!"

"Get some glows!" Fiona shouted, her voice echoing around the Weyr.

"I've got some here," Jeriz said, handing down a basket from above.

"Don't get too close to the edge," Fiona warned, looking up at the sound of stones landing nearby. She knelt down, moving to one side to let Bekka and Seban in to examine the fallen weyrwoman.

"How is she?" Fiona asked, just before her eyes fell to Jeila's crotch. "Is that blood?"

"Out of the way, out of the way!" H'nez bellowed, accompanied by the sounds of bodies being pushed away.

"Kindan, stop him," Fiona ordered. The harper rose quickly and turned to block the wild-eyed bronze rider.

"Wait man, let them help her," Kindan said, physically blocking and then grappling the tall, wiry rider. H'nez tried to plow through him, but T'mar had arrived and added his weight.

"You can't help her, let them do their work," T'mar urged.

"But she's just a girl!" H'nez cried, waving a hand toward Bekka.

"She's a journeyman!" Fiona called back, standing up and moving to confront H'nez. "And she knows about this, she's Jeila's best hope."

Some of the wildness went out of H'nez's eyes.

"I wouldn't let anyone but the best treat her, H'nez," Fiona told him softly. She glanced back over her shoulder, her eyes bright with tears, and turned back again, "And she's the best."

"Journeyman?" H'nez repeated blankly.

"Just tonight," Fiona assured him, reaching a hand to his arm soothingly. "You need to get back to Ginirth, he needs you, too."

"You'll do everything?" H'nez repeated, his voice pleading.

"Everything in my power," Fiona swore.

H'nez nodded and allowed T'mar and Kindan to lead him back to his dragon.

With a sigh, Fiona turned back to the group around the fallen weyrwoman.

"How is she?" Fiona asked as she came to squat next to Bekka.

"I think she lost the baby."

SIX

Dawn shows them
Man brought them
Never varying
Always querying
Dawn Sisters
In the sky.

The sun rose steadily, in the sky. Keeping pace with it, a trio of lights glowed, always in track with the dawn. The Dawn Sisters.

They traveled alone, brilliant orbs of the morning sky. For five hundred Turns and more they had lit the morning sky of Pern. Alone.

A flicker of movement appeared beside them, so small that no one on the planet below would have noticed. But, for the first time in hundreds of Turns, the Dawn Sisters had company.

Lorana looked silently at the three huge shapes floating near her. Only one was close enough to see clearly and it hung almost above her, brilliant and blinding.

Her breath grew cold and it became harder to breathe.

Come on, Minith, back.

And, presently, the Dawn Sisters were alone once more.

▼ ▼ ▼

Back from the cold of *between*, Lorana took several deep breaths, favoring the warm air near Igen while she plotted her next move.

That was fun, Minith told her. *Are we going again?*

Are you ready?

Soon, Minith said. Lorana laughed at the queen's honesty. As her understanding of Minith grew, Lorana began to wonder more and more about Tullea, past, present, and future. The queen was comfortable with her and not overly worried about being away from her rider—that had to say something good about Tullea. And then there was B'nik. The Benden Weyrleader was a fundamentally good man and devoted to Tullea. Prickly, difficult, stubborn, opinionated, vengeful—yes, those were all parts of Tullea. But kind, loyal, loving, and honest were also in her character.

I'm ready, Minith announced. Lorana chuckled and climbed back onto the queen's neck, shelving her consideration of the queen's rider for a later time.

Very well, Lorana thought, forming the image of the coordinates in her mind. *Let's go.*

This time they arrived not in the glare of the large ship but in its shadow. Lorana had learned from the previous two jumps that they would have minutes before the air turned too cold and thin to breathe. On the first jump, she'd brought Minith as high into the sky as she could imagine, looked at the bright lights of the Dawn Sisters and had re-imagined the image as closer and brighter to get even nearer to them. With the view from their second jump, she was now able to bring them this close.

In the great ships' shadows, Lorana could look down on Pern below her without being blinded by the reflected glare of the Dawn Sisters. She took a quick look up at the ship closest to her and saw that it was named *Yokohama*. The name tripped off the tongue easily.

Below her, in crystal clarity, lay Pern. She could make out the eastern coastline, bathed in the light of morning, and, farther westward, the dim shadow-shrouded middle of the continent with Telgar and Igen. She tried to pick out the Weyrs but couldn't: The distance was too great and clouds added some confusion to her view.

The snowy wastes of the north reflected the sun brightly, nearly blindingly, and Lorana looked away from them quickly, blinking to clear her eyes.

It's time, she said, as she felt the first chill in the air around her.

Back once more on Pern, Lorana found herself looking at everything with new eyes. She had never truly realized how beautiful her planet was, how amazing that it could hold life, that it held all of them protected from the harsh chill of space.

She realized that, following the Dawn Sisters, it would take a full day to see all of Pern. No, she thought to herself, not a full day—just parts of one. The sun lit a full third of the planet—say, a quarter if allowing for the confusion of the shadows of sunset and sunrise. If she timed it right, it would take her only four more jumps to see all of the planet.

I'm tired, Minith confessed. *Can we rest?*

We've got all the time we need, Lorana assured her, climbing down and leaning against the queen's belly. *We should go carefully, we're going far higher than is safe.*

I could feel it, Minith agreed. *The cold coming in and the air getting bad.* After a moment she added with a tone of surprise, *I think I can hold the air longer, keep the cold out.*

You hold the air? Lorana repeated in surprise.

It comes with us, Minith said. *When we go* between, *we bring it and it comes with us when we come out of* between.

And you could hold it? Lorana asked. Something nagged at her, something more than just the beauty of their homeworld, something more than just the peril of their time. She shook her head and the moment passed. Holding air, Lorana thought as she closed her eyes with a deep sigh. Something to do with holding air.

I could, Minith agreed sleepily.

They awoke when the sun had set and it turned cold.

Ready? Lorana asked Minith as the queen roused herself.

Cold, the queen told her. *I'll need to eat after.*

We've missed a meal, Lorana agreed and she climbed up and strapped herself in firmly. *Can you hold the air this time?*

I'll try.

Minith cupped air, leaped upward, and, with Lorana's sure guidance, went *between* between one downbeat of her wings and the next.

The Dawn Sisters were above them once more, the great *Yokohama* nearest. Below them, Benden and the east coast were dark, dim. The west of the continent was now bathed in sunlight from the edges of Telgar all the way to Tillek Tip. Lorana picked up the spot where she knew Tillek Hold lay, but could make out no sign, except perhaps splotches that marked different fields outlying the hold. She looked down the length of the coast, toward Southern Boll, shimmering on the horizon, nearly out of sight.

It was so beautiful she felt her heart ache with joy and love for her planet.

No one has seen this in five hundred Turns! she thought to Minith in awe. *And it's beautiful.*

I'm holding the air, Minith said excitedly. *Can you feel it?*

I can, Lorana said approvingly, not the least perturbed that the queen deemed the vista spreading beneath them less noteworthy than her own very remarkable feat. It was clear that somehow Minith had brought even more air with them or was *holding* it better than before. *Well done, Minith.*

Lorana took another long look down, sighing at the beauty beneath her. She had seen all the northern continent, her home. Aside from the snowy wastes, she could see no place that was not already fully occupied where it might be possible to raise weyrlings to maturity.

Besides, there's the food, Lorana thought to herself, realizing how her stomach was grumbling.

Come on, Minith, let's eat, Lorana said, imagining the perfect place for the queen to hunt. It would require going back in time some more—to a time when the game she wanted would be plentiful—but Lorana could easily imagine it and they would make it in one slightly longer jump *between*.

Eagerly the queen agreed and they winked out, leaving the Dawn Sisters once more in sole possession of their vantage point over Pern.

Lorana allowed herself a pleased smile as Minith bugled in pleasure as she sighted her prey. The queen leaped and pounced, tearing down one of the large, unwary, herdbeasts that had grazed for Turns unmolested in the canyons and plateaus near the abandoned Igen Weyr.

Game was plentiful here, far more so than she'd been led to believe from Fiona's tales of Igen Weyr—the settling of which was some months still in the future of *this* time. Perhaps, it was just that Fiona, daughter of a Lord Holder, wasn't as well-versed in managing herd-beasts as Lorana, daughter of a herdmaster.

She felt Minith's delight as she gorged on the hot blood of the fresh kill, felt her tearing into the warm flesh and savagely ripped meat from the carcass as she slaked her hunger.

Lorana's stomach rumbled, reminding her that the queen dragon wasn't the only one who needed food. She'd drunk her plenty from the nearby stream that fed the Igen river, but, thirst quenched, her hunger redoubled.

I could get you a beast, Minith offered with a flash of joy mixed with pride as she imagined herself hunting and tearing down another one of the large herdbeasts.

It would be a waste, Lorana said. *I don't eat as much as you.*

Minith gave the mental equivalent of a draconic shrug and contin-ued happily chewing on her meal, freely relaying every hunger slaked, every morsel of meat torn.

There had to be traders nearby. They would have fire-lizards, too, Minith could track them on those—fire-lizards liked talking with dragons.

Fire-lizards. Lorana closed her eyes and sighed as she thought of

Grenn and Garth. She was still immensely pleased to know that Grenn had survived the fantastic trip back in time, the evidence of which was in the three-linked locket that Tullea had found in the Ancient Rooms when they'd been working on the cure for the dragon sickness.

Tullea had only given Lorana the locket when she'd come back from High Reaches Weyr with her queen cured of the illness. That locket had included Grenn's picture—he was perched on the shoulder of a scar-faced man. Was Minith protected from disease now that she had had the cure? Should Lorana worry about re-infecting the queen?

She thought for a moment and shook her head. The cure made the sickness impossible. The disease could not spread to Minith, her body had been so completely changed. Someday, perhaps another illness might come that could affect the dragons, but it would be thousands of Turns at least. For now, no dragon inoculated with the cure could catch the sickness. That much, Lorana admitted with a bittersweet feeling, she'd accomplished.

Lorana, Minith spoke to her softly, *look up.*

Lorana peered upward and saw a small green figure hovering above her.

Hello, Lorana thought to the fire-lizard. *Are you hungry?*

I've plenty, I can share, Minith added. The fire-lizard turned toward the queen in the distance, squawked in surprise and disappeared *between.*

Minith, Lorana added thoughtfully, *could you kill another for the fire-lizard?*

It won't eat as much as you, Minith remarked, even as she leaped into the air, searching out a fresh kill.

Kill it cleanly, please; it's going to be my lunch, too, I suspect.

I thought you liked yours only after you'd flamed it all smoky, Minith responded, her tone tinged with curiosity.

I suspect I'll get my smoky fire and cooking soon enough, Lorana said, rising to her feet and scanning the horizon. *Your kill will give me something to trade.*

Soon enough, Lorana spotted the distinct shapes of several trader drays lumbering on the horizon. She was in a cool, grassy spot while they still toiled with their wide wheels in the desert sand and heat.

She waited. The green fire-lizard returned, skittishly scouting the area out. He gave a small sound of delight as he noticed the fresh kill, but at Minith's urging, he took a bite only from the queen's leftovers. Minith said approvingly, *That's right, the other is for the humans.*

The humans arrived soon enough. A very tall man, with shoulders so broad and muscled he looked as though he could lift one of the workbeasts himself, left the lead dray and approached her slowly, his eyes squinting against the light. From Fiona's description, she knew he was Azeez, the trader who had helped—or would help—the injured dragonriders and young weyrlings who would shortly come back in time to Igen Weyr to recover and grow into maturity. And he had piercing green eyes, so like those that Tenniz had spoken of when describing his wife.

Standing back by the dray was a tall, lanky boy. He was younger than when she'd last seen him, but very recognizable as Tenniz.

"Is Javissa your daughter, then, that she is with Tenniz?" Lorana asked as the man came within earshot.

The man's eyes widened and he stopped, taken aback. He glanced beyond her to the gold hide of Minith.

"I do not know what you are talking about," the man replied haughtily.

"That's Tenniz beyond you," Lorana said, pointing. "He sees the future." She sighed, her expression sad. "He and I will meet in the future."

"In the future?" Azeez repeated. He gestured for Tenniz to join them. Tenniz rapped on the side of the dray and, as he moved to join them, a figure emerged from within the dray, taking guard. Lorana caught a glimpse of green eyes, a smattering of freckles on a swarthy face, jet-black hair, a trim figure.

"Javissa," Lorana breathed, surprised not only at the accuracy of Tenniz's description of her, but also of her beauty. She was truly as remarkable, with her pure, piercing green eyes and delicately etched face, as Tenniz had said.

"What did you say?" Azeez asked, moving closer toward her so as to keep the others out of her sight.

"I said Javissa," Lorana said, moving slightly to one side so that she could see beyond him and nodding toward the lithe form climbing down to take guard position beside the dray. "She is beautiful." She cocked her head at him. "She's your daughter?"

"She is," Azeez admitted. "But how do you know this?" Azeez had a good reason for the question. His dark eyes were nothing like his daughter's, his features were more broad, and his build was large and massive, while Javissa's was thin and light.

"Tenniz," Lorana said, gesturing to the approaching youth who raised his head at her naming.

"How long have they been married?" Lorana asked.

"They've been together for most of their lives," Azeez said. Lorana detected some hidden feeling in the older man's voice, as though he didn't approve of their union, but had resigned himself to it. "They've been partnered now for three."

"And they *have* just *one* child?" Lorana asked, her eyes going to Javissa's figure, spotting the signs of a nursing mother; signs that in her slim shape were only subtle hints. Lorana saw the way Azeez tensed nervously and she stretched her arms out at her side, palms out.

"I'm sorry, I know this may be a great shock to you," she said. "In this time, we've never met, but I've heard about you." Her eyes cut toward Tenniz. It was hard to see this young man with the memory of the cairn at Red Butte still fresh in her mind. "And I've met you already."

"In the future," Azeez breathed, his eyes going wide and worried as he turned his gaze from her to Tenniz behind him and back again.

"You are the beacon!" Tenniz said as he took in Lorana fully. He raced up toward her and dropped to one knee in front of her. "How may we help you?"

"I thought to trade," Lorana said, smiling down at the serious young man and wondering what he could possibly mean by "beacon." Behind him, she heard Azeez gasp in surprise—the word clearly had significance to him. Her stomach growled, reminding her to attend first to her business. Explanations could wait for later.

"Minith was kind enough to dispatch a large herdbeast, I was hoping to trade you the raw meat for a cooked meal, and perhaps some conversation." She paused and looked beyond to the dray. "Is Mother Karina with you? I would like to meet her."

Not long afterward, Lorana found herself in a circle with eight traders around a small fire, its flames barely visible in the afternoon sun. Lorana watched as they prepared the carcass, carefully saving the skin and other choice pieces, while carving the meat into smaller, manageable portions.

In the shadiest spot, Mother Karina sat on a stool and, nearby, Javissa, also ensconced on one of the light canvas stools, was feeding her baby.

"She's the one?" Mother Karina asked Tenniz.

"Yes."

Mother Karina eyed Lorana for a long while. "Do you have any trader blood?"

"My father was a beastmaster, we roamed between Benden, Bitra, and Lemos," Lorana said, shaking her head. She was surprised by the knowing looks exchanged between some of the traders.

"The Plague?" Mother Karina asked.

"No," Lorana said, deciphering her cryptic question. "My father was killed after by a blow to the head from a frightened beast."

"Your mother?"

"Mother, brother, and sister were all taken by the Plague," Lorana said, the pain of that loss welling up once more in her heart. She could take Minith to see them, save them—her lips tightened and she shook her head slightly as she banished the thought: if she could have done it, she *would* have, just as J'trel had told her over a Turn ago—rather, Turns in the future still to come. You cannot break time, she reminded herself, her eyes straying sadly to the young Tenniz.

"So, you said you wish to trade," Mother Karina said.

"I thought just—" Lorana broke off, remembering spatterings of conversations with Fiona. She hadn't heard all about their trip back in time to Igen, but she had heard enough, and more when she'd been given Tenniz's locket. Her hand twitched and she moved to place it out of sight under her tunic.

Her movement was her undoing, for Tenniz gestured toward her, asking, "May I see it?"

"Do you know what it is?"

Tenniz frowned. "I see snatches of the future," he admitted, "not all of it." He shook his head as though giving up on his chance for one fragment of the future. "I know it is important."

"It is dangerous to know too much about the future," Lorana cautioned.

Tenniz smiled and nodded firmly. "*That* I understand."

Lorana found herself grinning back, almost able to forget her last moments with him; moments in her past, but still in his future.

"It does no good to cry about what will be," Lorana murmured to herself, struggling to hold back tears.

At that moment, Tenniz broke into a wracking cough. Lorana recognized it and was surprised that she hadn't heard it from him before now—clearly the cough got worse as time went on.

"True," Tenniz said when he recovered, glancing swiftly at Javissa and then back to Lorana, "but it is also foolish to hold back grief when it comes."

"So we should cry today for what will be tomorrow?"

"We should cry when we hurt, let the tears cleanse us, and move on," Tenniz replied.

Mother Karina cleared her throat loudly, catching their attention and said somewhat emphatically, "Perhaps *I* should let you two conduct the trade."

"I've said that before," Tenniz agreed dryly. Karina glared at him, but the younger man did not flinch.

"You would give away everything," Karina swore.

"And what's the harm in that," Lorana wondered, "if the one you trade with does the same?"

Karina and several of the traders looked astounded at the notion.

"Profit comes when both feel they had fair bargain," Lorana said.

"You are a trader!" Karina exclaimed.

"My father used to say it," Lorana said with a shrug. "I thought it only common sense."

"Common sense among traders," Azeez said, eyeing her intently. "Among crafters and holders, the thinking is different."

"Worse, with dragonriders," one of the others muttered darkly.

Lorana searched for the speaker but could not identifty him, so she chose to speak directly to Mother Karina. "*I* am a dragonrider, I was the daughter of a holder, and was considered by many to be a crafter."

Karina's eyes picked out the offending speaker, glaring, "Abab, you need to learn more of silence. Speak not for another month, and trade not for thrice that."

Abab lowered his eyes, his face dark with shame.

"He has shamed us," Javissa spoke up, shifting her baby from one arm to the other. She turned toward Lorana. "We are in your debt."

"If hot mouths were not allowed to speak, there'd be no breezes," Lorana said, dismissing the issue. Again the traders exchanged surprised looks. Lorana creased her brow. "Is that another trader saying?"

"It is," Mother Karina agreed. "But Javissa speaks rightly in this."

"Listen to her," Tenniz said, his voice sounding odd, full of vision.

Lorana laughed, raised a finger and shook it at him. "Never pretend, you'll fool no one!"

Tenniz flushed, but across from him Javissa's voice peeled with laughter and she had to use both hands to hold her baby as she giggled. "I told you!"

"When you have told me your visions, they have had a sense of Power behind them," Lorana said to the young man. "A sense of rightness, a strength that cannot be denied." She frowned for a moment, adding, "It is akin to the dragons' power."

"You are not here by accident," Mother Karina said. "What sent you?"

Lorana quickly glanced away from Tenniz, her eyes straying toward Javissa but the green-eyed woman was quick-witted and her eyes widened; she knew what had sent Lorana. Lorana shook her head at the girl, willing her to hold the secret, and Javissa gave her an imperceptible nod in response.

It was all for nothing.

"I did," Tenniz said. His eyes met Lorana's. "Our paths have crossed once already for you."

"Yes," Lorana agreed softly. "Some Turns in the future."

"*She's* the one?" Javissa blurted suddenly, her eyes on Tenniz.

Tenniz nodded bleakly.

"Why is it that *you* are to spend the last night with my husband?" Javissa demanded of Lorana.

"Instead of you?" Lorana guessed, shaking her head. "I do not know."

"That's not your dragon," Tenniz said suddenly, as if fitting pieces of a puzzle together.

"Tullea is Minith's rider," Lorana agreed. "She offered her to me in exchange for—" Lorana broke off, not knowing what to reveal.

Tenniz didn't hear her, his expression changing swiftly as he intoned, "*The way forward is dark and long. A dragon gold is only the first price you'll pay for Pern.*"

"Is this true?" Karina breathed, looking at Lorana, then Tenniz, as the lad recovered from wherever he had been and sighed deeply with fatigue. "Have you paid with a dragon gold?"

Lorana nodded, the tears flowing from her eyes and she bowed her head into her hands, unable to look at the traders anymore, unable to think of anything save Arith and her own empty womb.

Arms surrounded her in silence. She smelled the warm, wet baby breath of little Jeriz, felt the kind warmth of Javissa, felt the strength of Azeez gathered behind her, felt Mother Karina's arms on her shoulder, in her hair, caressing it while crooning wordlessly, felt Tenniz in front of her, his hands on her knees.

"In the name of all traders, I claim this one," Karina spoke in a voice that was deep, melodious, authoritative.

"We hear this claim," the traders chanted in response—even Abab spoke, clearly released for this from his silence, his voice firm, unwavering.

"Lorana is ours, flesh of our flesh, blood of our blood, until the ending of the days," Karina continued.

"Flesh of flesh, blood of blood," the others chanted back.

"As her heart wills, so shall we do," Karina said. "Her price is our price, nothing is too great."

"Her heart wills, we will pay the price," the others chanted in response.

"I name you Beacon, the light of the way," Tenniz's voice spoke up, strong and vibrant.

"Beacon," the traders agreed.

"Ask what you will of us, your price is paid," Karina said, ending the ritual.

Lorana opened her eyes slowly in wonder, staring at the eyes surrounding her. In the distance, she felt Minith's strong approval, the queen's sense of rightness in this moment, of her own commitment.

"I cannot ask too much of you," Lorana said out loud, meaning her words for Minith.

You hear my heart, Minith corrected her. *You hear all the dragon hearts.*

"There is nothing you cannot ask," Javissa spoke for the traders, leaning closer to Lorana. She lowered her voice for Lorana's ears alone as she explained, "The only offense you can give is not to ask in need."

"I would not have you lose by it," Lorana said.

"Of course," Tenniz agreed. "But you are Beacon. Traders will square accounts."

"What do you mean by Beacon?" Lorana asked him.

Mother Karina answered, gesturing toward Tenniz. "Once in a

generation, if we are lucky—and we try to be lucky—we are gifted with one who can see something of the future."

Lorana nodded, she'd learned this already from the future Tenniz as well as from Jeila, Shaneese, and Fiona.

"In the hundreds of Turns since we've been on this planet," Karina continued, "our seers have spotted several Beacons."

Lorana gave her an inquiring look.

"One was Torene," Azeez said.

"She could speak to any dragon," Lorana said, recalling her Teaching Ballads. "Is a Beacon one who can speak to dragons?"

"More," Karina said. "More even than we understand. All we know is that when we find a Beacon, we support her."

"Always to our profit," Azeez added.

"Sometimes in ways that take time to reveal," Javissa said.

"But always to our profit," Karina concluded. "So we know that supporting you will be to our benefit."

"Which makes it easy to offer our help," Tenniz said. He shook his head at Mother Karina.

"So, what help can we give you, Beacon?" Karina asked.

"Firstly, call me Lorana," Lorana said. She paused then, as she remembered what Fiona had said about her journey to Igen Weyr and how the traders were ready for them, had laid in supplies.

"I think there *is* something you can do," she said. "And I think it will be to your profit."

Quickly she explained what she wanted, sketching out the details as she recalled. She spoke of medical supplies for the injured, of gathering food for about one hundred and fifty—she couldn't quite remember the exact number and wondered if that was good enough or if she should go forward in time—

"Oh!" Lorana said, suddenly startled by her own thought. The others looked at her expectantly. She shook her head and apologized, "I hadn't realized something."

"You've no fear of secrets with us," Karina vowed.

"Sometimes it is dangerous to know too much of the future," Lorana said.

"True," Tenniz agreed.

"Continue," Karina said, nodding in acceptance.

"You will have to keep your fire-lizards from them," Lorana said, continuing her train of thought. Moments later she was finished, having recalled all she could. As she waited for them to digest her proposal, certain looks and movements that had occured amongst them while she'd talked took on a new meaning, and she said, "You've been using Igen as a depot, right?"

Tenniz chuckled at the expressions of surprise on Azeez's and Mother Karina's faces. "Beacon!"

"We have," Azeez agreed. "Do we need to stop?"

"It would help if you could clean the quarters somewhat," Lorana said. "When they arrive, they'll have injuries and younglings."

"I see you didn't answer the question," Azeez said, eyes twinkling. "But we will do as you ask."

"Thank you," Lorana said. "And when you see them, say nothing of me."

"Of course," Karina agreed. "But it is getting later, we've had our meal, our custom is to rest in the shade before nightfall and then move on."

Lorana yawned at the notion.

"Why don't you join us?" Javissa offered. "You can sleep here, or in the caravan."

"Here would be cooler," Azeez noted.

"A nap would be good," Lorana agreed.

It took a while to settle, partly because Jeriz was fussy. Lorana held her arms out in offer to Javissa, who passed the baby over shyly and with only a trace of reluctance. Jeriz whimpered at first in the taller woman's arms, but then smiled and drifted to sleep, rocked quickly to drowsiness by Lorana's greater height, which gave her rocking motions greater sway.

"He *never* does that with strangers," Javissa said in an awed whisper as she took him back and lay next to him on the pile of cushions that the other traders had set out.

"He's nearing two, isn't he?" Lorana asked, eyeing the boy. He was not large, his bones thin and small like his mother's.

"People think he is younger," Javissa said, with past affronts remembered.

"You are hoping for another?" Lorana said, just turning her words into a question at the last moment. Javissa nodded shyly. "A girl?"

Javissa smiled. "Is that a seeing?"

"Most mothers want at least one girl if they've got a boy," Lorana said, dodging the question. She yawned once more and closed her eyes, easing her breathing. Beside her she heard Javissa yawn in sympathy and then the ligher sounds of her breathing and the faster, much lighter sound of the baby.

It was near dark when she woke and she looked up suddenly, startled. Tenniz was staring down at her.

"I have seen you like this," he said in a low voice laced with wonder and fear.

"You have," Lorana agreed.

"You were sick, you needed help," Tenniz said. "And I had everything I needed."

"Yes."

"I have an image of you crying, cold hard rocks, a flat high place," Tenniz continued. Lorana lowered her chin in a nod, and sighed deeply, near a sob. "This is when we first met?"

"Yes," Lorana said.

"And it makes you sad," Tenniz observed with an expression of apology on his face.

"It was a good thing," she assured him. "You helped more than you know."

"Be careful when you say that to a seer!" Tenniz told her with a chuckle.

Lorana's lips twitched upward in agreement.

"I couldn't tell you at the time," Lorana said, rolling to her side and propping herself on one arm. "I want you to know now that you helped me a great deal."

"Thank you," Tenniz said. "That's a comfort."

Lorana moved and pushed herself into a squatting position. Her head was slightly above Tenniz's, but she met his eyes. "What do you know of that future?"

"That I can tell you?" Tenniz asked. Lorana nodded. "You've been there already." Lorana nodded again. Tenniz shook his head in wonder at the notion. "Is it hard to travel through time?"

"Not so much physically as it is emotionally," Lorana said, "at least, for me."

Tenniz's eyes took on a slightly wistful look, but he shook his head and cleared them before saying, "I know that I die before my daughter is born."

"Is Javissa pregnant already?"

Tenniz shook his head. "We're trying; soon."

"What else do you know?"

"How do I know that I won't tell you something you don't know already?"

"I'll stop you if you try," Lorana swore.

"And will you tell me things I don't know?"

"Perhaps," Lorana said. "If it seems right."

"Fair enough," Tenniz said after a moment. "I know that when we meet, I will die." Lorana nodded. "And you will bury me." Lorana's eyes clouded with tears even as she nodded, her lips trembling. "And *that* will be a great honor. No seer has been buried by a Beacon."

"It's an honor I would prefer you avoid," Lorana told him.

"Yes," Tenniz agreed. He gave a sad sigh, then continued, "But we cannot break time."

"J'trel tried; he failed," Lorana agreed.

"Rides a blue in Ista, correct?"

Lorana nodded. "He saved my life."

"All honor to him."

The rest of the camp stirred. Jeriz was tetchy and calmed, once more, in Lorana's arms. She passed him back reluctantly, saying, "I must go."

"Will we see you again?" Karina asked.

Lorana shook her head. "I don't know," she said truthfully. Then, with a grin, she pointed at Tenniz. "Ask him."

*W*here are we going? Minith asked as they rose above the clearing in the star-lit night.

The Dawn Sisters, Lorana told her. *Let's see what they see.* She formed the image in her mind, and Minith took them *between.*

Lorana paid no attention to the great ships above and beside her, peering instantly over Minith's neck to view the ground below. As she'd hoped, Tillek tip and the west coast of Pern were just barely visible as dark smudges on the horizon. Below her, bathed in sunlight—

"I never heard of this!" Lorana said in astonishment. She was about to order Minith down to the new land spreading below them when she felt it.

Something stirred nearby. She turned in her seat, craned her neck up, looking for movement. Only the three great ships, *Yokohama* nearest. The ship appeared no different but it *felt* different.

Almost . . . Lorana tried to recall a memory of a similar feeling. Yes, almost but not quite like what she'd felt at Tillek when they'd returned the ancient artifacts to the sea. Something had been alive there, in the deeps off Tillek tip.

Tentatively she stretched her senses. Nothing. Or perhaps . . . something sleeping, dreaming deep thoughts unlike any she'd felt before.

Minith, do you feel something?

Cold, the dragon replied instantly.

Let's go, Lorana said, setting in her mind a closer image of the lands she'd seen below.

▼ ▼ ▼

They arrived at a promontory and began a long, slow sweep of the land beneath them. It was lush, green, luxuriant. There were no clearings or any sign of the presence of man.

This will do, Lorana said, urging Minith back *between*. She had work to do now. *We have the place, let's see if we can use it.*

Lorana patted Minith affectionately as they glided silently into Fort Weyr's Bowl in the dark of night. The watch dragon had been happy to let her rider sleep and agreed to forget their arrival. It was cold, snow clung to the top of the heights, decorated the Weyr Bowl below, muffling all sound.

Minith touched down with exquisite delicacy. Lorana stretched her senses and smiled. *Fiona.*

She felt the much younger girl wake, even as she felt Talenth's alert questioning mind, not all that much different from the full-grown queen she would meet in the future at Telgar Weyr. But now both rider and queen were young, untested.

No one else arrived stealthily in the dead of night to join her, so Lorana *knew* that it was up to her to lead Fiona back in time to Igen Weyr.

Lorana spoke to Talenth, heard Fiona's question, the queen's response even as she climbed down from the Benden queen and sent silent orders to the dragonets in the weyrling barracks. Presently, Lorana saw the small form of the new queen rider stick her head out of the queen's weyr. Lorana, used to the slightly taller and much more self-possessed Fiona of Telgar times, was amused by the hesitancy she saw in this younger counterpart.

She smiled to herself as Fiona came down the queens' ledge and toward them.

"Get dressed," Lorana said, feeling tendrils of curiosity emanating from Melirth's weyr. "We must be quick. We can't wake the others."

Lorana restrained an urge to hug Fiona; to feel the kind heart and brilliance of the younger woman again would be almost like . . . home. She saw Fiona looking at her, trying to determine her features.

"Why? Where are we going?" Fiona asked.

"Igen," Lorana said, challenging Fiona into action.

"I can't leave Talenth."

"She comes, too," Lorana said. "And the weyrlings." She glanced at the barracks, urged the dragonets to speed. "They're coming now." She saw doubt in Fiona's eyes. "We have to hurry. They need to see you and Talenth go or they won't follow."

"Follow?"

"They need to come with you to Igen."

"How do you know?" Fiona asked.

"It's already happened," Lorana told her.

"You're from the future!"

"You must hurry," Lorana said, suddenly worried that something would go wrong, something Fiona hadn't mentioned.

"Xhinna," Fiona cried, turning back toward her weyr. "I need to—"

"She stays." Lorana turned, alerted by Minith, toward a figure racing from the Living Caverns. Again, she had to keep herself from calling out with joy as Terin, much younger, still a child, raced toward them. "You may come."

Talenth crept out of her weyr, glancing furtively at Melirth's quarters, and hopped from her ledge onto the soft snow below.

"We can't go *between*," Fiona protested. "And Talenth is too young to carry my weight."

"You'll ride with me," Lorana said, wondering why she hadn't thought of this beforehand. "As for *between* . . . you'll have to trust me."

Lorana turned as she heard noise from the weyrling barracks and spotted two boys.

"Hurry!" she told Fiona, charging back to Minith and climbing quickly to her neck. She leaned down and held a hand out to Fiona. "I know *when* we're going!"

"Talenth will be safe, won't she?"

"My word on it," Lorana said, grasping Fiona's hand and pulling her up. It was strange having the weyrwoman riding behind her. "Quickly, they must see us go *between*."

Talenth!

I have the image, I can see where to go, Talenth responded calmly.

"Doesn't she have to be flying?" Fiona asked.

Lorana smiled. "Talenth, jump!"

They went *between*, Lorana feeling for and holding the little queen's presence firmly in her mind. She heard Fiona call frantically, *Talenth!* and heard the queen's unfazed response: *I am here. We are fine.*

It will be longer than normal, we are going back in time, Lorana told Fiona to calm the girl.

Don't you need to go to Igen now *first?*

I've already been there, Lorana said, surprised at how familiar and yet, how different, Fiona's mind felt. She felt the young girl's growing sense of wonder, felt her wonder to herself if perhaps Lorana was really Fiona, herself, from the future.

In a way, Lorana thought, she's right. It was strange, Lorana thought, how much of what Fiona is learning from me now, I learned from her later. She took heart in that, pulling forth Fiona's unconquerable optimism and armoring herself with it.

*W*hee! *Look how high I am!* Talenth exclaimed with joy as they burst out into the warm morning Igen air, slightly more than ten Turns back in time from when they'd started.

Careful! Just glide down, Fiona cautioned.

Okay, Talenth said, disappointed.

"This is Igen Weyr," Lorana called over her shoulder. "Your new home."

"It's awfully warm. I thought it would be cold and windy, even here."

"We are slightly more than ten Turns back in time," Lorana said, remembering Fiona's exclamation when she'd recounted the tale Turns from now. "I thought you'd prefer to start with warmer weather. This is the second day of the seventh month of the four hundred and ninety-eighth Turn since Landing."

Minith landed lightly and Lorana turned to Fiona. "Get down."

As soon as Fiona touched the ground, Lorana urged Minith back into the air, eager for the next stage of the journey.

Lorana and Minith returned to Fort Weyr and quickly arranged the weyrlings.

"Fiona is waiting for you," was her response to any objection. F'jian and J'nos rallied any waverers and soon they were following the strange queen *between* back in time to Igen Weyr and the lonely Fiona.

F'jian spotted Fiona as she ordered Talenth out of the way of the swarm of weyrlings. "Did you see us?" he called as Ladirth came to a halt. "We flew!"

"We only glided," J'nos corrected as he slid down his brown's foreleg. "But we went *between*!"

Lorana was pleased when F'jian told Fiona, "If we hadn't seen you do it, we wouldn't have dared to try."

"Where is everyone else?" J'nos asked, looking around the Weyr expectantly.

Lorana listened to Fiona and the weyrlings gabble in a distracted manner until Fiona steeled herself and came to her.

"Hello!" Fiona called up. "Can you bring back the other injured dragons and riders?"

Yes, Lorana thought. Instead, she said, "For that I'll need help."

"I don't think we could give you any help," Fiona said reluctantly, gesturing to the dragonets. "They're too small; it's a wonder they managed to get here at all."

"Oh, it's no wonder," Lorana said with a laugh. "And I'm sure you'll be able to help with what needs doing."

Lorana urged Minith upward and *between* once more.

She arrived again in Fort Weyr. This was the moment she had been waiting for, ever since she realized who it was who brought Fiona back in time to Igen Weyr. Now she would get the answer to the question: Who had helped her with the injured dragons and riders? Who was the other mystery queen rider?

As Minith sloped her way toward the ground, Lorana saw that the bowl was full of activity, all quiet, all muffled by the night and the snow.

Her heart leaped when she felt Talenth's touch and she cried with joy when she saw Fiona look up and wave at her. She landed right beside the queen and rider, racing to give her a hug.

"It's so good to see you!" the two women said simultaneously, falling into each other's arms with relief and tears. It did not last long. Fiona broke the embrace first. "We have to hurry."

"So it *was* you," Lorana said. "The second queen rider."

"And did you notice our accomplices?" Fiona asked, waving a hand toward the others. Lorana recognized J'nos and J'gerd.

"Where's F'jian?" Lorana asked in surprise.

"I can't tell you," Fiona said, her face abruptly void of expression. Then her humor slipped back into her and she grinned. "But *when* you find out, you'll be pleased."

Quickly they arranged for the injured riders to be carried, the injured dragons to be escorted, and, with the merest leap, all went *between* to the warmer climes of Igen, to rest, recover, and grow.

They stayed only long enough to deposit their charges and for Lorana to see young Fiona waver, wobble, even as the older one seemed to shrink in on herself. *Too many me in the same time,* Fiona apologized, jumping *between* with the others as soon as she could. Lorana followed suit, but did not follow them.

It was a merry meeting, Lorana told herself as she considered her next steps now that she knew that she could bring young weyrlings safely through time.

SEVEN

Weyrwoman, to your duty hew
With honors many and comforts few
Bronzes may your queen outfly
As you soar about the sky.

They made Jeila as comfortable as they could and Fiona insisted on staying with her until H'nez was free from his duties.

"How is she?" the gaunt dragonrider, eyes hollow with fatigue and worry, asked when he relieved her.

"The bleeding's stopped," Fiona said. "Bekka's sure there's no lasting harm." She met H'nez's eyes. "She could get pregnant again."

"But—just a fall!"

"It was exactly the wrong type of fall," Fiona said. "It put too much stress on an already stressed body." She grimaced. "Bekka says that sometimes a person will miscarry because stresses are too great, times too hard."

"I see," H'nez said. He looked down tenderly at the sleeping weyrwoman, then glanced questioningly at Fiona.

"She's still concussed," Fiona said. "She'll feel awful in the morning, but we can't give her any fellis until we're sure she's recovered."

H'nez nodded. "Thank you, Weyrwoman."

"Call me if you need anything," Fiona said, rising from her bedside seat. At the exit into Ginirth's weyr, she turned back. "H'nez, I'm sorry."

The tall rider had already taken Fiona's seat beside Jeila and was gently stroking the unconscious weyrwoman's hair. He waved a hand in acknowledgment. With a sigh, Fiona left.

The injured were all tended, the task ably handled by Birentir and Bekka. Kindan was shepherding the weyrlings back to their quarters. T'mar was in Shaneese's care; Fiona suspected a lot of wine was involved.

Having run down her list of responsibilities, Fiona turned toward Terin's quarters.

Jeriz sat beside Terin's bed, much the same as Fiona had sat with Jeila earlier. He started when Fiona laid a hand on his shoulder.

"How is she?"

"Sleeping," Jeriz said. He looked up at Fiona with worried eyes. "And Jeila?"

"The same," Fiona told him.

"Is she still pregnant?"

"No," Fiona said, shaking her head. She looked down at her still flat stomach and smiled ruefully. "It appears I am the only one with that honor, now."

"Shaneese," the boy corrected softly.

"I should say that I'm the only weyrwoman," Fiona agreed.

"What will happen with her?" Jeriz said, nodding toward Terin.

"We'll stay with her, keep her company, help her recover."

"You've never had this happen to you."

"No," Fiona said. "But I know a little of what she's going through." The young trader boy cocked an eye in her direction, so she explained: "All my brothers and sisters—save Kemin—died in the Plague."

"He died saving T'mar, warning the others," Jeriz said. "That was brave."

"It was," Fiona agreed. Something puzzled her. How did he know?

"Terin's still the same," Fiona said the next morning as she met Shaneese for breakfast.

"It will take a long time for her, she was very much in love," Shaneese said.

"When I came in this morning, Jeriz was in the bed with her," Fiona said, smiling at the memory. "He's barely half her size, but he had her head on his chest."

"I cannot believe he did that," Shaneese said, a bitter tang in her voice.

"Jeriz?" Fiona asked, surprised.

Shaneese shook her head. "No, F'jian."

Fiona made a face, but said nothing.

"He swore on his dragon's egg that he'd be there when she needed him," Shaneese said. "Either he lied about everything or . . ."

"Perhaps he was too distraught," Fiona said. "Perhaps he discovered that he was going to die and he said whatever he could to Terin, to let her know how much he loved her."

"The way I see it, either he was telling the truth all the time or he was lying about everything," Shaneese declared flatly.

"But if he was telling the truth, where is he now that Terin needs him most?"

Jeriz came rushing in, raced up to Fiona, a broad grin on his face.

"Where's Terin?" Fiona demanded.

"She's okay," Jeriz said as he grabbed a roll and wolfed it down.

"She needs someone to be with her all the time," Fiona said, rising from her chair, ready to rush to the other woman's side.

"She's got someone," Jeriz said, smiling broadly.

"Who?"

"F'jian," Jeriz said. "He's giving her a bath right now."

"What?" Fiona cried, racing toward the Weyr Bowl.

"She was in the bath when I woke, and she told me she was all right."

Talenth! Fiona roared. *Tell T'mar to see to Terin.*

"I'll talk to *you* later," Fiona swore as she raced off toward Terin's quarters. As soon as she was in the Bowl, Fiona shouted, "Bekka! Terin!"

"Coming!" Bekka shouted back from several levels up.

Fiona raced up across the Bowl, up the queens' ledge, through Kurinth's weyr, and into Terin's quarters to find the young girl in a robe, sitting on her bed, bawling and shouting up at T'mar.

"He was here, I swear!" Terin shouted.

"Terin," T'mar said in a kindly voice, shaking his head, "I saw him. He didn't survive." His voice broke. "He saved my life. He didn't survive."

"He was here," Terin shouted back. She spotted Fiona. "Make him understand."

T'mar turned to Fiona with a beseeching look on his face. Shaneese came bustling out of Terin's bathroom.

"There's no one here," Shaneese said. She glanced at T'mar and Fiona as she added, "But there are enough wet towels for two."

"I told you," Terin said triumphantly.

"What happened?" Fiona said, moving forward and seating herself beside the younger weyrwoman.

"I was sad," Terin said. "I was so mad at him because he broke his promise and then—there he was."

"What did he say?" Fiona asked, gesturing for T'mar and Shaneese to leave.

"He said that he loved me," Terin told her. "He said that he couldn't be with me often, but that he would be with me forever."

"Forever?"

"He said he would be there when I needed him most," Terin continued, nodding in agreement with Fiona's question. "He said that if he didn't come it was because I didn't really need him."

"I see," Fiona said. "And how did he look?"

"Tired," Terin said. "Not as tired as I last saw him." She reflected for a moment, then added, "And he was so apologetic. But then we took a bath and we played and—" She broke off, smiling at Fiona. "It was so great to know that he was there! That he kept his promise and that he loves me."

"Terin," Bekka's voice came softly from Kurinth's weyr as the young healer moved forward, "sometimes when we've been through something terrible, we get confused."

Terin gave Bekka a troubled look.

"Is it possible," Bekka said as she sat on the other side of Terin and grabbed her free hand, "that you dreamed this?"

"There were two sets of wet towels," Terin said.

"Sometimes we want something to be real even when it isn't," Bekka said. "And we want it so much that we don't realize how we're convincing ourselves that it's real."

"Ask Jeriz," Terin said.

"Did he talk with F'jian?" Fiona asked.

Terin shook her head. "F'jian winked at me and shook his head when we heard him wake up. So I told him that I was okay, that F'jian was here and he should get some breakfast."

"And he said that he'd come back when you needed him the most," Bekka asked.

"Yes," Terin said, her eyes shining with joy at the thought. "He said that he'd always be there when I needed him." She shook her head. "I'm sorry I ever doubted him."

"So he kept his word," Bekka agreed in a neutral tone.

"He did," Terin agreed.

"And you're all better now."

"No," Terin said, shaking her head. "I still hurt, I still wish he were here all the time but . . . at least I know that he'll be there when I need him."

"That's good," Fiona agreed.

"How's Jeila?" Terin asked. "I'm so sorry she got hurt; is she all right?"

"She's recovering," Bekka said, again in that carefully neutral voice.

"Can I see her?"

"No," Bekka said. "I think you should rest today and I know she'll need rest, too."

"Thread falls at Fort Weyr in two days' time," Fiona said. "I imagine B'nik will send them a wing to help. If that's so, we've got nearly a fortnight of rest before the fall over Igen Weyr."

"Can someone help me feed Kurinth?" Terin asked. "I'll have to get dressed, first."

"I'll help," Bekka offered.

"I'll talk with T'mar," Fiona said, rising. Terin held on to her hand so Fiona turned back to face her.

"Tell him I'm sorry I shouted," Terin said.

"Of course," Fiona replied. She waved at Bekka, leaned down to kiss Terin on the forehead and cautioned the younger woman, "Don't rush things, you've been through a lot."

"I won't," Terin promised.

"I won't let her," Bekka added.

T'mar's expression was grim as Fiona sat down beside him. Kindan was seated opposite the Weyrleader, his expression equally troubled.

"She could be hysterical," Kindan suggested. "Grief can do that."

"She could be telling the truth," Fiona said with a touch of waspishness in her voice. She saw T'mar and Kindan exchange looks. Angrily, she spun in her chair and called, "Can I get some food?"

Shaneese bustled up and set out fresh rolls, a pitcher of juice, and a bowl of fruit.

"Thank you," Fiona said, adding, "I'm sorry if I sounded rude."

"You did," Shaneese agreed, lowering herself into the chair next to T'mar. Fiona pushed the pitcher toward her. Shaneese unbridled enough to give her a nod of thanks.

"These two are convinced that Terin's imagining things," Fiona said, waving at the two men.

"And you?"

Fiona shrugged. "I once went back ten Turns to a place called Igen Weyr."

"So you think her F'jian went back in time?"

"Forward," Fiona said. She noticed T'mar shudder at the notion and continued, "It could explain why he'd been so tired the last sevenday. And even the strange woman."

Kindan sighed, glancing at her but not meeting her eyes. "And who do you think that woman is?"

"Lorana," Fiona said, feeling his incredulity growing stronger. "She's the only one who knows time that well."

"Knows time?" T'mar repeated.

"She not only hears all the dragons, she has an uncanny sense of time," Fiona said, glancing at Kindan for confirmation.

"She did," Kindan agreed woodenly.

"She *does*," Fiona insisted. Kindan's lips twitched, but he said nothing, clearly finding it difficult to agree with her, but unwilling to argue the point.

"How are you feeling?" Shaneese asked. Fiona shrugged questioningly. "You're in your sixth week."

"The twins are doing fine," Fiona said. "They haven't so much as twitched yet, but Bekka and all the healers say it's still too early to feel anything, even with two."

"And you?"

"I'm hungry, tired," Fiona admitted, adding emphatically, "and *irritated* that anyone would think my wits addled."

"Forgive me, Weyrwoman, but have you ever been pregnant before?" Shaneese asked her. With a heavy sigh, Fiona shook her head. "And so how can you be so sure your wits aren't addled?"

"Because they're the same wits I had yesterday," Fiona returned quickly, spreading a glare amongst the three. "And the day before that, as well."

"You'd tell us if you felt differently?" T'mar asked, but his tone sounded certain.

"Of course!" Fiona said. She glanced at Shaneese, but said nothing of the other woman's pregnancy; as Shaneese had said, it was too early to be certain and no one needed the extra worry at this moment. The headwoman caught her gaze and held it.

"I'm not worried about your wits, Weyrwoman," Shaneese declared. "But I am worried about Terin."

"So am I," Fiona agreed emphatically. "And I understand wondering if her vision of F'jian might not be similar to when Lorana came to draw me." Her eyes fell toward Kindan and she saw him jerk as the comment hit home. "And it *could* be that I only imagined it." She paused a moment. "But that's just as likely that D'gan and the rest of Telgar will return from *between*."

"For nearly four hundred extra dragons, I'd even be happy to see him," T'mar said.

"So many of them were sickly," Shaneese said, her eyes going dim with memory. "There was a chorus of coughs even as they went *between*."

"We've got plenty of syringes still, and healthy dragons to pick from," Kindan said. "We could cure all of them."

"The man was arrogant, wouldn't listen to reason," Shaneese said, shaking her head sadly.

"K'lior said that C'rion and M'tal thought he would do all right, given time," T'mar said.

"Well, he didn't get it," Fiona said. "And we've got to deal with what is now, not what we wish."

"You really *did* see her?" Kindan blurted suddenly.

"On my dragon's egg, I swear," Fiona told him, seeing the hope dawning in his eyes.

"And she drew you with colored pencils?"

"Yes," Fiona said. "She said that you'd given them to her."

Kindan frowned.

"What, still doubt me?"

"It would be easier to believe you if I didn't know that those colored pencils are still back at Benden Weyr," Kindan admitted.

"*Now,*" Fiona pointed out. Kindan stared at her for a moment and then burst out laughing.

"Now!" he agreed when he could breathe again.

Jeila looked up at the noise outside her weyr and called out, "Yes?"

A long moment later a short head poked around the entrance, looking in worriedly.

"Weyrwoman?" a boy's piping voice asked softly.

"I can't see you," Jeila said.

The boy stepped out of the weyr and into her quarters, close enough that she could make out his piercing green eyes. They were amazing. She took in his thin frame, his dark skin, his jet-black hair.

"Desert trader," Jeila said, sitting up in her bed.

"Northern trader," Jeriz said, rushing forward and going to his knees in front of her. "I have a great boon to request."

"Not trade?" Jeila asked, surprised.

"Carte blanche," Jeriz said, looking up to meet her eyes. "Whatever you wish, whenever I can give it."

"First give me your name," Jeila said in the time-honored trader tradition.

"Jeriz, son of Tenniz and Javissa," he replied formally.

"Tenniz?" Jeila repeated, eyes going wide. "You are his son?"

"Yes."

"You have the Sight?"

"No," Jeriz said, making a face. "That goes to my little sister, Jirana."

"Jirana?" Jeila asked, surprised at the naming.

"My parents had Lorana's permission to honor her," Jeriz said. In a lower voice he added, "She is the Beacon."

"The Beacon?" Jeila said. "But she's gone."

"Fiona doesn't think so," Jeriz said. "And my father said that it would be hard to know with her because she has the gift of time and place."

"What do you want of me?" Jeila asked, rising and gathering her robe around herself.

"Can you fly, you and your queen?" Jeriz asked.

"I'll get my things."

"I see drays," Jeila called over her shoulder, pointing down to a trail of dust rising slowly in the midday air. "They're heading south."

"Then we should turn around and head north, my lady," Jeriz said. "They've probably already dropped them off."

"Who?" Jeila called back, but, before Jeriz could respond, Tolarth made a sudden lurch, twisted on a wing tip, and started spiraling down.

"Them?" Jeila asked, spotting two small dots struggling north-ward from Southern Telgar Hold.

"Yes."

Tolarth had just landed when Jeriz, with a complete disregard for all custom, rolled out of his seat and slid down the side of the great queen, rushing toward the woman and throwing himself into her arms.

"Momma!" the boy cried as he smashed his face into her belly, his arms snaking around her waist. "I brought her, Momma, just like father said I would."

As if the words recalled him to his senses, Jeriz pushed away and turned back toward Jeila, rushing to Tolarth's side to offer his aid as the dimunitive rider gingerly climbed down.

"Mother," Jeriz said, turning them both toward his mother and sister, "this is Jeila."

"Trader of the north," Javissa said, bowing slightly. Beside her, the small girl bowed in following. "I give you my sympathies."

"Trader of the desert," Jeila said, her dark eyes widening, "I greet you but ask, why the sympathy?"

"My husband said I'd meet you when you were hurting most," Javissa said, casting her eyes down to Jeriz.

"He said to me: *You will know the right time*," Jeriz said. He nodded toward Jeila. And spoke to his mother, "This is the right time, Momma. She has just lost her baby and Terin, the other queen rider, has just lost her man."

"Oh!" The word burst from Javissa, full of shock and sympathy. She let go of the girl's hand and rushed toward Jeila, reaching out to her. "Weyrwoman, I am so sorry. I know how hard it is."

"You do?"

"Twice," Javissa said, her eyes dropping to the ground to keep her pain from showing. She grabbed Jeila's hand and pulled the other woman toward her. "It hurts, I know."

Jeila found herself resting her head on the other woman's shoulder, tears flowing silently down her face as she gripped the woman tight enough to squeeze the breath out of her. Javissa stroked her hair with one hand and patted her shoulder with the other. "Time, dear heart, time will ease the pain."

A long time later, when Javissa felt Jeila's sorrow ease and the woman stiffen against her uneasily, she pulled back. They were of similar height and build; Javissa met Jeila's eyes on the level. She smiled as she looked into the beautiful dark, near-black eyes, now so full of sorrow but, she could tell, so easily full of life and mischief. Eyes that, oddly, reminded her somewhat of Tenniz though, even now, she could see that Jeila had none of the Sight, for there was no awareness of future pain, no sorrow born of excess knowledge. Raw, elemental, firm, steady, that was the normal stance of the woman in front of her. And beautiful, very beautiful, a beauty more in keeping with the desert than with the cold north.

"We must be related, you and I," Javissa said softly.

"Because we're so short?" Jeila asked with a touch of her normal humor.

"That, too, but because of our builds and bones," Javissa said. Jeila nodded and Javissa continued, "But we can talk lineage later."

"Your son asked a boon," Jeila said, glancing at Jeriz, who was busy distracting the young Jirana. The girl looked very much like she could have been Jeila's own child, heartbreakingly so. She had the same thin bones, the same dark, near-black eyes, the same dusky skin.

"Tenniz said that I would take the dark road to Telgar," Javissa said, "and that I would know when the time was right."

Jeila glanced again at Jirana. Javissa saw her look and shook her head. "It is not yet her time," she said of her daughter. "He said that she would find her Sight in a far land."

"Telgar?"

"No, I don't think so," Javissa said. She saw Jeila's look and explained, "Tenniz often tried to cloud the meaning of what he saw; he said it was so difficult to know that speaking clearly was the first mistake he ever made." She frowned. "He'd mutter something about spit soup, but he'd only smile and shake his head when I pressed him on it."

"He must have been a difficult man to live with," Jeila guessed.

"Oh, no," Javissa said, shaking her head. "He was the most marvelous man to live with." Jeila raised an eyebrow and Javissa moved close enough to whisper in her ear, "He knew his time was short and he made the most of it." She smiled in memory of the passion. "And he loved me every moment of every day."

"H'nez loves me," Jeila said, feeling almost compelled to defend him.

"He'd be a fool otherwise!" Javissa said with a snort. Jeila looked askance at the response, so Javissa explained, "For one, you are a trader child. For another, it is obvious—even through your pain—that you are one who finds a man and sticks to him."

"Fiona has many," Jeila said in self-deprecation.

"That is her way," Javissa said. She saw the weyrwoman's eyes widen. "We've seen her grow from child to adult down in Igen, we keep track of her." Her smile faded. "In truth, she has only two men, maybe three, and she shares her love with all."

"Yes," Jeila agreed. She shook herself. "I'd best get back, she'll need me."

"She has you in her spell," Javissa said.

Jeila frowned for a moment, then nodded. "I would die for her," the weyrwoman admitted.

"As she would for you," Javissa concluded. "She is one of those lucky enough to live in full love." Jeila gave her an inquiring look. "She is like Nuella, she spreads her love like air—and we all breathe the easier for it."

"Yes," Jeila agreed. She nodded toward Jeriz. "She opened his heart."

"His father gave him a terrible burden," Javissa said. "It is hard to be the son of a seer and not a seer yourself."

"He's a good lad, he's got a true heart," Jeila said. She smiled as she couldn't help adding, "And eyes that will break hearts throughout Pern."

"If he learns to control himself," Javissa agreed, blushing. Jeila looked at her. "I had a similar problem until I met Tenniz." She frowned. "It was hard to be judged only on my looks."

"What happened?" Jeila asked in wonder, referring to Tenniz's courtship.

"He asked me whether I'd be willing to live a hard life that I'd love, or a soft life that I'd hate," Javissa said with a wan smile. "I was his after that."

"That fast?"

"Well," Javissa temporized, "after that and our first kiss." She smiled at the memory. "*Then* I was his forever."

"And now?" Jeila asked softly.

"I have children," Javissa said. "And a responsibility." She gave Jeila a frank look. "I will have other lovers, I'm certain, but when I'm ready." She drew back a little and lowered her head in a trader's bow. "Weyrwoman, I request the shelter of the Weyr."

"I'd be glad of your help," Jeila said, offering her hand. Javissa shook it firmly. "Times are hard, the way is dark."

"Tenniz said it would be so," Javissa replied. She glanced at Tolarth. "Your queen is big, the largest on Pern, they say. Can she carry us all?"

Jeila laughed. "Let's see!"

"Should she be out on her queen after all that's happened?" H'nez asked Bekka worriedly. He'd tracked the healer down the moment he'd noticed Jeila's absence and had followed her with a pack of questions that the young woman had answered slowly and steadily.

"She was early enough that the loss is little more than her usual monthly, wingleader," Bekka told him kindly. "She might feel more cramping, but if she felt able to ride her queen—and her queen was willing because, as you know, Fiona has all the queens check with her—"

"She does?" H'nez asked in surprise.

"There are only three and only two of them can fly yet," Bekka reminded him with a shrug. "It makes sense that the Weyrwoman know what's going on with the queens in her Weyr."

"They won't rise for months yet," H'nez protested.

"Of course," Bekka agreed. "I think Fiona's just making it a habit and . . . I think it's just part of who she is, you know?"

H'nez snorted at the question and then gave it more attention. "Yes, I suppose it is."

"Anyway, she's on her way back with Jeriz and two others," Bekka said.

"You can talk to any dragon?" H'nez asked, eyes narrowing.

"No," Bekka said, smiling. "But I *can* talk with Talenth and she's happy enough to ask Tolarth a question and relay the answer to me."

H'nez eyed the blonde appraisingly. She'd always had a great deal of self-assurance, justifiably with her expertise in healing, particularly midwifery, but her new elevation to journeyman seemed to have cemented that confidence within her, giving external validation of her internal aspirations. She moved more surely, more confidently. She had, the wiry wingleader realized, found herself as an adult.

He heard the watch dragon bugle a challenge and Tolarth's response. "I'd best greet her."

"I'll come along," Bekka said. She cocked an eye at the taller bronze rider. "Do you want me to give out to her?" H'nez's eyes narrowed in confusion. "You know, scold her?"

"If you think it would help," H'nez said.

"It'll be easier if it's coming from me," Bekka said. "That way you can be sympathetic."

H'nez's eyes widened in surprise at Bekka's display of guile. "I would appreciate that."

Bekka snorted. "My mother taught me *that* trick, wingleader!"

"Wise woman."

"Jeila, what are you doing up?" Fiona called as she crossed the Bowl toward Tolarth. "And Jeriz, you and I need to talk."

"I brought them, Weyrwoman," Jeriz cried excitedly as he leaped down from his perch on Tolarth's neck. "I brought them!"

"Who?" Fiona asked, her smile broad in response to his clear exuberance. She glanced up and saw the two trader figures above. "More strays?"

She moved forward to help the woman and child climb down from Tolarth's high shoulder.

"Step here, then there," Fiona said, guiding the small woman's feet as she instructed. When the woman was down, she turned, and at that moment Fiona caught sight of her green eyes. Her smile faded. "You must be Jeriz's mother."

"Javissa, Weyrwoman," the other replied, hand outstretched, though caught off balance by Fiona's coldness. Even Jeriz turned his eyes toward her in surprise.

Fiona ignored the proffered hand, moving behind the woman to help the girl down and scooting her forward toward her mother while she helped Jeila dismount.

"Where'd you find the strays?" she asked Jeila. The dainty gold rider gave Fiona a startled look, surprised at her tone. "Jeriz asked a boon."

"Weyrwoman," Jeriz said, "this is my mother, Javissa, and my sister, Jirana." He paused and added, "Her name is in honor of Lorana."

"Lorana?" Fiona repeated sharply, glancing at Javissa. "How do you know Lorana?"

"My husband, Tenniz—"

"He said it would turn out all right," Fiona broke in accusingly. She turned her attention to Jeriz. "And you! How *dare* you leave, especially after Terin."

Jeriz visibly wilted in the face of her anger, his eyes smoldered, and his head lowered. "I only—"

"Enough!" Fiona cut across him, raising a finger and pointing toward Terin's quarters. "Go there, relieve Shaneese, and *stay* with her, no matter who comes or where she goes."

"Yes, Weyrwoman," Jeriz returned sullenly. He started off slowly, but Fiona barked after him, "Run!" Jeriz picked up his pace to a slow trot.

"I'll go with him," Javissa said, starting off after her son, clearly surprised at her harsh reception.

"I'm staying with her," Jirana said, pointing at Fiona. Fiona turned to say something to the girl, but the dark brown eyes met hers squarely.

"You're hurting," Jirana declared, as she stepped forward and grabbed Fiona's hand.

Fiona blinked once at the girl and then burst into tears. "Yes, yes I am!"

Jeila took charge and bustled them over to Fiona's quarters, shushing the distraught Weyrwoman. Jirana never left her side, gently holding Fiona's hand as though her touch gave the blond weyrwoman comfort and, as far as Jeila could see, it did.

She got the younger weyrwoman to sit on her bed, then, with a decisive sigh, she forced Fiona out of her clothes and into her nightdress.

"You need rest," Jeila declared, surprised at herself. "You've been carrying this Weyr on your shoulders for too long." She gave Fiona a measured look and shook her head. "You may be taller than me, but you're not *that* tall."

"I've got to."

"You've got to rest, too, you know," Jeila told her softly. "You've got the babies to care for."

"I've got the only babies now," Fiona said, suddenly blubbering again. She grabbed for Jeila's hand and kissed it. "Oh, Jeila, I'm so sorry! I so wanted our babies to grow up together."

"And they will," Jeila promised. "I'll have more, you'll see."

Somehow alerted, Bekka arrived. She gave Fiona one look, gave young Jirana a considering glance, and declared, "You need to rest, you're going to drink this, and you're going to sleep until you wake up." She turned to Jirana and said, "She's a funny one, our Weyrwoman, she uses her friends like blankets and pillows—would you be a pillow?"

Jirana giggled at the notion and nodded silently.

"Good!" Bekka said. She turned toward Talenth's weyr. "Talenth!" The queen raised her head and craned it in through the entrance, eyes whirling steadily. "She's to sleep, don't let her fret. And let me know if she needs anything."

As you say, Talenth replied.

"Peel out of your stuff and get into this," Bekka said, finding one of Fiona's tunics and throwing it at Jirana, "and then crawl into bed with her." She saw Jirana glance around and added, "Don't worry about tidy, the floor's clean, throw it there."

Jirana's eyes widened, but the child silently obeyed and was soon dressed in Fiona's soft tunic. She lifted the fabric closer to her and sniffed. "It smells nice."

"That's Fiona smell," Bekka said with a smile. "She does smell nice, I think it's a Fort Hold trick."

"I smell of Koriana's bed," Fiona confessed as she slid into her bed. "I've kept the scent ever since I learned that Kindan liked it."

"Who's Koriana?" Jirana asked.

"She was my sister," Fiona said. "She died in the Plague."

"Oh."

"Scoot in bed there, young one," Bekka said in a kindly voice.

"I'm only a little sleepy," Jirana confessed. Fiona yawned and the girl caught it, yawning wide, and gave the Weyrwoman an accusing look.

"Sorry," Fiona said.

"Did you ever want a little sister?" Jirana asked.

"Yes, I've been begging my father ever since I could talk," Fiona said, turning to peer into the bright, dark eyes of the girl beside her.

"My father's dead," Jirana said with a touch of sadness. "He died before I was born."

"I knew him, he was a good man," Fiona said, yawning once more.

"That's what everyone says," Jirana confessed. "And they say he had the Sight, he could see the future."

"He could."

Jirana's voice lowered as she admitted, "They say that I'll see the future, too, when I get older."

"Oh," Fiona said, at a loss for words.

"I'll leave you two," Bekka said, "and see how Terin and Jeila are doing."

"I'm sorry to be such a mess," Fiona said, yawning once more and giving the little girl an apologetic look as she yawned in sequence.

"You're pregnant, you're under a lot of stress," Bekka said with a dismissive gesture. "I'm only surprised you didn't collapse a seven-day sooner."

"This is normal?"

"Nothing, Weyrwoman, is normal with you," Bekka said, smiling. She walked back and leaned over Jirana to kiss Fiona fondly on the forehead. "That's why we love you so."

"Check on Shaneese, too," Fiona said, eyeing the midwife carefully. She was not surprised at Bekka's lack of reaction—she was certain that Bekka had already discerned Shaneese's pregnancy.

"I will," Bekka assured her, straightening and beating a quick retreat. At the entrance to Talenth's weyr she turned back. "Rest, Weyrwoman. You'll feel better."

Fiona closed her eyes obediently. She heard Bekka's footsteps fade in the distance and thought of opening her eyes, but the fellis-laced wine was working on her and she was tired, so tired. She heard Jirana's breathing beside her and reached out to touch the girl on her shoulder.

"You could be my sister if you'd like," Fiona said.

With a half-cry, Jirana threw herself into Fiona's arms. "I'd like that, very much, please."

"Good, then it's settled," Fiona said, kissing the crown of the girl's dark hair. "Sisters it is."

Startled by Fiona's outburst, Jeriz was reticent about introducing his mother to Terin, but Jeila had no reserves, explaining all that had occurred as they made their way up the slant of the queens' ledge.

"I understand," Javissa said when Jeila had finished. She took a deep breath and closed her eyes. "Such losses are hard on anyone."

"How did you manage?" Jeila asked softly.

Javissa gave her a half-smile. "I had special help."

Jeila gave her an inquiring look, but the other trader woman shook her head. "I'll tell you about it later."

Terin met them in Kurinth's lair. She was feeding the queen, aided by a gaggle of small weyrkids.

"Gently, Kurinth," Terin called as the queen lunged toward a bite temptingly offered her by one of the younger boys. To the boy she said, "It's better to just throw it toward her."

"That doesn't seem very respectful," the boy said.

"She's little," Terin replied. "She doesn't mind." She bent down and stroked Kurinth's eye ridges. "Do you, greedy guts?"

The children giggled at her choice of words, but Kurinth paid them no mind, cheerfully chomping on the next sliver of meat offered. Terin heard the noise of Jeila's approach and turned toward her.

"Are you all right, Jeila?" she said, moving toward her. "I'm so sorry!"

"It's over," Jeila said, looking up at the younger woman and gesturing toward Javissa. "This is Javissa, Jeriz's mother and—"

"Tenniz's mate?" Terin asked in wonder. "I don't think we saw you when we were in Igen."

"I was busy with child most of that time," Javissa admitted. Jeila cast narrowed eyes in her direction; there was something that the woman wasn't saying.

Terin pointed to the far wall where a large leather set of riding gear was stowed. "He had that made for me—the gold fitting there. He said—"

"'This is yours and no other's,'" Javissa finished, smiling at the young woman as Terin's mouth opened in a look of surprise. "He told me about it, when he had it commissioned."

"Traders trade," Terin said. "How can I pay this debt?"

"You have, many times over," Javissa assured her. "And again, just now."

Terin's lips worked anxiously. "It was a great gift he gave me," she said. "It gave me hope."

"I'm glad," Javissa said. "Don't lose it."

"Did he say something more to you?" Terin asked, pouncing on the other woman's words for a hidden meaning.

Javissa shook her head. "No," she said, "he was careful not to reveal too much to me."

"And how did you get here, on this day at this time?"

"He told me that I would know when to take the dark road," Javissa said.

"And he left word that I would find a home where none has ever been, but that first I would have to go to Telgar and save the queens," Jeriz said.

"Save the queens?" Jeila repeated, glancing at Terin.

"I'd say he has," Terin said, reaching up and tousling his soft, dark hair. "You, me, and now Fiona."

Terin saw Javissa's eyes narrow and looked toward her questioningly. "She's holding up as best she can," the red-haired weyrwoman said in apology for Fiona's outburst.

"She is," Javissa agreed. Her expression softened. "Tenniz and Mother Karina spoke so highly of her—"

"That you were shocked at her explosion," Jeila finished. She shook her head. "I've heard of her exploding a time or two before. It's been necessary, although not always directed in the right direction."

"But why me?" Javissa asked with less passion than curiosity.

"Because of Tenniz's words to Lorana," Terin said, gesturing for them to move away from the weyrkids. "And his words to her."

"His message was: '*It will turn out all right*,'" Javissa recalled.

"Which is why she's so angry," Terin said, smiling sadly. "First Lorana, then F'jian, and then—" her expression crumpled as she saw Jeila.

"Good to see you up and about," Bekka said, having listened in quietly on the conversation. She flicked her eyes toward Jeila. "You're well enough, will you join Birentir with the wounded?"

Jeila opened her mouth, eyes flashing angrily, then thought better of it and nodded, reaching out to pat Bekka on the shoulder. "As you wish, Journeyman."

"Weyrwoman," Bekka said, nodding respectfully but not giving on her determination. She looked at Javissa. "Can I leave you with Terin? Fiona's right that Jeriz shouldn't have left her alone, no matter what she said."

Terin gave the healer an angry glare and growled, but Bekka was having none of it. "You've been through a lot, you haven't finished grieving." Bekka nodded toward Javissa. "She knows something of grief."

"I promised Fiona—" Jeriz began.

"And broke that promise," Bekka rode over his words. She smiled at him for a moment. "We all make mistakes and Fiona knows that. She knows you meant the best, too. But you've got to show us now that you've learned the lesson and won't make the mistake again."

Jeriz eyed her for a long time and then nodded. "I'm sorry," he said to Bekka, then Terin, then his mother. "She sounded so happy."

"And why wouldn't I be?" Terin demanded. "I saw him again and he said he'd be there whenever I needed him."

"Most," Javissa corrected absently.

"Pardon?" Terin asked, goggling at her.

"Didn't he say that he'd be there when you needed him the most?"

"Yes," Terin agreed slowly, surprised that this new woman had known that. "How did you know?"

"One day, I will tell you," Javissa promised. "But for now, we cannot break time."

"You've met Lorana," Terin, Jeila, and Bekka said in chorus. "When?" Jeila added accusingly.

"Turns back," Javissa told her. Her eyes took on a sad look as she added, "A lifetime ago."

Fiona woke to the sound of voices. A girl's and a woman's. She opened her eyes.

"Fiona, would you sit for me?" the woman asked her.

"Lorana?"

"She looks older than the last time," Jirana said by way of agreement.

"Kindan says the colors are at Benden," Fiona said drowsily.

"They are," Lorana agreed. "But I've got them here, too." She paused and smiled at the younger woman. "If you could sit up for me, you don't have to get out of bed."

"Can I lean on Jirana here?" Fiona asked even as the little girl prodded and pushed her into position.

"She's my sister," Jirana said proudly.

"Then I'm your sister, too," Lorana said, her eyes suddenly wet with tears.

"Really?" Jirana asked in surprise, her eyes going from the dark-haired almond-eyed woman to the blond Weyrwoman with the sea-green eyes and back in surprise.

"Really," Fiona agreed fervently. "We are sisters in heart."

"Father said that you would help her grow her heart back," Jirana said, leaning against Fiona. "Can you do that?"

"I'll try," Fiona said, glancing at the teary face of her friend. "Are you back for good?"

Lorana shook her head, her tears coming more freely and reaching out a hand imploringly toward Fiona. Fiona took it and leaned forward, stroking it against her cheek. Softly, Lorana tugged it free. "Let me draw you now, so that we have this memory."

"Frozen in time," Fiona agreed, leaning against Jirana and cupping the child closer toward her with her free hand. She did not bother to question why Lorana wanted to draw her again because she knew she would get no answer. There was something tragic in Lorana's actions, like she was feeling pain or a compulsion to draw Fiona now.

Lorana sketched quickly, glancing up at them for a moment, then down to her work as she drew with bold, strong strokes.

"What happened to your face?" Fiona asked, eyes narrowing critically. She noticed a line on her cheek, a thin scar. Threadscore? A knife cut?

"Nothing," Lorana assured her.

"You didn't look like that the last time—" Jirana hushed when Lorana raised a finger toward her in caution.

"What did I say?" Lorana reminded the youngster.

"You cannot break time," Jirana said in depressed tones. But she lifted her eyes once more and added, "But sometimes you can cheat it."

"Shh," Lorana said, with a wink, even as her other hand sketched more quick strokes. "And remember."

Lorana finished quickly, kissed Fiona on the forehead, did the same with Jirana and had them lie back down.

"Sleep!" Lorana said when Fiona protested. "You need your rest."

"They think you're dead," Fiona told her in a troubled voice. "They think I'm imagining you like Terin's imagining F'jian."

"You're not," Lorana said. "And she's not."

She was gone before her words registered with Fiona. When they did, Fiona cried out, "What do you mean?"

"She's gone, Fiona," Jirana said, trying out the Weyrwoman's name with some trepidation.

"Do you know what she meant by that?"

"I'm only little," Jirana said. "She talks like my father sometimes."

"Your father died before you were born," Fiona reminded her absently.

"He did," Jirana agreed, sounding sad. "But I've seen him several times since then."

Fiona closed her eyes, confused, wondering why a child's imagination should be so full of strange things. Slowly, mind still churning, she drifted off to sleep, secure in knowing that she was comforting her "sister."

"Fiona, you were fellis-drugged, there was no way you'd wake up," Bekka assured her irritably for the third time at lunch the next day.

"Ask Jirana," Fiona said.

"Jirana has seven Turns," Bekka reminded her. "She's a lovely child, and certain to be like her father, but at the moment you're lucky she's not collecting tunnel snakes for pets."

Fiona fumed at the healer.

"Look," Bekka said, "I've got to tell you how I feel and what I know. And what I know is that you were fellis-drugged, you were exhausted, worried, and tired. It's far more likely that you imagined all this than that it really happened." She paused, seeing the fire in Fiona's eyes. "Besides," she added with sympathy, "I asked Jirana and she said she didn't remember."

"She didn't?" Fiona hadn't seen the child since she'd woken that morning.

"No," Bekka said, shaking her head. "She seemed rather shy about the whole thing." Bekka made a face. "Maybe I shouldn't have forced you on her the first night in a new place."

"We're sisters," Fiona said.

"You're sisters with all the women on Pern," Bekka said, her voice full of mixed condescension and love. "You've got a big heart, you are never upset, and always hopeful." She took another breath and patted the Weyrwoman's hand. "And you're pregnant and likely to imagine the most amazing things, even when not fellis-drowsy."

"Isn't the fellis bad for the babies?"

Bekka shook her head. "Your worry is worse and the dose was low."

"So I could have woken up, couldn't I?" Fiona asked, pouncing on this information.

Bekka pursed her lips in thought, then shook her head. "Possible," she admitted. "But really unlikely."

F iona found Terin with Jeriz, watching the weyrlings drill across the Bowl.

"Aren't you two supposed to be working with them?" Fiona asked.

They both gave her looks of surprise.

"Aren't we all supposed to be working with them?" she added ruefully, glancing around. "Where's Jeila?"

When neither had an answer, Fiona said, "Terin, please have Kurinth ask Jeila if she and Tolarth would like to join us in a bit of flying." She saw their looks and explained, "I'm going to look for Jirana. Then we'll tack up Talenth and give these weyrlings some inspiration."

"Can I ride with you?" Terin asked.

"No, I'd like you to ride with Jeila," Fiona said, shaking her head apologetically. She turned to Jeriz. "I'd like to bring you and your sister with me."

"If it pleases you, Weyrwoman, my duty is with Terin," Jeriz said with stiff formality.

Fiona pouted, then sighed. "Jeriz, I apologize for my outburst yesterday."

"You were tired," Terin said. "Bekka was right, you were overdue for a meltdown."

"'Meltdown'?"

"Like when Ellor destroyed that pot she'd set empty over the fire," Terin said, mimicking molten metal sprinkling over a fire. "Meltdown."

"Thanks," Fiona said. "So now I'm an empty pot that's sitting on a fire."

"Nah," Terin said, glancing toward Jeriz and winking. "Jeriz here took you off before you got too hot."

To their surprise, the boy giggled at the notion. Fiona reached forward and tousled his hair.

"Thank you, young trader, for the gift of release," Fiona intoned in mock formality.

"I didn't mean to upset you," Jeriz apologized.

"We all make mistakes," Fiona said dismissively. "But you are right, your place is with Terin." Jeriz nodded even though it was obvious that he regretted missing out on his chance to ride on a queen. "So we'll ask Jeila if Tolarth can carry you both, and ask Talenth if she'll take me, my sister, and your mother."

"Your sister?" Jeriz asked, looking around in surprise.

"I'm sorry, did I tell you I was borrowing your sister as my own?"

"You can have her," Jeriz said emphatically.

Terin and Fiona shared a laugh.

Fiona found Javissa with Bekka. She saw the trader's eyes widen and how she braced herself, but Fiona bowed her head low, saying, "Javissa, I ask forgiveness for the offense I gave you yesterday."

"Fiona—" Bekka began with a trace of exasperation in her voice.

"Your husband was a valued friend of ours and I am ashamed at how poorly I returned his kindness," Fiona continued, ignoring the healer. "I offer my apology, the courtesy of the Weyr, and my heart in penance."

"Shards, Fiona, you really go overboard, sometimes," Bekka said. She was rewarded with the glare of a piercing set of sea-green eyes. Bekka shook her head and groaned. "Javissa, this is Fiona. Fiona, this is Javissa, she's had two children, she understands about pregnancy, and she's heard all about *you*."

"And my meltdowns?" Fiona asked, feeling somewhat chagrined.

"Tenniz spoke highly of you," Javissa said, reaching out her hand once more. Fiona took it gratefully.

"I came to apologize and to offer you a ride on Talenth," Fiona said. "Also, I came to ask if you would let me adopt your daughter as my sister." She dimpled as she added, "I suppose that'd make you my mother."

"Oh!" Javissa exclaimed, slumping against the wall.

"Are you all right?"

"Yes," Javissa said, recovering and standing up. Her lips quirked upward.

"Tenniz?" Fiona asked, her eyes narrowing suspiciously.

Javissa nodded, barely suppressing a laugh. "He said that I would be mother to a Weyrwoman taller than I am."

"He had a terrible sense of humor," Fiona observed.

"Oh, Weyrwoman, you don't know the half of it," Javissa said in fervent agreement. "As for your offer, I'd love to ride with you."

"And my request?"

"Bekka's already told me all about it," Javissa said. She cocked an eye toward Fiona consideringly. "You know she squirms."

"Not as much as Jeriz," Fiona countered. She lowered her voice as she added, "And she's scared."

"About her gift?"

Fiona nodded. "I don't know what I can do to help, except be there for her, and offer 'sisterly' support."

"That's more than Jeriz can offer," Javissa said. She lifted her head to meet Fiona's eyes. The taller Weyrwoman met them frankly, still startled at how amazingly green they were. Javissa nodded as she made her decision. "I'm sure that Jirana will be happy to be sisters with you."

"Thank you!" Fiona said. "Now, if you'll follow me, we need to get you some riding gear."

It took longer than Fiona had hoped, especially as Javissa was a conscientious mother who made certain that both her children were properly garbed before allowing them to mount.

"We nearly froze the last time," Javissa apologized to Fiona.

"Part of that was *between*," Fiona assured her. "It gets cold, flying, but not that cold."

The two queens rose into the air with their properly attired, properly strapped-on passengers and circled upward, climbing gently toward the watch heights. The watch dragon bugled at them and Fiona was delighted to see how Jeila returned the formal salute. And then, coordinating with Kindan through Xhinna's Tazith, they began a series of steep glides into and out of the Weyr Bowl, banking up sharply as the sheer face of the cliff came toward them and twirling on wing tip to repeat the circuit.

Fiona was surprised to see the whole Bowl fill with weyrfolk, young and old, looking up and pointing as the two queens worked in sequence from east to west across the Bowl, up to the heights, back around to the Star Stones, and diving again for another pass.

When Kindan told them they were done, the weyrfolk below clapped in admiration of the maneuvers.

"They like us!" Jirana exclaimed from her place in front of Fiona and behind her mother.

"Yes, they do!" Fiona agreed, laughing. With a stroke of praise, she asked Talenth to bring them back to the ground.

The queen obliged, landing daintily with not even the slightest jolt.

Well done! Fiona thought.

That was like a weyrling drill, Talenth thought wistfully.

Maybe we should talk to T'mar and see if we can't do it again, Fiona thought. Talenth agreed wholeheartedly as she ambled over to the queens' ledge.

The next three days passed with a slowly building sense of dread for the impending Threadfall at Fort Weyr. Fiona heard from Ista's senior queen rider, Dalia, that Ista would fly the Fall with Fort. She and T'mar talked about it in private.

"They're almost as strong as Benden," T'mar said.

"But their leadership is weak after the loss of C'rion and M'tal."

"They're only loaning a wing." T'mar sounded no more certain than Fiona felt. "And it's a morning Fall."

"True," Fiona agreed, not bothering to point out how the sun could easily blind riders to Thread falling above and behind them, similar to the way that the evening Fall that T'mar had survived had so surprised them.

"We need to conserve our strength," T'mar said regretfully. "I've spoken with K'lior and he agrees."

"Cisca said the same to me," Fiona admitted with a grimace. "It's just that—"

"It'd be nice to help our friends," T'mar guessed.

"And I hate to be always begging for help," Fiona agreed.

"It would be nice to be able to offer it," T'mar said. "Especially as it seems so—"

"Inept," Fiona concluded, hastily adding, "And you're not, you've done nothing wrong."

T'mar shook his head ruefully. "I wish sometimes it didn't feel so much like it, then."

"We started this Pass two thousand dragons short," Fiona reminded him. "It could never be easy."

"Especially after we lost D'gan and Telgar," T'mar agreed with a frown.

"The weyrlings are doing well," Fiona said, changing the topic in hopes of brightening the mood. T'mar nodded. "Kindan is handling them well."

"Yes," T'mar agreed absently. He grinned as he added, "Are you and Jeila doing your circuits again today?"

"I don't know," Fiona admitted. "I thought if things go badly at Fort, we might offer help."

T'mar tightened his lips and nodded. "It won't be long now."

"Hours yet, Weyrleader."

"Hunh," T'mar said, pushing himself from his seat. "Then I guess we've got time to do some drills."

"I'll get Kindan to have the weyrlings practice with firestone," Fiona said, rising to join him. When he gave her a look, she added, "It'll keep their minds off the Fall."

"And how are their minds?" T'mar asked, pausing for her answer.

"Muzzy," Fiona replied. "All of them."

"Terin more than most."

"I'm not so sure."

T'mar made a face, but shook his head, avoiding further conversation by moving off with a parting wave.

Fiona joined Jeila, Bekka, and Birentir on their rounds. They returned three more dragons and their riders to fighting duty. The three were glad for the release; they'd all been badly mauled and had had to wait at least sixty days watching their companions fight without them. They were all eager to get back into the air and do their part.

Jeila seemed in better spirits, although Fiona felt she could detect some hidden melancholy in the older woman. Bekka had warned her that that was natural; it would take time for Jeila to work through her grief.

They were finished looking at the last of the injured on the seventh level when Talenth reported that Fort had met the leading edge. They walked back down quietly, with Fiona and Jeila glancing at each other from time to time as the reports were relayed by Cisca's queen, Melirth.

The first dragon lost was Istan, and Fiona winced at the report.

Back down in the Weyr Bowl, the weyrlings were stacking firestone while T'mar had the fighting wings drill in low passes, inspired, he'd admitted, by Fiona's and Jeila's tight flying in their circuits. "C'tov was particularly impressed," T'mar had told Fiona when they'd discussed it. "He thinks it will build cohesion."

"It'll certainly breed caution," Fiona said, shaking her head ruefully. "If you're not careful in timing when to pull up, you can easily find your dragon trying to run up the walls of the Weyr."

T'mar chuckled; he'd seen how Fiona had nearly misjudged one circuit the day before.

Another casualty, this one from Fort, was reported by Melirth, and Fiona sucked in a breath in sorrow. Two lost, now one injured. Three ducked *between* with Thread. Fiona heard Jeila's sigh of relief when all three returned to the fight unscathed.

The difference in times meant that Fort's morning Fall occured in the afternoon for Telgar and lasted through to early evening.

Fiona found herself crawling into bed with Kindan and Jirana, exhausted by the stress and sorrow of the Fall. In the end, Fort had lost only two dragons outright, but Ista had lost three and between them the two Weyrs could count another eight dragons out of the fight. Fort now could call on only seventy-nine fighting dragons; Ista on ninety-four.

The mood the next morning was grim. T'mar called his wingleaders to the Council Room. Fiona, Jeila, and Terin joined them, the young redhead insisting, "It's my duty, too."

Kindan came in both his capacities of weyrlingmaster and harper.

"Right now we have seventy-six fighting dragons," T'mar began.

"As well as twenty-two mauled and recovering, eight lightly injured and recovering," Fiona added.

"High Reaches has seventy-four, Fort seventy-nine, Ista ninety-four, and Benden has the most with one hundred and fifteen," Kindan reported.

"They've got a total of one hundred and twelve mauled dragonpairs and seventy-three injured," Fiona said.

H'nez's brows furrowed as he worked through the numbers. "So with the weyrlings and the injured we'd have nearly another Weyr's strength."

"And we've somewhat less than a full Weyr's strength on all Pern," C'tov said.

T'mar spread a look between Fiona and Kindan as he asked, "Any idea how much longer we'll be able to fight?"

"Just by the numbers, there'd easily be another hundred Falls," Terin said. The others looked at her. "We're losing about four dragons each Fall, and we've got more than four hundred fighting."

"But at some point, there'll be too few to fight anything, even if we time it," H'nez reminded her.

"But we don't know what that number is," Fiona said. "If we decide that a Flight is the least number, then we've . . ."

"Around eighty-five more Falls," Terin responded. "That would be a bit less than ten months from now."

"Even taking every risk, the weyrlings won't be able to fly for two Turns," T'mar said with a grimace.

H'nez began, "So we'd be defenseless for—"

But Fiona raised a hand, turning her head sharply toward the Weyr Bowl.

"B'nik and Tullea are coming," Fiona said. She frowned as she communed with Talenth. "So are Sonia and D'vin."

"Dalia, J'lian, and S'maj have just jumped *between* at Ista," Jeila reported.

"Cisca and K'lior are coming with my father," Fiona said. She rose from her seat and raced toward the Bowl.

Talenth, warn Shaneese.

▼ ▼ ▼

As it was, Fiona and T'mar were able to greet their unannounced arrivals with all due courtesy.

"Cisca!" Fiona called, racing into the taller woman's arms and grabbing her in a firm hug.

"Fiona," the Fort Weyrwoman said as she recovered, "I thought you were pregnant."

"Nothing stops her from greeting friends," Bekka called out sourly from her vantage point. Cisca smiled at her and Bekka nodded back until the Weyrwoman noted Bekka's new rank knots and her eyebrows rose approvingly.

"Father!" Fiona cried as she let go of Cisca. Lord Bemin greeted her with a tight hug and a kiss on the head.

"Is she a terrible patient, Bekka?" the Lord Holder asked over his daughter's head.

"Unless I sit on her, my lord," Bekka said. "And then she becomes biddable for a short while."

Bemin's eyes sought out Kindan and he addressed the harper solemnly. "Masterharper Zist sends his regrets and asks if you will sit in his place."

"Is he ill?" Kindan asked in sudden alarm.

"He's old, lad," Bemin said in a sad voice. "I think he knows he's failing."

Kindan frowned. Fiona moved beside him and touched his arm lightly. She knew that Zist had hoped to promote him to Master, and guessed that the old harper saw Kindan as his successor. She knew from her childhood at Fort Hold that none of the current Masters—Kelsa, Nonala, Verilan, nor any of the others—were the slightest bit interested in becoming the Masterharper nor, as Fiona had heard her father say, were they up for the political duties involved. Kindan had demonstrated that ability long ago, and not just during the Plague, but also with the handling of Aleesa, the old WherMaster. She was equally certain that Kindan did not feel as capable for the role as the Masterharper did.

"I will return as soon as I can," Kindan swore.

"Soonest would be best," Bemin agreed. He turned to T'mar and Fiona. "I stand for all Lord Holders in this meeting."

"And what, my lord," Fiona asked with a formal bow, "is the purpose of this meeting?"

"We need to know what to do," Bemin said. The others all turned toward him. "We must make plans."

"We will fight to the last dragon," Fiona declared.

"But when do we start feeding the queens firestone?" Sonia asked challengingly. "When the last of the bronzes, browns, blues, and greens are all gone?"

"Or before then?" Cisca asked.

"You're too many for the Council Room," Fiona said, gesturing toward the Kitchen Cavern. "We'll meet there."

"We were just talking about this," Terin said as she walked beside Fiona. "How did they know?"

"In hard times, the same thoughts come to many," Bemin responded as he matched his stride with theirs.

"These are hard times," H'nez agreed.

"The first dragonriders dealt with harder times," Fiona said staunchly. "Sean and Sorka survived."

"They had help," Kindan said. "Don't you recall those flying machines that the Ancients used?"

"But at some point the flying machines wore out," Fiona said. "And then they had not many more dragons than we."

"How did they survive, then?" Bemin wondered.

"The holders all lived in Fort," Kindan said. "It was only when their numbers were great enough that the dragonriders spread out across the rest of Pern."

"But what about Thread?" Sonia asked.

They entered the Kitchen Cavern and Fiona saw that Shaneese had already set the high table with a range of foods from snacks to full meals to meet the varying hours of the Weyrs.

"Perhaps the fire-lizards helped," Fiona suggested after they'd all been seated. "They could have caught a lot of Thread on their own— it was known that they hunted it."

"Or the watch-whers," J'lian said.

"There were fewer watch-whers than dragons," D'vin said, shaking his head.

"I don't know, Weyrleader," Kindan said, "we've never had a good grasp of their numbers and how quickly they breed."

"Which brings up another question," Sonia said, glancing around to be certain she had everyone's attention. "By my Records, our queens should have been rising twice a Turn for the past three or more and yet they haven't."

"Could they have sensed the illness coming somehow?" B'nik wondered.

"We won't know if they'll start rising more often for a while yet," Fiona said. "It's not been quite half a Turn since the last mating flights."

"True," Tullea agreed. "But even if they do, it won't help us now."

"Why not go back in time like before?" Bemin asked.

"We've no place to go that's safe, Father," Fiona said. "All the time in Igen's been used and there are only so many places one can put a dragon."

"And feed them," Bemin agreed sadly. He noticed the way the Weyrleaders looked at him and he shook his head, adding, "Not a complaint, Weyrleaders, merely an observation of fact."

"What we need are two thousand fighting dragons," T'mar said. "From the egg, it takes three Turns to raise them to fighting strength."

"At a herdbeast every sevenday that adds up to a large number of beasts," Bemin said.

"They eat less when they're younger," Terin said, her face bearing an abstracted look as she thought of her queen. "But, roughly, that's three hundred and twelve thousand herdbeasts."

"We holders are expanding as fast as we can, but after the Plague, we're still not up to those levels."

"One hundred and fifty-six thousand a Turn at full strength," Terin added.

"Well, at least you're not some invisible voice this time," Tullea remarked sourly, recalling Terin's presence at the last High Council.

"That's correct, Weyrwoman," Terin said with an edge to her voice. Fiona smothered a laugh as she saw Tullea and Sonia eye the young redhead warily, clearly upgrading their image of her from young child to woman in her own right.

That's right, Fiona thought, don't underestimate my friends.

"Lorana will have an answer," Fiona blurted on the heels of her thought.

Her comment was greeted with pained looks around the table.

"I'm not sure that we're . . . ready . . . for Lorana's answer yet," Dalia said into the silence that fell.

"She'll come," Fiona declared.

"I wish she'd come soon, then," Tullea said. "I'm tired of riding on someone else's dragon."

"Fiona," Bemin spoke up, his tone carefully modulated. Fiona turned to her father and he continued slowly, measuring his words, "Even were she to return, what help could she bring?"

"Are you sure you're not pinning your hopes on her simply because she helped us so much the last time?" Sonia asked gently.

"I've seen her," Fiona said. "She drew my portrait, twice now."

"I can see how *that* helps!" Tullea snorted.

"If you've seen her," Sonia said, "why hasn't she remained with you?"

"And sent back my dragon!" Tullea snapped.

"She wouldn't say."

"For the moment, we must do what we can without her," T'mar inserted smoothly, trying to move the conversation back on topic and away from a potentially painful and embarrassing outcome for his Weyrwoman.

"Look," Fiona continued, undaunted, "it makes sense. Lorana went to get aid. That's why the queens aren't rising as much, they know that there will be enough dragons when we need them."

"Perhaps," Kindan allowed, his expression grim. "Or perhaps she knew that there was no hope and grief overcame her."

"She was carrying a child, Kindan!" Fiona protested. "Your child. Do you think she would throw that away?"

"If she thought the alternative was worse, yes," Kindan told her grimly.

"And she took my dragon with her!" Tullea snarled, turning angrily toward Fiona. "If her purpose was so pure, Weyrwoman, why didn't she send back my queen?"

"The only way to go *between* is on a dragon," Fiona reminded her.

"Or a watch-wher," Kindan added. Fiona accepted his small aid with an angry shake of her head.

"No one can live *between* without a dragon or a watch-wher," Sonia said, giving Fiona a sympathetic look. "If she'd wanted to go *between* forever, then she would have had to do it a-dragonback."

"And, consider," Kindan added, meeting Fiona's eyes squarely, "by your accounting, she'd seen K'tan go *between* forever—"

"Saving B'nik!" Fiona protested.

"—saving B'nik," Kindan allowed with a nod. "So she had an example in front of her." He paused, shaking his head. "Why couldn't it be that she felt there was no hope and decided to follow him, to go where her Arith went."

"She wouldn't," Fiona said, shaking her head firmly, her eyes wet with unshed tears. "She loves you too much, Kindan, she'd never leave you."

"Never leave *you*," Kindan said, shaking his head. "You can't believe that she'd leave you."

"Harper—" Bemin began warningly.

"I'm sorry, Fiona," Kindan said, "but all your life people have been leaving you, they left before you were born. Perhaps you just can't let them go."

"Kindan . . ." Fiona said, her voice fading into sobs as she dropped her head into her hands.

"Harper," Bemin repeated, "if you are counseling despair, I think you've succeeded."

"'Step by step, moment by moment,'" Fiona said, suddenly on her feet, eyes flashing, hand raised with a finger pointing accusingly at Kindan. "'We get through another day.'

"Listen to your words, Kindan," Fiona spoke, her voice rolling through the room with power so great the dragons outside roared. "We *must* survive, we must find a way."

She glanced at the Weyrleaders and Weyrwomen. "Maybe Lorana is gone, maybe not," she told them. "The harper is right that she must, for the moment at least, be out of our thinking." She glanced at Kindan. "It was foolish of me to pin my hopes solely on her." She shook her head. "So we must find another way. *That* is our duty to our weyrfolk"—she nodded toward Shaneese and the others who stood rooted by her outburst—"to our holders"—she nodded to her father—"to our crafters"—and she looked toward Kindan and then down to her chest as she finished with—"and to our children." Her eyes went to Kindan again.

The harper rose and moved toward her. She held him back with a hand.

"We have yet to consider the watch-whers," Fiona said. "I spoke with the Mastersmith some time ago about building sunshades dark enough that they might fly in the day."

"I know something of this," Kindan said. The others looked at him and Fiona waved a hand for him to continue. "Master Zellany reports that they have delivered a pair of these shades to Nuella." He paused for a moment. "Nuella tells me that Nuellask tried them and could use them for an hour just before sunset. Otherwise, the sun was too bright for her."

"Can Zellany make them darker?" Sonia wondered.

"He's trying," Kindan said. "It will take him another month to prepare a darker set."

"Have him make three sets of different darknesses," D'vin suggested.

Kindan nodded in agreement with the suggestion.

"What about the fire-lizards?" Terin asked. Everyone turned toward her questioningly. "Well, if they helped Sean and Sorka, could we not get them to help us?"

"The sickness—" Kindan began.

"But we've a cure for that," Terin said.

"Indeed," Bemin agreed. "But I'm afraid that since they were sent to Southern, many of them would have already sickened and died."

Terin blanched.

"So, where does that leave us?" Sonia asked.

Before anyone could answer, they heard the bellow of the watch dragon issuing a challenge and the voice of a queen bugling in response.

"Minith!" Tullea cried, jumping out of her seat and racing out to the Weyr Bowl.

"Lorana!" Fiona called in triumph, glaring at Kindan on her way after Tullea.

Outside, a crowd of weyrfolk were clustered around the gold.

Benden's queen had returned.

Riderless.

EIGHT

Holder, crafter, harper know
Every dragon's loss is a blow
To strength and power of the Weyr
And the hope of all everywhere.

Tullea insisted upon departing immediately with her queen and demanded that B'nik come with her. "We don't know how long she's been gone if Lorana's been timing it; she might be ready to rise any time now."

The departure of Benden broke the quorum of Weyrleaders and Sonia and D'vin of High Reaches departed soon after, followed by the Istans. Cisca and K'lior remained long enough to let Bemin say farewell to his daughter and then they returned to Fort. Cisca promised to be in touch, but Fiona noticed how the Weyrwoman kept her eyes more on T'mar than herself.

"I'd better see to the weyrlings," Kindan said to T'mar, keeping his face from Fiona.

"Yes," T'mar agreed in a cold voice, "do that."

"I'm coming with you," Terin said, darting after the taller harper. Kindan paused, gesturing to the young weyrwoman invitingly.

When Terin caught up, he checked his stride to match hers.

"She's the Weyrwoman, you must respect her," Terin said in a tight voice as they strolled across the Weyr Bowl.

"I do," Kindan said.

"She's right more than she's wrong."

Kindan nodded in agreement. "She's strong-willed."

"Stubborn," Terin allowed.

"She doesn't give up."

"Nor did you," Terin said, glancing up at him challengingly. "Are you so upset now because she's learned from you too well?"

"She didn't learn from me," Kindan said with a frown. "She learned from the ballads."

"The ballads?"

"Songs become more than truth," Kindan told her. She gave him a questioning look. "I was scared during the Plague. I didn't know what I was doing, I wasn't sure that we'd survive."

"But you didn't give up."

"Because I couldn't," Kindan said. He shook his head at the memory. "I was much younger and I wanted to impress Koriana, to impress Lord Bemin . . . and I wanted to live."

"And you did all that," Terin reminded him. "Because you didn't give up."

"I didn't give up because I couldn't," Kindan said with pain in his voice. "After Koriana died, baby Fiona was bawling her head off, Bemin couldn't remember where he'd put her"—he stopped and met Terin's eyes squarely—"it was for her that I didn't give up."

"So why are you giving up now?" Terin asked him softly. "She's here, she's fighting with all that she's got, doing all that she can, and she's probably carrying your child."

"I don't know how we'll survive," Kindan admitted bleakly. "We're being worn down, dragon by dragon. At some point, we'll have too few to fly a Fall and they'll all die gloriously and then the queens will chew firestone and die gloriously and—"

Terin's slap was as hard as it was unexpected. Kindan raised a hand to his face in surprise and gave the redhead a wide-eyed look of astonishment.

"That's enough," Terin told him harshly. "You are going to go over to those weyrlings and you're going to train them. And *we're* going to survive. That's all there is to it." She heaved a deep sigh. "And if you can't figure out how to save us, Fiona will."

"Yes, weyrwoman," Kindan said. Then, to her surprise, he leaned over and kissed her on the forehead. "You are right; I was wrong. We'll figure it out even if we have to send you and Fiona to the Red Star to stomp out the Thread strand by strand."

"Do you think we could *go* to the Red Star?" Terin asked, with serious consideration in her eyes.

Kindan gave her a worried look. "I think we'd be wiser to stay as far from it as we can." He thought on it a moment more and added hastily, "And whatever you do, don't mention it to Fiona or she's likely to try."

"Good point," Terin agreed.

Mekiar was waiting for Fiona when she entered Talenth's weyr.

"You heard?"

"News travels fastest when shouted," the ex-dragonrider explained. Fiona made a face. Jirana came out from Fiona's quarters and saw her expression.

"Why were you crying?" the solemn-eyed girl asked.

"I heard something that made me sad," Fiona said, not wishing to distress the youngster.

"What?"

Fiona sighed, realizing that Jirana would continue to ask questions until she got to the bottom of the matter. "The others think that my friend was too sad to continue and that she went *between* forever."

"They're stupid," Jirana declared with childish certainty.

"How so?" Mekiar asked, peering down at her with a kindly expression.

"You're talking about Lorana, right?" Jirana asked. Fiona nodded. "Well, it's not her time."

"How do you know?" Fiona asked, feeling hope ready to rise within her once more.

"Father told me," Jirana said.

"He told me it would turn out all right," Fiona said morosely.

"He said that it's always darkest before the dawn," Jirana said as if in response. Fiona cocked her head at the youngster and Jirana explained, "If it's going to turn out all right, doesn't it have to turn darkest first?"

"She has the right of it," Mekiar said with a dry chuckle. His expression sobered as he added, "But we can't be sure that it is darkest just yet."

"Even so," Jirana persisted, "if my father said that it will turn out all right, it will."

Fiona smiled and nodded. "I suppose you're right," she said, trying to keep her voice cheerful.

"In this much, Weyrwoman, she's correct: We still have hope," Mekiar said.

"While we have you," Jirana agreed, turning her gaze to the older man with interest. "Your eyes are sad, but your mouth smiles."

"This is Mekiar," Fiona said, making introductions. "He works the pottery wheel and if you're very nice, he might teach you."

"What color was your dragon?" Jirana asked.

"I rode a brown," Mekiar replied with just the slightest waver in his voice.

"I'll bet you were good," Jirana said. "When I get my dragon, will you teach me?"

"You're a bit young yet to be thinking of dragons," Mekiar temporized.

"My father was the seer for the traders," Jirana said. "I'll be a seer too, when I'm older."

"Is that so?" Mekiar asked with the polite tone that adults use with children they don't believe, but don't feel pressed to correct, either.

"It is," Jirana returned with aplomb.

"Mekiar, are we keeping you?" Fiona asked, offering the older man a way out of the conversation.

"No, you're keeping a wheel from its work," the pottery master told her with a small nod of his head. He smiled wryly at Jirana as he added, "Perhaps two of them."

"Did we schedule a time?" Fiona asked, eyebrows narrowed as she rubbed the back of her neck, trying to recall the appointment.

"No," Mekiar told her. "The time is always yours, Weyrwoman, but I thought that perhaps this would be a good time for you."

"Okay," Fiona agreed. "I don't think there's much else I could do anyway."

"If I make something, can I keep it?" Jirana asked, spreading her question amongst the two adults.

"If you wish," Mekiar said.

"Could it be mine for always and forever?" Jirana persisted, suddenly becoming all bouncy child again, fidgety with excitement and worry.

"Always and forever," Fiona agreed.

"Then I will make something for you," Jirana said, nodding toward Fiona. "For you to keep always and forever."

"And I will make something for *you*, always and forever," Fiona said, reaching for the youngster's hand. Jirana gladly took hold and, swinging arms together, the two traipsed back to the Kitchen Cavern and Mekiar's pottery wheels.

Much later, when the sun had gone down and the Weyr recovered some semblance of calm, Fiona and Jirana returned to her quarters. Their "gifts" were still drying, to be fired in the kiln. Neither was extravagant; Jirana had managed a passable mug and Fiona had designed a nice plate, but the young girl was thrilled with the thought of painting her finished work over the next few days.

Fiona was getting ready for sleep when footsteps announced the arrival of a pair of people at Talenth's weyr. It was Kindan and Javissa. Javissa smiled at her daughter and gestured for her to come with her.

"You'll stay with me tonight, little one," her mother said. Jirana turned a gimlet eye on Kindan and warned him, "Don't make her cry."

"I'll try."

"Don't try," Jirana said sternly. "Your word as harper."

"My word as harper," Kindan responded in all seriousness. Jirana bit her lower lip while she considered him, then nodded, slipping her hand into her mother's and tugging her out along behind her, exclaiming happily, "I made a mug today, Momma!"

The sounds of the happy banter died away, leaving Fiona alone and awkward with the blue-eyed harper.

"Terin tore strips out of me," Kindan said into the awkward silence that fell. Fiona said nothing and Kindan strode forward, reaching for her hand, which she allowed him to take, unresisting. "If our child is a girl, I hope she takes after you."

"Children."

"Pardon?"

"Children," Fiona repeated. "I'm having twins so they're our children."

"Isn't one T'mar's?"

"Will anyone know?" Fiona asked. "And do you seriously believe, Kindan of Telgar, that you can turn your heart on to one and off to another?"

Kindan frowned, shaking his head. "No."

She pulled her hand out of his. Kindan stepped back, shocked, worried. Fiona smiled and shook her head at him, raising her hand to stroke his cheek.

"It's late, let's get to bed," she said, lowering her hand. Kindan grabbed her lowered hand and brought it back to his lips, kissing it. He heard her sigh of joy and pulled her toward him, kissing her deeply.

"'Step by step,'" Kindan said by way of apology.

"Shut up, harper, and get into bed," Fiona said, throwing off her tunic, and sliding under the sheets. "I want your apology in silence."

Kindan paused only for a moment as he absorbed her meaning. Then, with alacrity, he turned the glows, shucked his tunic, and climbed in beside her. Gently, he stroked her cheek, traced the line of her nose, caressed her ears, lowered his lips to hers.

In the end, she was demanding and she would not rest until she got his complete and abject apology—three times over.

"Where is she?" Tullea's harsh voice bellowed and echoed around the Bowl walls early the next morning.

Fiona woke in surprise and quickly threw on her robe in the dim light, rushing out to join Kindan, who, by his absence, must have roused sooner than she.

"How can we help you, Weyrwoman?" Fiona called when she spotted Tullea stalking grimly up the slope of the queens' ledge.

"You can give me that dragonstealer so I—"

"Minith is gone?" T'mar asked as he stepped blearily out of the spare queen's weyr that was his quarters.

"No, not Minith," Tullea snapped, pointing toward the bulking outline of her dragon in the distance. "Where did she take Lin and the others?"

"What others?" Fiona asked, her eyes going toward the weyrling barracks with a sudden sense of dread. *Talenth, where's Kurinth?*

She's not here, the queen reported a moment later. Miserably she added, *None of the hatchlings are here.*

T'mar must have received a similar report from Zirenth, for he turned toward Fiona with a look of alarm on his face. "They can't all have gone *between*, could they?"

"And taken Kindan with them?" Fiona replied, shaking her head.

Tullea observed their exchange first with surprise and then with growing comprehension even as Fiona asked Talenth to take tally from the other Weyrs.

"All the weyrlings, queens included, have left all the other Weyrs," Fiona told T'mar. "As well as their riders and several other—" She broke off abruptly then shouted loudly, "Jirana! Where are you?"

A moment later she heard a muffled sound followed by Javissa's voice. "Weyrwoman, what's the matter?"

"Is Jeriz with you?"

"No, he was with Terin," Javissa called back a moment later. She darted out of the dormitory into the Weyr Bowl, bustling over to the queens' ledge. From the ground she looked up to Fiona, Jirana holding on to the side of her nightdress and swaying with fatigue. "Is he in trouble?"

"Or dead," Tullea snapped, her eyes flashing back toward Fiona. "Maybe your precious Lorana wanted company *between*."

"Oh, please!" Fiona said wearily. "If she'd wanted that, she would have left you, B'nik, and Caranth behind half a Turn before when we lost D'gan and Telgar."

Tullea gave the younger woman an affronted look, shocked that anyone her junior would take her on so sharply.

Fiona raised a hand, gesturing toward the Kitchen Cavern. "It's early our time, but our night staff should have something warming, why don't you join us and we can discuss this further?"

Tullea thought for a moment and nodded. She looked suddenly lost and helpless to Fiona's eyes. How much of the woman's irritating manner was a shield for her?

"Javissa, if you and Jirana can't go back to sleep, we'd welcome your company, too," Fiona said, looking down at the trader woman. Javissa nodded once, bent down, and picked up her daughter, ready to carry her, but Fiona leaped down and rushed over. "Please, could I carry her?"

"She's heavy," Javissa cautioned as she passed the girl over.

Fiona placed Jirana easily on her hip and shot a grin toward the surprised trader. "My father made it a custom that I should offer myself to sit the young ones in return for all that their mothers had done the same for me."

"A wise man, a good custom," Javissa allowed.

"She's lighter than most her age," Fiona said. "She's quite a charmer."

"She has her father's temperament," Javissa agreed with a chuckle.

"And Jeriz favors his mother?" Fiona asked teasingly even as she turned politely and waited for Tullea to join them.

"Why are you carrying that child?" Benden's Weyrwoman asked suspiciously.

"This is my sister," Fiona explained. Jirana lifted her head enough at Fiona's words to nod silently, then laid it once more on Fiona's shoulder. "We adopted each other."

"I see," Tullea said in a tone that clearly proved she did not. They took a few more steps and then Tullea said with ill-concealed longing, "Would you like me to carry her for a bit?"

"Is that okay, Javissa?"

"I'm not sure she's awake enough to know the honor of being carried by *two* Weyrwomen," Javissa said, even as she nodded permission.

Fiona passed the small child over to the older Weyrwoman and gently instructed Tullea in the art of centering Jirana's weight on her hip.

"Why, she weighs nothing!" Tullea exclaimed, even as she moved to hike Jirana up and closer to her. She glanced down at the sleepy head resting on her shoulder and Fiona could feel the fear melting in the other woman's heart, feel Tullea's wonder at her tenderness grow.

"I could take her back, if you wish," Fiona offered a few steps later.

"No, it's fine," Tullea said, trying to maintain her chill poise. Fiona exchanged a glance with Javissa; the other woman's eyes danced in amusement. Several paces later, Fiona was not surprised to hear Tullea muse hopefully, "Do you think I might have one this small?"

"I imagine a child of yours would be taller," Fiona told her diffidently. "Especially if she were to favor B'nik."

"They all get bigger over time," Javissa offered as she noticed Tullea's look: It was apparent that the Weyrwoman was having second thoughts with this mention of size. "Your baby would be much smaller to start, and she'd probably not get as big as Jirana here until her fourth or fifth Turn."

By the time they were seated at a table and *klah* was on its way to them, Jirana had so completely beguiled Tullea that the Weyrwoman refused to give her up even when it was obvious that she was uncomfortable in her seat.

Fiona neither asked for her back nor argued with Tullea's silent possession, seeing the serene look in the older woman's eyes. It was the trust, Fiona decided, the total trust that sleeping Jirana bestowed upon Tullea. It was a special insight to the mind and makings of Benden's tetchy Weyrwoman; here was someone who returned trust with fierce loyalty.

Javissa's efforts to arrange her daughter more comfortably on the Weyrwoman were all met with stiff though polite rebuff, as though Tullea were afraid to yield this moment of bonding.

"You must love her very much," Tullea said, turning her head to kiss Jirana's dark hair softly. "She's such a kindly soul."

"She has her moments," Javissa agreed.

T'mar and Shaneese joined them then, Shaneese's eyes going wide when she saw Jirana on Tullea's lap. The headwoman gave Fiona a wry look, which the Weyrwoman returned sanguinely.

"All our weyrlings and dragonets are gone," T'mar reported.

"And several others, too," Fiona said. On a hunch, she asked, *Talenth, is Bekka here?*

No, Talenth said. *I cannot hear her anywhere.*

Not to worry, Fiona assured her. *She's with the others, safe.*

"Lorana took them someplace," T'mar said, his tone making his words a statement.

"Obviously," Fiona agreed, still looking serenely toward Tullea and the small Jirana. For some reason, she felt it vital to lodge the image firmly in her mind so that she would never forget this moment when she saw the Benden Weyrwoman for who she truly was—a loving, kind person who hid her fear in brash armor. A child would help her out of that armor, Fiona thought to herself, just as Jirana is helping her now.

As though awakened by the intensity of Fiona's thoughts, Jirana opened one eye and nuzzled more firmly against Tullea's warmth.

"Can I borrow a jacket?" Tullea asked, looking toward T'mar and then to Javissa. "I don't want her to get cold."

T'mar took off his own jacket and, at Tullea's urging, laid it over both of them. Satisfied, the Weyrwoman snuggled the young child closer to her and closed her eyes, absorbing the new sensation with relish. Tullea opened her eyes just long enough to say to T'mar, "Thank you." A moment later she turned to Fiona. "Would you meet them outside? I don't want to disturb her."

Fiona nodded and rose, imagining that Tullea would next ask them to land softly, for she'd felt the tension rise in the Bowl with the sudden presence of the other Weyrwomen and Weyrleaders. T'mar raised an eyebrow questioningly and she jerked her head for him to join her.

"You might want to set out refreshments at another table," Fiona told Shaneese as she made her way past.

"Of course," Shaneese agreed in an amused tone.

Fiona could never afterward quite decide how she'd managed to calm the others, set a soft tone, and get them all seated without their even glancing at Tullea, two tables over. Perhaps it was something less spoken but more understood by women, some unvoiced feeling of motherhood that made it clear to all that Tullea was having a special moment that required silence and respect.

However it was, all the voices, male and female, never rose above a polite murmur.

And even though Tullea never once stirred from her position with Jirana perched in her lap, Fiona felt certain that it was her serenity that made it possible for the others to believe Fiona's claim that the weyrlings were all right, unharmed, somewhere and some*when* with Lorana.

No one argued the point with her; instead they accepted it, merely trying to imagine this secret location and purpose.

"We were gone less than three days," T'mar recalled, raising a hand to stifle a yawn. "And we had three whole Turns in which to raise the weyrlings."

"I didn't know they could go *between* so early," Sonia said softly.

"'*And in a month, who seeks?*'" Fiona quoted quietly.

"Do you mean to say that the Ballad says when they can go *between*?" D'vin asked.

Fiona nodded. "It would be something they'd have to know back in the old times of the first dragons."

"Why?" Sonia asked.

"Well, I'd imagine that in those early days, they'd have to know how quickly they could move the dragonets from one place to another," Fiona said. "And, from what Lorana said about the Ancient Rooms, the Ancient Timers knew a lot about how dragons work."

"And the woman who brought you back to Igen?" Sonia asked. "Do you think that was Lorana?"

"It could have been Lorana," Fiona said. With a shrug, she added, "Just as easily, it could have been me."

"She's the likely one," Tullea called softly from her seat. "You do your defiance openly; she's more subtle."

"Father said—" Jirana's voice piped up only to be silenced by Tullea's soft shushing.

"I didn't mean to wake you," Tullea apologized.

"Father said that it's always darkest before the dawn," Jirana said, yawning and curling up tighter against Tullea. "And the sun lights everything."

"Shh," Tullea said, rocking as best she could in her chair. "Yes, that's right, it's darkest before dawn, then bright with sun."

Fiona reflected on Jirana's words and rose slowly from her seat. She moved out toward the Weyr Bowl where the sun was even now rising. Silently, Cisca followed her. Sonia came next, then Dalia, T'mar, D'vin, and K'lior. B'nik remained behind, furtively eyeing Tullea and reflecting on the change in her.

"What is it?" Cisca asked as she saw Fiona looking up into the morning sky. Fiona shook her head and shrugged. Cisca craned her neck up, scanning the lightening sky. The other Weyrwomen joined suit, followed by the four Weyrleaders.

"There!" Fiona cried suddenly as a bright light flashed in the morning sun. "That's where she went!"

▼ ▼ ▼

"I can't see how anyone could live up there," Tullea objected again when Fiona explained her reasoning to her for the third time. Javissa had politely but forcefully relieved the Benden Weyrwoman of her daughter, backed by gentle assurances from B'nik, and now Tullea seemed ready to revert to her old form.

"I don't think they can," Fiona agreed. "Although I could be wrong," she added with a puzzled expression. "Don't the Teaching Ballads say that our ancestors crossed the stars in the Dawn Sisters?"

Tullea nodded.

"So they must be large enough to have housed thousands of people."

"But not dragons," Tullea objected. "And even if they had herd-beasts with them, I can't see any living there now."

"True," Fiona agreed. "And I'm not saying Lorana took the dragonets there."

"So where and when did she take them?" Tullea demanded.

"I don't know," Fiona confessed. "But I think if I go up to the Dawn Sisters—"

"You might lose the babies," Shaneese broke in. Fiona's mood deflated abruptly.

"I'll go first," T'mar offered. "If it's safe enough, then you can come."

"I think Telgar has enough glory," D'vin observed. "Why not let us go?"

"T'mar," Fiona cut through the growing rancor, "just go!"

Cisca gave the younger Weyrwoman a wry look and raised her brown eyes to Sonia's green ones. "Feisty."

"Better let her have her way," Sonia agreed with a shake of her head.

"She has earned the right," Tullea allowed. "That is, if she's correct in her guess."

"We'll know soon enough," T'mar said, nodding toward the others and striding back out into the Weyr Bowl even as Zirenth came rushing toward him.

"I'm not catching falling riders!" Fiona called after him. "Nor drag-ons." A moment later she corrected herself softly, "Well, maybe falling dragons."

Cisca glanced at her and shook her head ruefully.

*Y*ou *know where to go?* T'mar asked his bronze dragon once more as they circled the Star Stones.

To the Dawn Sisters, Zirenth agreed affably. *They are not hard to find.*

But we want to get close to them, make them big in our sight, T'mar cautioned his friend.

Of course, just like Lorana did, Zirenth agreed.

You know that she went there? T'mar asked in surprise. *How?*

When you thought about it, I thought about it and remembered that she'd been there, Zirenth told him innocently.

Show me your image, T'mar said. He closed his eyes and felt the image form, the image of three large shapes, different from any ship he'd ever seen but still obviously ships, even if ships for the stars. *Very well, let's go.*

Take a deep breath.

A moment later, they were *between.*

Between lasted longer than three coughs, but less than the time it had taken them to go back ten Turns in time. And suddenly bright lights assailed T'mar's eyes and he raised a hand to shield them, looking down and—

T'mar gasped in wonder as he saw Pern laid out below him, moun-tains and trails etched into the surface with a clarity he'd never seen before. He could almost spot Telgar Weyr, could easily make out Crom and Telgar Holds, could follow the Igen River down toward the sea.

How long he stared down in awe he could not say. Suddenly he felt very cold and his vision started to gray.

Let's go! Back!

▼ ▼ ▼

"T'mar!" Fiona shouted, racing toward the falling dragon as Zirenth hurtled, lifeless, toward the ground.

Talenth! Tolarth! Ginirth! she called and then suddenly she felt a surge of power, felt more voices respond to her, felt all the dragons arrayed in the Weyr rise up form a bridge, a cushion, a descending line that guided rider and dragon softly to the ground.

Too much! she heard a voice cry to her. *You can't lose the babies!*

And then Fiona felt her knees buckle, felt her head wobble toward the ground until—

"I've got you, lean on me," Jirana said, forcing herself under the Weyrwoman even as K'lior and Cisca raced to her aid.

"He's not breathing!" D'vin shouted from a distance.

"I'm on it!" Birentir called, his feet pumping hard on the packed ground as he sped toward Telgar's Weyrleader. "He's blue, he's been without air, give him room."

Fiona found her own breath, reached down to steady herself on Jirana, gently pushed on the small shoulder until she got her legs under control, and then gave Jirana a gentle squeeze in thanks as she stood back up.

"Get me to him," Fiona said to her, Cisca, and K'lior.

"Lean on me, then," Cisca said, taking all of Fiona's weight on her side. Cisca waddled them over to T'mar, half-carrying the smaller Weyrwoman.

T'mar sputtered and sat up, waving aside further aid just as Fiona reached him.

"Not enough air, eh?" Fiona asked. "And cold, too?"

"Only later," T'mar agreed.

"What did you see?" D'vin wondered.

"Telgar, Crom, Igen—it was beautiful."

"And deadly," Sonia reminded him sternly.

"Only when I ran out of air," T'mar protested, trying to stand and discovering that his legs refused to move. "Next time, I'll be more careful."

Shaneese arrived at that moment, glaring down at him.

"And why would there be a next time?" she demanded.

"Because I haven't seen it all." His eyes sought and found Fiona. "It's beautiful."

"Well then, when you're rested, we'll go look," Fiona told him. "Shaneese can ride with me."

In the end it was decided that Cisca, K'lior, and Fiona would go next and then, on their return, Sonia and D'vin of High Reaches Weyr, Dalia and S'maj of Ista Weyr would go. Shaneese, to T'mar's evident relief, decided to remain behind. Tullea was quietly insistent that she and B'nik also remain behind.

"Someone's got to handle things if you get lost," Tullea declared.

"We need to handle this like altitude sickness," K'lior warned the two Weyrwomen as they prepared for their jump.

"Any sign of chills, tingles, and we jump right back," Fiona said in agreement.

"What are we looking for?" Cisca said, looking toward Fiona.

"Someplace suitable for weyrlings," Fiona replied.

They climbed their dragons, rose in the air, gathered by the Star Stones and went *between*.

Fiona followed Zirenth's coordinates, adjusting for the change in time so that Fort and High Reaches were bathed in the morning light that had yet to roll toward them. She paused only a moment to gaze in wonder at the great, blinding ships hovering soundlessly above her, then craned her head over Talenth's neck, instinctively grabbing tighter to her riding straps as she peered down to the planet so far below.

She could see the coastline, could see the sea beyond and—*Go there!*

A moment later they hung alone in the sky, still hovering near the Dawn Sisters but later in the day, with the far side of Pern below her.

That's it! Fiona declared. A moment later, Cisca on Melirth and K'lior on Rineth burst into existence beside her.

You scared them! Melirth relayed in an aggrieved tone.

Sorry, Fiona responded. *Look down.*

Dragons and riders looked below.

We've found it, Fiona thought. *Let's tell the others.*

A moment later only the great ships remained, still silent, still watching.

They were not alone for long, as Sonia, D'vin, Dalia, and S'maj took their turn, looking down in surprise and awe at the beautiful blue planet below.

"It seems a waste that our ancestors could come all this way and not foresee the Red Star," D'vin said when they'd all gathered in the Kitchen Cavern to relate their experiences.

At Fiona's urging and their general acceptance, the Weyrleaders and Weyrwomen shared their reminiscences with everyone who wanted to listen.

Talenth, Fiona cautioned, *be certain that no dragon goes to the Dawn Sisters without my permission.*

I have told them.

And?

They wonder why anyone would wish to make the journey, the queen said. *I told them that it was cold and the air went bad quickly.*

Fiona smiled, wondering if Talenth had chosen her words to dissuade the others.

"It was so beautiful it made your eyes water," Cisca explained to a group of interested riders.

Beyond her, D'vin waxed eloquent about the huge ships that had brought them so far. "They were white, brilliant, blazing white in the sunlight, yet there were darker places, perhaps where windows looked out to the stars."

"But why, if that island is so great," Tullea wondered, "has no one ever been there before?"

"Maybe they didn't have a need," B'nik suggested.

"Or our ancestors were too busy settling this continent to worry about the other," Fiona said with a shrug. "It's much smaller than ours."

"Wouldn't that make it easier to defend?" Tullea persisted, her eyes narrowed in suspicion. "And there's no hint of it in the Records."

"Not all Records survived the fire at the Harper Hall during the Plague," Fiona reminded her, feeling a pang out of loyalty to Kindan. "And, again, it may just not have seemed as important to preserve that Record as it was to preserve others."

"So Lorana's taken all the weyrlings to a place no one's ever been before," Tullea mused, sounding much like her normal sour self. "How safe is that?"

"I suppose the better question, now that we know where she's taken them, is *when*?" T'mar put in.

"Well, there's one way to find out," Fiona said, rising from her chair and alerting Talenth as she strode toward the Weyr Bowl.

"How?" Tullea demanded.

"I'll ask her."

T'mar and the others opened their mouths to begin the many reasonable objections that Fiona knew they would raise—that she was pregnant; that she didn't know where to find Lorana; that it was too risky. Fiona didn't wait. She would be careful, but before anyone could give voice to their objections, Fiona climbed on top of Talenth and, with a single leap, they went *between*.

"How can she know when to go?" Tullea asked crossly.

"She knows where she was," T'mar said, rising himself and signaling Zirenth to meet him. "If you'll excuse me."

H'nez followed him out. "What should we do in your absence?"

"I won't be gone long, I promise," T'mar told him with a smile. "But in the meantime, I'd like you to be senior leader; coordinate with C'tov and don't forget that he's the older."

Surprisingly, the tall wiry rider took no offense at T'mar's words. "I'll do my best."

"Good man!" T'mar called as he clambered up Zirenth's side and hoisted himself into position. Checking to be certain the area around him was clear, T'mar urged Zirenth up and instantly *between*.

They arrived in the dead of night, gold leading bronze. Fiona waved over her shoulder in acknowledgment as they glided to a landing. She urged Talenth to bring them to the Hatching Grounds at Telgar. Zirenth followed.

"What now?" T'mar asked as he climbed down to stand beside Fiona.

"We wait," Fiona told him. She slumped slightly as the drain of being in the same time more than once crashed in on her. "And try to stay awake."

"I'll take first watch," T'mar offered. Fiona nodded, leaning lightly against him.

They did not have to wait long, no more than an hour passed before Fiona felt a terrible pain in her head and grabbed T'mar's shoulder both for support and in warning. Even as he reached to steady her, they saw the shape of a large dragon glide to the ground and a lithe figure dismount.

"You'd better ask her," Fiona managed in a hoarse whisper, her eyes full of pain.

"Why?"

"Because that's me over there," Fiona told him, even as her knees buckled. "Be quick, she can't feel any better about this than I."

T'mar walked briskly toward the gold rider who seemed to know he would be there and was moving in his direction already.

"You've got to go," the other Fiona called urgently. "It's too much, you've got to go! There are three of me here at this very moment."

"When did you go?"

"Three Turns," the other Fiona told him, wincing at the sound of his voice. "Now take her and go, go quickly!"

Even as she said this, they spotted a figure walking quickly down the queens' ledge toward them. It was Kindan.

T'mar glanced at him in understanding, then nodded to the other Fiona and raced back to the Hatching Grounds. His Fiona was on the ground, heaving. Gently he raised her up and helped her climb to her position on Talenth's neck, strapping her in tightly.

"I'll give the coordinates," T'mar told her. Fiona managed a bare nod, her whole body trembling.

"Quickly!"

T'mar raced back to Zirenth, strapped himself in, and urged the bronze out of the Hatching Grounds even as he relayed the same order to Talenth. Together the pair of riders and dragons took a quick leap and, on T'mar's image, went *between*, back to the sun of Telgar the morning after.

"Shaneese!" T'mar roared as soon as Zirenth came to a stop. "Help Fiona!"

"What's she done now?" Shaneese asked, running out and gazing up at the Weyrwoman worriedly.

"She was in the same place three times last night," T'mar explained as he leaped down from Zirenth's neck, bracing his knees to absorb the impact.

D'vin and Sonia lent a hand and soon they had Fiona seated in the Kitchen Cavern with a cup of fresh-squeezed juice by her side.

"Well," Fiona said weakly, "we knew when they went."

"But why only three Turns?" D'vin wondered, shaking his head.

"We'll have to ask them when we get there," Fiona said. T'mar gave her a rebellious look and she smiled at him weakly before closing her eyes as the room started to spin.

NINE

*West of Tillek, east of Benden
Halfway around the world.
Far lands, strange lands,
Large lands, Great Islands.*

Lorana had Minith land carefully on the driest, stoniest part of the ground near the shore and waited, still perched on the queen's back for several minutes, just listening.

She was fortunate to have had enough experience with J'trel to have learned something of woodcraft and knew that it was perilous to move too quickly or act with too much assurance.

"The first mistake will be your last," her father had once told her. It was sad and true both; he'd been talking about herdbeasts—and it had been his mistake with the crazed herdbeast that had kicked him in the head that killed him. He'd been working with the animals all his life; it had taken only the one mistake to end it.

"Let's try farther up the coast," Lorana said, guiding Minith back into the air. They glided up the coast, with Lorana urging Minith to take occasional forays inland before returning to the coastline once more. When she spotted another rocky outcropping, she had Minith hover above it for several minutes. Something about it looked forbidding, Lorana had no idea what until, after a few minutes, she saw something streak across the rock and leap toward them.

Up!

Minith responded instantly to Lorana's order and beat her way high into the air even as Lorana craned her neck over, trying to identify the strange attacker.

What would consider attacking a dragon?

This was a place to be treated warily. Lorana had Minith wait several more minutes to see if she could spot further movement, in vain.

Can we go back to the first spot? Minith asked. *I'd like to rest.*

Let's go back to Red Butte, Lorana said. *We can rest safely there.*

Lorana was shocked when they arrived to realize that, ten Turns back from the start of the Third Pass, there was no rock cairn to mark Tenniz's resting place.

He was still alive.

It was early in the summer's day she'd chosen, the sun was high enough that the rocks had been warmed and the early breeze had died down to wisps of wind. Lorana and Minith soon found themselves stretched out, the ex-dragonrider leaning against the exhausted queen and, in short order, they were asleep.

They woke late that night, cold but rested. Lorana took them forward to the next day, near Igen, where she found several strong wild herdbeasts. She had Minith catch one and they hauled it back to what she had started to call the Great Isle. She let the beast go on the barren spot of rock they'd found and returned for another, repeating the effort until she'd brought a good dozen, half of whom were male, judging by their horns.

Now, let's go see what we find, Lorana thought to the queen as she imagined the same place seven Turns in the future. The weyrlings would need the three Turns before the start of the Third Pass in which to grow to maturity, but she wanted to give her small herd enough time to grow and populate the island before she brought in dragon hunters.

The leap forward in time was a long one, though not as long as her leap to the end of the Pass. She noted that Minith was pale with exhaustion at the end of it and regretted how hard she'd treated the willing queen.

It is necessary, Minith thought back, as they circled the island. Lorana was thrilled when she first spotted one of the herdbeasts descended from her flock. They followed it until it met up with a large herd that ran away from the dragon above them, joining with a larger herd and then a larger herd until it seemed that the whole plain teamed with herdbeasts.

Lorana was amazed at their numbers. *Could all these have come from my dozen?*

Suddenly she felt a warning from Minith and then the air crackled as a dragon burst from *between*. The rider grinned and waved at her. Lorana gave the rider a startled look—it was Fiona and her heart leaped with joy as she waved back.

Talenth says to turn north, toward the camp, Minith told her.

Let's go!

Lorana was surprised to see a large and well-formed camp near the dangerous rocks she'd marked out on her first foray into the Great Isle, but she was glad to land, hopping off Minith to race into Fiona's arms.

"I knew it!" Fiona cried, her face wet with tears. "I knew you wouldn't quit, you'd never give in."

"Of course," Lorana agreed, hugging her fiercely. "I couldn't let you down." She glanced around as she added, "Or Kindan."

"He's here," Fiona told her, grabbing her hand and dragging her along. "He'll be delighted to see you, he needs to see you." She raised her voice to a bellow and called, "Kindan!"

The harper appeared from within a group of drilling weyrlings and his jaw dropped as he spied Lorana. In an instant he had his arms around her, was hugging her tightly and babbling, "Never, never leave me again!"

"I won't, I won't," Lorana swore just as fervently and just as teary-eyed. When they'd both cried themselves out, Lorana pulled back, glancing from Kindan to Fiona and back again. In a small voice she said, "I lost the baby."

Fiona reached out to her and grabbed her tightly. "Yes, dear," she said, "we know."

"**W**e thought of the same thing and came up with the same solution," T'mar explained when Lorana got to the part in her tale where she mentioned moving the herdbeasts back in time.

"At least now we know why we were all so muzzy-headed," Fiona said with relief. "We are not only back in time here, but also back in time at Igen as well."

"Knowing why helps, but it doesn't stop us from feeling the effects," T'mar said.

"I'll be glad when we get to normal," Fiona agreed. "At least now, though, I don't have to doubt my sanity." Fiona explained about how she fainted when she met her future self and how she nearly fainted again when, as her future self, she went back in time to organize the weyrlings for their jump back to this time and place.

"What about the injured?" Lorana asked, noting the small size of the camp.

"We decided this time to bring them back when the weyrlings were older and could provide more help," Fiona said. "That way our young dragonriders don't have to split their time so much."

"So we'll have two Turns here by ourselves, and then we'll get the injured back with us to heal," Kindan said.

"And then we'll have another three hundred and forty-one dragons to add to our strength," Fiona said with pride.

"That might still not be enough," T'mar cautioned, in a tone that sounded like he was rehashing an old argument.

"It's the best we can do," Fiona said. T'mar frowned but nodded.

"What do you need me to do?" Lorana asked.

"Well, first, if you don't think you need her, you should probably send Minith back to Tullea," Fiona said. "She's nearly desperate without her."

Lorana nodded vigorously. "I worried about her," she said. "I hope she'll forgive me." With a frown, remembering the Tullea of the far future, she added, "But I doubt it."

"Did you learn anything about the wildlife here?" Kindan asked. "We've only been here two days ourselves and we're still getting sorted out."

Lorana shook her head. "I didn't learn much," she told them, describing her original survey of the land.

"Something tried to attack a dragon?" T'mar repeated, in surprise and glancing questioningly at Kindan.

The harper shook his head. "I don't recall any Records of that."

"Nor I," Fiona said. She made a face as she added, "We've been hearing some noises from the woods, some deep *mrreow* sound that we've never heard before."

"I think what I met was different," Lorana said with a shake of her head. "This creature made no noise. It seemed like a tunnel snake. Large and very fast."

Kindan and Fiona exchanged a look. "I suppose if there was nothing hunting tunnel snakes they'd get large," Fiona said.

"And the faster ones would survive longest," Kindan said, "and grow largest."

"Large enough to attack a queen?" T'mar asked, his tone dubious.

"Need breeds desperate action," Fiona said.

"Well, we'd best keep guard," T'mar said grimly. "A weyrling is much smaller than a—"

A sudden *mrreow* broke through his speech, followed immediately by a dragon's cry of pain and a chorus of shouts. The group rushed out to see a large furry beast running off, and a group of youngsters gathered around a bellowing dragonet.

Talenth! Fiona cried.

It struck before we could spot it, the queen replied.

Fiona rushed back to the tent for her aid kit. When she returned, Lorana and the others were gathered around the young blue dragon whose left wing was badly mauled. B'carran looked up anxiously, asking, "Will he be all right?"

It was a nasty wound, Fiona noted as she reached for her gear.

"Let me," a young woman said as she knelt next to Fiona. "Jassi, of Ista."

"I've heard of you," Fiona said, then leaned closer to murmur for the young woman's ears alone, "What do you think?"

"It's bad," Jassi said as she examined the wound. She point to the worst spot. "The sail's completely away from the bone here."

"Nasty," Bekka said as she shouldered her way through the crowd. "What did this?"

"One of the Mrreows," Fiona said. Bekka pursed her lips tightly.

"We'll need to build a large wall," T'mar said, turning to Kindan. "Let's organize some crews."

"Lorana," Fiona said, turning toward the taller woman, "would you take Talenth to help? I'm going to be busy here."

Lorana gave Fiona a measuring look as thoughts raced through her head, then nodded. Fiona smiled back at her in gratitude for accepting Fiona's wordlessly delivered plan.

Lorana moved away from the crowd and called to Minith.

It's time you went home, dear, Lorana thought fondly to the queen.

I do miss my rider, Minith admitted, sounding wistful, but still willing to remain with her.

She misses you, Lorana agreed. She turned her attention to Talenth. *Can you follow us?*

Of course, Talenth said, but Lorana could feel the slight sense of worry from the younger queen.

"I can fly her," a voice spoke up from beside Lorana.

"Bekka?" Lorana said, reaching for the young blonde and giving her a quick hug. "Aren't you needed with Mayorth?"

"I think Fiona and Jassi will do fine," Bekka said. "But I'm worried about Talenth going *between* by herself."

"Very well, if Talenth's willing, you can fly her with me," Lorana said after just the slightest of pauses.

Talenth was happy to carry Bekka and before long the two were airborne. Lorana confirmed coordinates with Talenth, having learned from Bekka when Minith returned to Tullea, and together they went *between* forward in time.

They had not quite been *between* for three coughs when they heard a male voice cry toward them: *The Weyrs! The Weyrs must be warned!* And another voice, female, cried, *Can't lose the babies, can't lose the babies!*

Lorana felt a tug on her heart as she tried to fathom the pain of the two voices, but she felt Bekka's rising panic and, with a surge of will, they broke beyond the cries, forward to Telgar Weyr and back once more into the light.

Lorana jumped off Minith and raced over to Talenth where Bekka gave her a hand up. They were in the air and *between* before anyone noticed.

"He'll survive," Fiona told B'carran as she finished the last of the bandaging on Mayorth's injury. "The damage was bad and it'll take several months to heal, but he's young and he'll make a full recovery."

B'carran nodded absently, his eyes straying toward the Istan girl, Jassi.

"The Weyrwoman's right, B'carran," Jassi told him, then she shook her head in apology to Fiona.

"If you say so, Jassi," the young rider said in relief, reaching down and scratching the young blue's eye ridges. "You'll be fine, Mayorth, Jassi says so."

"The two of you need to get rest," Fiona said, motioning for them to move on.

"Sorry about that, Weyrwoman," Jassi apologized after the blue dragon and his rider had departed. "They're used to me at Ista."

"And they trust you, with good reason," Fiona said, gesturing for the other woman to follow her. "I take it you've been at Ista for a while, then?"

"I came when the sickness started," Jassi said. "I wanted to help the dragonriders; when I was little, it was J'trel who found the fruits during the Plague to nurse me back to health."

"You knew J'trel?" Fiona asked in surprise. "Did you ever meet Lorana?"

"I did, once, before she went aboard the *Wind Rider*," Jassi admitted. Shyly she added, "My father's still got one of her drawings in his tavern."

"Come with me!" Fiona said, her eyes twinkling. Talenth had just returned and Fiona picked up her pace, urging the older woman to keep up, so that they met Lorana just as she was helping Bekka down from Talenth's neck.

"Lorana?" Jassi asked in surprise.

"Jassi!" Lorana exclaimed with a wide smile, moving forward to hug the woman tightly. Jassi squeezed her back with equal force.

"When we heard about the *Wind Rider*, I cried," Jassi said, tears starting in her eyes. "And then we heard about you and your queen and"—she broke off, gesturing back toward the weyrlings—"you could have my queen, if you want."

"I think Talenth might have something to say about that," Fiona said, patting her queen's foreleg possessively. "She's quite partial to Lorana."

Lorana laughed suddenly at some hidden joke, and the others all looked at her in surprise. "Falth"—she said, pointing to Jassi—"and Talenth"—she pointed to Fiona—"both say that while they would happily carry me anywhere, they are quite attached to their riders and would not want to lose them!"

"I think all dragons are partial to her," Bekka said. She looked up at the dark-eyed woman and said, "If *I* ever Impress, I'll let you ride my dragon."

Lorana smiled back at Jassi and shook her head. "As you can see, I've got too many dragons to ride already."

"But doesn't it *hurt*?"

"It does," Lorana admitted, her voice catching on a sob. "I miss my Arith every moment of every day." Fiona grabbed her hand and clenched it comfortingly. Lorana squeezed back as she continued, "But the dragons keep me company and that makes it a bit easier."

"I heard," Jassi began hesitatingly, "when the sickness was the worst that C'rion said you heard every dragon die."

Lorana nodded bleakly.

"How can you survive such pain?"

"It's hard," Lorana said. "But it would be much harder to abandon those who remain, to give in or give up simply because it hurts."

Bekka moved toward her, raising a hand to rest on her shoulder. Lorana smiled down at the young woman.

"I think it'd be harder, not being able to share their pain," Lorana said. "But I don't know."

"It's hard," Bekka said. "Sometimes I go into a corner and just cry and cry after a bad Fall."

"You, too?" Jassi asked in wonder. "I thought I was the only one."

"I think we all do," Fiona said. "But mostly they get better, so it's not too bad."

Jassi cast her gaze out to the lush undergrowth that surrounded them. "But these creatures, these—"

"Mrrreows, I call them," Bekka said.

Jassi considered the term, then nodded. "These Mrrreows are nasty."

"Now that we know they'll attack dragons, we can guard against them," Fiona said.

"With weyrlings?" Jassi asked.

"No, our old weyrlings will manage," Fiona assured her with a smile. "You may recall that I went back to Igen Weyr with Fort's weyrlings—"

"I heard about it, and then our weyrlings and injured followed you," Jassi said. "That's why I was willing to come here, so my Falth could grow and help with the next Threadfall."

Fiona nodded and continued, "Well, the weyrlings who came back with me all suffered from what we called 'muzzy-headedness'—"

"Tired all the time? Forgetful?"

"Exactly," Fiona agreed. "And now," she waved a hand at their current location, "that they're all grown up and ready to watch over our current batch of weyrlings, we know why."

"Why?" Jassi asked.

"Because they're here now and *there* in Igen at the same time," Fiona said.

"They all came?" Lorana asked, surprised.

"All except F'jian," Bekka said sadly.

"F'jian?" Lorana repeated, glancing around. "Where is he?"

"He was lost *between*," Fiona told her. "He died saving T'mar."

"But then why was he muzzy-headed?" Lorana wondered. Fiona shrugged and shook her head. "And Terin? How is she?"

"She *seems* in good spirits," Bekka said.

"Seems?"

"She claimed that F'jian came back to her, told her it would be all right, that he'd always be there when she needed him most," Bekka said, her face in a frown.

"You don't think so?"

"He's dead," Bekka said frankly. "I don't see how he could have come to her."

"We're keeping an eye on her," Fiona said, turning her head back toward the camp. "Jeriz is with her all the time—"

"Jeriz?" Lorana asked suddenly. "Tenniz's son?"

"Yes," Fiona said. "He was sent to Telgar, where he was driving Shaneese to distraction until she thought to make him my minder." Between Fiona and Bekka, Lorana was quickly brought up-to-date with all that had happened since she'd left Telgar Weyr, days ago and Turns in the future.

"And I was adopted by the Weyrwoman," a small girl's voice suddenly piped up. Lorana looked down into dark eyes and a dusky face so like Tenniz's that she could only be his daughter. "So you're my sister, too."

Lorana gave Fiona a quick look of resignation, then knelt down to the smaller girl and met her eyes, holding out her hand in greeting. "We haven't met yet, I'm Lorana."

"I know, I'm Jirana," the girl replied. "I was named after you." She took Lorana's hand and shook it as she added, "And we *have* met, maybe you just didn't do it yet."

"You've met?" Fiona asked, pouncing on the girl's words. "When?"

"If she doesn't know, I can't tell you," Jirana said apologetically.

"You're the new traders' seer?" Lorana asked.

"My father said I would be the seer when I got old enough," Jirana said.

"Is there something I should remember?" Fiona asked the child.

Jirana nodded solemnly. "Shaneese wants to know if you've eaten."

"Shaneese is here?" Lorana asked in surprise and delight.

"I wouldn't leave her behind," Fiona said. The older woman gave her a measured look and Fiona explained, "It wouldn't be fair to her or T'mar."

Fiona led them back to a spot just outside the tent and they met Shaneese, who insisted on hugging Lorana and then sat them all down, apologizing for the poor fare she had to offer them.

"Well, Lorana saw to the herdbeasts," Fiona said. "So I think it's only fair that we work out the rest."

"If we could make some nets, I'll bet there's great fishing to be had," Jassi said, looking out toward the seaward horizon.

"It's fruits and vegetables that worry me," Shaneese said as she deftly served the group.

"And spices," a voice piped up.

"And spices," Shaneese agreed, nodding toward Javissa who was tending one of the nearby pots.

"We'll all have to pitch in," Fiona said, glancing at Terin with a grin. "I wonder who we'll find to trade with here."

"I thought no one was here," Jassi said in confusion.

"You have to be careful with our Weyrwoman and her words," Shaneese told the well-built blonde. "She tends to talk in plans."

"Ah, you've figured that out!" Terin said. Shaneese snorted a laugh and nodded.

"And someone's got to dig the firestone," Fiona mused, turning to Lorana. "Unless you've managed that already?"

"Firestone?" Jassi asked.

"Not for at least two Turns yet," Terin assured her. "There's no use doing it before—oh! You mean *that* firestone mine!"

"Someone cleared it out and mined it," Fiona reminded her. "And I think we were the ones who made it happen."

"Again," Terin agreed. Under Lorana's questioning, Fiona explained about the firestone mine they'd discovered back in time at Igen Weyr, clean and ready for use, with firestone already stacked for them.

"That reminds me," Lorana said. "Have you ever heard someone speaking in *between*?"

"Speaking in *between*?" T'mar echoed as he and Kindan wandered back from their latest efforts. He glanced at the harper, but Kindan shook his head.

"What did you hear?" Kindan asked.

"I wasn't sure, it might have been my imagination, but when I came forward to return Minith to Telgar, I heard two voices," Lorana said. "One a man's, the other a woman's."

"What did they say?" T'mar asked.

"Did Bekka hear it, too?" Fiona asked on his heels.

"I didn't ask her," Lorana confessed.

Talenth, did you hear voices? Fiona asked her dragon.

Yes.

"Talenth heard them," Fiona said. "What did they say?"

"The woman's said something like: 'Can't lose the babies!'" Lorana said. "And the man said: 'The Weyrs! They must be warned!'"

"That was D'gan," Kindan said instantly, looking at Lorana. "Don't you remember? He said that when Telgar went *between* forever."

"Could they still be there?" Fiona asked, horrified at the thought.

"We didn't hear them when we came forward from Igen," Terin said.

"We came back in time before they were lost," Fiona reminded her. Abashed, Terin nodded in recollection.

"Why didn't we hear them coming back?" T'mar wondered.

"And what about the other voice?" Kindan asked. "A woman's."

Lorana looked at Fiona. "I thought it was you."

"Me?" Fiona asked as a chill of fear swept over her. She shook it off angrily. "After all we've been through, I'm going to be certain that I'll have my babies *here*."

"Babies?" Lorana repeated in surprise.

"Bekka thinks I'm having twins," Fiona told her.

"Which is why as soon as you eat, you'll take some rest," Shaneese told her. "And Jirana will keep an eye on you."

"I don't know how I can sleep in this heat," Fiona said. She saw Terin start to speak and rushed on, "It's not like Igen. I'm *sticky* all the time."

Terin nodded in understanding. "There's too much water in the air, I feel like a fish."

"It feels like home to me," Jassi confessed.

"In the desert, we learned the ways of the desert folk," T'mar said, nodding at Shaneese and Jirana. "What advice, sea person, do you have for us?"

"Wide windows, lots of fans, dress loose and cool," Jassi said, ticking each point off on a finger.

Lorana's eyes narrowed and she looked at Kindan and T'mar, asking, "I'm curious, why did you choose this location?"

"We found a rocky promonitory, but it was too small," Kindan said with a shrug. "This is slightly better."

"When we start building," T'mar added, "we'll build more inland, clearing the trees and undergrowth."

"You'll have to keep trimming it," Jassi cautioned. "This island is wetter than Ista and it takes constant effort there to keep the brush back."

"Are you familiar with any of the vegetation here?" Lorana asked the blonde.

"Is there anything we can eat?" Shaneese added.

Jassi frowned. "I haven't seen much, yet."

"We've been busy just settling in," Fiona explained. "We've only been here two days; this is just a camp until we figure out where to settle."

Lorana nodded. Fiona grinned at her. "Perhaps you and Jassi would be willing to scout around?"

"I can come," Kindan offered. Fiona glanced toward T'mar, who frowned for a moment in thought. "I can make and shoot a bow," Kindan added as he saw the Weyrleader's hesitation.

"Very well," T'mar agreed. As they started to move, he held up a cautioning hand. "But you've got to turn over your Weyrlingmaster duties to someone while you're gone." Kindan nodded readily, but T'mar wasn't finished. "And then you've got to teach everyone what you know of woodcraft."

"I know some, too," Lorana added.

"Good, then you can teach together," T'mar said with a grin. To Kindan he said, "Who should take over as weyrlingmaster?"

"Terin," Fiona said immediately. The young weyrwoman made a startled sound, but Fiona waved a finger at her peremptorily. "And Lin, and Jassi, and—who are the other queen riders?"

"Oh," T'mar said, his eyes widening in delight. "Very good, well said, Weyrwoman."

Jassi and Terin both looked perplexed. It was Lorana who spoke first. "That way none of the weyrlings will feel confused, seeing their own queen riders, and you will all get experience in leading—which will stand you in good stead later."

Fiona nodded and smiled at the older woman. "If you get confused or need help, look to Xhinna and her mate, Taria. They're good at organizing younguns, they'll handle the weyrlings just as easily."

"Garra is from Fort, Indeera from High Reaches," Lorana told Fiona. "Their queens are Niloth and Morurth."

"Oh, yes!" Fiona said, smiling again. "If you get really lost, have your dragons bespeak Lorana. All the dragons talk to her."

As Lorana started away, leading Kindan toward Talenth, she paused and glanced around. "Where's Seban?"

"Father stayed behind," Bekka said with a sniff. "He said that we'd be gone a long time here, but only a wink for the rest; he was afraid that he'd be too old when we got back."

"That makes sense," Lorana agreed. She looked at Bekka's shoulder, and pointed to the journeyman knot. "And we've clearly got all the healers we need."

Bekka's lips curved upward in pleasure at the compliment.

By the end of the month, they'd staked a location, sketched out and designed by Fiona and Jassi, who both had the most experience in setting up living quarters, and had laid out a ring of stakes from the trees they'd removed, set close together to provide protection from the marauding Mrreows. Inside the Weyrhold, as Fiona had taken to calling it, they had finished some crude buildings and were starting on a more complex stone building.

The dragons had to weather the rains that swept in frequently, which pleased no one, but all their scouting had revealed no location any better than the one they'd chosen—nothing at all like a proper weyr or a even a decent mountainside.

"I suppose, if we can figure it, we can build into the ground," T'mar had suggested. Jassi shook her head. "If the weather's like it is in Ista, the ground will be too wet and it would flood in a heavy rain."

"So how are we going to protect the dragons?" Fiona wondered.

"We could build large houses for them," Jassi suggested.

"If we could get enough canvas, we could rig tents," Javissa said.

"How much canvas would we need?"

"About four dragonlengths long by one dragonlength wide for each dragon," Terin said. "Assuming you're willing to put up with openings at each end and a height just high enough for a dragon to stand under."

"The weyrlings won't need that much space," Kindan said.

"They will when they get bigger," Fiona said.

"Then we'll need seven hundred and eight square dragonlengths of canvas," Terin said.

"I doubt all the Masterfisherman's crafters make more than fifty dragonlengths of canvas a Turn," Jassi said.

"I think I understand why our ancestors chose to use the Weyrs," Fiona said with feeling.

"And perhaps also why they chose not to come here," Kindan said.

"If we went back in time to the time of Igen, and the clothmakers doubled their work, they could make seven hundred dragonlengths in those seven Turns," Terin suggested.

"They'd need half of that for the ships," Jassi pointed out. She shook her head, adding, "I don't recall any order like that, or anything close in the past seven Turns."

"And it's not something that wouldn't be noticed," Kindan agreed grimly.

"So we need a different solution," Fiona said. She looked at Kindan. "Could we quarry enough rock?"

"How would you make the roof?" T'mar challenged.

"We use leaves," Jassi said, eyes going wide. "The shore is full of palms, and sailors have used them for ages to make quick shelters."

"They'd dry out," Kindan objected.

"So we replace them," Fiona said with a dismissive shrug. She turned back to Jassi. "How many would we need?"

"I'm not sure," Jassi admitted. "There's an art to making that sort of covering."

"Are there any among your weyrlings who might know?" T'mar asked.

"We should ask them," Fiona said, gesturing outside their shelter.

"It's nearly dinner," Shaneese said. They'd had luck enough in finding several patches of tubers, some of which they'd transplanted into their compound, and Jassi had located several edible vegetables, but they were running low on spices and had yet to find a decent stand of *klah* trees. Fiona didn't mind that nearly as much as the others, content to drink the plentiful juice from the various succulent fruits that had been found scattered readily throughout the island.

"Maybe tomorrow we should scout the western half," Lorana suggested, "maybe we'll find a better place there."

They had stopped at the great river that stretched nearly the whole length of the Great Isle, splitting it into western and eastern halves. The explored eastern half was nearly as large as all the Telgar plain. In all of it, mysteriously, they had spotted no animals larger than the herdbeasts they'd imported Turns before. They'd found several clutches of wherry eggs, but had found few wherries themselves. Half the wherry eggs Kindan had tried proved to have been already eaten by the ever-present tunnel snakes. He'd only managed to find two in all their exploration that were unhatched and had brought them, triumphantly, back to be cooked and served to Fiona, who craved them with a passion that surprised her.

In fact, if Fiona hadn't thought herself properly pregnant before, she was making up for it now in her ninth week of pregnancy. Smells began to affect her and foods she'd never liked she now craved, while those she'd adored she found she could no longer stomach.

"And I think they're fighting in there," Fiona had complained to an amused Bekka after one night of terrible heartburn.

Unbeknownst to her, Bekka had spoken with Lorana, Kindan, and T'mar. She'd invited Javissa to join them, as the older trader had the most recent practical experience with growing children.

"We're beginning to run out of medicines," Bekka told them. "I'm worried about what Fiona's eating, she'll start to get cravings—as will Shaneese—and we may not have what she needs on hand."

"We need something to trade," T'mar said. "And we need to do it in such a way that no one will notice."

"There's no one here to trade with," Bekka reminded him.

"I know that, child." T'mar smiled at her and shook his head. "So we'll have to trade with the Northern Continent, discreetly."

"Those brightfish might fetch a fair mark," Lorana said. The brightfish were the catch of choice amongst both rider and dragon. The meat was not fishy, being pink in color and tasting tantalizingly of the best meat—with just a little something different and spicy. Jirana had said it best when she'd said that it tasted like a smoked meat. But the fish itself was bright and easily spotted from the air, so the name brightfish was given to it and quickly stuck. "And we could maybe work with the fishermen or traders to the fishermen so there'll be no questions." She frowned for a moment as she remembered Colfet, the man who had saved her when the sailship *Wind Rider* had foundered. What had happened to him?

"Whitefish, too," Bekka said. "It's less tasty, but it goes well with the tubers."

"When fried and served with vinegar," Kindan agreed, his eyes going wide with pleasure.

"Cromcoal would help," Shaneese pointed out. "And we'll need some wine or we'll have to make it ourselves if we want more vinegar."

They'd found some wild grapes growing, but had only harvested them as fruit as they were too few for a decent batch of wine.

Fellis they'd found in plenty and numbweed, too.

"We need something small that we can trade," T'mar mused.

"What about ice, from the Snowy Wastes?" Kindan suggested. "That worked well before."

"There's a thriving ice trade already," T'mar said.

"How do you know that's not us?" Lorana asked with a ghost of a smile.

T'mar frowned thoughtfully, then shook his head. "It might even be, when the weyrlings are old enough to fly, but not now—we've got too much work for our grown dragons as it is."

"I'm beginning to understand tithing much better," Javissa said grudgingly. The others looked at her. "Even without Thread falling, it's too much work to raise dragons *and* provide for them at the same time."

"We did it in Igen," T'mar said with a shrug. "Fiona figured out a way."

"Maybe we should ask her again," Bekka said. The others stared at her and she shrugged. "It's not like others don't need these supplies and she's still got her wits, even when pregnant."

"Why don't we wait until we've checked out the western half before we ask her?" Kindan asked. "Maybe we won't have to worry her."

"Very well," T'mar agreed.

Fiona's shriek startled them all out of bed before dawn the next morning. T'mar and Shaneese rushed in to find Kindan, Lorana, and

Jirana anxiously consoling the Weyrwoman. Bekka dashed in a moment later.

"What is it?" Bekka asked, looking from one person to the next for an answer.

"We got a message," Fiona said, gesturing to Kindan, who passed a slate over to the healer.

"'Stay east of the great river,'" Bekka read. She glanced sharply at Fiona. "That's your writing."

"It is," Fiona agreed. "But I don't recall writing it."

"That happens sometimes in a pregnancy," Bekka allowed with a shrug.

"But look at the slate," Fiona said, gesturing for her to examine it again. Bekka looked down at it and then up again, confused. "We don't have slate here," Fiona told her. "It has to have come from another place. Probably another time."

"So you sent yourself a note from the future?" Bekka guessed. "And why should we stay east of the great river?"

Fiona shook her head, shrugging. "There must be a reason that we'll find out in the future."

"So we need another solution," Kindan said to T'mar.

"For what?" Fiona demanded. With no preamble, Bekka told her. When she was finished, Fiona nodded. "We could trade brightfish and whitefish, if we were careful." She paused for a moment, then added, "Probably with traders who are used to trading with fishermen, and don't ask questions."

"We thought of that," Kindan said.

"It's bulky, but we can catch it easily enough," Fiona continued. She frowned thoughtfully. "The easiest thing to trade is information."

"Judging by this slate, telling anyone about where we are is not a good idea," Bekka said. The others nodded.

"Come along, we're up, so's half the camp," Shaneese said, "we might as well break our fast."

They made their way to the firepits that had been set outside the wooden building. A weyrling was on watch, tending the fire and the warming brew stewing in a pot. They had not found *klah*, but they'd discovered several very large varieties of brewable herbs from which to make tea.

Bekka and Shaneese both waved for Fiona to take the nearest seat while Shaneese and Lorana brought out one of the clean pots in which to start some breakfast cereals cooking.

"Not information," Fiona said, "but perhaps some of the plants here could be traded." The others nodded. "What we really need is something valuable, something rare, something like . . . gems."

"What about that clay?" Bekka mused, thinking of the rich deposits of clay they'd found near all the riverbeds.

"It's good clay," Fiona agreed, wishing she could get Mekiar's opinion on it. "We could trade it, but it's heavy, even for a dragon."

"Aren't finished goods even better?" Kindan asked. Fiona nodded, her eyes narrowed questioningly. "Well, couldn't we set up a pottery wheel and kiln and make finished goods?"

"We'd need more than one pottery wheel to get a decent set of trade goods," Fiona said. "And we'd want to find some decent glazes, too."

"We'd do better with leather from the herdbeasts," Lorana said. "We've got plenty to spare."

"We could trade that for a lot of things," Kindan agreed. He looked toward Bekka. "Could we use the leather for our coverings?"

"You think we could get hundreds of *dragonlengths* of leather?" Bekka asked incredulously. Kindan thought on that for just a moment before letting go of the notion with a soft chuckle and a shake of his head.

"There are greenstones in some clays, aren't there?" Fiona asked, looking toward Kindan for confirmation.

"Sapphires," Kindan agreed. "But green's not a popular color."

"What about that blue-green stone we found near the beach?" Lorana asked suddenly. "It was pretty."

"It certainly was," Kindan agreed. "I'd never seen its like before."

"It could be used in jewelry," Shaneese said. "I know several holders who would like it."

"Wait a moment," Fiona said, her eyes going wide with amusement. "We're talking about trading what's rare, aren't we?"

Shaneese nodded.

"And haven't we been eating the best fruit we've ever tasted?" Fiona asked.

"Fruit," Kindan repeated dully. "You'd trade fruit?"

"In winter," Fiona said. "When it's not available."

"Or where it's not available," Shaneese said, eyes widening.

"And I know the perfect person to do our trading," Fiona added, turning to Jirana. The girl was too sleepy to notice, but she perked up when Fiona said, "Sweetie, can you wake your mother for us? It's important."

It was Jassi who came up with the ultimate solution to their housing problem.

"Ships!" she declared one day as she raced toward Fiona. The Weyrwoman was dozing in the midday heat and feeling large and heavy with children.

"What, are they here?" Fiona asked, trying to understand how ships could have come this close to their shore without being grounded.

"We bring ships, my lady," Jassi said, eyes full of excitement.

"Dragons will carry anything just as easily," Fiona assured her. "They can carry great weights."

"No, my lady, we buy ships and bring them here," Jassi told her, waving her hand around the camp. "They don't have to be new, they can be old and mastless."

"Slow down, slow down," Fiona said. "I don't understand."

It took a while for Jassi to make sense and, infuriatingly for Fiona, even longer for the Weyrwoman to comprehend her.

"So we buy old ships without the masts, small ships, and have the dragons fly them from the shore here onto the land."

"Exactly," Jassi agreed. "We might want to dig out the ground to give them an even keel, but then we could put all the people and supplies in them—it'd be just like living aboard a ship." Jassi paused. "We'd need about nine or ten small ones, maybe less if we could haul a bigger one—they could easily hold a wing of riders or more."

"And the dragons?"

"They don't mind sleeping out," Jassi said, gesturing around toward several clumps of stray dragons dozing in the sunlight.

"They're tough," Fiona said.

"And they think it's fun," Jassi added.

"What about the sails?" Fiona asked, perking up. Jassi looked at her in surprise. "If we bought the ships, they'd come with—what?—two sets of sails, right?"

In the end, it took a combination of ships, sails, and palm trees to provide enough housing and they found eleven ships in all, keeping one afloat to help with the fishing.

Lorana and Jassi were the principle sailingmasters, aided by the one person Lorana trusted back in this time with their secret—Colfet.

She'd been delighted when Jassi had told her that the old sailor had survived the wreck of the *Wind Rider* and had insisted on taking Talenth to meet him. Their reunion had been joyful, but Lorana had seen how hard the wreck had been on the man; his arm had never healed quite right so he'd eked out a living repairing fishnets and sails. He'd been perfect for the mission and thrilled to be able to help her once more.

His enthusiasm had faded somewhat when he'd discovered how poorly some of his students absorbed his teaching, but he was old enough to take the long view and shortly, even the worst of his "crew" were able to do their duties to his satisfaction.

Fiona had dispatched T'mar and Terin to borrow the Igen Weyr Records, which she insisted upon using for teaching materials with Jeriz—she had not forgotten her promise to teach him reading.

Jassi suggested that they borrow the Records from Ista, which might have suggestions more suited to the humid, wet climate they inhabited, but Fiona vetoed that idea.

"What we really need is a smith or access to their Records," Fiona mused one day after Kindan had brought back a bit of silver. "That'd teach us something about smelting silver."

"We need to talk to the Masterminer about mining the ore and what to look for," Kindan countered.

"Why not both?" Lorana asked. The two turned to her. Jirana was already asleep on one of the hammocks that Fiona would never use—they made her seasick—and the group had the large stern cabin to themselves, as Colfet had refused Lorana's offer, saying, "The side cabin's all I need, lass."

"How could we do that?" Kindan asked.

"Harpers are permitted anywhere," Lorana said blandly. "And you could copy anything we need that you found." She glanced toward Fiona and winked. "Take Jeriz with you, he could use the practice."

"You'd have to pry him away from Terin," Fiona said. She'd only managed to teach the lad to read by arranging for the young weyr-woman to be with them. Fiona got the impression that, were the green-eyed boy older, he would have sought instruction from Terin directly.

As it was, Kindan managed to get Jeriz to agree to go along only if Terin could accompany them. So, Lorana, Kindan, Jeriz, and Terin departed on Talenth, leaving Kurinth in Fiona's care.

When they returned, it was all Kindan could do to thank the younger pair and release them before he and Lorana burst into laughter. "You should have seen him," Kindan told Fiona, "you would have thought that Verilan himself was watching his every stroke."

"Did he do well?"

"Marvelously, if terrified for fear of not impressing Terin," Lorana allowed with equal mirth. She shook her head and sobered, telling Fiona, "I think you made an inspired choice with that pair."

Fiona said, "Yes, I did, didn't I? I can't wait to see my own children at that age."

She could not say the same thing six months later. She was great with child, expecting any moment, sleeping fitfully in a bunk in the captain's cabin, attended by Bekka, who was aided by Jirana with Javissa and Shaneese, and with Lorana on call.

Bekka examined her after her water broke and Jirana went for her mother and Shaneese. At Fiona's behest, Lorana, Kindan, and T'mar came, but the cabin was too small for all of them, so they took turns comforting her.

"I'm never, never, never doing this again!" Fiona screamed as a contraction rippled through her.

"You're doing fine," Shaneese assured her.

"I don't feel FIIINE!" Fiona shouted as another contraction shook her.

"T'mar, get behind her," Bekka ordered, all her calm tone suddenly replaced with a commanding voice of cold precision. "Fiona, you know what to do."

Fiona, with T'mar's guidance, found her way to the birthing stool and squatted as she'd practiced for the past two months. T'mar knelt behind her and she leaned back onto his chest. Lorana came to one side and Kindan to the other.

Bekka examined the position of the babies with her hands on Fiona's stomach and grunted in satisfaction.

"You're doing fine," Bekka assured her. "Next contraction, push hard."

"Anything!" Fiona wailed, squeezing Kindan's hand tightly.

Another contraction rippled through her and another. Fiona yelled loud and long, took another deep breath.

"I don't think you're yelling loud enough," Bekka told her calmly as she examined the birth canal. "Can't you do better?"

"Bekkkaaa," Fiona warned with a ragged breath. "Don't tempt me."

"Are you afraid?" Bekka taunted, eyeing Fiona's stomach carefully. "Remember, you've got two coming. The time to have avoided this was ten months back."

"They're not forty weeks," Fiona said, panting to regain her breath. "They're thirty-seven, so that's not much more than nine months."

"Stop talking," Bekka snapped. She saw the contraction start, and ordered, "Push!"

With another yell, louder this time, Fiona pushed with all her strength. Bekka reached up to guide the baby and caught it deftly.

"Shaneese, the knife," Bekka said.

"What!" Fiona wailed, eyes wide with surprise.

"The first one's out, I'm cutting the umbilical," Bekka told her, making the cut and tying the tube. She pulled the baby away and handed it to Shaneese, who cleaned it quickly, and, following Fiona's instructions, showed it to her.

"You have a beautiful girl, Fiona," Shaneese told her.

"You and Lorana know what to do," Fiona entreated, gasping for breath and feeling as though she'd been punched repeatedly. Another contraction rippled through her. She felt so awful that she was glad to know that she'd arranged with Lorana and Shaneese that they would watch over the child if anything happened to her. And, with twins, she was glad that one would be getting immediate maternal attention, leaving her to deal with birthing the second.

"The other one's getting ready," Bekka said, feeling gently around Fiona's tense stomach. "You're lucky, you might only have another hour."

"Another hour!" Fiona wailed in dismay. She gestured feebly to Shaneese. "Show me the baby again."

Smiling, Shaneese brought the baby girl up to her mother. Fiona looked at her, then squeezed Lorana's hand for attention. The other woman looked at her.

"Swear to me, both, that you'll be her mother," Fiona said.

"Fiona!" Bekka growled.

"Swear as foster-mothers," Fiona said.

"Nothing's going to happen to you," Lorana assured her. "But I claim this child as kin of my heart, blood of my blood, life of my life, for all time."

"This child is ours," Shaneese said in agreement. "She shall grow strong with the care of her mothers. I shall call her my own, tend her wounds, cheer her triumphs. Blood of my blood, heart of my heart, life of my life."

"Thank you," Fiona breathed with relief. "Kindan, T'mar."

"I'm here," Kindan told her, squeezing her hand lightly.

"I'm here," T'mar said, running his hands over her strained shoulder muscles, soothing them.

A contraction rippled across her belly before she could speak. Kindan gestured to her reassuringly; they had spoken of this long before, he knew what she wanted.

"I claim this child my daughter," Kindan said formally.

"As dragonrider of Zirenth and Weyrleader, I do claim this girl my own, heart of my heart, blood of my blood, life of my life," T'mar said.

"I name her my own, heart of my heart, blood of my blood, life of my life," Kindan concluded.

"Here comes another contraction!" Bekka warned. Fiona yelled as the next contraction rippled through her. Bekka looked up at her sternly. "Shards, Fiona, you're not even trying!"

"I . . . am . . . too!" Fiona swore between breaths. She concentrated on breathing for several moments, then continued in formal tones, "I, Fiona, Weyrwoman of Telgar, do name you, heart of my heart, blood of my blood—oh!"

"Push!" Bekka ordered.

Fiona pushed, even as she squeezed Lorana's hand imploringly.

"As her mother, I name this child in a mother's voice: Tiona," Lorana said even as Fiona bellowed with her next contraction.

"Shaneese, see to her," Bekka said, nodding toward the baby.

"We'll be right here, Fiona," Shaneese assured the Weyrwoman, "so Tiona can meet her sib."

Fiona didn't hear her, as another contraction tore through her and she yelled once more, pushing with all her lagging strength.

"Well done," Bekka said. "The head's out." She glanced down and gestured for Kindan to join her before she looked up at Fiona, her eyes full of concern. "I need to get one arm out, I'm going to have to guide it."

"Tell me what to do," Fiona said, beads of sweat dotting her forehead, her hair dank and lanky with exertion.

"Until I say otherwise, hold off on pushing," Bekka said even as she began to ease a hand up through the birth canal to feel for the baby's arm.

"Okay," Fiona agreed, leaning back against T'mar and taking slow deep breaths.

"You're doing fine," Shaneese assured her. Kindan looked to Bekka for guidance and saw the concern in the younger woman's eyes.

Javissa came up to take Kindan's place, bringing a damp cloth that she used to cool Fiona's head.

"Hold my hand tight," Javissa told her. She felt Fiona's hand grip hers tightly in gratitude.

"This is going to hurt," Bekka warned as she eased her hand over the offending limb. Fiona bellowed in pain. "Good, I've got my hand where it needs to be," Bekka assured her. "When you feel the next contraction, push as hard as you can. And yell like you mean it this time!"

"That won't be HAAARRRDDD!" Fiona's shouted as she writhed through another contraction. "AAAHHH!"

Her pain peaked and just as suddenly dropped to a dull, aching throb. She heard a funny sound and Bekka gave a slight yelp of glee.

"Javissa, the knife," Bekka said. She glanced up at Fiona, her blood-smeared face split in a wide grin. "Congratulations, Fiona, you have a son."

Fiona made a sound and then found her voice. "Trust a boy to be last."

And then she fainted.

"You're fine, your son's fine, your daughter's fine," Bekka assured Fiona the instant she woke up. "You lost a fair amount of blood, but nothing to be worried about." She paused as she turned a glow halfway to give the cabin some thin illumination. "How do you feel?"

"Sore, thirsty, and full," Fiona said, even as she noticed how easily she could move and how much it hurt.

"Kimar is here," Lorana told her quietly.

"Give him to me," Fiona said urgently. As soon as she had him, he started nursing, much to her relief. "Where's Tiona?"

"Here," Kindan said, moving forward with another bundle and guiding her to a good nursing spot.

"Help me sit up," Fiona said, as she tried to deal with two hungrily nursing babies. Bekka, Kindan, and Lorana rearranged her pillows so that they supported her back, but it wasn't enough, so Kindan got behind her to provide back support and help hold one of the babies.

"They're beautiful," Bekka told her with warmth in her voice. "You did a wonderful job."

Fiona nodded, not saying anything as she absorbed the painful-pleasant sensation of her two babies as they nursed.

"I'm hungry," Fiona said suddenly.

"Feed them first," Bekka advised her. "Then they'll sleep and you can eat."

"Why does that sound so much like raising a dragonet?" Fiona asked.

"Well," Bekka said with a shrug, "it is."

As the months passed, Fiona found herself yearning for the time when the twins could be weaned. She loved her time with them, even the incessant nursing, but she was restless to get moving, to be seen, to organize things. T'mar twitted her on it. "You've got to learn to delegate."

Lorana took over many of her duties, sliding easily into the role of senior Weyrwoman. Fiona was careful not to overtax her co-mother and set Terin and the other queen riders to helping as much as they could.

Often Fiona would find herself out in the center of the camp, watching the weyrlings drill from her seat, feeling more like a Lord Holder than a Weyrwoman as the babies napped nearby or fed quietly in the shade.

She soon had company, for Shaneese delivered her baby boy right on schedule. Together the two of them exchanged groans about the whole process, smiling at the beautiful babies when they thought no one would notice, and complaining about all their difficulties when they thought someone would.

Between them, Shaneese, Fiona, and the three babies had all the help they could want and soon found themselves strictly rationing it.

Xhinna, Taria, all the queen riders, and the other three women who had Impressed were constantly stopping by, many to coo over the babies and some to look wistfully.

This brought a new concern to Fiona and she and Shaneese spent much of their time working out plans to handle the babies they expected might soon join theirs. The women riders realized that as their dragonets were growing to soon join the fighting ranks, this was the best time for them to have their children and get their families started. The queen riders were less keen.

Of them all, Terin was the least happy. She was thrilled at Fiona's joy, hugged her friend and helped with the babies, being certain to exercise Jeriz's talents with diapers as well as honing her own, but Fiona could see the younger woman's sadness rise nearly day by day as Terin dwelled more and more on her loss.

"It's what she cannot have, that's why she wants it so much," Shaneese declared when she and Fiona talked about it one day. The babies were crawling around in the specially constructed play area, filled with sand and lined with rocks.

"Maybe she's just beginning to realize that F'jian won't be coming when she needs him," Fiona said, shaking her head sadly.

"We should start planning the nursery," Shaneese said, changing the subject.

"A nursery?" Fiona repeated, surprised. "That seems a bit grand for just our three."

"They won't be alone for much longer," Shaneese reminded her with a grin. "Some of the green riders have been inspired by our example."

"Who?"

"All of them except Taria," Shaneese said. "Helena has been working on J'gerd for months now and, from her smug look, she's succeeded."

"And Vellany?" Fiona asked, referring to the sturdily built green rider who had surprised everyone when she'd Impressed Delanth, as she'd seemed the least interested of all the Weyr's young women. She'd been far more interested in spending time with J'gerd and other riders, so it was no surprise when Shaneese continued, "She finally managed to get J'keran to stay awake long enough."

"Are you sure?" Fiona asked, peering out from under their shade, trying to locate the woman among the drilling weyrlings.

"Bekka is," Shaneese said. Bekka's ability to spot a pregnancy early was so well-known throughout their camp that some of the women had taken to avoiding her for fear that she would suddenly fix them with her knowing look.

"And Seriya?" Seriya was a shy sort with large eyes set alluringly in a delicate face.

Shaneese laughed. "V'lex!"

"Really? How?"

"I have no idea," Shaneese admitted. "And I'm not certain how she managed to keep V'lex from pining after J'gerd long enough to—" She stopped, shaking her head in amusement. "V'lex is beside himself with joy and J'gerd—"

"That could cause trouble," Fiona said, peering off into the distance thoughtfully.

Fiona remembered to mention it to T'mar and Kindan as they stopped by for lunch. Tied to the babies as they were, Fiona and Shaneese had taken over as much of the cooking as they could, aided by Jirana, Javissa, and whoever else was detailed to them for the day.

"Ho, so that's what's going on!" T'mar chuckled when he heard. "I've seen the way they've been looking at each other."

"And?"

"And they'll sort it out," T'mar told her. "Seriya, for all her shyness, is a sweet person who gets what she wants."

"It might be a problem," Kindan said. T'mar glanced at him and he explained, "Well, their dragons will be just old enough to start flying when they're either most pregnant or have just given birth."

"Stick Jeriz on one and Bekka on the other," Fiona said with a wave of her hand. "For that matter, get Colfet aboard the third."

Colfet had proved himself a master of all trades and invaluable to the camp. He'd become the older person that everyone found themselves consulting. He was always willing to listen politely, say nothing, or bark a quick order as needs be. At this moment he was out overseeing a party setting up the kiln works, while another party was digging out silver ore, and a third party was at work smelting it. Between him and Kindan, the island had turned profitable, exporting the luscious fruits that Fiona and Shaneese consumed in bulk, as well as the pretty sea-green stone set in various silver fashioning—necklaces, bracelets, rings, and hilt pieces being the most common.

Javissa's connections with the traders had given them ready access while Colfet had managed to secure fishing gear in exchange for the much-treasured brightfish and whitefish.

Fiona was still uncomfortable with their open surroundings, preferring the solid confines of a proper Weyr; the humidity was a constant annoyance as were the strange flying insects that seemed to buzz around incessantly, although, thankfully, they kept well clear of the dragons.

The old ships, half-buried in the ground, looked utterly incongruous in their surroundings, but had proved survivable. Wood was certainly more comfortable than cold stone, even if it was prone to retain damp air.

Fiona had dismissed the notion that some of the younger weyrlings had of calling their camp "Eastern Weyr"—it was far too pretentious and sounded far too permanent for such a temporary arrangement, but that hadn't stopped the name from spreading so much that she'd had to catch herself when she'd started to say it.

"You'd have Colfet fly on a dragon?" Kindan asked. "I'm sure he'd be much happier on a ship any day."

"Well, then, Bekka and Jeriz at least," Fiona said. "They're likely to Impress."

"Why not Lorana or Shaneese?" T'mar asked.

"Lorana's riding Talenth," Fiona reminded him.

"Only because her own rider is too lazy," T'mar teased. Fiona glared at him, but said nothing: There was too much truth to his words. As she reflected more on them, Fiona realized that there really was nothing to prevent her from flying more with her queen; the babies could easily be tended by Shaneese or Javissa. Even little Jirana was getting old enough to keep an eye on them, able to alert Talenth or one of the adults in need.

The first time it had happened, Fiona had been surprised. She hadn't thought that Talenth would hear the little girl, but Talenth's urgent message from Jirana had brought the Weyrwoman racing to the playground just in time to stop a small tunnel snake from darting after the babies.

They'd set a more careful watch after that and Fiona herself had gone on a few secret hunting missions; she'd found these eastern tunnel snakes to be much more vicious than those she'd killed as a child in Fort Hold.

Talenth had been unfazed when she explained that she kept a mental "ear" open for all of Fiona's friends. Apparently the queen had adapted to her rider's open ways by being more open herself.

"Dragons and riders influence each other," T'mar had said when Fiona had told him. "It's not surprising."

"Those greens would probably be more happy with women riders," Fiona said now, cocking her head toward Shaneese. "I can watch the babies if you want some exercise."

In the end, both suggestions were adopted. Shaneese rode Vellany's green Delanth with the woman's approval, while Javissa rode Seriya's Firunth and Lorana or Fiona switched off with Sidrath and Talenth.

The women's children were born within a month of each other and pronounced healthy by Bekka who, now nearing her fifteenth Turn, had grown mature in her healing. She had been turning heads nearly since their arrival in the camp and now, Fiona noticed with amusement, the blond healer was turning her head from time to time.

"I'm not getting pregnant," Bekka assured Fiona when they had a moment together privately. "We can't afford it."

Fiona raised an eyebrow at her challengingly, even as she bounced an oblivious Kimar on her knee.

"Oh, I'm going to have children," Bekka told her airily. "And I'll make you diaper them, too!" Then she shook her head firmly. "But not now. I'm not ready and there's no other midwife."

"Javissa," Fiona suggested.

"When I have a baby, I'm going to have my *mother* midwife and my father standing beside her," Bekka declared.

When asked, Bekka had assured her that Lorana could still have children. The older woman seemed content to play with Kimar, Tiona, and Shanar. As a second mother, Lorana was perfect, but she seemed to want nothing more than that for the moment.

As for Fiona, she found herself torn between the joy of her growing children and her own desire to get back to the fight.

She arranged, without telling T'mar, to gather the old Igen riders together—she was certain that it was they who had met with Lorana and had brought the old Fort injured riders back to the hot desert Weyr to begin their long recovery. And it seemed to her that the time was right to make that journey.

T'mar surprised her, though, when she and the others were ready to take off in the dark of night.

"Thought to leave without me?" he asked as he approached, dressed in riding gear, with Zirenth gliding in behind.

"How did you know?"

"I figured you'd try something like this," T'mar told her. "So I asked myself when would be the best time for the Weyrwoman to fool the Weyrleader?"

"Oh," Fiona said, shaking her head. "It would have to be a night when she'd arranged Javissa for babysitting, Kindan and Lorana for a night alone, and told Shaneese to have a good night's rest."

"Exactly," T'mar agreed, his teeth showing bright in the night's gloom. "So I merely waited until those conditions were met and asked Zirenth if he knew where Talenth was going."

"And she told him," Fiona said, sighing. She hadn't thought to caution her queen on the need for secrecy.

"So here we are," T'mar agreed. "And now, are we ready?"

"Yes, Weyrleader," J'gerd said, standing forward with the others. "We're ready."

T'mar says you're to give the image, Talenth said when they were airborne and ready to make the jump between.

Check with Lorana, she'd know best, Fiona said, even as she pulled together an image of Fort Weyr, later on that morning when she'd gone back in time to Igen Weyr with the unknown queen rider—the rider who she now knew was Lorana.

Your image matches, Talenth said after a moment.

Are you ready? Fiona asked. Talenth said that she was and Fiona urged her to pass the image on to the other dragons and, when they were ready, they went *between*.

They arrived in the dark of night, over Fort Weyr. They had jumped not quite three Turns into their future and shortly would be jumping ten Turns back into the past, shepherding the severely injured dragons and riders with them.

As Talenth silenced the watch dragon with a quick response, Fiona wondered if she were the gold rider who her much younger self had seen waving at her. She pulled the hood of her cloak up, while all around her, the other riders echoed her motion to disguise their identities.

"Quickly!" Fiona whispered as the riders landed and fanned out toward the various Weyrs. Her urging was unnecessary, each had already selected the dragonpair they would aid, their choice helped by their memories of the carping the older dragonriders had made when they'd arrived back in Igen Weyr so many Turns in their past.

Quickly, but not as quickly as any would have liked and not without a few heart-stopping coughs and scuffles echoing through the night air, they gathered the injured dragons and dragonriders and shepherded them *between*.

Their trip through time to Igen Weyr ten Turns in the past was longer than Fiona liked and she was tired at the end of it, finding less joy in waving at her younger self—had she been *that* small?—than she would have thought. She was grateful when they jumped back *between* to their present time and their Eastern Weyr.

But she was also very tired. Fiona collapsed the moment she got off Talenth, falling straight into T'mar's arms.

"I'm sorry," Fiona apologized.

"Nothing I hadn't expected," T'mar said as he carried her back to their quarters. The ships were still high enough that stairs had been constructed to reach the deck, but they'd been built wide enough for three people to walk side by side so that the heavier goods could easily be carried; T'mar had no trouble climbing up with Fiona in his arms.

When they reached the deck, he glanced down at her, smiling. "You know, the stars are quite pretty this close to morning."

"They are," Fiona agreed gazing up at him tenderly.

"Shaneese is already asleep," T'mar said.

"Was she expecting this?"

"No, but I had Zirenth explain to her before we left," he told her, as he squatted down on the deck, lowering her gently.

"And what did she say?"

"She said that you and I hadn't been spending enough time alone together," he told her, still holding her around the waist.

"And what, bronze rider, do you think we should do with our time?" Fiona asked coquettishly.

"Perhaps we can think of something," he said as he bent down to kiss her.

Fiona wrapped her arms around him as their lips met and when they broke free again, she said, "Perhaps."

With all the adult company surrounding the children, it was not surprising that they learned to speak early and well. Tiona spoke the first word of the three. Kimar was the last of the children to speak, even though Shanar was a month his junior.

Dark-haired and blue-eyed, there was no mistaking Tiona as

T'mar's daughter, although her ebullient manners and charming ways were clearly inherited from her mother. At turns this both delighted and exasperated Fiona, who discovered a girl "just like me" could be a handful, much to Bekka's obvious amusement—everyone else was too cautious to produce more than a studied lack of expression.

Shanar was sturdy, steady, and friendly, very much like his mother. He had her dark eyes and darker skin, but he freckled, reminding everyone of Jeriz.

Kimar was blond-haired and had his mother's sea-green eyes. But his manner was more like that of his obvious father, Kindan. The boy would watch everything, move slowly, but always with grace.

When Kindan fashioned them simple pipes, all three children were ecstatic, but only Kimar slept with his every night.

Colfet, at Fiona's request, had built a large bed in their quarters, large enough for three adults and three children—or four adults in a pinch—but as they grew older, Tiona started to exhibit a definite desire to sleep on her own like the big girls, pointing toward Jirana. Fiona and Shaneese worked to redirect that desire to something more obtainable—like having a sleepover with Jirana. Tiona, somewhat reluctantly, allowed herself to be diverted.

The young trader girl, now nearing her ninth Turn, was in parts both ecstatic at the toddler's desire and apprehensive. She agreed to Tiona's request to sleep with her one night, but the two were so ill-suited that Jirana found herself quietly begging a sleepy Fiona to take her daughter back or, failing that, to let her sleep in the big bed. Fiona thought only for a groggy moment before pulling Jirana in with the others and asking a drowsy Talenth to keep an "eye"—really, a mental glance—on her wayward daughter. Jirana's bed was not so far away that Fiona wouldn't be able to hear if the child needed her, but it was nice to know that her queen was also keeping watch.

The next day, Fiona explained the situation to Colfet who, with a merry laugh, promised to have Tiona a bed of her own by nightfall.

The children were a special source of pride to the old seaman, whose own children were all grown and starting families of their own. These dragonchildren were, for Colfet, a treasure of unimaginable wealth.

Whenever he could, he would watch them, and he was practically encouraging all the women to have more children, seeing each pregnancy as a further sign of his own success.

Fiona finally understood when she coaxed Lorana into telling her the full harrowing tale of their misadventure in the *Wind Rider* and Colfet's sacrifice for her.

"J'trel had thought I'd be safe on the *Wind Rider,* but some of the crew had other ideas, particularly when they stranded Captain Tanner at the new Half-Circle Sea Hold," Lorana told her. She explained how the *Wind Rider* had been caught in a storm, how Colfet had smuggled her off into the launch, and how she'd fallen out of the launch into the sea when a rogue wave had hit her.

Gently, but unerringly, Fiona tugged the whole story out of the older woman. She learned how guilty Lorana felt over sending her fire-lizards away—"Even then they were sick, I should have known!"—how Lorana had despaired of life, how she'd woken up in Benden Weyr and had Impressed her queen, Arith. How she'd lost Arith to her own error, how the loss of the Telgar Weyr riders under D'gan had provided her with the chance to bridge time to give those in the distant past the vital clue they needed to provide *her* with the right tools to save the dragons of Pern, and of how, in the end, she'd been given the locket that proved that one of her fire-lizards had made it back through time to the First Pass—and had lived.

Fiona kept encouraging her to remember until Lorana finally shed the tears that Fiona knew she needed to release—over the loss of her fire-lizards, the loss of her queen, the loss of her pregnancy. Fiona hugged her tighter then and released her long enough to kiss the other woman on both cheeks and forehead before hugging her once more.

Hearing her story, Fiona understood how Colfet felt involved in saving the dragons of Pern and how their every increase increased his own pride in Lorana—and in his decision to aid her.

"You are my life, my blood, my heart," Fiona told her feelingly. "I could not be without you."

Lorana hugged her back tightly, at a loss for words.

"I'm worried about Terin," Bekka said as she met Fiona and Shaneese for lunch.

"She's keeping to herself," Fiona said in agreement.

"Jeriz is with her and she's doing her drills with the weyrlings," Shaneese pointed out.

"Halfheartedly," Fiona said. She glanced at Bekka before being distracted by a noise from the latest additions to the nursery. Seriya raced over to scoop up her baby, but Fiona called back, "Leave him, he's fine."

The green rider shot Fiona a worried look but held back and watched as the baby dusted himself off and went back to playing happily with the others.

"You've got to let them see if they're all right," Fiona told the other woman with a grin. Beside her, Javissa snorted, for it had been the trader woman who had taught that to her. "If you come the first time they fall, they'll come to believe that they're hurt worse than they are."

Seriya nodded in understanding.

At two Turns, Shanar, Tiona, and Kimar were the eldest in the nursery, the others ranging from nine months to slightly more than a Turn. The six alternated between playing and fighting. The older three were somewhat better at playing, but they'd had more practice.

"She's afraid her dragon will rise," Fiona said, in answer to Bekka's earlier statement.

"Isn't it still too early?" Bekka asked.

Fiona shook her head. "There's a chance any time after the first two Turns. It's more likely in the third Turn, though."

"What about the greens?" Seriya asked worriedly. "Could they rise?"

"Yes," Fiona agreed. She frowned as a new thought struck her. "And they haven't chewed firestone."

"So they'd be fertile?" Bekka asked.

"Why hasn't Talenth risen already?" Shaneese wondered.

"I don't know," Fiona said, turning fondly toward where her queen was sleeping contentedly in a warm spot near the nursery.

"It could be because of them," Bekka said, pointing toward the nursery.

"The Records show that many Weyrwomen had babies while their queens were mating," Fiona said, shaking her head.

"How many had twins?" Bekka asked.

Fiona made a face. "None."

"It's possible that the extra effort required from you has inhibited her."

"Or something else has," Fiona said, frowning thoughtfully.

She tested this idea out on T'mar later that night. He frowned and shrugged. "Either explanation is possible," T'mar agreed.

"We should have thought of this when we came here," Fiona said. "Talenth hasn't much of a choice if she were to rise." She turned to where Zirenth lay curled on the ground just before the bow of their ship. "No offense, Zirenth."

"He's not offended," T'mar assured her. "And why would you want more choice, when you've got him and ten weyrling bronzes?"

"The Records show that the greater the choice, the longer the flight, the more blooded kills, the greater the chance of a large clutch," Fiona told him. She reached a hand to him and touched his shoulder gently. "Not that I want her to be flown by another bronze; I'm just not at all certain that I'd want her to be flown by one of the youngsters."

"You've read the Records," T'mar told her seriously.

Fiona nodded, getting his point. "It's possible for a queen to stay with just the one bronze," she reminded him.

"Possible," T'mar agreed grudgingly. "But very rare."

"And not always to the good of the Weyr, either," Fiona said. "But what my queen does is not always a reflection of what I want."

"And what do you want, Weyrwoman?"

"Right now, I want answers to our questions," she told him. "And I want you to know that I love you."

T'mar's expression softened. "I do."

"And remember that I will always have a place in my heart for you."

"And others."

"Like Shanar and Kimar," Fiona reminded him.

"So much competition," T'mar teased, shaking his head.

"It's only competition if there's a prize."

Wisely, the bronze rider said nothing.

"**B**etween the tunnel snakes and the Mrreows, I don't know which is worse," Colfet said early one morning after he had completed inspecting the hull of one of the ships.

"What's up?" T'mar asked. He, Kindan, Lorana, and Fiona were seated nearby. T'mar and Kindan were due to start more drills with the now mature weyrlings.

"The tunnel snakes tore a new hole in the side of the *Istan Harvest*," Colfet said, shaking his head, referring to one of the older ships. "They got into the stores and we probably wouldn't have found them except one of those fardling Mrreows came chasing after it."

"Was anyone hurt?"

"They were all scared out of their wits with the racket but no other harm was done," the seaman replied.

"Should we organize another hunting party?" Kindan asked. "The pelts fetched a fair price, last time."

"The pelts weren't worth the three injured," Fiona said, shaking her head. Kindan absently stroked his left forearm: He'd been among those injured.

"And we were lucky that Mayorth ever recovered," Lorana reminded them. "We can't risk another injury when we're so close."

"Well, we've got to figure out what we're going to do," T'mar said. "We're nearing the time when we should bring the injured here."

"We've got another couple of months, surely," Fiona said.

"True, but if they were here earlier, we'd have more bronzes," T'mar pointed out. "And more experienced riders to help with the training."

"But we'd have the injured to tend and more to feed," Fiona countered.

"So what do you suggest?"

"Well," Fiona said, pursing her lips for a moment before continuing, "I think we should consider our firestone needs and get that sorted before we bring the fighting dragons here."

"The queens could rise any day," T'mar reminded her.

"They could but, aside from Talenth, they'd still be pretty young."

"Honestly," T'mar told her, "I was rather surprised she didn't rise when we were in Igen."

"And I'm surprised she hasn't risen here, yet," Fiona told him, recalling their conversation weeks past. "Do you suppose it has something to do with timing it?"

"I doubt it," T'mar said, taking a bite of the melon that he'd tackled for breakfast. He looked at it with distaste, saying apologetically to Shaneese, "I never thought I'd say it, but I'm getting tired of fruit."

"Well, we've no holders to till fields," Fiona replied, "so unless you want to take *more* weyrlings from training and set them to the fields, we'll have to make do with what we've got."

T'mar grunted an agreement and finished his melon in silence. Fiona, too, was silent while she ate and for much the same reason— melon once a sevenday was a rare treat, melon morning, noon, and evening was more of a torment.

Jirana was watching the toddlers, but she came racing when they finished their meal. "Are we flying, Weyrwoman?"

"Of course!" Fiona assured her. "Have you got your gear?"

"I'll get it," Jirana chirped, racing toward their ship. It had become a habit for Fiona to bring her up with her whenever she flew Talenth, just as Jeriz rode with Terin whenever she drilled.

"She's eager," Shaneese said approvingly even as she moved closer to the playground to take over minding the toddlers.

"She loves flying," Javissa agreed with a touch of worry.

"She can always fly with me," Fiona told her. "Even when we return."

An angry growl and a child's shriek electrified them.

"Jirana!" Fiona and Javissa cried at once, racing toward the ship. They reached it together and found the girl crumpled on the deck, a large gash in her leg. One of the Mrreows ran off at their approach, something dangling from its mouth.

"Baby!" Javissa cried as she gathered her youngest in her arms. Fiona knelt and examined the bloodied leg, her expression grave.

Talenth, get Bekka! She called even as she located the artery behind the girl's knee and applied pressure to reduce the blood loss.

"I hurt, Momma," Jirana whimpered.

"What happened?" Fiona asked, looking up and smiling at the dark-eyed child. "Can you tell us?"

"I was going toward the stairs when the tunnel snake charged at me," Jirana said. "And then I was hit from the back and heard the Mrreow and I screamed." She turned to her mother. "I think the Mrreow tried to save me."

"I think it was just trying to get the tunnel snake," Kindan said when Fiona recounted the tale to him and T'mar later, after Jirana's wound had been stitched. She'd been given fellis and brought to the center of their camp, near the nursery, so that she could be kept under constant watch. "It pushed her out of the way because it was hungry and the tunnel snake was the smaller prey."

"I suppose," Fiona said without much enthusiasm. Kindan quirked an eyebrow upward questioningly. "Well, it just seems that these Mrreows came with the colonists." She raised a hand to tick off her reasons, "They've got fur like the canines. And they've four limbs, not six, their eyes aren't like any of the eyes the six-limbed Pernese have."

Kindan pursed his lips and nodded. "It could be," he agreed. "But why haven't we seen them before?"

"Why do they attack dragons?" T'mar demanded. "None of the canines or herdbeasts do that."

"Maybe the dragons are too much like the tunnel snakes," Lorana replied.

"But we've got canines that go after tunnel snakes, and not dragons," Kindan objected.

"The dogs have to be trained," Fiona reminded him. "They don't attack the tunnel snakes without training."

"That's because they're smart," Kindan replied. "Those things are nasty." He shook his head. "I still can't believe you used to hunt them when you were little."

"I didn't know any better," Fiona admitted. "And I think if the tunnel snakes back home were like these, I probably wouldn't have."

"Well the question remains, what are we going to do about them?" T'mar said.

"The bigger question is whether hunting the Mrreows is helping or hurting us," Fiona said, glancing toward Kindan. The harper had his bow at his side and a quiver of arrows on his back. "If the Mrreows are keeping the tunnel snakes in check, perhaps we should just leave them be."

"And hunt tunnel snakes?" Kindan asked.

Fiona shrugged. "They're almost impossible to find in this soft soil. They have no trouble at all burrowing through it."

"There's no decent rocky place on this half of the island," T'mar remarked, glancing challengingly at his Weyrwoman. She shrugged; she still hadn't written that strange note warning them away from the western half of the Great Isle, so she had no reason to know if the restriction was still necessary.

"And there's no guarantee we'd find better elsewhere," Fiona said, shaking her head. "And even if we did, it would take at least a month, probably more, to move our camp now."

T'mar blew out a sigh in agreement.

"Regardless," Javissa spoke up, "what are we going to do about the children?"

"I think we'd better have them sleep here," Fiona said. "And we'll need to set up a guard."

The attack on Jirana had unsettled everyone in the camp, and the setting of a permanent guard was met with a feeling of relief.

"Did you notice Delanth at drill tonight?" Kindan asked T'mar as they made their way back to their ship for the evening. The Weyrleader nodded.

"Proddy, wasn't she?" Fiona asked. T'mar nodded. Being proddy—irritable and snappish—was a sign of a green about to rise.

"You know, they haven't chewed any firestone," Kindan said.

"Yes," Fiona agreed. "But that might not be so bad."

The others looked at her. "Well, even if all the greens had eggs, how many would that be?"

T'mar shrugged. "No one knows."

"If they had twenty eggs each, we've only forty-four, so we'd have just eight hundred and eighty eggs," Fiona said.

"And just how, Weyrwoman, would you expect us to feed that many hatchlings?"

"And where would we find all the Candidates?" Kindan asked in surprise.

"Well, we don't even know how many they'd clutch, so I think we're counting our dragons before they hatch," Fiona said.

"But if they could," T'mar said with a sense of hope, "we could repopulate all Pern."

"With greens and blues," Fiona reminded him.

"I suppose that must have been another one of Kitti Ping's thoughts," Lorana said.

"Actually," Fiona said, "I think the fire-lizards figured it out on their own and our ancestors just kept it."

"We'll talk on this in the morning," T'mar decided, patting his Weyrwoman tenderly on the head. She bristled at him and then leaned up for a kiss that he returned briskly before going to his cabin. He was back a moment later, saying to Fiona, "Where's Shaneese?"

"With the children," she told him with a dimpling smile. "Why, dragonrider, are you afraid of sleeping alone?"

Lorana chuckled and T'mar went wide-eyed, nodding. "Very afraid," he assured her. "What should I do?"

"Perhaps we'll think of something," Fiona told him, turning to hug Lorana and Kindan in turn. "Why don't you and I discuss it Weyrwoman to Weyrleader?"

Their pleasant night was shattered at first light when Fiona woke, eyes wide.

"She's rising."

"Talenth?" T'mar asked, surprised and reaching to touch Zirenth's mind. The bronze was still sleeping.

"No, Delanth," Fiona said, pushing herself up and putting on her robe and slippers.

They met Lorana and Kindan as they left their cabin and together the four of them went to the center of the camp and the nursery.

"Lorana, can you be with Vellany?" Fiona asked. "I'll handle the queens and the other greens."

"They're all so close to rising, it might be a good idea to have them go elsewhere," T'mar suggested.

"Exactly my thinking," Fiona said. She grabbed her gear, while warning Talenth. The queen met her at the bottom of the ship. They were about to take off when Jirana rushed toward them. "Come on!" Fiona called.

The little girl scampered up, Fiona strapped her in and with a quick image to Talenth, took them all *between*.

"This is where my father died, isn't it?" Jirana asked as Fiona and the other queens and greens circled down for a landing on the Red Butte. Fiona mentally kicked herself for her choice—it was instinctive, one of the earliest drilling points the Igen riders had learned.

"Yes," Fiona said, wondering if she should bring them all elsewhere. But the mood of the younger greens and queens was too nervous and it took all of her and Talenth's efforts to get them organized and arrayed around the plateau. "This is also where the dragonriders arranged to provide food to the holders during the Plague."

"It's a nice place," Jirana said as she looked around, scanning. "Can I see where my father is?"

Fiona nodded silently, relaying orders through Talenth assigning the other queen riders responsibility for overseeing their greens. She jumped down first, reached up to hand Jirana down, and looked around.

It had been at least four, perhaps five, Turns since Lorana had built the cairn.

Terin saw and joined them, leading Taria, Helena, and Seriya, as well as the other green Telgar riders with her. As if by some unspoken command, Lin, Jassi, Garra, and Indeera followed and soon more than forty riders were behind Fiona.

The Weyrwoman nodded at the other queen riders, then stopped and knelt down beside Jirana. "Is it okay if the others come with us?"

Jirana looked around solemnly at the others grouped silently nearby and nodded slowly. "I think my father would like that."

"Jirana is looking for the cairn Lorana made for her father," Fiona told the others after she stood up. Terin moved forward and rested her arm comfortingly on the young girl's shoulder. Lin came up on her other side while Jassi, Garra, and Inderra stood behind.

Fiona led the way, even as she checked with Lorana about the flight.

We're at Red Butte, Fiona told the other woman with a tone of apology in her voice. *Jirana wants to see her father's grave.*

She felt a trickle of shock from the ex-dragonrider, then a calm supportive acceptance. *Of course,* Lorana thought to her. *I've told Javissa. She approves.*

Fiona nodded to herself absently even as she sent a grateful thought back to Lorana; she hadn't thought about asking Jirana's mother. A moment later, Fiona turned with a certainty and headed toward a pile of rocks in the distance.

"Your father lies here," Fiona said, going to her knees beside the girl.

Jirana looked around the plateau and closed her eyes. She swayed with the wind, her nostrils going wide as she took in a deep breath, savoring the scent on the wind. After a long moment she opened her eyes again, peering at the ground between the stones of Tenniz's cairn.

"Do you think purpleflower might grow here?" Jirana asked, turning to Fiona.

"It's very dry up here," Jassi said, coming to squat beside the young girl on the other side. "But I think you could find some that would thrive."

"When we come back, can we do that?" Jirana asked.

"Of course," Fiona promised. "Should we bring your mother?"

"No," the little girl replied. "Father told me that it would make her sad."

"He told you?" Fiona repeated, eyes narrowing. Jirana nodded. "Just now?"

Jirana made a face. "No, silly, he's dead! He told me before; the last time we met."

"Jirana," Fiona began with the slow patience of an adult trying to break bad news to a child, "your father died before you were born."

"Yes," Jirana said. "But he told me when he saw me the last time."

"The last time?" Terin repeated, dropping down beside Fiona and exchanging a quick worried look with Fiona. "When was that?"

"When he told Jeriz that he had to go to Telgar," Jirana replied simply.

You can come back, Lorana told Fiona. *Winurth flew her.*

"We should get back," Fiona said, looking first to Terin and then to Jirana. The little girl nodded in quiet acceptance.

"So what does this mean?" Shaneese asked when they gathered back once more and were able to take a break.

"It means that J'gerd is going to have a lot of explaining to do," Kindan predicted.

"He'll do fine," Fiona said. "He's good with words and well-liked."

"I meant about eggs," Shaneese said. "Will Delanth clutch?"

"Perhaps," T'mar said, looking toward Fiona.

"If greens are like queens, then we'll know in twelve to fifteen weeks," Fiona said, "when she clutches."

"We haven't got a suitable hatching ground," T'mar said. "Will the eggs even harden without the heat?"

Fiona shook her head. "What we could do is bring more sand up here, cover it at night, and expose it by day when it's not raining so that it will gather heat."

"The sands are always hot," T'mar said. "What will that mean to these eggs?"

"I don't know," Fiona admitted, turning a questioning look to Kindan.

"You've read more Weyr Records than I," he told her.

"So we don't know if she'll clutch and, if she does, we don't know if her eggs will hatch on this ground," T'mar concluded.

"Worse," Fiona said, and the others turned to her apprehensively, "we know that this mating flight will spark others."

"The bronzes are old enough," T'mar said, flicking a hand open dismissively.

"They may be old enough, but are there enough bronzes for all these queens?" Lorana asked.

"And what do we do if more than one rises, green *or* queen?" Fiona asked. Lorana and T'mar shook their heads; they had no more of an answer than she.

"We can send the others to Red Butte," Kindan suggested. "That would help."

"But if two or more rise?" T'mar asked.

"Then we'll have to handle it," Fiona declared. "We can't lose any dragons."

The next morning, Fiona woke with a hot angry feeling roiling inside her.

Talenth! Fiona's cry roused Lorana and T'mar just as the bronzes roared expectantly.

"Come on!" Fiona cried, racing out of the cabin toward her suddenly ravenous queen. She heard Lorana follow after, felt the dragonrider pull herself away from the queen even as Fiona found herself fighting to maintain control.

No! Blood your kills!

Talenth's bellowed response was not that of her normally kind, docile friend. Now she was a full queen, roaring her challenge to the entire Weyr.

The bronzes roared in response and then—another dragon bellowed! Another queen!

How dare she!

Who, who could challenge her? Talenth shrieked in anger. Fiona felt confusion, fear, terror, panic—but none of it from her.

Terin! Kurinth! Lorana's voice rolled through her mind.

Help her, Fiona called, even as she poured her will toward Talenth. The queen rose with an angry bellow and dropped immediately on the nearest buck, snapping its neck.

No! Fiona rasped at her queen. *Only blood your kills!* Talenth rebelled, angry, fighting back, ready to eat her way to combat strength—she would teach this challenger, she would kill any who stood against her rightful position.

For an instant Fiona wavered against the pressure, felt herself ready to give in, to see claw against claw, fang against fang, to rend, tear, rip to victory.

No! Fiona cried, her will flowing like fire into her queen. *She is our friend!*

Talenth raged back, tearing down another buck, sucking it dry and rising again only—

—there was another queen in the air, too, challenging her. It was Kurinth.

Lorana reached Terin just as she heard the bellow from her queen.

"Terin!" she cried. "You must control her, you must take her away from here, don't let her gorge, get her away."

"No," Terin said miserably, shaking her head, eyes streaming but unseeing. "He's not here, it's not right, it's not right, it's not right." Her expression altered and she took on a fierce expression. "Hate her, she's stopping me. She can't stop me, hate her." She shook her head again and wailed, "F'jian! F'jian, help me!"

Above, a throng of dragons bellowed in the morning air. Lorana reeled as she felt the power, reeled as she felt her legs turn to rubber. She sank to the ground even as she saw Terin's eyes go wide.

As the last of her strength drained from her and she felt darkness overtake her, Lorana cried out, *I can't control her!*

I can't control her! Fiona heard lashing through her mind. And then she heard nothing. *Lorana?* She called, her concentration on her queen totally broken.

Freed, Talenth tore her way toward the usurper, ready to rend and tear.

Dragons creeled in anger, and Talenth found her way blocked— there were other queens between her and her prey.

Fiona, hold her! a voice cried.

Lorana?

Hold her, the voice called again. *Help is coming.*

Fiona reached for her queen and hauled her back under her control, surprised and confused by Lorana's sudden return, stronger and more determined and—riding Talenth?

Go here! Lorana called, picturing an image that Fiona and Talenth both caught. In the image there were several alluring bronzes, far below, looking forlornly up, trying to match her speed and—

Suddenly they were there. The Red Butte was beneath, the bronzes struggling vainly to match her glory and—

Talenth soared. Fiona rose with her, freeing her dragon to reach for the highest heights.

Up! Up! Fiona called. *Leave them behind!*

▼ ▼ ▼

"Terin, Terin, you must control her!" a voice was shouting in Terin's ear. It was a scared voice, a tired voice, the voice she wanted to hear most—

"F'jian?" Terin said, opening her eyes and looking up. "F'jian?"

"I'm here," F'jian said. "I'm here, love, just like I promised."

"Kurinth?"

"Go with her," another voice urged quietly. "Flow with her, follow her in your mind, see where she is."

"Ladirth!" Terin cried as she saw the world through her queen's eyes. "What's he doing here?"

Does he think he can catch me? Kurinth asked, looking back with both longing and disdain as the sturdy bronze pursued her. She saw others, good strong bronzes, trying vainly to outfly her and failing.

She taunted them with a roar and climbed, climbed, climbed— suddenly at ease with the world, full of her power, certain of her future.

Beneath her, a bronze broke off, winded. And another. She bellowed at them, the poor, small piteous things! And she looked down at Ladirth. There was a great bronze. She dove toward him, feeling compelled, feeling anxious, feeling—

And suddenly he turned on his side and caught her as she came toward him and together they fell, fell, fell, and—

Together. They were together and it was everything. They were the only two on Pern, gold and bronze.

TEN

Queen and bronze fly entwined
Heart, spirit, soul, and mind
To the Weyr's strength assure
That the eggs will endure.

Fiona found herself in the arms of T'mar and she nuzzled tightly against him even as she felt her sated queen gliding toward the landing of the Red Butte. The other bronzes had departed. Only Zirenth remained. When they landed, gold and bronze, they settled near each other, necks entwined.

She reached across land and ocean toward their camp, trying to find the feel of Lorana and failing.

"We must go back. Lorana's fainted and I don't know what's happened with Terin," Fiona said, pulling herself away from T'mar with ill-concealed regret. She reached out and—a sudden welling of passion overtook her and she clutched at T'mar for balance.

They lost it.

Later, when they recovered, Fiona found herself lying on T'mar's shoulder. Cautiously she reached out once more, feeling for Lorana.

Come home, she heard.

"**A**re you sure you're all right with this?" Lorana asked Fiona a seven-day later as she prepared to climb onto Talenth's back.

"She'll be too egg-heavy soon enough," Fiona said. "And, once she's clutched, she'll not want to leave her eggs."

"This has never been done," Lorana cautioned.

"I trust you," Fiona assured her. "You're the only one to do it." She smiled at the taller woman as she added, "After all, you can't break time."

Lorana smiled at her, gave her a quick hug and mounted Fiona's queen.

They rose into the sky, circled once, and winked *between*.

"I need to borrow your mate," Lorana said when she located Javissa. The journey had been less effort than she'd imagined, even though she knew that this was only the first of several journeys she needed to complete before she returned with Talenth to Eastern Weyr. It was a time after they'd first met. Javissa was large with child. The traders were at the same oasis where she'd first met them, traveling with only a domicile dray.

"Borrow?"

"I'd like him to meet some people," Lorana said. She saw Javissa start to ask and shook her head. "I can't tell you who."

"How long will you be gone?" Javissa asked. "His cough is getting worse."

"I know," Lorana said. "Soon he will go to the place he dreamed and meet me there, but I won't know him."

"But not now?"

"No," Lorana said. "When he goes, he'll need food for two for three nights."

"What sort of food?"

"I can't tell you," Lorana replied. "I'll have him back in no time at all, but he'll be very tired and need to sleep."

"And you?" Javissa asked. "You won't be tired?"

"I'll manage," Lorana said.

"Javissa, what is it?" Tenniz's voice came from behind the dray.

"It's Lorana," the trader woman said. "She wants to borrow you."

"Borrow?" Tenniz called back, as his voice came toward them and he stepped into view. He looked at Lorana, then back to Javissa. She met his eyes and some secret communication passed between them.

"We were wondering," Javissa said slowly and not without some misgiving, "if you would do us an honor."

"Whatever you wish, that I can do," Lorana promised without hesitation.

"Would you allow us to use your name in our daughter's?" Tenniz asked. He glanced shyly at Javissa and took her hand. "We were thinking of Jirana, if it wouldn't offend you."

"I'd be honored," Lorana said, dipping her head.

"Thank you," Javissa said. She looked in Lorana's eyes for a long time. "Tenniz says that I will be seeing you again."

"You may be sure of it," Lorana promised, turning toward the seer.

"And you will not keep him long?"

"When do you want him back?" Lorana asked.

"Give me time to make camp, so that he can go straight to sleep," Javissa said.

"Twenty minutes?"

"That would be enough," Javissa agreed.

Lorana nodded and extended a hand toward Tenniz. "I thought you would like a chance to go a-dragonback."

"Thank you," Tenniz said, taking her hand and following her toward the queen.

He eyed Talenth intently and said, "This is not the same queen you were on last."

"True," Lorana nodded. She guided him up and strapped him in.

"Where are we going?" Tenniz asked as Lorana silently guided Talenth skyward.

"When," Lorana corrected. The trader craned his neck around to look at her. "Would you like to see your daughter?"

"My daughter?" Tenniz said with a sob. "But, lady, we cannot break time."

"True, but sometimes we can cheat it," Lorana said, silently ordering Talenth *between*.

▼ ▼ ▼

They arrived much less than a Turn into the future. Lorana spent a few moments orienting herself and then Talenth whirled down to the ground near a trader's caravan. It was night, but the caravan had not circled up as was the usual trader precaution.

From the domicile dray there came a woman's cry. Tenniz's eyes widened and he scampered off Talenth, rushing to the dray. Lorana waited outside while Tenniz was with his wife for the birth of their daughter. She was surprised when Azeez came outside to greet her.

"You have brought my daughter a great gift," the man said with tears in his eyes.

"It was the least I could do," Lorana assured him.

"You are clearly the Beacon."

Lorana waved the compliment aside. "Please tell Tenniz that we cannot tarry long."

Azeez nodded and returned to the dray. Minutes later, Tenniz returned, his eyes gleaming.

"Thank you, weyrwoman, for this gift beyond price," Tenniz said.

"It is not much I can give you," Lorana replied. She gestured toward Talenth. "Climb on."

"We're going back?"

"We're going," Lorana told him with a twinkle in her eyes lit by the night's stars.

Again they went *between* and this time they returned to another caravan, this one circled up in the customary fashion.

"We are two Turns in the future," Lorana said.

"How do you know when we are?" Tenniz asked. Lorana smiled and pointed up to the night sky. "Oh!"

"The traders taught Fiona," Lorana said. "She taught me."

"'Our gifts are always returned many fold,'" Tenniz said, quoting trader lore. His brows puckered as he asked, "But how do you know where to go?"

"Talenth and I scouted before we came to you," Lorana told him.

"So you know what we'll find?"

Lorana shook her head. "I only thought to offer you opportunities."

"Thank you," Tenniz said with feeling, deeper than mere words. "And what opportunity do you offer now?"

"I thought you might want to talk with your children," Lorana said, gesturing to the caravan.

When Tenniz returned this time he shook his head in awe and hugged Lorana fiercely. "She spoke to me," he said, "Jirana spoke to me."

Lorana nodded and gestured for him to mount Talenth once more.

"Now we go back?" Tenniz asked.

Lorana shook her head. "A friend of mine tells me that the third time is the best."

Again they went through time and returned in the night, above a caravan. Talenth bugled a warning as she descended and the caravan halted, heading south from Southern Telgar Hold on its way back to the desert.

"Jeriz has nearly ten Turns now, Jirana just seven," Lorana said as the trader gave her an expectant look. His eyes narrowed at her tone, but she said no more, gesturing for him to head on.

Close to an hour later he returned.

"I had a sight: Jeriz will go to Telgar," Tenniz said. Lorana nodded. "You knew?"

"I knew that he would go, not that you would see it," Lorana said.

"And do you also know about Jirana?"

Lorana smiled. "Are you ready to return?"

"Yes," Tenniz said. "I can return now." He mounted up. "It will be easier to face my fate knowing that my children will be safe."

*H*ow *are you feeling?* Lorana asked Talenth as they climbed once more into the night sky, having brought Tenniz back in time before the allotted twenty minutes had passed.

I am fine, Talenth assured her.

Very well, let's go, Lorana told the queen lovingly. *And remember, say nothing to Fiona.*

They winked *between*. Again, Lorana was surprised to feel something tugging at her, hear voices crying in pain. *Can't lose the babies! Can't lose the babies!* And: *The Weyrs! They must be warned!*

She collected herself and fought through once more, propelling herself and Talenth as if through muddy water toward their destination.

Five coughs later they appeared above Telgar Weyr. Talenth silenced the watch dragon and glided to a landing beside the queen's ledge.

Ladirth, be ready to come with us, Lorana said, sending the sleepy bronze the impression of hot flying, tense moments. The bronze perked up immediately, even as Lorana stepped over into Kurinth's weyr. The young queen was sleepy, sated from a meal. Softly, Lorana moved into Terin's quarters and tapped F'jian on the shoulder.

The bronze rider woke, startled, but Lorana put her finger to lips and gestured for him to follow her. With a backward glance at the sleeping Terin, F'jian followed her out into the sleeping queen's weyr.

"I need you and Ladirth to come with me," Lorana said.

"Is this important, my lady?"

"Yes," Lorana told him. "But I will not lie to you, it will be tiring."

"I should stay with Terin," F'jian said, turning his head to peer back at the sleeping weyrwoman.

"You'll see Terin," Lorana said. "Bronzes are blooding their kills."

"Their kills?" F'jian repeated, glancing around, senses stretched. "Where?"

"Come with me," Lorana said. "Terin needs you."

"Terin?" F'jian repeated blankly. He glanced toward the sleeping queen. "But Kurinth is too young."

"Now," Lorana agreed. "Come with me, it's your only chance."

Before she went *between*, she called Tolarth, Minith, Melirth, and Lyrinth to her, giving them the coordinates. The queens obeyed her summons, sensing her urgency.

Taking a deep breath, Lorana urged the queens and F'jian *between* forward into the future.

A fury erupted around them and they heard the screams of angry queens preparing to fight for their rights to the bronzes.

"F'jian!" Lorana called. "Go to Terin, she needs your help!"

The bronze dragon dashed to the ground long enough to drop his rider and then rose into the air, taking one herdbeast from the pen and sucking its blood in a frenzy before taking to the sky. Lorana dispatched the queens and Talenth to separate the passion-flamed Kurinth and Talenth, then had Fiona, T'mar, and the others send their dragons to the Red Butte to separate them from Kurinth and her flight.

Knowing that she—her earlier self back in time—had fainted from her fruitless efforts, Lorana stayed clear of Terin's quarters. She felt Kurinth and Ladirth make their brilliant union and, moments later, felt Talenth and Zirenth join triumphantly over the Red Butte.

As Kurinth and Ladirth returned to the ground, necks twined, Lorana felt the tensions ease out of the dragons. Much later, Lorana said to Ladirth, *We cannot tarry too long.*

F'jian came out of Terin's quarters not long after, his fingers twined in hers.

Tell F'jian that whenever she needs him most, he'll be there, Lorana said to the bronze dragon.

F'jian's head snapped to face Lorana as his dragon's words registered. The bronze rider gave her a questioning look, one filled with an infinite sadness. Lorana nodded in response: She meant the promise.

We must return, Lorana said. Sadly, F'jian let go of Terin and mounted his tired dragon.

They followed her once more back to Telgar Weyr. As Ladirth flew up to his quarters for a needed rest, F'jian and Lorana walked back to Terin's quarters.

"How long do I have?" F'jian asked softly.

"I cannot tell you," Lorana said, shaking her head sadly. "And you cannot tell Terin."

"Why?" the bronze rider asked.

"Because, no matter how much we want, we cannot break time," Lorana said.

"So I am to die?"

Lorana said nothing. The young man turned toward the sleeping girl.

"Will I see you again?"

Lorana nodded. "And remember, I don't know this yet."

"Why are you doing this?"

"We cannot break time," Lorana told him quietly. "But we can cheat it." She waved him toward the sleeping girl and turned back once more to the Weyr Bowl.

Talenth, let's go, Lorana said.

"This isn't anything like a proper Hatching Ground," T'mar said as he surveyed the result of two sevendays' worth of effort. The dragons had worked tirelessly, scooping up fine sand from the shore and bringing it back to pile atop and beside the old nursery into the newly stone-lined makeshift Hatching Ground.

"It's the best we can do," Fiona said. She shook her head. "Who ever thought we'd have all five queens and four greens ready to clutch at the same time?"

T'mar shook his head. "How will we feed so many weyrlings and hatchlings?"

"We'll send the older ones back," Fiona said. "Keep a few for work and wait until the rest are old enough to return to the Weyrs."

"Hmmph," T'mar said, not satisfied with her solution but unable to counter with anything better. "What about Candidates?"

"*That* is a problem," Fiona agreed. She turned to Kindan and gave him a questioning look. "Will Lorana stand, do you think?"

"Will you stand?" T'mar added, glancing at the harper.

"He has no choice," Fiona declared. Kindan glanced her way and gave her a resigned look. Fiona chuckled and reached out to pat him on the shoulder. "He's a wise man."

"I don't think it matters, really," Kindan said with a shrug. "No Records I've ever read mention someone my age Impressing."

"But if you *can* Impress, then maybe we can get some of the others who have lost their dragon to stand on the Hatching Grounds again," T'mar said. "Think how that would be."

"I've nearly thirty Turns now," Kindan said. "Aren't I too old for this? Shouldn't someone younger have the honor?"

"The dragons will decide," Fiona said.

"And you'll keep your word?"

"Yes, if you are not chosen this time, I won't ask you again," Fiona said. They'd talked about this ever since the mating flights. At first, Kindan had refused outright, but when Lorana had merely suggested it was probably moot, the harper had relented on the condition that he would not be asked again.

"Otherwise, I'll be as old as Zist and standing on the sands!"

"Well, we have some time to find Candidates," Fiona said. "No one's clutched and it will be at least five weeks from then to a Hatching."

"If they hatch," T'mar said grimly. "No one's tried such cool sands before."

"We do what we can," Fiona said with a shrug. "We expose them to the sun when it's shining and protect them from the elements when it's not."

"But day to day they'll be hardly more than warm," T'mar groused.

"I think that any additions to our strength would be worthwile," Fiona reminded him.

"True," T'mar agreed. "But I wonder if we wouldn't be wiser having Talenth and the other queens return to their Weyrs."

"Or maybe we can find a proper Weyr on the west side of the island," Kindan added.

Fiona shrugged. "It's worth considering, but we'd better be quick."

"Six queens, four greens; how many Candidates will we need?" T'mar said again. "And where will you find them?"

Fiona shrugged once more. She, Lorana, and the other queen riders had discussed the issue with no more resolution than now. Terin had done the numbers: At the best, there would be nearly a whole Weyr's worth of eggs looking to Impress. Even at the most conservative estimate, the ten clutches could see over a hundred eggs on the sands—nearly a quarter of the total strength they had in the camp now that they'd brought the injured riders back in time with them to heal and recover.

That decision had not been taken lightly but, as Fiona pointed out, the right time was before the queens clutched and before the eggs hatched; when the Eastern Weyr—she had given up arguing against the name—had fewer dragons to feed and enough trained bodies on hand to tend to the needs of the injured riders and dragons.

The addition of over four hundred mouths to feed—half human, half dragon—had put a huge burden on the existing population that was only met by having the now-mature weyrlings and their riders spend most of their time providing sustenance or succor but, as Fiona and T'mar had agreed, the fighting Weyrs would be able to more easily integrate the suddenly grown weyrlings into their wings if they had also trained with the soon-to-be-healed riders and dragons with nearly a Turn of Thread-fighting experience behind them.

What neither Fiona nor Lorana could explain was the strange lack of concern expressed by the queens. Fiona had only her experience of Talenth's first Hatching, but she found it odd that the queens weren't more anxious to provide for their offspring.

It will be all right, Talenth had assured her calmly.

"We've got some in the camp who can stand as Candidates," Fiona said now, "and we can probably find some from the traders and the wherhold who'd be willing to stand."

"We're near enough to our proper time that we would not arouse too much concern if we rode a proper Search," T'mar reminded her.

Fiona made a face; they'd been through this before. "Let's wait until they clutch."

"Would you look at that," Shaneese said as she shook her head in admiration at the ranks of eggs of all sizes and shapes dotting the sands before them. The dragon females had all clutched within a sevenday of each other, digging, burrowing, and otherwise arranging their own individual nests out of the oversized Hatching Ground that had been made. She turned to Terin. "How many?"

"Kurinth laid twenty-three," the weyrwoman told her proudly. "And one's a queen!"

"Yes, but how many altogether?" Javissa asked, gesturing toward the nesting queens and protective greens.

"Oh." Terin sounded less concerned. "Between them all, we have two hundred and fifty-three eggs, including five queen eggs."

"The green eggs look smaller; will they hatch?"

"They're about the right size for green or blue eggs," Terin replied, shrugging. "We'll know soon enough if they'll hatch."

"**W**e can't even feed a thousand!" Fiona complained when T'mar trotted out his suggested number for Candidates. "Much less find them."

"But with that number we'd have less than four Candidates for each egg, we really should have more," T'mar objected.

"Well, we *can't* get more than twenty right now," Fiona said. "And if you take a wing off in Search, how will we feed everyone here and still keep training?"

"Which is more important?" T'mar demanded of her with an angry shrug.

"Yes, which?" Fiona replied with nearly as much force.

"Could we time it?" Kindan asked. The others looked at him. "When we find out how many are hatching, we time it to find enough Candidates."

T'mar and Fiona exchanged speculative looks.

"That sounds too much like breaking time," T'mar said finally, glancing toward Lorana for confirmation.

"I'm afraid so," the queen rider agreed. "What you're saying is that we'd know before we know, as it were."

Kindan blew out a sigh of resignation. "If we can go forward in time to provide help, why can't we go forward in time to get help?"

"It didn't work for Lorana," Fiona reminded him grimly.

"It seems we can only know what we thought to ask," T'mar said. "And now that we've thought to ask, why can't we find out?"

"Fine, *you* try it," Fiona told him, gesturing toward the outside and Zirenth in the distance. "Let me know when you get tired."

"You've already tried?" T'mar asked in surprise. Fiona and Lorana both nodded.

"Perhaps you can go, but neither of us could," Fiona told him.

"It's like J'trel said, there's no *there*," Lorana added.

"Does this have anything to do with your voices?" T'mar asked Lorana. She had told them all about her encounters with the strange voices going forward in time. No one had any satisfactory explanation.

"I'd be happier if we could find answers instead of more unanswered questions," Fiona said resignedly.

"Well, in the meantime, we should at least arrange to get as many Candidates as we can and have them ready at a moment's notice," T'mar said.

"But that won't be near a thousand," Fiona said. "Perhaps a hundred at most."

"It would be a terrible tragedy to have all these hatchlings and not enough riders to Impress them," T'mar said.

"There are a lot more girls in the Caverns back in Telgar than boys," Terin said. "They keep secrets better, too."

T'mar gave her a doubting look that he hastily abandoned when both Fiona and Lorana chimed in unison, "She's right."

"We could probably contact the other girls," Terin said. Bekka beside her nodded. "I know some at Fort would love the chance."

"Nerra's been taking in so many orphans since the Plague that Crom's practically bursting at the seams," Kindan said. "You'll find more girls than boys there, too, but you'll still find plenty of boys."

"And we can tell the traders," Fiona said, glancing at Shaneese, who returned her look with a grateful nod. She smiled at the headwoman as she added, "They seem to be rife with rider blood."

"Or riders are rife with trader blood," Shaneese countered mildly. Fiona shrugged, willing to cede the point.

"We should check with the other Weyrs, beyond Telgar and Fort," Kindan said. "Mixing blood from the Weyrs, Holds, and Crafts has always been the custom, but with dragons and riders from all five Weyrs, we can really exchange customs and ideas."

"So that's settled," Bekka declared, cocking an eye at Fiona. "Are you ready for our rounds, Weyrwoman?"

Fiona nodded, turning toward Shaneese, who assured her of the babies' safety. "I've got my eye on them, Jinara's got *her* eye on them, and we've dragooned Jeriz to keep *his* eye on them, too—they'll not escape this time."

"Actually, perhaps we should take one with us," Fiona said. Shaneese gave her a surprised look. "Well, you know how much everyone loves a baby, I was thinking if Shanar would accompany us, he could be poked and admired while we got on with the business of tending to wounds and being stern."

"And it's good for morale," Shaneese guessed before Fiona could open her mouth to continue her pitch. She chuckled, shaking her head. "Very well, Weyrwoman, he's yours."

"Always was, always will be," Fiona said, going to the relocated nursery on the far side of the center pavilion and calling for Shanar. The dark-eyed boy, whose skin favored his mother's but whose features favored his father's, trotted over readily enough and jumped up excitedly when Fiona made her offer. In a moment he was squirming in her arms, in another he was on the ground, in a third back in her arms again—all before Fiona returned to the group.

"Very well, let's go!"

The "morning tour," as Fiona liked to call it, of the injured dragons and riders had quickly become a ritual; it had taken only the once before Fiona and the rest had recognized how much good the sight of one of the toddlers was for the morale and emotions of the injured, rider or dragon.

Dragons loved the gentle emotions and pure honesty of the very young, their riders loved seeing proof that Pern would continue, that their great efforts were not without reward, and—most of all—everyone secretly loved seeing Fiona struggle to teach the squirmy infants manners.

Fiona was quick enough, particularly with her breeding as a Lord

Holder's daughter, to pick up on that, and she capitalized on it shamelessly, being certain always to bring with her a change of clothes, particularly diapers, and a bag for the soiled clothes. Sometimes she would change the child herself, other times she would spend minutes moaning and murmuring to wheedle a rider into doing the deed for her.

Lorana and Kindan both were privately amazed at her ability to judge emotions correctly; Fiona seemed to know which rider most needed to see that the Weyrwoman wasn't above getting her hands— and even her clothes—dirty, and which riders wanted to prove to themselves that their fingers weren't so clumsy, their voices weren't so hard, their fears weren't so great that they couldn't change the diaper of a crying baby and return it laughing merrily.

For Fiona, it was as easy as breathing; she was never certain, but she always had an inkling of another's emotions. This morning M'del, the grizzled old rider from High Reaches Weyr, was too sore to do more than gaze at Shanar while he gritted his teeth as Bekka gently changed the bandages on his hand.

He'd taken a scoring on the left side, his hand and thigh. Fiona learned from his brown Oranth that the rider had actually tried to push the Thread away from his dragon with his hand. Wind and motion had pushed it onto his leg before they had gone *between* and it had frozen off.

The hand was not much more than bone and seared muscle on the outside, which made matters worse as the muscles on the palm were still vigorous, making recovery all the more difficult. Bekka, Lorana, and Fiona all feared that he'd never regain full use of his hand, but they were determined to do the best by him.

"There," Bekka said lightly as she finished replacing the bandages. She cast a meaningful look toward Fiona: They were almost out of bandages. Ever since they'd brought in the injured riders, they'd been plagued by one shortage after another. Work had slowed as grown weyrlings were drawn off the mines and fields to tend to the injured while still maintaining their drill.

Jeriz, now having nearly thirteen Turns, had been dragooned into everything. Fiona noticed that it was easier to get the best out of him when he was around her or Terin and suspected that the young lad, who had started to draw more attention as he reached his maturity, harbored feelings for the two of them. Terin seemed both flattered and amused.

Fiona wasn't certain how she felt. She understood about crushes; she'd managed to turn hers on Kindan into a solid reality, so she could hardly fault the lad for hoping for the same.

Terin was much nearer him in age. Still, Terin was enlivened with the knowledge that F'jian had come when she'd needed him most and that he would come again when she needed.

Fiona and Lorana had spoken, again in private, about what the queen rider had done to arrange this, and Fiona had promised Lorana that she would honor Lorana's vow as her own. That Lorana had said nothing, had unconsciously expected Fiona to do just that, was another sign to Fiona of how much they loved each other. More than sisters, lovers of the same man, heart bound to the same queen, intent on the same destiny. There was a place, Fiona knew with certainty, where they drew upon each other's strength just as they replenished each other. She had something similar though less secure with Shaneese; their partnership was based more on words spoken than on emotions shared, but it was still much the same partnership.

"We should send Bekka to Nerra," Fiona said now quietly to Lorana as they moved on toward their next charge. The dark-haired, almond-eyed woman smiled softly in response and Fiona snorted. "You were waiting for me to say that!"

"I thought it was a good idea," Lorana said. "And if it was, I was sure that it would come to you."

"Hmmm."

"Can I go now?" Bekka asked. "I might be able to get Nerra to spare some of her stores."

I am ready, Talenth said. The queen was still clearly besotted with the blond healer.

"All right," Fiona said. Bekka glanced over at her, eyes narrowed. "I know you'll be careful."

"Extra careful," Bekka assured her, in response to Fiona's evident worry. "Should I not go?"

"I'm just worried about those voices of Lorana's," Fiona said.

"Maybe I should bring Lorana."

"No," Fiona said, "none of the weyrlings here seem to have any problems going *between* and she only noticed it going through time as well."

"So I'll stay in the same time," Bekka promised. She caught Fiona's look and added, "And I'll check in when I get there and before I leave."

Fiona and Lorana both kept an "ear" open for the queen, who duly reported each step of their journey. Bekka was greeted warmly by Nerra and Fiona got the impression that their offer through Bekka was met with much relief—even Nerra had found it difficult to house all the orphans that had come to Crom Hold.

Everything went well, but Fiona was truly relieved only when she stood beside Talenth herself, scratching the queen's eye ridges and joining her in looking out over the sea of hardened dragon eggs.

Kurinth and Talenth had determined to clutch together, as if in compensation for their lust-driven fracas, and they took turns watching over the combined clutches and communicating with each other, to the amusement of Lorana and the surprise of Fiona. Terin had apologized profusely over the mating flight; Fiona had waved the issue aside. The only change that surprised them was the pleasant discovery that Terin was pregnant.

Lorana had remained noncommittal on whether F'jian would be available for the delivery, explaining when Fiona asked that, "There were only so many nights before F'jian took his final flight. If we use them too quickly . . ."

Bekka's success with Nerra had prompted Lin and Jassi to make equally furtive forays to their home holds and, at Fiona's connivance, they had arranged to have Candidates gather at locations for pickup at the end of a sevenday.

"A sevenday?" T'mar said in surprise when Fiona told him. "You're taking a risk, aren't you? We don't know if they'll hatch tomorrow or a fortnight from now."

"We'll time it if we have to," Fiona told him. "As it is, a sevenday is the best guess we've got."

"And if they don't hatch soon, we'll have to leave them while the rest of us go back to our Weyrs," Shaneese observed. "Our herdbeasts are getting very thin."

"Another reason to visit our home continent."

"Well, perhaps we can feed from strays when we go back to our continent for flaming drill," T'mar said thoughtfully. Inderra, the young queen rider of Morurth, had been greeted with cheers when she'd reported from her mission to the holds of High Reaches Weyr that not only would Pellar and Halla send their daughter, Jepara, for the Hatching, but that they'd agreed to the dispatch of miners to help clear the firestone mine near Igen.

A mixed wing of older recovered riders and those with the now-mature weyrlings of the nearly three Turns past were dispatched under the leadership of J'keran to open the old mine that they'd found near Igen Weyr when a much younger Fiona had gone back in time from her old Fort Weyr. Back then, they'd found the mine already opened and worked, little realizing that their mysterious benefactors would be themselves from Eastern Weyr—Turns older, but still living in the same time. Fiona had insisted on taking enough time when they were done to write the note her younger self had seen at the opening of the mine so many Turns before, finding a perverse pleasure in remembering how the note had so confused her so many Turns ago in her own life.

"When can we start drilling with the firestone?" Taria asked. She'd grown to become quite a competent rider in her own right, matching Xhinna in everything except leadership; where Xhinna was competent and had the natural inclinations of a good leader, Taria was content to follow—not that she did not speak her mind or stand her own ground when she felt it necessary, but always from the position of a wingsecond at best, never more.

"Tomorrow, I hope," T'mar told her.

"If the eggs don't hatch," Fiona reminded him. He shrugged off the question.

Lorana woke in the middle of the night, alarmed. Something had disturbed her and she came awake with the instant alarm of a mother adopted. She listened first only to hear the sounds of the three sleeping children, the calm slow sounds of Kindan's heavy breathing, and the sweet, softer sound of Fiona's breath coming somewhat quicker.

Something was in her hand. Surprised, she slid out of the bed and moved toward the glow. It was a slip of paper. There was a note on it: *Don't let the greens chew firestone.*

"It's my handwriting," Fiona admitted later when they gathered for breakfast in the center pavilion that had become the camp's version of the Kitchen Cavern. "But I haven't written this."

"Yet," Bekka said, examining the paper and passing it to Terin.

"That must be very confusing," Lin said as she reached for the paper.

"Timing it has many dangers," Fiona agreed with a frown. "So why don't I want the greens to chew firestone?"

"So they'll make eggs," Jassi guessed. She glanced out of the raised side of the pavilion to the field of eggs beyond. "Although why we'd need more than we have now . . ."

"We need to start drills if they're to fight," T'mar said, frowning once more in the direction of the note, now in Inderra's dainty fingers. He looked to Fiona. "What do we do?"

"Have I been wrong before?" Fiona asked archly, then swatted at T'mar as she saw his eyes twinkle. "All right, I've been wrong, but I don't think I've made it a point to send a note back in time about it."

"This is now two mysterious notes from the future," Kindan said. "I'd be happier if we could get an explanation for at least one of them."

"We will," Fiona said. She was not surprised when Terin, with a big grin, joined her in unison to say, "in time."

"I'll be glad when we can get back to our own time and stay there," weyrwoman Indeera declared. She glanced hastily to Fiona, her face going red. "No offense, Weyrwoman, it just seems so confusing and wearying."

"None taken," Fiona said cheerfully. "For myself, I agree," Fiona said. "I'll be glad when we can bring our charges—and our new weyrlings—back to the Weyrs."

"So, we'll drill without the greens," T'mar said.

"The young ones," Fiona corrected. "The ones who already have chewed firestone should not be excluded."

"That's not what the note says," Lin objected. She was the most literal-minded of the five junior weyrwomen. That she was willing even to contradict Fiona was a great step forward in bringing the young woman out of her shell and into her role as Benden's junior weyrwoman. Fiona was glad to see the changes in Lin's demeanor, changes that she, Lorana, and Shaneese had secretly nursed, aided by the more ebullient Bekka and Terin.

Just as Terin had F'jian for her Kurinth's mating flight, so had each of the weyrwomen found themselves with their favorite candidates for their mating flights. Fiona was even more pleased with the outcome that paired Jassi with J'lian. He was no youngster, but after the devastating losses in the Istan leadership, he was the obvious future leader of Ista Weyr and his Neruth's mating with Jassi's Falth meant that, on her return to Ista, he would become the true Weyrleader, just as she would inherit the senior Weyrwoman role vacated by Dalia.

Jassi and Fiona had formed a tight bond in their time together, and Fiona was almost more pleased with the way the forthright younger woman agreed with her thinking than she was with their success with demure Lin. Jassi's quiet competence had allowed Fiona to slough off many of her own responsibilities without overburdening Terin or the other queen riders, and her easygoing nature had meant that she hadn't seen it as a reduction in power when Fiona returned more and more into her own role as the twins grew older.

Javissa was another of Fiona's quiet triumphs. The woman was slightly older than Shaneese and there had been some friction between the two at first, but their similar backgrounds and natural kindness had rubbed that off, leaving two women who coordinated all housekeeping chores effortlessly while maintaining the control that only a headwoman could manage. Terin had been quite openly impressed with the pair of them and said so; Fiona had been secretly amused to note that both Jassi and Indeera had quietly tried to recruit the trader woman to come to their Weyrs when they all returned to their homes.

Javissa was younger than Kindan, so Fiona had set other plans, being certain to point out various eggs to Javissa even as she was ostensibly pointing them out to Jeriz. There certainly were enough eggs to go around. Even with their planning, Fiona was nervous about the number of Candidates they'd be able to present and had the occasional nightmare of creeling hatchlings going *between* forever, unable to find their mates.

"Fiona?" Terin prodded gently.

"Oh, sorry," Fiona said, recovering from her thoughts. Terin nodded her head at Lin as a reminder and Fiona smiled, first at her friend and then at the serious Benden weyrwoman. "No, if I'd meant that the older greens shouldn't chew firestone, I would have said so."

"Perhaps we could convince the older riders to trade off with the younger ones so they'll get a feel for flaming," Kindan suggested.

"And we weyrwomen can practice with the flamethrowers," Fiona said. They'd borrowed a complete set from the wherhold. Zenor had asked no questions, handing them over with full loads of agenothree.

"If you keep timing like this, you'll be older than I am soon," he'd warned when she'd made her quick visit.

Fiona had laughed and kissed him on the cheek before departing. "We'll see you soon!"

Now was the first day Fiona had found it practical to drill the flying queens with the agenothree-equipped flamethrowers. She'd tackled Kindan for suggestions and the harper had reluctantly agreed to drill the queens only after Lorana had softened him to the notion. Traditionally, the senior queen rider conducted the drill, but Fiona decided it was more politic to inveigle the weyrlingmaster into the duty.

"At least they're not all like you," Kindan had teased. "Some of them will actually listen to what I say instead of arguing all the time."

"I don't argue *all* the time," Fiona had said, pouting.

Now, as T'mar organized the fighting dragons for aerial drill, Kindan arrayed the queen riders for ground drill. They had grown used to drilling together on the ground in the nearly three Turns since they'd come to the Eastern Weyr and now, with their queens full grown and clutched, they eagerly approached the challenge of the bulky apparatus with the firm hopes that one day soon, each Weyr would be able to field the customary queens' wing.

Fiona's alternative had been an easy sell. "And until then," she'd said, "we can form impromptu wings among the weyrs."

"Isn't that what we're doing now?" Lin had asked in confusion.

"But not with the queens," Jassi had corrected her. Lin's face lit with excitement and they'd spent several minutes working out the proper protocol to use in the future. All were agreed that it was an excellent idea and wondered why they hadn't thought of it sooner.

"Because with only one queen in each weyr, it was too risky to try," Fiona had told them, simply.

They'd all learned how to load the flamethrowers, using water for practice until Kindan and Fiona were satisfied that they could progress to the live acid, and they'd practiced with that on the ground, as individuals and in groups, but today was the first time they would fly their queens together.

"Who should lead?" Jassi asked, turning toward Fiona.

"I think Lin should lead us first," Fiona said. The shy brown-haired woman blushed and shook her head, but Fiona persisted. "You'll have to do it one day. Now, with this company, is the best time to practice."

The others had weighed in and Lin and her Lith had taken the lead position.

Lith was more secure in herself than her rider and Lin changed the moment she was with her queen, just as she'd changed from shy, demure youngster to passionate, heated, demanding lover during the mating flight when her Lith had been flown, surprisingly, by J'lian's Neruth. Fiona had quickly quashed any notions that the queen's eggs might go to Ista, and Jassi had agreed. It would be hard enough for Tullea to accept the deed, but impossible if it had resulted in a loss for her Weyr.

In the air, Fiona was glad to fly on the rear of the left wedge of the wing, with Jassi far across from her on the right. She waved and the other woman waved back before she turned to her left, carefully positioning her thrower so that its acid would fall out and to the left of the wing.

While dragons flew up to flame Thread, queens flew down to catch the trailers that had been missed by the fighting dragons, so their natural target was something below them, not above.

At Kindan's request, they were flying low over treetops to the south of the camp, their agenothree strong enough to help cut a clearing between the camp and the trees so that they would increase the arable land they could use for crops.

"You can never tell when you'll need more," Shaneese had said when they were planning the day's work.

"And it's good practice," Lorana had agreed.

So Fiona was looking down and leftward when she first saw a streak of tawny cross the clearing, racing away from the falling agenothree—and toward the camp. She cried out a warning as she peeled off and down after the Mrreow, Talenth bugling with her.

The Mrreow moved with astonishing speed and leaped over the poles that had been placed around the camp's perimeter, its goal unwavering.

Have Shaneese get the children! Fiona cried. She spotted another Mrreow and a third suddenly break cover heading toward the camp. *Lorana, Mrreows are attacking!*

The other queens had recovered and, at Jassi's urging, had reformed behind Fiona.

Falth says: "Can we use the agenothree?" Talenth relayed.

No, it might hurt someone, Fiona responded at once, adding a visual emphasis by raising her arms over her head and crossing them. At Fiona's urging, Talenth dived for the nearest Mrreow and grabbed it even as the beast flailed and tried to wriggle out of the queen's grasp.

Bring it back to the forest, Fiona said.

Why not to the rocks?

Far in the forest, Fiona reiterated. For some reason, she couldn't bring herself to kill the beasts, who were probably only hungry and acting from instinct. Even so, she kept the nozzle of her thrower pointed at the tawny hide as it struggled in Talenth's claws. If it looked like it might hurt her queen, Fiona would have no difficulty in flaming it to cinders; sympathy was one thing, stupidity another.

They flew swiftly and made it to the far side of the forest before Talenth dove and released the creature, which struggled for a moment to regain its feet and disappeared. Behind them as they climbed, Fiona heard another Mrreow and the third as Jassi and Lin dropped their catches.

"What were they after?" T'mar wondered that evening as they took their dinner.

"If they were after the children, they were dead," Javissa declared, matching looks with Shaneese, who nodded in similar determination. Neither of the traders understood or condoned Fiona's actions in releasing the beasts—both preferred Talenth's suggestion of dropping them from far up onto the rocks of the distant promontory.

"If they were after the eggs, they were dead, too," Terin said.

"I can imagine them going after the children," Fiona said, "but they would have been addled to consider the eggs—they're too big." But even as she said it she wondered. She and everyone in the camp found the notion of eggs just lying out bare to all the elements very disturbing. Talenth and the other queens were similarly disturbed, but neither man nor dragon had a better suggestion of how to place eggs on the soil of their plain.

"The sooner they hatch and we can return to the Weyrs, the happier I'll be," Fiona admitted.

▼ ▼ ▼

Fiona awoke instantly the next morning.

"They're hatching!" she cried, rousting Kindan, Lorana, and the others out of their shared bed. "Come on."

I'm coming, Talenth! Fiona called as she pulled on trousers under her tunic and slipped her feet into her boots. She raced over to T'mar's quarters and rapped on his door.

"We're coming," the Weyrleader's voice responded. She ignored him and burst into the room, reaching for Kimar even as Shaneese hoisted Shanar to her side. Fiona reached out a hand for Tiona and the little toddler grabbed it and held on until they entered the hallway where she released it and raised both her arms imploringly to Kindan, who hoisted her up with the practice of a well-trained parent.

"The eggs are hatching, come and see," he told her, his eyes shining brightly in the dim ship's hallway. Tiona slipped her arms around him and clung tightly.

They raced up the ship's passageways and down the stairs onto the camp.

Bronzes gathered around the perimeter of the sands, and more dragons came to join them, their throats opened wide in the deep thrumming that anticipated the hatching.

Go, go, go! Fiona cried to the queens in turn as they left with their assigned wings and returned with the prepared Candidates gathered at Crom Hold, up at Fire Hold in the north, and various trader camps around the continent. Wave after wave arrived as the sun rose in the morning until finally the sands were a mix of white-robed Candidates and mottled eggs.

Outside the camp, ominously, a deep-throated Mrreow roared as if in challenge or perhaps calling together its companions. Fiona nodded in satisfaction as she heard Lorana dispatch a patrol to drive them off.

And then the sun was in the sky, red and rosy. The air, still cool from the night, slowly grew thick with moisture. One by one, the bronzes stopped humming and the riders looked around, eyes wide with confusion.

Suddenly, there was a shout and someone pointed toward an egg. It wobbled feebly, then cracked. A dragonet emerged, creeling in panic and hunger. Steadied by the older dragonriders, the knot of candidates mostly stood their ground although some fled in confusion.

One, an older lad from the Smithhall by his knots, ran toward Fiona, which she thought odd.

"Weyrwoman!" the lad cried when he was close enough. "Are there tunnel snakes here?"

"Yes," Fiona said, a sense of dread clutching at her even as she replied.

"I think they've got the eggs," the lad said, lowering his head respectfully.

"We've been guarding them," Fiona said, shaking her head adamantly.

"For a feast like this," he said, stretching his arms out to indicate the massive hatching sands, "they'd tunnel for months."

Fiona looked at the nearest clutch, one of the green's, and noticed that none of the eggs were rocking. Here and there, further along, she saw one or two hatchlings but far, far fewer than she knew they should be seeing by now.

She went to the nearest egg and rocked it. It was hard to get it to budge in the sand, but even as she felt it move she knew the smither was right—the egg was lifeless, empty, too light.

Aghast, Fiona turned toward the other eggs near her but could not move.

Fiona? she heard Lorana call worriedly.

The eggs, Fiona said, suddenly finding her feet moving as she gained motion and speed with one destination firmly in mind.

Talenth!

Only a very few of Talenth's eggs had hatched. Kindan saw her dart by and followed her. "Fiona, what is it?"

"The tunnel snakes!" she cried. "They got the eggs!"

"What do we do?" Bekka asked, turning hastily around. Scenes of destruction played all around them.

"Get to the good eggs," Fiona said. "Find them, get them Impressed, and get them away from here."

Bekka nodded and sprinted away, grabbing white-robed Candidates and dragonriders with her as she went, dropping groups here and there to stay on guard against tunnel snakes—and hope for an Impression.

She was just about to swing back around when she heard the unmistakable sound of a shell cracking. She whirled toward the sound and saw a large egg. She turned around quickly, looking for Candidates to send to the hatchling and realized that she was alone.

"No!" she cried, rushing toward the egg. "We can't lose you! I won't lose you!"

I am Pinorth, the small gold hatchling said as her head broke through her shell. *You shall never lose me.*

"By the First Egg, yes!" Bekka shouted, her eyes blazing with pride, joy, and fierce protectiveness.

Kindan stopped and turned, nearly dropping Tiona as he saw Bekka rush toward a hatchling and help her out of her egg. He had no time to rejoice, for a hatchling's cry distracted him and he stopped, scanned the large sands and suddenly noticed how many eggs lay unhatched, motionless. He was just about to move on when the egg nearest him cracked.

"Get it!" Fiona cried, circling back, desperate to salvage anything from this disaster for her queen and for all Pern. "Help it!"

Kindan turned and passed Tiona off to her mother and then was all arms and feet, pounding and tearing through the thicker shell membrane to free the dragonet.

Another sound broke through the morning and Mrreows raced onto the sands, attacking human, hatchling, and tunnel snake without regard.

Talenth! Fiona cried, ordering her and all the queens aloft. Talenth stretched one claw and grabbed one of the tawny things, snaring it and then throwing it high in the sky where it was caught by a vengeful blue and thrown once more out of the camp to fall, crushed, among the rocks in the distance.

"Kindan!" Fiona cried as she saw a Mrreow leap toward him—only to snag a tunnel snake that had erupted from the sands, snapping after Kindan and the hatchling both.

Fiona had one fleeting instant to wonder if the Mrreow had gone for the tunnel snake or the man before she was equally transfixed by Kindan's cry.

"No, no, no!" he cried. "Not me, there are others!"

Fiona moved toward him and bumped his shoulder, her eyes flaming even as her humor overtook her, "Why does everyone I know *say* that?"

Kindan looked at her for a moment longer, and then sighed heavily, reaching the tiny creature in one swift movement and pulling it bodily out of its egg.

And then, with a dozen brilliant memories of Kisk, of Valla, of all who had gone before, K'dan looked into the eyes of his dragon and knew that there would be nothing so marvelous, so wonderful, so *right* as that one moment when he realized that Fiona and Lorana were absolutely correct—there *was* a dragon for him and his name was—"Lurenth, I greet you."

And I you, the small one said with grave dignity. The moment was fractured when Lurenth burped and added plaintively, *I'm hungry.*

"That's the last of them," J'gerd reported woodenly to T'mar late that evening. "We've thrown the eggs into the sea and as many tunnel snakes as we could kill."

"And?"

J'gerd shook his head. T'mar had been there when the avenging dragons had dug through the sand to the huge tunnel that the snakes had excavated, a tunnel so large that a man could almost stand up in it.

"This ground's too soft, all we can do is hope to fill the tunnels in for a time," the brown rider told him.

"We should leave this place," Shaneese said. "It has brought us nothing but sorrow."

"Not all was sorrow," T'mar said, stretching out a hand to stroke her forearm soothingly. "But we should leave."

"It's not as easy as that," Fiona spoke for the first time since settling K'dan and Lurenth on the upper deck of their ship. "The new hatchlings are too young to go *between* and there are things here we should preserve."

"Leave them behind with a guard and take the rest," Indeera said, her eyes still red from crying.

"How many did we save?" T'mar asked, turning toward Fiona.

"None of the green eggs," Fiona said, grimacing. "Partly because their shells were thinner, partly because I don't think the greens are as good at guarding their eggs, and partly because—well, I think the greens let the queens tell them where to put their eggs and that meant the green eggs were more likely to be in the most exposed locations."

T'mar nodded wearily and gave her another look.

"Of the two hundred and fifty-three eggs, all queen eggs hatched, including Bekka's Pinorth, and most of the bronzes." Fiona sighed. "Twenty-three."

"Bronzes?" T'mar frowned, trying to recall that many.

"No, twenty-three hatched altogether," Fiona said. "Jeriz—no, J'riz—saved the only green." She did not need to add that J'riz's Qinth was badly injured by an assault of tunnel snakes that had pierced the poor dragonet's shell before she'd even managed to crack it. They all heard J'riz's pained cry; in all her reading, Fiona had never heard of a dragon Impressing *through* her shell, but her need was great and J'riz had risen to it, smashing the egg open, pulling her out, and had single-handedly throttled two tunnel snakes before others rushed to his aid.

"Anything," he'd cried pitifully, "I'll do anything if you can help her! Save her, please, Weyrwomen!"

Fiona, Terin, and Lorana had rushed to the hatchling's side. She had a nasty gash in her chest and it looked as though a tunnel snake had started to gnaw her innards before she'd been rescued.

"Shouldn't we then say twenty-two?" T'mar asked grimly. "She can't make it through the night."

"Oh yes, she can," Fiona said firmly. "Lorana's with them now, then Terin, Bekka's got her queen bedded with them, and I'll be there as soon as I'm done here." She flashed her eyes at him. "We're not losing her."

"There isn't enough firestone on all Pern for those tunnel snakes," T'mar growled. "In one stroke we've lost a Weyr's strength."

"Well, we have to work with what we have, not what we want," Fiona said, reaching out a hand toward him. He smiled and took it.

"You're right," he admitted. "And what do we have?"

"We have nearly three hundred and forty-one fighting dragons, six full-grown queens, six hatchling queens, and seventeen other weyrlings," Fiona told him.

"So with our strength we'll nearly double the fighting strength of the Weyrs," T'mar said, his eyes glowing. "When can we leave?"

"The better question is when can we get there?" Fiona reminded him. She turned toward the headwoman and said, "Shaneese and I are still working out detailed plans, but there's no reason that all the fighting dragons—save one wing for protection—couldn't go back to the future tomorrow."

"Good," T'mar agreed. "And when we will return?"

"They've got a Fall over High Reaches tip next," Fiona said.

"Then we'll fly with High Reaches and send our wings home from there," T'mar declared.

"We haven't enough firestone," Fiona reminded him.

"The sun rises earlier at Telgar," T'mar said. "We'll go there first, load up, and fly on."

"You'll be all right?" Fiona asked Lorana worriedly the next morning.

"I'll be fine," she assured her friend.

"You'll come straight back, you won't go off to the future or any-thing?" Fiona persisted.

Lorana laughed, sobering immediately at Fiona's worried gaze. "I won't be going anywhere unless you send Talenth for me."

"And you'll keep an eye on K'dan?" It was both very hard and very easy to remember to contract Kindan's name with the honorific. She'd called him by his longer name for so long she sometimes stumbled, but she always smiled when she got it right.

"And Xhinna and Taria and R'ney and all the other new weyrlings until they're old enough to go *between*," Lorana said. R'ney, who had been Raney before he'd Impressed his brown, had been the astute smither lad who'd run to warn Fiona of the tunnel snakes. He'd managed to Impress the very last hatchling—a brown—after having found a shovel he'd used both as a hammer with which to shatter shells and as an ax with which he severed the heads of a dozen tunnel snakes, his rage rising to berserk levels.

When his rage had cooled, he had been one of the first of the new weyrlings to bring his dragonet and set up his camp beside the injured Qinth. Xhinna and Taria were already there, quiet sentinels who slept not a wink the whole night. Taria had smiled shyly at the brown-eyed, rusty-haired lad, and they'd quickly struck up a conversation into which Xhinna had occasionally wandered, seeming surprised that her shy mate would find the smithcrafter's company so enjoyable.

Fiona rushed over to Xhinna, who was holding Kimar for her, and hugged her tight even as Kimar cried, "Mommy, you're crushing me!"

Taria plucked the boy from between the two women and set him on her shoulders. Tiona raced up and demanded the same attention only to be diverted by R'ney, who was a head taller than Taria.

"Take care of her," Fiona whispered to Xhinna, so that Taria wouldn't hear. "Take care of them all."

"My word on it, Weyrwoman," Xhinna said.

"Blue rider," Fiona said, touching the dark-haired woman on the shoulder as they parted. "Come on, kids, we've got to get you up on Talenth, we're going home!"

"But this is home," Tiona cried. "And I want Xhinna."

"You'll have me soon enough," Xhinna said, waving her away. "Now be off with you and mind your mother until I get back."

"She minds *us*," Tiona declared, finding one of Fiona's legs and wrapping her arms around it possessively. "I'm only little, that's the way it's supposed to be."

"Yes it is," Fiona agreed. "And now it's supposed to be that you go with me back to Telgar."

The wings and flights arrayed themselves behind T'mar and his impromptu wing of bronzes. Between them and the rest, Fiona had arrayed the queen's wing, insisting that they return in all their glory.

Three hundred and forty-one fighting dragons and six mature queens circled their home of three Turns once and then winked *between*.

One, two, three—*The Weyrs! They must be warned!*

Fiona felt T'mar's confusion, felt the bronze rider begin to doubt, felt something pulling at them, holding them, leeching from them, angry, scared, confused.

The Weyrs! They must be warned!

Those words! Fiona remembered them. She'd heard them before. *D'gan?*

The Weyrs! They must be warned!

Suddenly a fear welled up in Fiona. In front of her, strapped securely in their own harnesses were her children, her babies. She couldn't lose them.

In the dead silence of *between*, Fiona screamed: *Can't lose the babies! Can't lose the babies!*

And she heard it again: *The Weyrs! They must be warned!*

And again she screamed, *Can't lose the babies! Can't lose the babies!*

Trapped. They were trapped.

The Weyrs! They must be warned!

Can't lose the babies! Can't lose the babies!

I can't lose the babies, Fiona told herself. She knew what she had to do, her fingers worked furiously at her clips, unhooked them, and with one final, anxious cry, she stood and leapt—into the nothing of *between*.

Talenth! Go to Lorana! Go to Lorana, Talenth!

And then she was alone. All alone.

The Weyrs! They must be warned!

Can't lose the babies! Can't lose the babies!

ELEVEN

A dragon gold
Is not the only price
You'll pay for Pern.

"Talenth!" Lorana cried as the queen burst forth, bugling anxiously, her cry disturbing the entire camp. "What are you doing here?"

The queen wheeled in for a landing in front of Lorana and turned, as if inviting her to climb aboard. Lorana heard the twins crying loudly in fear and panic. K'dan raced over to her even before Lorana had climbed up to calm the twins.

"Mommy's all alone!" Tiona told Lorana through her tears. "She jumped off and left us!"

"I'm sure she had a good reason," Lorana said even as she calmed them and lowered them to the waiting hands that reached upward.

"I'm here, little one," K'dan said to his daughter as she met his arms.

"I'm scared, Daddy, I'm scared," Tiona said, burying her small face into his shoulder. "Mommy was so scared and she jumped off Talenth."

Kimar was sent down into Xhinna's waiting arms and she held him tightly, shushing and soothing him even as he shook in her arms from the weight of his tears.

Talenth? Lorana asked.

She said to go to you, Talenth told her, clearly sounding torn between her rider's orders and her own sense of duty.

You did right, Lorana assured her, even as she tried to imagine Fiona's logic.

We could not get through, Talenth told her. Lorana turned back to K'dan. "They could not get through."

"I'm not a baby," Kimar murmured into Xhinna's ear as his sobs lessened. "I'm not a baby."

"No one said so," Xhinna assured him. "You're very brave."

"Mommy said so," Kimar replied. "I heard her, I heard her in my head."

"In your head?" Lorana repeated, glancing toward K'dan. "Love, what did she say?"

"She said, 'Can't lose the babies!' over and over," Kimar said.

"She said that because she loves you more than life itself," Lorana said with a sob. She turned to K'dan. "I must go," she told him firmly. "On your word, take care of our children."

"My word," K'dan said, reaching forward to embrace her. "I love you, I always will."

"I know," Lorana whispered back softly, kissing his cheek once more. She climbed up Talenth and looked back down once more to her family, the one Fiona had built for her, had fought for, would always fight for.

The one Fiona had bet her life on.

Come on Talenth, let's go.

T he Weyrs! They must be warned!

Can't lose the babies! Can't lose the babies!

Lorana heard both cries, heard the pain in them, felt the fight, the wills exerted.

Fiona? No response. She tried pulling against the voice of D'gan, lost so many months before but now here, in this same time, in this same sliver of *between*, trapped with Fiona, who was herself locked in her own moment, her own fear, her own leap of faith. *Can't lose the babies! Can't lose the babies!*

Fiona! It's me, I've come to get you! Lorana shouted, trying to find her friend, her sister/daughter/mother/fellow-wife in all the torment, anguish, confusion, fear, and anger. She couldn't. She needed to free them all, to break the logjam. She pulled, she reached to D'gan locked in the moment of his worst fear, his worst nightmare, and found that she could no more break through now than she could when she'd found the power of all the Weyrs—the Weyrs!

With a final push of will, Lorana pulled herself and Talenth through *between*, past the time when D'gan and old Telgar Weyr had collided with Fiona and the new riders.

She found her lungs heaving for air, never feeling so warm as when she broke out in the skies above Telgar. Beneath her, Talenth bugled an alert that was taken up instantly by all the dragons, who came out of their weyrs bellowing.

Lyrinth! Minith! Melirth! Bidenth! To Telgar! she ordered even as she urged Talenth down to the Weyr Bowl. The air was clean and warm, and Lorana drank it in, recovering her power as she urged Talenth to a quick descent and gentle landing.

Jeila rushed out of her weyr, with H'nez behind. C'tov came racing down the steps from an upper level and Birentir ran out of the Kitchen Cavern, aid bag in hand.

"What is it?"

"They're trapped!" Lorana cried. "We must help them." The air was alive suddenly with queens and bronzes as the Weyrleaders and Weyrwomen of the other Weyrs arrived.

"Lorana!" Tullea cried. "We thought you were dead."

"Not yet," Lorana said drolly. "But if we don't move fast, six hundred dragons and riders will be lost forever."

"What?" Cisca cried, looking around. "What happened?"

Quickly Lorana explained about the voices, about Fiona's desperate maneuver, about Talenth's warning, about her belief that the two Weyrs' worth of strength were caught in some fragment of *between*, unable to move forward or backward, stuck repeating their moment of time over and over.

"What do you need?" B'nik asked, clearly convinced and prepared to offer all aid.

"I need all of us to go there and free them," Lorana said.

"You couldn't free D'gan before, why do you think you can now?" Sonia asked.

"Because now he's locked with Fiona and the others," Lorana replied. "I think I couldn't move him until the time *between* when he was locked with her." She paused as she glanced at the others. "We'll be the key, the guide that breaks the hold of that moment and frees them."

"They've been there for almost half a Turn," K'lior said, "can anyone survive that long?"

"D'gan's voice was still alive when I got here," Lorana said.

"If you got here from your time, why couldn't T'mar and the others?" D'vin asked.

"I broke free," Lorana said. "I was the only one, I—" She stopped and shook her head wearily. "I don't know. But I need your help."

"Benden rides with you and always shall," B'nik declared, sending the word to his Weyr.

"I will not leave them to die in the cold of *between*," Sonia said, glancing at D'vin. The High Reaches Weyrleader nodded in agreement.

"Nor I," Cisca told K'lior. He smiled at her. "Ours are on the way."

"And Ista," Dalia said quietly.

"And when they come, what then?" H'nez asked.

"Then we find them, break the binding, and bring them back home," Lorana declared.

Wing by wing, pitifully small numbers of riders and dragons formed the ranks of the five remaining Weyrs of Pern.

At your command, Talenth relayed from the other queens.

Very well, let's go, Lorana said.

And all the dragons of Pern winked out at once, *between*.

Lorana guided them through, back to the time when she'd found—

There! Lorana called, reaching out, feeling dragons and riders numb and cold with the shock of their entrapment *between*.

She spread her power out, felt the dragons that had come with her array and group themselves, gathering the trapped dragons and riders, physically touching them.

It wasn't enough. They were still trapped, locked in a cycle of fear and panic. And it was spreading.

Can't lose the babies!

The Weyrs! They must be warned!

They are warned! D'gan, you saved them! Come back. Come back, D'gan! Lorana eased Talenth over to D'gan's bronze Kaloth and reached out in the darkness. She engulfed the dragon in a sense of calm and felt it spread to the rider.

They're safe? Kaloth asked for his rider.

Safe, Lorana thought firmly. *And now we must get back.*

Can't lose the babies!

The babies are safe! Lorana thought on the special link she had to Fiona. Instantly she felt the other calm, felt a surge of gratitude, joy, relief.

Lorana turned her energies toward the others who were slowly coming out of their fear, their worry. The dragons and riders of the other Weyrs followed her example, radiating calm, soothing thoughts, adding their mental voices to hers.

And the cycle broke.

They were ready to go back, free of the fears that had trapped them *between.* Lorana felt her heart ease as she realized that they had done it, they'd saved the lost dragons.

Fiona, we're safe, Lorana called out. *They're all safe. Guide me to you and we'll go home.*

Silence.

Fiona? Lorana called again. Beneath her she felt Talenth rumble with unease.

We need to go, Cisca's Melirth told her.

We've got everyone, Sonia's Lyrinth added. *We cannot tarry, they are cold from* between.

No! Lorana roared back. *No, we have to find Fiona!*

She isn't here, Melirth responded gently. *None of us can hear her.*

We can't leave her! Lorana called back, her voice full of pain and tears. *We can't leave her here in this cold. We can't!*

She felt the other queens surround Talenth, their love enveloping them even as the queens touched them and pulled them out from *between*.

"NO!" Lorana shouted as they burst forth over the cold Telgar heights. "No, let me go back! I can find her! You have to let me go!"

But the queens held fast and pulled dragon and rider down into the Weyr bowl.

T'mar and the Weyrleaders raced over to her as Talenth touched the ground.

"Let me go back!" Lorana cried, writhing on her mount above Talenth who creeled just as piteously. "Let us go back, we have to find her!"

"Lorana, she's gone," T'mar called up to her, tears streaming from his eyes. "She's gone," he repeated as his eyes met hers. "You must stay here, with Talenth. We need all our queens to save Pern."

"No," Lorana repeated feebly, her energy sapped, her heart shattered, her will gone.

"Come on down," T'mar urged, reaching a hand up to her. Others climbed up beside him and between them, Weyrleaders all, they carried Lorana back to the ground where Cisca, Sonia, Lin, Dalia, and even Tullea embraced her in a tight, comforting hug.

"Cisca," Lorana said in a small voice as she caught the taller woman's brown eyes. "Let me go find her, please?"

"Shh," Cisca said, pulling Lorana's head under hers. "She's gone, love, she's gone."

"You can't break time," Tullea added, patting her softly on the back, tears streaming down her face. "You know that."

Lorana looked up as she heard steps rushing toward her. It was Terin.

"Terin?" Lorana called out, her voice breaking mid-syllable.

Terin pushed her way through the other Weyrwoman, grabbed Lorana's hand, and pulled her free.

"You can't break time," Terin told her as she urged Lorana into a sprint back toward Talenth. "But you can *cheat* it!"

"Cheat it?" Lorana repeated, a faint glow of hope warming her voice. "But she's gone!"

"And she *would* be, if you went back and *got* her!" Terin glared at T'mar and the Weyrleaders still grouped protectively around Talenth and called, "Get out of the way!"

She barreled through them and pushed Lorana back up on Talenth's neck before they could react. Dropping back down to the ground, Terin called up to her, "Go! Bring her back!"

With a triumphant cry, Talenth went *between* just after she'd cleared the grasp of the other dragons.

Find Fiona, Talenth, Lorana called even as she reached out with her senses and called, *Fiona? Fiona, we're coming for you!*

She felt a faint answer, as if distant in time, and Lorana grabbed at it with her will and pulled—she pulled hard, pulled herself and the great queen through the nothing of *between* to the time when she heard Fiona's voice.

We're here! Lorana called.

I knew you'd come! Fiona replied, her voice weak with exhaustion. *The others?*

We've got them, Lorana replied, guiding Talenth closer and closer to the small living mote in the vast void of nothing.

No, Fiona said anxiously, pushing back at Lorana urgently. *No, no they're still here! I can feel them! We can't leave them, no one will find them if I'm not here!*

We already found them, Lorana said. *We've brought them back, now we've come for you.*

Now?

Now, Lorana assured her. *We're cheating time.* She felt Fiona's acquiescence, felt the blond rider reach out toward her and Talenth, providing a slim flicker of thought to guide them.

A foot struck Lorana gently in the cheek and she reached up and grabbed with all her strength, pulling the younger woman into her arms.

Let's go, Talenth!

▼ ▼ ▼

A gold burst back into the sky over Telgar, bugling in triumph, racing down to the ground even as the other queens darted up toward her, their cries full of surprise and glee.

Talenth fell until the last minute then brutally cupped her wings, beat once, and hit the ground hard. A dust cloud settled around her.

"Help her!" Lorana called to the throng racing toward her. "She's cold."

Ready hands reached up to guide Fiona down, but they received a limp, unresponsive, cold body.

"She's not breathing!" Lorana heard the cry rise up from beneath and jumped off Talenth's neck.

She beat her way into the crowd surrounding Fiona. The blond Weyrwoman's skin was blue and cold, her eyes closed, her chest still.

"No," Lorana said fiercely, reaching forward to lift the base of Fiona's neck and tilting it back.

"I'll pump," T'mar said as Lorana opened Fiona's cold lips and leaned down to blow life-breath into the still form.

Lorana sealed her lips over Fiona's, exhaling a deep breath and watching to see the younger woman's chest rise. She repeated it twice and nodded to T'mar who started to pump Fiona's chest, massaging her heart.

With a cough, Fiona's eyes flew open and she looked up at Lorana. Feebly she reached up, dragged the older woman back down to her, and whispered fiercely, "I *knew* you'd come."

Lorana encircled her with her arms and drew her close. "Of course."

EPILOGUE

It will turn out all right.

Third Interval

"Terin?" F'jian called in surprise as he spotted the red-haired girl climbing up the ledge to the queen's wing. The girl stopped and spun in place and he could see instantly that she wasn't Terin.

"No, I'm Torina," the girl said quickly, scowling at him with all the indignation of a woman just leaving childhood. Her eyes widened as she took him in and, in a whisper of surprise, said, "Grandfather?"

F'jian looked closely at the girl in front of him, with scarce more Turns than Terin had at Telgar Weyr, and saw the subtle differences in her face. He could see Terin's features—and even his own—reflected and melded with other, unknown features to produce someone who was undoubtedly both Terin's and his own grand-daughter.

The young woman recovered before him and reached out, grabbing his hand and tugging. "Come on! Mother's waiting!"

"Mother?" F'jian repeated dully, allowing himself to be led in a way that was so heart-breakingly similar to Terin's marvelous, brilliant, brisk manner.

Torina shot a look over her shoulder, still tugging him behind her. "You know, your *daughter*."

F'jian had a moment of panic. "Am I too late?"

"You'll see," Torina said, sounding all too much like her grand-dame. She craned her neck back once more, catching his eye and adding honestly, "I'm so glad you came, I was afraid I'd never get to meet you."

The weyr they entered was not the same one that Terin and Kurinth had occupied so many Turns ago, and F'jian was surprised as the dim gold queen raised her head wistfully to greet him.

Greetings, Kurinth said. *She was hoping you'd come.*

"Father?" a silver-haired woman of later years said and rushed over, wrapping her arms tightly around him. F'jian hugged her back, as surprised at her frail bones as at the fierce love he found in her embrace. As if not to be outdone, Torina turned back and hugged her grandfather as soon as her mother had stepped aside.

"Come on," Torina said, regaining F'jian's hand and dragging him behind her once more into the weyrwoman's quarters. F'jian shot her mother a bemused look, but she just smiled at her daughter's staunch possession of her too-young grandfather.

With all the bustle F'jian had come to expect from Fiona or Terin herself, his granddaughter broke through the large throng gathered quietly around the weyrwoman's bed.

A silver-haired man, his face lined with age and Threadscore, caught F'jian's eye and nodded to him in greeting. "C'tov?"

C'tov smiled and reached over. "We've missed you," the old bronze rider said. His lips twitched up as he added, "She and I would argue sometimes over who missed you more."

"I'm sorry," F'jian apologized.

"Don't be," C'tov told him firmly. F'jian thought to say something more, but his old friend shook his head once more and gestured toward the bed.

"Terin?" F'jian said as he knelt down at the edge of the bed.

"You're still beautiful," an age-strained voice spoke back, and he heard others reach out to help his only love sit up in her bed.

F'jian lifted his eyes to meet the green eyes of the age-wrinkled, white-haired woman in front of him. "So are you!"

Much later, after the toasts were drunk and elderly weyrwoman and elderly bronze rider took their dragons *between* on their last journey, F'jian returned to Ladirth and the rider astride him.

Quietly he climbed up and took his position.

"Are you ready?" Lorana asked him softly.

F'jian nodded. "I am."

As Ladirth circled the Star Stones, Lorana said, "It will be a long cold journey *between*."

"No it won't," F'jian corrected her. "Not with all these memories."

As the blackness of *between* gripped them, Ladirth relayed a message from F'jian to Lorana: *We might not be able to break time but we can cheat it!*

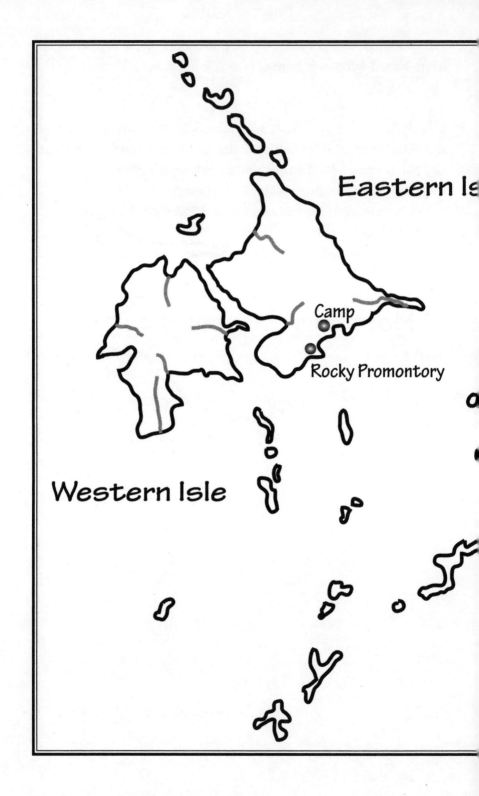

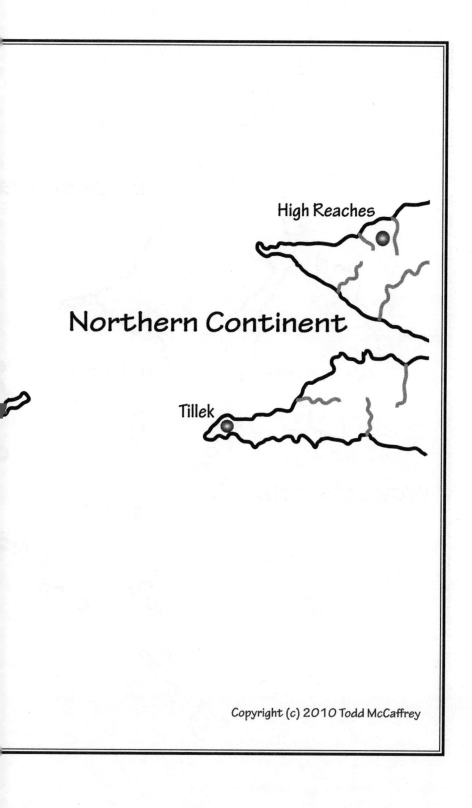

High Reaches

Northern Continent

Tillek

ACKNOWLEDGMENTS

No one truly labors alone, authors in particular, and we'd like to acknowledge those who helped bring this book to fruition.

We'd like to thank Don Maass, Todd's agent, for asking us to think outside of the box—it allowed us to take Pern in a direction we had never before considered. We'd also like to thank Diana Tyler, Mum's agent, for her untiring enthusiasm and support in the writing of not only this book but its sequel, *Dragonrider*.

Angelina Adams, Margaret Johnson, Susan Martin, and Pam Bennett-Skinner were our brilliant first readers.

Shelly Shapiro, once again editor *par excellence* at Del Rey, did not shy from her role of demanding the very best we could give, and Martha Trachtenberg performed a marvelous job of copyediting. They are definitely a great team and we *know* how lucky we are to have them!

Judith Welsh, our editor at Transworld, once again provided her insights and support, working seamlessly with the editors at Del Rey to allow us to produce one consistent editorial voice.

Despite everyone's efforts, there are probably some errors in this book—that's just the nature of the beast. When two authors work together, it is usual to "let" one handle the final edits, copyedits, and proof edits. In this case, I, Todd McCaffrey, was given the job. As a consequence, all errors not uncovered rest solely upon my shoulders. (Don't worry, Mum won't beat me up too much over them as she knows how mistakes get by the best of us.)